Morse Code For Cats

Tom Conyers

Laguna
PRESS

MORSE CODE FOR CATS
Copyright © Tom Conyers 2008
morsecodeforcats.com.au

Published by Laguna Press
P.O. Box 406
Burwood - 3125
lagunapress.com.au

First published 2008
Reprinted 2009

National Library of Australia
cataloguing-in-publication data:

Conyers, Tom Gregory, 1975–
Morse code for cats / Tom Conyers
A823.4

ISBN: 978-0-9805871-0-4

Edited by Judie Litchfield
Cover Design by Ali Dullard
Printed in Australia by Griffin Digital
Cover photographs by Ali Dullard/Matt Wood

Laguna Press

Morse Code For Cats

Tom Conyers was born in England in 1975. He has lived in Australia for most of his life. *Morse Code For Cats* is his first book.

'Proof absolute that in competent hands the coming of age yarn has a few good miles left in it yet. Delivered as they are, in complex and compellingly gritty shades of grey, it's impossible to be unmoved by Conyers' perfectly flawed, all too real characters, as they document universally awkward, agonising and occasionally exquisite, tentative first steps into adulthood. You'll remember *Morse Code for Cats*.'

Mark White, *choreographer, The Adventures of Priscilla, Queen of the Desert*.

'Conyers has, in Sam, created a sweet and instantly likeable character … Equal parts funny and affecting, *Morse Code for Cats* is an enjoyably tumultuous journey.'

Nick Bond, *co-editor/journalist, Southern Star*.

'You show-off smart arse bastard. I'm only on page 5 and already I hate you because it's so f**king good.'

Joanne Brookfield, *stand-up comedian*.

'A pleasure to support a novel that doesn't seek to titillate but, rather, provokes thought. The author has presented in a confronting manner my belief that places such as ''The Peel'' should not need to exist.'

Tom McFeely, *owner, The Peel, Melbourne, Australia*

This book is dedicated to my friends,
family and acquaintances,
for when I told them I had some talent in me,
they replied that I was full of it.

Chapter One

Perhaps I should start at the beginning.

Not the beginning, beginning. No one cares that far back. Just the beginning of this story.

But it's going to be hard to tell it right. The whole story, I mean. The whole story of that long year and a bit leading up to the millennium party, 2000, 'cause although not much happens in a pot-boiler kind of way, there's still a lot went on. For as my friend Zane would say, 'Sam, with young people, everything's a drama – even life!'

So you'll have to bear with me 'cause, well, I find it pretty scary getting things out. When I get closest to people, that's when I feel furthest away. You know just what can be said but, worse, how much *can't* be.

A writer's supposed to be good at expressing things, but I reckon writers are the funniest lot in the world, and they've got it worst when it comes to communication. They can't say how they feel except in stories. That's just it, you see. Stories, stories, stories. They don't write things straight out – they won't. It all has to be suggested or, at least, not everything said. But in the end they

1

communicate best, 'cause you remember what they say: the important bits stick.

So when I say writers don't talk straight, I mean it. They can't. Never get too close to one. They're hopeless. But I reckon writers can reveal a thing or two. In the most artsy-fartsy way in the world, of course, but when they get it right, it's true. And that's what I fear worst. That you can't ever just say something and someone will understand. You have to be understood. So I'm sorry if this takes time. It has to.

This story's about me mostly, 'cause it's through my eyes (can't be helped!) and I guess it's about … well, it's about people and things that choke you up.

Okay, I'll shut up about that now.

Getting selected for District Cricket in Melbourne was how I got out of the country. That was my Superman, swooping me up before I got stuck on the ground for good. It got me off the farm and into the city. Cricket's about the only thing I showed promise in at school. In the city, the stars might not hang above you, but at least they're all around.

I got into Melbourne in early December 1998. The season had well and truly started, but some colt had shied from the game two months in and they needed a replacement. I had a week or so to get settled, and then I'd be into it.

First thing I did was get a place in inner-city Melbourne over Wally's Bar. Single room, shared amenities, which sucked. Tried to keep outdoors mostly and rarely went downstairs for a beer 'cause, well, you don't drink where you shit, right?

The first night was kind of lonesome. The shadows of the trams on the street below played noughts and crosses on my ceiling.

In the morning I made my way by about a million forms of transport to Balwyn Oval to try for my position in the batting order. The fellers were practising in the nets, with a tall muscly guy (who was obviously the coach) standing watching.

When I walked up, they all gave me the twice-over. This guy with a bit of a goatee and mullet eyed me up most. Turned out his nickname was Dizzy (not *the* Dizzy, but some wannabee). He was standing next to this other guy called Tubby, who had a bit of a paunch. (They fancied themselves a bit, these blokes).

When I put in my box, the celebrity duo smiled like I was going to need it. The coach had Dizzy bowl his quickie best at me. The ball wasn't five seconds out of his hand before it was outside the oval. Needless to say, Dizzy was pretty rubbed up, but I noticed Tubby had a bit of a smile. All ten people on all five adjoining pitches stopped their practice. They turned their heads from where the ball had landed to me.

After Tubby and the coach exchanged nods, the coach threw me a key. It had a number on it: six.

'Okay, Big Feller, you can open with Arny.' The coach nodded at a guy in the adjoining net. Through the wire veil, I saw the guy smiling at me. He had curly black hair and the nicest smile.

The coach called it a day and we all retired indoors. The clubhouse was a red-brick building, with benches, lockers, the odd poster, but not much else. I guess with so many teams using it, it wasn't worth the effort and risk of theft to outfit it beyond that.

At the lockers afterward, I found my spot. The locker door to the left of mine had 'Vice-captain' written on it. It swung closed, revealing Arny.

'We're neighbours,' he said and shook my hand.

It wasn't too firm a grip and it wasn't too limp. A shake so right it was almost secret. Next thing I knew, Tubby appeared. He owned the locker to my right. Boxed in.

'Hey, Sam!' said Arny, 'Have you met our captain Arnold?'

'Another Arny?' I asked.

'That's why they call *me* Tubby,' and Tubby gripped his stomach with a laugh. He retrieved his bag pretty quick then turned back to me, paunch stuck out.

'Man, that form you showed out there, that was the shit.'

I just about slugged him.

'It's okay, Sam,' said Arny, putting his hand on my back. 'Tubby doesn't mean it was *shit* shit but *the* shit.'

'Big fuckin' difference, eh Arns?' laughed Tubby as he poked Arny in the ribs.

Tubby was making for the door already, but he kept shouting to us over his shoulder.

'With you two opening, this team might win a few.'

Arny finally dropped his hand from my back. I couldn't remember a guy ever being so familiar before. Maybe things were different in the city and besides it was kind of nice – in a manly way.

I must say, I got really lonesome by the end of that first week. And I didn't have my first game till a week after that, on the Saturday. At least cricket practice would help fill in some of those hours. The pay wasn't too bad, so I wasn't going to be totally broke, but I didn't know what you did for kicks in the city.

4

On the farm, it was pretty obvious. One of my faves was building rock walkways across the creek. The test was how long they'd last 'cause in winter, after a few beltings of rain, the creek would swell so much the bridge would be washed away. But in the city … well …

Sunday came and I caught the afternoon train back home. With the setting sun coming in sideways across the fields, it was like we had another train travelling with us, but a phantom one, just out of synch. A slide show but without the pictures; you just had squares of orange light. Real pretty, if you pick up on that sort of thing.

The station loomed with the attraction of an iron lung. Cinders was there, all black and white stripes and dyed orange hair. She wasn't going anyplace.

'What you fucking back for?' she asked. She was curled up in the waiting alcove, smoking a ciggy. Kev was half passed out next to her, his hands between her thighs for warmth. Even though it's hot in town during the days, a real chill wind can blow across nights.

'Well, what *you* doin', Cinders?' I asked. 'It's fuckin' freezing.'

I don't know why, but soon as I caught up with Cinders, I started saying fuck as much as her.

'Last night, my fuckin' mother come inta my fuckin' room, Sam. I'm already on the piss, yeah, and she says, looking all fuckin' serious: Cindy, what's this I found under your bed? Yeah, fuckin' what, Mum? Mum went off at me. Don't fuckin' talk like that to me, missy. Not when I found this under your fuckin' bed. Yeah, found what, Mum? Mum holds it up, right. And guess what she says?'

'Dunno.'

'I found your fuckin' boing.'

'Your what?' I asked.

'My boing.'

5

'Boing?'

'Couldn't fuckin' work out what she was on about. Then I got it. That's my fuckin' *bong,* Mother. Bong.'

I had a bit of a laugh, not that I knew much about dope at the time. But Cinders shook so much she nearly woke up Kev: a few sparks from her smoke twitched on his cheek. She heaved down to a standstill then smiled at me.

'Yeah, mums, they don't know shit.'

Cinders tried to push Kev off. A bit of drool frog-tongued onto her skirt. A train was roaring through the other side of the station, a freight one that didn't stop. Just tooted its high range horn for people to stand back.

'Gotta see the fam', Cinders!' I shouted.

'Well, gonna have a fuckin' beer with us after?'

'Sure.'

I turned and walked from the station.

Cinders was the closest I had to a friend. But that hadn't got me into her larger friendship group; even Kev didn't welcome me in. It eluded me why I couldn't be more successful on that score, what it was about me, why I wasn't taken up as one of the gang. Recess and lunch were always the longest times at school.

I passed the white brick houses, with their faded white slatted fences, red geraniums and pelargoniums sprouting from ground and pots, and the peppercorn trees giving the night air a lemony flavour.

In Melbourne, I'd make friends.

Normally I'd have a few ks walk to get to the farm, but Sunday was always barbecue at Dirk's place. I've got two brothers, Dirk and Ashleigh, both older than me. Dirk's the eldest. He lives near the station. I rolled up at his front door. Locked. The house unlit. That didn't mean much; Dirk 'lives' in his backyard. I walked down the side of the house. As predicted, the family was there. Had to pat about five dogs before I got to the people.

'Here he is!' they yelled. I made out the familiar faces in the firelight. The fire was in a washing machine tumbler; it blazed and crackled.

Dirk told me to get a beer from the tub. (They had a bathtub on the lawn filled with ice – an ancient bathtub with brass lion feet.) My brothers' girlfriends were also there, Janet and Tarlia. The whole family reunion thing, so something was up. I found myself a seat and started ripping up the cardboard boxes the beer came in, feeding them to the fire.

Dirk benches a few weights – his neck tapers off to a head. His hair, a short, grizzly black. A wide nose, slightly crooked. Ashleigh is slightly leaner, with longer, lighter hair. I guess my appearance back then lay somewhere between my two brothers. I hadn't yet filled-out. Janet's a peroxide blonde; Tarlia, a brunette with a bob cut.

Janet held her ring up to the fire so it copped a licking of light. She got Tarlia to hold hers up against it. So that was the fuss: double engagement.

'So when's Sam tying the knot?' asked Janet.

Dirk pincered her neck. 'He hasta get a girlfriend, first, babe.'

Ashleigh butted in with a few jokes, how he and Dirk would be tied down for the rest of their lives now and all, but it wasn't serious. All I could think was, here's Dirk and Ashleigh getting married and here's me, not much younger, with … well … I just hadn't met the right girl yet.

The smoke finally got around to annoying me in the circle.

Tarlia asked if I hadn't met any 'babes' in Melbourne.

'What's wrong with the girls round here?' asked Ashleigh.

Dirk piped in. 'Not good enough for Sam. Just 'cause you read all those books,' he directed at me.

My eyes were still smarting from the smoke. Dirk reckoned I was a snob. So did his girlfriend, Janet. I guess if you don't sign your name with a cross.

Janet's younger sister, Carlene, emerged from the side of the house, nearly tripping in the dark on the hose and assorted junk. I was glad of her arrival and moved away from the circle to meet her.

'Hello, cunt,' she said, scratching my chin. 'Look who's looking rough and manly.'

Carlene was wearing a red, short-sleeved, check shirt, brown cord trousers and black boots. A pretty cowgirl look. She held up her arms.

'It doesn't pouch when I do this?'

'No,' I said, 'it's a pretty shirt.'

Carlene and I were always pushed onto each other. Not that I minded. She was a swell girl. Always called me 'cunt' and 'bitch'. No one else much, so I guess that showed I meant something to her.

'So how's Carlene?' Dad asked when I went to refill our drinks; he was refilling the tub with ice. 'Saw you two chatting away.'

'Dad, we're just friends.'

'Oh right, just friends,' he said, winking at Mum.

The winks kept doing the laps. Soon I was jack of it. So I slunk off and walked up the dirt road a couple of k, using the dogs as an excuse. But I only took one – the most ladylike. That's how she got her name: Lady. At the station I looked about for Cinders. It was pretty dark with only a sliver of moon and the odd lamp to illuminate things, but I could see she was gone. I went to the six-pack (that's what we called the silos) and there she was, the red of her cigarette like a lone firefly. She must've dumped Kev back home at his boatshed. I asked Cinders why she was hanging about so much.

'My fuckin' folks had a bit of a blue. Would've waked the neighbours 'cept they were also fuckin' arguing.'

Cinders snorted. Lady took it for a friendly 'come here' in doggy-speak, and self-cranked her tailshaft to take-off speed. I called her back but Cinders gave up rolling her ciggy to give Lady tiny, circular pats.

'Why aren't you at Kev's?' I asked.

'Nah, fuck that. What a place! You wonder why I'm never fuckin' there, man. Fuck, when I do sleep, practically have to sleep with one eye open. Just to make sure the other eye isn't lifted, 'course. Playing fuckin' winkies all night, eh. But yeah Kev's there all right, he's there with his other woman.'

Other woman? Poor Cinders.

'Horse.'

Horse? Not the most attractive name. But then I got it: heroin. Where did heroin take Kev that this life couldn't?

'Yeah, he's screwed my brain with her. All the same, everyone treats 'im like God, Love and Heaven Sent. The only one that stands up for me in this fuckin' town is me. They wanna crucify me, I'm tellin' ya. What fuckin' Christ do they believe in, eh? Schizes me out. Can you tell me that, Sam? What fuckin' Christ do they believe in?'

I don't know why exactly but seeing Cinders like this, made me more than ever not want to miss out on life, whatever life was, or would turn out to be. Whatever Melbourne held, I'd stick with it. Coming back home, even after so short a time away, I knew my change of scene would be a good thing, because it might allow *me* to change. And I did need that change – even if I didn't know what form it would take.

Cinders pushed her hair away from her face. I wanted to get away, but I also couldn't leave her.

'Wanna come to this barbie we're having?' I asked. 'The whole friggin' family's there. Even Janet's sister, Carlene.'

She looked at me closely. 'What the fuck do you want me there for, Sam?' she snapped. 'So you can pass me off as your girlfriend?'

I practically recoiled, like she'd slugged me. What made Cinders say that? She didn't elaborate but felt a bit bad I guess and patted the space next to her. I sat down reluctantly. Straightaway, Lady docked her head in my lap for more pats.

'Wan' a ciggy?' asked Cinders, half falling against me.

I didn't but I took one anyway. As I formed a cave for Cinders to light the cigarette, I thought of Carlene waiting for me back at the barbie.

Everyone was pretty drunk when I finally got there. A quick look told me Carlene had gone home. I felt a relief that disturbed me. I mean, I'd just had this great revelation about embracing life. But if I wanted life so much, hadn't I walked away from it by walking away from a potential sweetheart? I put the question out of mind, or at least out of reach.

The remaining soaks were saying how they loved each other and all, their empty beer bottles cracking in the fire. Ashleigh tossed me a stubbie, fresh from the tub. Eventually I packed up inside, on the couch.

You never sleep well if you're drunk but somehow I made it to morning. At least when you're soused, you don't remember your dreams. And some of mine weren't regulation. Some of mine were …

Anyway, morning came, a kookaburra waking me with its laughter. With a bandaid yelp, I pulled my wet face from the imitation leather couch, then worked out the damage by excavating my jeans pocket, left: ten beer tops. Ten? I'd never drunk like that before, and it certainly hit me when I stood, giving my brain a good slap.

It was dawning on me that I never drank much because I didn't want to let my guard down.

No one was up. I was about to wake someone to say goodbye but decided a message on the fridge whiteboard would be simpler.

The train got back to Melbourne mid-afternoon. I sat in my cramped little room, hearing the trams outside, looking down on Lygon. Hey, it wasn't so bad. I'd found myself a good place, really. Melbourne was okay. And I would make the best of it, making sure not to avoid life any longer. The next girl that showed interest in me, I wouldn't run away. Because if I'd learnt anything from all the books I'd read, the books Dirk teased me about, living meant loving.

The next Saturday, the last before Christmas, I went to the oval for my first match. People were nesting in the stands and spreading out on the lawns, pecking at the grass to remove stones and bottle tops, then flicking out blankets and settling down. We had a home game against Camberwell.

In the clubhouse, Tubby and Arny were padding up. Dizzy looked from his watch to me and back about ten times. Okay, so I was a tad late. Tubby undid his pads and threw them at me.

'I'm not an opener,' he said.

'Then why "Tubby"?'

'Well, it's not for my batting prowess,' he said, like I was stupid. He knocked Arny on the helmet. 'Plus we can't have two Arnys now, can we?' he added less blisteringly.

I quickly got changed into my whites and batting gear.

Arny and I walked onto the field. We played a good game. Well, all right, a brilliant one. Arny and I opened and never went out, scoring 5.6 an over. When it was Camberwell's turn to bat, they didn't have a hope. There was a fair bit of cheering once the game wrapped. In the clubhouse, with everyone getting showered and changed, Dizzy said Camberwell were a crap team anyway. Me and Arny wouldn't do so well against Brunswick, who we were scheduled to play in the new year. He knew 'cause he knew Brunswick's captain, Charles Acton-Heath, and a few of the other players, and had watched them play. They were an unbeatable team.

'Fuck that shit!' yelled Tubby, towelling his hairy belly. The guy didn't mix it up. 'We rocked. Camberwell sucked. And we'll rock even harder against your mate Charles Acton-Heath if our bowling is better.'

Dizzy was stung. He turned to Arny and me, involuntarily I'd say, as we turned to each other. Perhaps we shouldn't have smiled. I made my way out of the steam and quickly got dressed.

At the end of a beery night at the nearby pub – only six beer tops for me this time – Tubby asked if I wanted to go away with them for New Year's Eve. The big '99, practice party for year 2000. His girlfriend's family had a holiday shack near Woodend.

Dizzy nudged Tubby, spilling some of Tubby's pint. 'Tubs, there won't be room in the van.'

12

Arny, who was sitting my side of the long table, ignored Dizzy and turned to me. 'You can come in my car.' From the beery smile on Tubby's face, I could see that settled it.

I was due back at my parents, though. That was the plan: Tuesday to Saturday in Melbourne, Sunday and Monday on the farm. Plus I was always there for New Year's Eve.

The next morning, I rang Mum from a payphone on the street corner near my room.

'Some of the boys have asked me to go away with them for New Year's Eve.'

'But you'll come for Christmas first?'

'Sure.'

'You left before I could give you some money,' Mum said. 'I'll give it to you Christmas Day.'

'Thanks.'

My forty cents ran out.

On the Thursday after Christmas, last day of the old year, Arny drove by after work, honking his horn. (I told him to do that – my humpy wasn't too flash, and I didn't want him coming up.) Pretty nice car he had, too: Holden Barina. I hopped in. The wool seat-covers smelt good in the sun. There were a few manila folders at my feet which Arny told me to throw in the back.

'They look serious,' I said.

It turned out Arny was an accountant, if you can believe it. He looked more like Superman than Clark Kent, even in his work suit. In his jocks, well …

Well, anyhow, we got on the Calder and were soon out of Melbourne. Tubby, Dizzy, another guy (Joe) and their respective girlfriends were being troop-carried in Dizzy's van, according to Arny. Arny and I were the rear flank.

13

The drive up was kind of nice. First I couldn't think what to say. Arny didn't seem to be even trying. He looked happy just to be minimising the bends with deft steering. Then I mentioned something about the ring-barked trees looking like sun-bleached coral on a desert reef.

That got Arny grinning.

Soon we were outgunning each other for arty descriptions. We passed a dead tree that had fallen over, its roots yanked out of the ground, disturbed dirt beneath.

'A beached squid,' I said. 'A pool of ink seeping out from beneath its tentacles.'

Arny reckoned that was the winner.

The holiday shack was pretty cute, I must say, the way it was cut into the side of a steep hill and all. I got introduced to the girlfriends over some beers on the porch. (More alcohol; I'd have to watch it!) Tubby's girlfriend was Beth; Dizzy's, Jane; and Joe, who I'd hardly said a word to, had Kelly. They were a funny pair, those two. Joe was beach-boy blonde, Kelly crustacean red, and it was hard to tell whether they loved or hated each other.

Either way, it added up to one very coupley occasion. Hell! Felt more like spring than summer. I did another scan of the tandem tricks. Somewhere in that one-eighty pan I reckon I saw Dirk and Ashleigh with their girls, Janet and Tarlia. But I didn't really. Just felt like it. My eyes came to rest on Arny's. From his look, I reckon he must've just done the same pan as me, but starting from the opposite end of the arc, and now our eyes idled on one another's with a reflected smile. We were so out of pattern with the rest … A pity there weren't two single chicks. Or if only Arny was a …

Geez, my mind needed burning back. I should explain what I mean by that. One of the best times on the farm was in winter when Dad would give me, Ashleigh and Dirk a stick each, wrapped at one end with a rag and dipped in fuel. He'd light them one by one before we'd stick them in the blackberry bushes. Burning back, he called it. Now and then a rabbit would race off. Kind of sad, destroying their homes like that. But Dad said they were an introduced pest and besides he needed more grassland freed up for our sheep.

There weren't any blackberry bushes on *this* property, not that I could see from the porch. It was pencilled in with trees.

Beth suggested we climb the hill. Tubby complained that it was a ruse of hers to get him to lose his paunch. With that gone, his name wouldn't fit. Beth countered that it was a great view from the top. I could see it was all in fun, and thought it was kind of sweet. Affectionately baiting in front of an audience.

Suddenly, we were all on our feet.

'You'll come, won't you, Sammy?' Arny nudged me.

Since when was I Sammy? I tried to think if I'd introduced myself that way. Nup. No way. Sammy? No one called me that.

It was odd, him asking me specially like that. Particularly after the general call had been put out. He told me to wait till he got changed.

I stepped off the porch.

'Isn't this great,' said Dizzy, 'how we're all in couples!'

He looked sideways at me and half put his hand over his mouth as if to say 'careless me'. Tubby flicked him a backhander. I felt pretty uncomfortable. It's awful when you join a group and someone takes an instant dislike to you. What had I done, except maybe smash his bowling around? I'd had the same problem back home, with Kev not liking me for one reason or another. It meant my exclusion from Cinder's gang. I hoped like anything that Dizzy's aggression didn't mean I was going to be left out the same way among the cricketing guys.

Beth walked over and talked to me while the others got their shoes on. She was pretty nice. Joe joined us as well, to give him credit.

Arny came back out, tucking his shirt in. He'd put on a baseball cap. Curly black hair like tendrils under a shell. He had a grubby white T-shirt with a long-sleeved grey T-shirt underneath.

We climbed the hill with its little terraces the sheep had marked out: trails with a fishtail patterning.

'I think we got it right, Sammy.'

'What?'

Arny was walking beside me. Big stomping steps. He laughed and pointed back.

'Going straight up. Rather than sideways.'

I looked back at the others. They'd doubled their climb, really. By zigzagging. Me and Arny were almost at the rim.

When we got to the top, we looked around. It was your typical country Victoria vista: ridgeback hills, Rottweiler valleys. Arny was pointing this way and that. That's Melbourne over there, with its smog halo aura even non-mediums could see. That was the bubble-gum stretch of highway we'd driven on. He said it was good to get on top of things, and a hill was a good start. Pretty obscure stuff. It was one of those conversations where you didn't quite know what the other person was getting at, but you wished to hell you did, 'cause you liked them.

It turned out Arny hadn't joined the cricket club much earlier than me, scoring the job of vice-captain over the veteran Dizzy. Maybe that partly explained why Dizzy was so worked up. Arny came from Canberra. Even that little journey made him want to travel further.

'Overseas, Sam. See the sights, visit the galleries. Have greasies with the Mona Lisa.'

Arny was born in England, so he had dual citizenship. Which meant an EU passport, even better. Working overseas would be easy for him. He could even live in England if he wanted to.

The others caught up.

Dizzy got me to photograph the couples against the sky, like they were in front of a red velvet drape in a photographer's studio. Tubby and Beth posed hugging; Dizzy and Jane all over each other; Joe and Kelly with a chasm between. Then Dizzy kicked the football he'd brought, and they were all hurrying down after it, zigzagging again because of the slope.

At the time, I hadn't been overseas but I have since. In Paris, I remember getting in this queue to see this famous statue of some goddess. You had to wait hours and then, when you finally got to see her behind her thick glass monocle of protection, you'd first be surprised how small she was, but then take as long as you could before the breathing of some feller behind you buffeted you forward. The funny thing was, how so many people, when they finally got their turn, would just pull out their camera, take a snap, and walk on, without even looking at the picture! Why bother coming from overseas? The reproductions in art books are probably better anyway – no tank glass in the way. That's the sort of people these cricket guys were, Dizzy especially. They'd climb all the way up a hill, take a photo of themselves against the background, then race down again. Then, when they showed their friends, they'd say how you couldn't really get the feeling of space from the photo.

I hung back.

Arny looked at me.

'I think I'll stay,' he said.

The others were already three sheep trails down. I mumbled something about getting back myself. Arny smiled and leant back, putting a straw in his mouth. It was so American Midwest.

He was staring at the horizon, face varnished gold. An Old Masters painting, enigmatic as any Mona Lisa yet 3D. *He* wasn't taking any photos; he was taking it all in. Me, I was doing the tourist thing, getting down as fast as I came up.

I kept looking back, all the way down that hill. Reckon Arny turned up nearly an hour later, when it was all dark. Don't know how he ever got down.

Later that evening, I somehow found myself one side of the fireplace, feeding the flames woodchips. I'm a bit of a pyromaniac. Once I start, I can't stop. It wasn't too nippy, being summer and all, but you don't always light a fire for warmth; there's cooking and ambience. Arny walked over.

'Sammy,' he said.

Sammy again!

'Let me make you a hamburger. I've put two meat patties on to cook.'

I sort of waved him away. He sat the other side of the fireplace, skewering the two sides of the bun and holding them into the flames.

'You need something longer,' quipped Dizzy from the other side of the room, grooming his goatee with one hand, and Jane with the other.

Arny smiled at me. He was deliberate with the toasting, doing one side, then the other. I got up and sat next to Beth on the couch while Arny went into the kitchen to put the meat patties and fillings in the bun. Beth was talking to Joe and Kelly who were sitting on the opposite couch and didn't appear to be talking to each other. Arny returned, giving me the hamburger. I could see him looking for a space between me and Beth. I spread my legs to fill the gap. But the unbelievable happened. Arny took a pillow and threw it at my feet. I wanted to yell, 'No! What are you thinking?' but I was under water. Arny slumped down on the damn thing. All eyebrows in the room made a Mexican wave. I chomped into my hamburger.

Actually, I have to admit, he'd toasted it to perfection. Pretty good, considering what he had to work with. A crackling fire and a bent fork. He'd rolled it round, making sure it was crisped every side, licked hard on the outer but soft inside. A class job.

I could do nothing but eat it. Best hamburger I've ever eaten and I don't generally care for them much. Maybe 'cause of that multinational variety and how it makes you feel like you're in the 51st state. I could see the others looking at me. *He* was looking at me. Arny. Rather than lean back, he leant forward, head tilted up. Funny effect somehow.

Midnight ticked over. We were now one minute into '99. I wondered, like you always do, where I'd be in a year's time, when I'd forget, like you always do, what I was doing a year before.

Rooms were divided up among the couples and I was to have the fold-out couch in the main room we'd been sitting in. I felt pretty out of it, being the new kid and all. Beth helped set up then I got into my sleeping bag. Arny unrolled his, and said he'd kip with me. Tubby, Dizzy and

Joe looked at him. 'To stay by the fire,' Arny said and lay on the floor next to it. The others cleared off to their rooms. I could see Arny was getting quite toasty. I was lying to one side of my big bed and we both looked at the empty space.

'Why don't you ...?'

'All right.'

And before I could think about it, he was next to me.

We lay turned in towards each other, the green hood on Arny's sleeping bag an oval frame for his face. We didn't speak. Every time I opened *my* eyes I saw him just closing *his*.

The fire crunched the logs. Bits of red spittle were lost to the dark. The smell of must, of smoke, and ... and him ... a real live human lying next to me.

A log fell out of the fire.

'Almost had an incident,' Arny said next morning.

I coughed my cereal.

We were sitting on the porch with the others.

'But me and Sammy saved the day,' laughed Arny, leaning forward in his plastic chair. 'We had these three logs we piled up high. To stay warm all night. Well, I knew one would roll off when it got a bit charred. Did too. We'd just gotten to sleep and "collumph".' He rolled his arm. 'But it hit the grate. That's why we have them, kids,' and for a moment he spoke to a porch full of them. 'Let that be a lesson to you. Remember the grate.'

This got a laugh.

'Might have been nothing left,' I put in.

'Nope, and me in my nylon slipper.'

'Could've been shrink-wrapped. That would've been a tragedy – '

Arny's face was all teeth.

'I mean …'

But it was too late; I'd said it.

Somehow the morning dipped into day. Arny and I were back on the foldout bed we were both too lazy to fold away. We were poring over a coffee-table book of aerial photographs from around the world, so abstract they were like modern paintings. Except for Beth, everyone else was outside playing footy.

Beth called out from the bathroom, 'Arny?'

'Yes'm?' replied Arny.

Beth popped her head round the door, pink toothbrush in her mouth.

'No, not you, Arny,' she said. '*My* Arny.'

She meant Tubby, but Arny played on the mistake.

'Boo hoo hoo,' he cried, rolling about, 'I'm nobody's Arny.' And he looked at me.

'You're your own Arny,' I said. I don't know why – I just blurted it out.

Beth turned from me to Arny and raised an eyebrow. The two shared a smile. Despite this, I couldn't stop myself.

'Beth's Arny is Beth's Arny,' I went on. 'But you're your own. You're Arny's Arny.'

Arny looked kind of sad at that but he smiled and put a hand on my knee. Beth turned back to the bathroom with a flutter. I stiffened. I felt sick. I smiled but it was the twisted-est smile ever. I couldn't get it right. I wanted it to say 'righto' but it just said 'red' – scarlet.

I got up, shaking Arny's hand off my knee and peered through the windows for the others. Their game must've migrated down the hill. Arny joined me by the window. He had this funny way about him. Rather than just shouting something across a room like the others, he'd

21

walk right up to me, stand a metre away or less, straight on, hands in back pockets, and talk like that. His hair was mussed from sleep.

'Do you want to go for a walk, Sammy?' he asked.

A walk! Actually, I thought, that's good. Outside I'll tell him. Tell him … well, not to stand so close and all. Hell, that would sound silly. Christ, I couldn't even say what he was doing exactly. I just knew, with him around, I was feeling the funniest ever. Like I wanted to take off or something but couldn't get a run-up.

No, that sounds good. It was bad. Something he was doing was bad.

He was mesmerising me.

I mean, I couldn't take my eyes off him for more than a second. Why …? This was … It was too scary. There *had* to be a reason …

Ah! That was it! I'd worked it out. So obvious. Nothing to sweat over at all. It was simple. The guy had the perfect-est features you ever saw. Perfect mannerisms, so goofy, so fleet. Right-on voice, camphor and sweet. Perfect hands, perfect body, perfect package …

I wanted to look like him, that's all.

Hell, I'd noticed that about myself. The way I'd eye up guys. That was normal enough. I mean, the way I'd look at guys all the time. Well, that was why. The reason was simple: I didn't feel too special myself. If I'd been a looker, I'd be eying up girls – crotches to cranium and back – pretty much secure they were doing the same in return, but no, I was checking out the saucy guys to see what I didn't have myself. You can rise above most things, but you can't rise above your looks. A bit of styling mousse, maybe.

But did that explain the dreams …? I'd never slept well anyway. Not surprising, really.

I was still staring at Arny.

Hell, those curls, each one looping back, all in love with his head. *My* hair can't wait to get away from me. Talk about the white afro.

Arny was outside by this time. I could see him standing by the clipped-wing gate, waiting for this walk I'd said I'd accompany him on. I'd told him I had to get my shoes on first. Beth had come back into the room and was washing up. Clink, clank.

Arny, hair wriggling in the wind. Hell, he was the sort of guy anyone would look at, right? Girls, guys, anyone.

I stood up, feet firmly sutured. Twelves stitches per boot.

'Hey, um, Beth …' I began.

Beth swivelled at the neck, hands still in the sink so the water wouldn't comb down the carpet.

'Um, why hasn't Arny got a girlfriend?' I asked.

She cocked her head at that. I had to make it normal.

'I mean,' I blurted, 'you'd say he was pretty attractive and all. I can't really tell with guys, you know, but …'

And my words ran out like coins. Ten cents short for the Coke. Beth turned right round, snow suds adrift.

'So you think Arny's hot, do you?'

Her playful tone and smile frightened me. It was like she was playing matchmaker. She must've seen how uncomfortable I was and backed off, turning back to the dishes.

'Well, Sam, I suppose he's not *too* bad-looking,' she said to the window in front of her, obviously trying to sound flippant. 'Guess it depends on your type.'

Depends on your type ...?

That would mean he was my …

No!

That clinched it. I'd have to get out there quick smart and tell Arny to stop it. Once and for all. It was sick.

Seducing a feller. What was he playing at? And what made him think I was like that anyway? I was sporty, daggy, a regular bloke. Apart from the book-reading, just one of the guys. Or hoped to be …

In the barn, he kissed me.

Again and again and again.

That night, stuck in my cramped room above Lygon, I tried to get to sleep but couldn't somehow. My head felt saddled to the pillow. Eventually, I hugged the pillow to me and that was enough, just, to canter through the night. *Arny* kissed me. Or had *I* kissed *him*? No. We'd kissed each other. In the barn. The light slicing the boards. The others' footsteps outside in the grass. On instinct, me pushing him away. Arny falling heavily. Then the door opening. The cricketers and their girlfriends standing there.

'You've got it wrong,' I said with all of us there, in tableau. 'I'm not a fucking faggot.'

Arny got up and left the barn. We followed him out and watched him walk to his car.

Dizzy told how he'd seen us walking to the barn together, close, a little *too* close. That's why he'd gathered everyone for the hunt.

We watched as Arny fumbled for his car keys.

'He tried ta come onta ya, Sam,' said Dizzy in my ear.

'Yeah, I know.'

'Lucky I saved you.' A little louder: 'He could've fucked your arse right up.'

'I know.'

'You owe me one.'

24

'I know.'

Beth went over to Arny and tried to make him stay. She turned and yelled at Tubby to make Dizzy shut up. Dizzy started another crack but Beth cut him off. She pleaded with Tubby to say something, take control of the situation, lead.

Too late. Arny drove off, taking a swig of the horizon. A coffee dreg on the porcelain sky was all he left.

I got a lift back in the troop carrier with Tubby, Beth, Dizzy, Jane, Joe and Kelly. Beth sniped at Tubby from time to time. I couldn't hear what it was about but I knew: Tubby not coming to the aid of his best friend, Arny. Joe tried shooting the breeze with me but Dizzy turned the music too high for talking comfort.

I'd managed to break into a friendship group – tenuously, yes, but enough to be invited away with them. Not only was I messing that up; I'd created rifts in the group.

They dropped me the other side of Edinburgh Gardens. I felt like the walk.

We'd just had a whiff of summer rain that had wet the grass to a crew-cut, and there was me, walking the footpath, telling myself how lucky I was. Geez, a little bit later and … he might of … we might of … I thought of those hills, and how there was something I wanted, something I wanted to get so badly, but couldn't for cucumber eyes. But I'd been saved. Must remember that. Something terrible could've happened. I'd let my guard down and I wasn't even drunk! A minute or two later and … and … My cheeks felt wet. Before I knew, it was raining. Like it never had since I was a kid. A full-on flood. Seemed to flow right through me, lifting my organs and dumping them on higher ground, my heart in my mouth and my life downstream. I shivered; barely made it off the footpath and onto a seat. I had only one thought, and it was pretty silly: hold myself. That's right, hold. Hard as could be. Otherwise I'd tear apart. I'd just about pulled the shoulders of my white shirt together at the front, double-breasted, when it ripped, with every cotton strand aching apart down my spine.

A lady walked past with soft pink impasto features. A lovely green scarf like seaweed caught on a jetty post.

'Son …?'

Just keep holding yourself, Sam. Hold.

'Son, have you hurt yourself?'

Injured? I looked at my knees. Maybe I'd tripped.

'Are you injured?'

Not a scratch.

'Have you hurt yourself?'

And I knew the answer.

Yes, I had. Deeply.

Back in my room, for some reason I thought about this effeminate guy at school, Carl. I hadn't thought about him in ages. The other kids teased him – no, I lie, *we* teased – so much his parents took him out of school and moved away. I was especially cruel. Reckoned we had nothing in common but maybe I feared we were too alike. It was the first and last time I teased someone about their sexuality. But I didn't reckon there was anything sissy about *me*. Nothing. I was – *wanted* to be – could *still* be – one of the guys.

The next day, Saturday, I forced myself to make the long journey to the clubhouse. There were general shouts of 'Here he is'. The coach told me he didn't want to lose both star openers.

'Both …?' I forgot to step back as I pulled my locker door open, getting a metal slug in the chin.

'Yep. Arny's done a runner.'

The coach walked outside. A great scythe had taken my feet but I was still standing. I saw Tubby on a bench, strapping on his pads, and something snapped. For the second time, I let my guard down, like I had finally let myself get drunk. Drunk all the time.

'Tubby, what's Arny's number?' I asked.

'What?'

'His number?'

Tubby, Dizzy and Joe just stared at me. I turned to Arny's locker. Maybe he'd left something with his number on it. But Dizzy was there, shoving his bag into it, then fumbling with the lock. Didn't make sense at all till he walked away with a smile, and then it did. I'd forgotten the 'Vice-captain' on Arny's locker. Dizzy had got his promotion.

But how to find Arny? Maybe when he had cleared out his locker, he'd thrown something in the bin. I looked. And sure enough: no number, but an old bill with his address on it. I put it in my pocket and ran outside, pushing through the others, who'd been watching me rummage like a dero, and past the coach who yelled at me, 'Where are you going?'

Arny's flatmate said he didn't know where Arny was either. But he sure as hell wanted to. The 'bastard' owed him on the electricity. I looked at what I'd rescued from the bin: an overdue notice.

I walked back to the game. The coach nearly hit me. He'd put Joe in to open with Tubby. But Joe and five more were already out and we'd only made fifty. Tubby and Dizzy scored fifty more between them before Dizzy was bowled out and I was sent in. At that point, we had to at least double our score for a chance of winning and, with the overs remaining, that meant better than one run a ball.

We were playing Brunswick, the team Dizzy reckoned was unbeatable.

I took the crease, then walked up the pitch towards Tubby for the usual chat, but he just stayed at his end. My stomach bunched up and I turned back.

Tubby tried to get a single down to long-on but was picked up in slips. A dot ball. The over finished, leaving me to face. The new bowler came on; the wicketkeeper moved in close; there was even a silly mid-on. Must have been planning spin.

The bowler marked out quite a log run-up. Medium-fast? He hurtled in. As he let go of the ball, the wicketkeeper whispered at me.

'Poofter boy.'

The ball hit the pitch short, a bouncer.

'Poofter boy.' This time it was silly mid-on.

I was distracted.

'Poofter boy.'

And didn't see it off the pitch.

I must've staggered pretty near the stumps 'cause the slips went up, but I hadn't knocked the bails off. My head hurt like hell where the ball had connected under my ear. The umpire's voice was a wet buzzing. I waved him away.

What was said? Before the ball came? Poofter boy, that's right! Poof? Strangest thing in the world. I mean, whispering that at me!

Tubby half walked up the pitch to me. I waved him back. The bowler got ready again. His arm cartwheeled, the ball was loosed.

'Poofter boy.'

Crunch!

My left elbow melted from solid to liquid state, and was aiming to go gaseous. Silly mid-on stepped in close. He put an arm on my shoulder. I looked round and he blew me a kiss. A kiss! Tubby yelled, halfway up the pitch. He must've seen. Then the wicketkeeper pinched my bum. What was that supposed to say? I was a girl or something?

Again, the whispering, 'Poofter boy, poofter boy.'

Just your regular sledging?

'You all right, Big Feller?'

The coach, I think. From the sideline. Everything was a dull cicada hum, and it wasn't the crowd.

'You all right?'

Maybe it was Tubby. I looked down the pitch, long enough for a runway, and saw Arny. A mirage, for a moment. We'd opened the last match and never gone out, retiring with a century for him and almost a double century for me.

'Have you hurt yourself?'

It was that lady in the park, with the pretty, green scarf.

'Have you hurt yourself, dear?'

The scarf blowing over one shoulder.

'Do you want the medic?'

It was the umpire, this time, definitely.

I shook my head at him. The world shook twice as hard back. Stay with it, Sam. The bowler winked at me before turning to find his marker. Tubby elbowed him as they passed and there was a bit of scuffling. The umpire shouted at them both.

The bowler merely shrugged at Tubby.

'You're the poonce, mate! Tubby yelled. 'With a name like Charles Acton-Heath!'

Charles Acton-Heath? Dizzy's mate.

The umpire motioned to get on with it.

Next ball. The run in.

'Fucking faggot.'

Whack!

My feet fell out. I sank to my knees. A direct hit to the stomach. Air, air – I needed air! I stopped wheezing and sucked, gentle as could be. The pain, the pain …

Tubby was yelling, the crowd shouting, and I could hear booing from the boxes where the rest of the team was up, standing.

Poofter boy? I mean … they were saying it … to me!

Me, Sam. I felt sick. Sickest I ever had, on top of the physical hurt. I felt exposed. Starkers in the middle of the oval. Practically a streaker. Maybe even the crowd were in on what had happened. I couldn't see how everyone knew about … Well, I suppose my running off to Arny's had done it. Guys just don't charge off after each other like that unless …

'Right, help this guy off,' said the umpire.

He and Tubby lifted me up.

'No,' I said.

Tubby squeezed my arm.

'Come on, Sam.'

'No.'

I threw off their arms. They walked back to their places. Three balls to go this over. I felt like a half-made house robbed of its struts.

My eyes on the pitch, I saw Arny driving away.

And it hurt. Ten times as much as it should've. I looked round at the fielders and saw what I'd lost, what it should've been. That memory, Arny. If it'd been boy and girl, not boy and boy, it'd be something else now, an altogether different time. It'd be my first real kiss, first love, something to think back on at eighty and smile about. The first real awakening of heart and hard-on, a tingling, a tantrum in the groin. But no, it was just pain. All pain. And no one wants to think back on that. No one, I tell you. I didn't want to hate.

Silly mid-on was whispering again.

I did hate.

Charles Acton-Heath loosed the ball.

Terribly.

Smash.

Silly mid-on was rolling on the ground, grabbing his groin. Snot and tears streamed from his face. Got him! There were yells and cheers all round. They took silly mid-on and replaced him with the twelfth man. No one was going to kick me out, no one was going to oust me from the game! Either this one or the game of life. I wouldn't be excluded any more. If I was gay, then I wouldn't hide it.

I smiled the meanest smile at the wicketkeeper. He signalled for a helmet. The next ball I stepped forward and hooked straight into him, hard as I could. He went to catch it, then tried to get out of the way, but couldn't do either. It caught him in the ribs, rolling him over and (I heard later) cracking two of them. There wasn't anyone to replace him.

The umpire lectured me. I ignored him, completely.

Next ball after that, I whacked a perfect cover drive. Charles Acton-Heath watched the ball straight into his forehead and fell with a crunch.

Tubby hardly got a bat the rest of the game. I made a hundred and fifty-three runs, not out.

Our rivals put on a good run-chase. Charles Acton-Heath was absent so someone batted twice. The wheezing wicketkeeper had a runner. In the end their 'good' wasn't good enough. We'd won.

I felt strangely elated. Justified. The opposition walked off, heads bowed. Tubby came up to me, took my hand and raised it in the air as the volume of the crowd rose. Tubby and I walked off to claps and cheering.

'You stayed in there Sam,' said Tubby, taking off his helmet. 'Man, you stayed in – you took control.'

I removed my helmet. The coach was staring at us as we approached the gate. Tubby's voice developed a wobble.

'Beth reckons I'm not much of a leader … for a captain,' he confided.

I turned but it was too late to say anything. The coach watched as we walked through the gate. I couldn't gauge his expression. Tubby and I made our way through the crowd and into the clubhouse.

Head down, I approached the bench, then realised Tubby was no longer beside me. When I turned, he was in the doorway, staring. I followed that stare.

'Dizzy!'

Dizzy turned around, surprised at Tubby's tone.

'What?'

'You told your mate Charles about Sam, didn't you?' spat Tubby.

'So what?' I could tell Dizzy was surprised Tubby was taking him on.

Tubby half-turned, looked like he was going to drop the matter, but then walked over and grabbed Dizzy, shoving him against his 'Vice-captain' locker.

'It isn't fucking cricket, that's what.'

This was captaincy! Beth could be proud of Tubby now. Tubby let go.

'Well, Tubs,' said Dizzy meekly, 'you tell Charles that. He's in hospital. Unconscious.'

The coach stuck his head in.

'Okay, Big Feller. Out here.'

I was sick to the core, elation gone. Knocking that guy out – I'd never gotten angry like that before. Always pictured the ball as my enemy. It was the missile, the

32

grenade I had to get away from me, far as I could. But now it wasn't the ball so much as the field. The whole thing had been target practice. What had I done?

I glanced at Tubby, then followed the coach outside.

We sat down in one of the now-empty stands. To my surprise, the coach lectured me on how smashing up the other side was none too nice but an indication of phenomenal talent. He went on so long, I couldn't get away. I was aware of the other cricketers leaving, their friends and families all gone. It occurred to me the coach was excited, like I had been, by how I'd batted. He was a big, toned guy, and to see those arms waving about like a kid's was a strange sight.

'This is what a coach hopes for in his career. Even if it occurs once.'

I finally got away, heading back to my room above the pub. But on entering the bar, I saw Tubby drinking beer and chatting to Wally over the counter. The fact he'd dropped by indicated he was still my friend. Certainly seemed like it, the way he'd come to my aid on the pitch, and his taking on Dizzy in the clubhouse. But I didn't know if I could face him right now. I'd cost him his closest friend and key player, Arny. And there had been an explosion in my life bigger than my explosion on field I needed to deal with.

So I slid out of the pub, making my way to the street and the phone booths. Even though mobiles were taking off in a big way, they still hadn't gotten round to removing most of the booths.

Tried calling Ashleigh but the line rang out. I couldn't quite talk to my parents yet. Don't know why. Nothing else for it, so I rang Dirk.

'Dirk, I … Dirk, I've fallen for a … for a guy.'

33

The phone booth window had been smashed. I remember thinking it was like a glass web. Silence. Then Dirk's gravelly voice.

'Me and Janet always thought you were a bit of a woolly woofter, Sam.'

'Prick.'

'What?'

'Nothing,' I mumbled.

If they thought I was a 'woolly woofter', why hadn't they ever said anything? Why had they gone on so much about me getting a girlfriend?

'Hey, you coming back, Sam? Drinks are at me and Janet's again. You bailed on us for New Year's.'

'Okay … all right. See you tomorrow.'

And I hung up.

I didn't get there till late – the afternoon train again. Cinders wasn't at the station but, then again, she didn't live there. The sun eased below the horizon, leaving a ripple of red. I walked to Dirk's. Noise carried from the backyard. I went round the side of the house, Lady and the other dogs greeting me. Dirk and his mates were getting the fire going, getting into their tinnies. Ashleigh wasn't there with Tarlia yet, Mum and Dad either. Dirk told me to get myself a drink from the tub.

I sat down in the circle. Again, I felt sick with nervousness. But it seemed to go okay – I kept up my end of the conservation, until Dirk said to fetch him a beer. I said *he* should. He went on, fuck, how he was always waiting on me, and stuff. Telling his friends he had a lazy sod for a bro'. It got pretty nasty.

'Steady on, you two,' said Janet.

I reckoned *I* should be the one waited on, if anyone was. Not like I was the birthday boy or nothing, still …

Well, it *is* kind of special in a way, like opening a tinnie. Don't know if it will just fizz or, if it's been dropped, whether half of it will foam away. Things got sore between us, that's all I'm getting at. Dirk reckoned he always had to do everything for me. Whenever he hung out with his friends, Mum and Dad always insisted he let his 'little brother' tag along. 'Only way Sam's gonna make friends,' they'd say to him. That always pulled me up short. Pretty sad when even your parents feel sorry for you.

Night was getting on, I could tell Dirk was still black with me, and people started telling jokes. Kev just told a funny one about a talking dog, when Dirk piped in – Dirk my own brother. 'I've got one,' he said. And he leaned forward into the fire.

'Okay, there's two fags fucking and one goes to the fridge to get a drink of milk.'

Straightaway, my stomach bunched up. I couldn't believe it.

'One of these fags, the one who's been butt-fucked by the other one, goes off to the fridge. He seems to be away forever. Finally, the other fag gets up to see what's taking so long. The guy's moppin' up this stuff on the floor. His bum-buddy says, "What happened? Spilt the milk?" "No," says his bum-chum. "I farted." '

Everyone laughed. Pretty hard. Even Janet. I could see she couldn't help it. I couldn't look at my brother. Couldn't look at his friends, either. I didn't even know if they knew about me yet. I didn't know what would be worse. If they did, or didn't. Dirk sure as hell knew. There was just one joke after the other, after that. He'd got them started. All pretty much the same theme. And I felt scared. Very scared. I'd felt scared sometimes before in similar situations, but I'd always thought: Geez, it's lucky I'm not gay in a place like this.

I got up.

'Hey, we're just telling jokes, Sam,' said Janet. '*Your* turn.'

I headed for the exit down the side of the house. Dirk yelled that Mum and Dad were coming over any minute but I walked straight out and down the road and caught the last train home. Yes, home. I would make Melbourne my place.

When I walked into the pub, Wally was holding the phone: Dad was on the line. People could ring in; I just wasn't allowed to ring out (Wally was onto the fact it wouldn't be local). Taking the phone from Wally's pizza crust fingers, I put it to my ear.

Dad wanted to know why I'd ticked off without warning. I said, well, what did he think of what Dirk had told him. Dirk hadn't told him anything, he said. Just that I'd taken off, no explanation. I could've killed Dirk.

'I'm gay,' I told him and hung up.

I'd done it now. I was gay and out. My family knew. The cricketers knew. I knew. How would I face anyone? I called in sick at training all week, and for the match at the weekend. Just stayed in my room and turned troppo.

Tubby caught up with me the following week. He'd been phoning the bar every day. (Wally was complaining about turning into my 'personal secretary.') But it was nice of Tubby. Seems I'd made one friend in Melbourne, at least. Could've been two with Arny. Tubby took me to the nets, for practice. That's why he was pursuing me: he still hoped I'd return to the club. No one bought my 'feeling ill' excuse.

I asked about Charles Acton-Heath.

Tubby broke his run-up.

'Man, you go and do something like that, which rocks, then you go and soil it all by feeling guilty. Don't feel guilty. Fuck the cunt.'

I certainly hadn't expected an approving response.

'Mild concussion, that's all,' Tubby offered at last.

The echidna in my stomach eased up slightly but then it scrunched up with my next question.

'Heard from Arny?'

Tubby looked at his feet. 'Yeah, he's gone overseas.'

I nearly cried. Don't, Sam, don't.

'Hey, Sam, he was always planning to,' said Tubby hurriedly. 'You … I mean … *we* just pushed his schedule forward.'

I liked Tubby even more for that touch but I didn't agree with it. 'We?' I asked sceptically.

'Yeah, well … maybe *I* should've come to his aid,' Tubby explained.

I tried to convince him it was all my fault, which was how I felt. He got ready to do his run-up but broke it again. He then said something else that surprised me.

'Man, maybe it was a little bit Arny's fault as well.'

I didn't understand that at all. I asked him to explain.

'Sam, *I* know what it's like to be called names. But, hey, *I'm* still here.'

I'm so thick, again I didn't know what he was getting at. He eventually had to explain it.

'Tubby!' and he slapped his belly.

That pulled me up short. It never occurred to me that the name hurt him. But he'd braved it out, even ending up by owning it. Maybe my problems weren't so big or rare.

'So, man, are *you* going to tough it out?' he asked.

This time, I knew immediately what he was getting at. I'd wanted to change, I'd hoped Melbourne would change me. It had. Now I had to decide to face people as the new Sam. Could I?

Tubby was still staring at me.

Swallowing drily, I nodded yes.

Tubby bowled his ball which I hit straight back into his hands.

'Anyway,' he said, the serious tone dropped, 'Arny will be back by the end of the year. No long-term harm done.'

Just under a year? It wasn't that long to wait. I lowered my bat, indicating I was ready to receive the next ball, but it was Tubby who wouldn't play. He got onto the real subject of why he'd called.

'Don't get me wrong. I'm not saying I go along with this whole thing. 'Cause I don't. No way, man, that shit ain't right,' he said. 'Copping cock like that. That shit ain't right. No way. That shit must really hurt. That arse must wink. Rise! Rise to the pillar of meat. Take a ride down that chocolate speedway. Do the hoola-hoop in his arse. Twenty cents, kids. Roll up, roll up. You too can ride the baloney pony.'

Tubby was unstoppable for someone who supposedly knew the pain of being called names. I didn't like the way he was making out I was some kind of girl. This is the way I'd reasoned it to myself: being gay made me even more of a man. I mean, I wasn't into girls. When you think about it, how girly's that?

'Christ, Tubby,' I yelled at last, 'maybe everyone should be fucked up the arse at least once. Hell, we might loosen up a bit.'

That got a quarter-inch smile. And from that I managed to create my own, the first in a while. I would accept this gay thing, even if not everyone around me could.

People amaze you, don't they? 'Cause the next thing I know, Tubby's confiding to me how he always wanted to sodomise a girl. I didn't really want to hear his fantasies; I was still working out my own. But all I said was, 'Listen mate, if you can't take it, then you shouldn't dish it out.'

'Nah, I'm never getting fucked up the arse.'

'Get Beth a strap-on.'

'Nah, fuck that.'

'Why not? Power to the pussy and all.'

I was actually having fun now. 'You'd have a strong back, wouldn't you …?' I started to say as I leant behind him, lifted his shirt, but he whacked my hand away, hard enough for a boundary.

'Fuck you!' I yelled, jumping. My arm really hurt.

'Just don't touch me,' he said.

That was the limit.

'Fuck you, Tubby. It's all right on the oval.'

Tubby looked away. I'd touched a nerve. He was always running up and hugging guys on the field. And because I'd caught quite a few balls in the slips, I'd had about a million bear hugs from the guy. I was jack of him, now. Being quizzed over your sexuality – it just ain't fair. I grabbed my polo bag, hitched it over shoulder left and made to lag out of there.

Tubby stood in front of me. I was about ready to rumble the bastard.

'Look, man, it's just … it's different now I know you're a …'

'No, it's not.'

I walked right through him like the fuck was a turnstile. When he stopped spinning, he called after me.

'Sam!'

'What?'

I couldn't believe I stopped; I even turned round to hear him out.

Tubby looked at the ground. 'Um,' he said, 'have you ever … er … fancied *me*?'

I just about tripped over myself in a rush to say no.

Tubby was just as quick to yell, 'Good.'

A long moment passed and then at last he looked at me. 'Why not?'

I reckon the stupid bugger was really cut.

Chapter Two

Tubby and I were in the coach's office. The coach squared me up with his quarter-pounder grimace. Tubby nodded to him that it was all right my being back; I was on the level. And besides, it was only one match I'd missed. The coach got up from behind his cheap, ply-board desk.

'All right, Big Feller,' he said, 'I'll forgive you this time, but never again.'

I thanked him then asked for the key to my old locker.

'You don't have it any more.'

With the slumping of my shoulders, my bag nearly dropped to the floor.

'Don't get excited, Big Feller. I gave your locker to Arny's replacement. You can have the one next to Dizzy's,' and from the rack of key-holders he took the last remaining key.

In the lockers, Dizzy was tying his shoelaces on the bench. When Tubby and I walked past he pirouetted faster than a figure skater.

'Quick, guys, backs to the walls.'

I stopped in the middle of the floor. The walls were lined with teammates. I made a quick promise to myself: not all jokes would be at my expense; I would make a few of my own. Tubby was blowing a speech-bubble of invective fit to burst, but I got in first.

'Dizzy, I wouldn't even fuck you with *his* dick,' and I nodded to Tubby.

Tubby was the first to laugh, Dizzy the last when he saw there was nothing else for it; the entire room had opened up teeth. I breathed easy. I'd own my name the way Tubby owned his. He was right – it was going to be okay. Probably the odd jibe in the showers, but I could handle that.

I took my locker. Standing in front of my old locker was its new owner.

'Hi, Sam.'

It was Joe. The guy must've been promoted up the order.

Joe and I opened against Keilor. He went out but not before scoring a quick-fire twenty. This time I didn't smash the balls, but still managed to stay in while the others made runs around me; the guy that frustrated the bowler.

'Trying a new kind of game there, Big Feller?' asked the coach when I was finally out, and making my way to the stands.

Maybe I was. I took a seat. Joe bundled down next to me, fringe of blonde hair swinging wide enough to reveal his blue eyes.

'Sam, I know how hard it is making friends when you move to a new city,' said Joe. 'Me and Kelly are going ice-skating tomorrow; you're welcome to come.'

I smiled broadly at him. Maybe I'd meet someone there who was gay. Joe smiled back.

Dad rang that night saying I couldn't just make this 'great revelation' to him and Mum about being gay then not come home and discuss it. Mum came on the phone. She said when you have kids, you want them to have the world, but as they grow up, you just want them to be happy.

'But are you happy, Sam?'

I was working on it.

Next morning I dressed up, adding more layers than the weather warranted, knowing it would be cold at the rink.

Luckily Joe's house wasn't too far from mine and I walked the distance in just over an hour. From the outside, his shanty looked pretty run-down and cramped; it *did* have a big yard but it was made smaller by the jungle growing in it. The flyscreen was open. Not that it wasn't open when it was shut; it had more holes in it than a piss-poor batting defence. I called out a few times but no one answered. So I walked in.

'Yes, hello?'

The girl shouting at me was giving a rabbit-in-high-beam impression. A good wad of her hair got loose from its band and fell over her face in wisps. Waving a paint brush in one hand, holding a turps rag in the other and wearing a paint-stained smock, she couldn't even use her sleeves to push aside her hair. I introduced myself.

'Sam …? I know you.'

I assured her she didn't.

'Perhaps your hair was combed the other times.'

'Look, is Joe here?' I was trying to get a glimpse of my reflection in the hallway mirror and see whether my part was holding.

She looked into the mess that was the back of the house and screamed, 'Joe!'

I must've jumped a metre 'cause she leapt back herself. She gave me a pointed stare then disappeared out back. Joe emerged from the same direction a moment later.

'That was my flatmate, Lydia,' he said. 'She's a painter.'

'Is she coming with – ?'

'Oh no,' said Joe quickly. But he then went on to say there'd be other friends who were going.

'They'll meet us at the rink,' he said, and suddenly I was very keen they did.

Joe's car was as messy as his flat. I could see the road rushing underneath through a tear in the floor. We had to yell to hear each other.

'So, Sam, what do you do?' yelled Joe.

That seemed a pretty daft question. He knew what I did.

'Play cricket.'

'Yes, but if cricket doesn't work out?'

That had never occurred to me. What would you do if your dream didn't work out? Crash pretty hard, I reckon. Joe was overtaking in zigzags. I forced myself not to grip the door handle.

Since *I* had no occupation beyond cricket, Joe got on to what he did, which was science. Geez, what sort of company was I keeping lately? First Arny the accountant, now Joe the scientist. How many others on the team clocked up degrees as well as runs? Made *me* look dumb.

Joe said he'd always liked science – loved it – at school.

'Only just got the marks to get in, too,' he said. 'One mark less and I wouldn't have. That was God telling me something …'

'God telling you …?'

'Yes,' said Joe, with that great smile he had. He had the most perfect set of teeth, almost as if they were fake and one size too big. But he *was* pretty attractive, I have to admit, in that pretty, attractive, way: tall, broad and blonde.

But God telling him to do science?

The skating rink was full of Joe's friends. Wouldn't you know: they were all seasoned skaters, which left me as the single novice. Joe booked me into a free class, which ran on the hour. While I waited and half shivered to death, Joe and Kelly and their friends performed their moves. Hmm, they'd been coming here for a while, that was certain.

Eventually the class started. The woman running it had two flawlessly round circles of red in her cheeks, and hair so black and silky she was a doll.

'My name is Rhada and I'm your instructor.'

We did a quick round of introductions – the five of us in the class, with us all holding the rails.

'Now, if any of you ski, you'll find ice-skating easy,' said Rhada.

'What if we haven't skied?' asked one of my older co-inadequates.

'Then you'll find it very easy once you've been ice-skating. So, who can show me a bunched-up fist? Anyone? That's right. Now, if we fall over, that's how we get ourselves off the ground. Much safer, I think you'll agree, than with fingers splayed out, especially with all those whiz-bang skaters around.'

I took a squiz at those whiz-bang skaters. Joe flew past himself – backwards. Show-off! He waved at me. That was rubbing it in.

45

'Oh well,' I said to myself and let go of the rail. Immediately I fell over.

After the hour was up, I got off the ice-skating rink, pushing my way out the gate. My bum was wet; my knees were wet; my knuckles were bruised and red. Plus my feet ached, my ankles ached – what am I saying! I nagged with pain all over. A whole lot of muscles I'm sure I'd never used before were mad at me.

There was this area where you could sit and the sun got in through big windows overhead, but I didn't get far. Kelly ran into me. She practically knocked her chest against me, she edged in so close. I stepped back.

'Hey, what ya looking at?' she asked.

'Whaddya mean?' I was taken aback by our collision and the schoolmistress tone. I'd only met Kelly on that weekend away with Arny and I don't reckon she and I had exchanged five words.

'Looking down my front,' she explained, looking down her *own* front!

Actually, I'd been staring off at Joe. He'd moved back to the outside rink. He was clocking the ks, too. I was wondering when he'd fulfil his role of host and help me out.

'I know you're cured,' said Kelly, 'because you've been looking at me.'

Cured? I bristled. Was that meant to be a joke? But I wasn't going to let insinuations get to me. I looked around for somewhere to retreat to but she had me cornered. She pushed herself even closer. She stared at her toes then ran her eyes up her body. When she got to her exposed bosom, she looked up at me, a finger-typist at last looking at the screen.

'Sam, you need to take a cold shower,' she said, placing hands on hips.

Pretty weird stuff. She was checking herself out and then projecting her leering onto me. Something was wrong, not just with that, but the whole situation. I got the same sense at Joe's house.

'Don't pretend you weren't looking, Sam.'

She hit me playfully.

'Dream on, boy.'

She shook a finger at me. What if Joe saw and really did think I was hitting on his girlfriend? He *seemed* pretty mild-mannered, but what did I know? And what if one of his friends noticed? Actually, a few were looking our way. Was that Kelly's idea, to create a scene?

'Kelly, what are you doing?'

Kelly drew in closer and adjusted the straps on her shoulders, moving them back and forth. The white had nowhere to hide. I don't know why, but I felt sorry for whatever white she had left. On her breasts. Her backside. Her ... Geez, this staring at her assets wasn't helping disprove her thesis.

Kelly bumped against me. I looked down. One of the black straps had fallen off her shoulder.

'Oops.'

She slowly stretched it down, revealed more of her chest. I saw Joe again, ploughing the ice. He was breaking! He'd stopped! He was standing the other side of the barrier. Kelly turned to him.

'Sam was trying to crack onto me,' she said.

'No, no, I wasn't,' I blurted.

Kelly pulled the black strap back onto her shoulder. 'I just seem to attract the guys. You'd better hurry, Joe. True love waits but *I* don't.' And she walked off all demurely like her blades were high heels or something.

Now I got what she was trying to do; I didn't appreciate it.

'So, Sam, are you having a great time?' asked Joe quite as if nothing had happened.

'Um, yeah, sure.'

'Perhaps I should come clean.'

If I was nervous before, that settled it. My stomach bunched up. What could Joe possibly have to come clean about? Then someone came up behind me, the oldest member of Joe's set: stodgy and with merino hair.

'Oh Sam, this is Shane, our group's "Guide",' said Joe. 'Shane's now happily married with four kids.'

What …? What an odd thing to say.

'What was he before that?'

'Well, Sam,' said Joe. 'Shane was gay.'

Shane waved his trotter vaguely. 'A lot of these people have thought they were too.'

At the cafeteria, I cradled my crap coffee. The floor was rubber, but it was still a hard job walking around on your skates – like little stilts. I made it from the counter to a table and sat down. Where was I exactly? We'd sure driven a fair way. How would I find my way back if it wasn't with Joe? Were all of Joe's friends ex-gay?

Despite the disaster with Arny, I felt I was breaking into life through my friendship with Tubby and acceptance by my teammates (barring Dizzy, though what did *he* matter?). But with Joe and his gang, I felt I'd just taken a wrong step.

A body loomed in front of me. It was Joe.

'Sorry, Sam, I should've told you.'

'Yes, you should've.'

He sat down.

'I'm sorry, it's just … watching what happened between you and Arny, I thought you might want help.'

'I've just come out of the closet; I'm not going back in.'

'It's more complex than that,' said Joe, pushing his fringe out of his eyes. 'A lot of people go through a phase – '

'Are you an ex-gay as well?' I cut him off. 'You've had higher education – you should know there's no helping who you are.'

What Joe said next didn't seem to follow, but he said it.

'Did you know, Sam, thirty per cent of science students are creationists?'

'Makes me wonder if we've evolved after all,' I muttered before sipping the last of my coffee.

'See!' smiled Joe. But it was he who didn't.

Melodramatically, I crushed the paper coffee cup in my hand.

'I want you to take me home, Joe.'

'But – '

'Home. Now.'

Joe stood up, wiping his sweaty hands on his sides. 'Just one more go on the rink, Sam. I'll go at *your* pace.'

Joe was a pretty good teacher, taking up where Rhada had left off. I was almost managing to glide one foot at a time. Still had to crash into the railing to stop, though. After one such head-on with the barrier, Joe glided in smoothly next to me to make sure I was all right. It was then, unsolicited, that I got the low-down on his 'situation'. Joe, it turned out, was a 'born-again' Christian, and so was just about everyone else in the group. Kelly he'd met at the rink. She wasn't Christian but she was warming to the idea.

'She's a … um, a very sexual person, Sam. Very … insistent.'

'Oh … okay,' I mumbled, embarrassed. First Tubby revealing his sexual peccadilloes, now Joe – what I was in for?

'Very sexual,' he went on. 'I haven't got there yet … but true love waits.'

I didn't understand waiting. 'If you've found true love, what could it possibly be waiting for?' I asked.

'Marriage.'

As for Lydia, Joe met her when he answered the ad for a room. She wasn't Christian either, and in her case it seemed there was no hope of her becoming one.

'I think she also fancies me.'

I blinked at this. Okay, so he had all the girls falling over him. So what?

Then there was me, from cricket.

And, finally, the 'ex-gays' he caught up with. With some of them whizzing past, I asked Joe for the second time if he was ex-gay himself. He looked down, around, everywhere but at me.

'I wouldn't say I was ex-gay yet, Sam, but I'm winning. I'm winning the fight.'

I couldn't imagine fighting to go back into the closet once you were out. Well, I could imagine it a bit. The moment I came out, I wanted to hide again, but not for long. The long fight for me had been to *come* out. Besides, there probably wasn't a better time to be gay. Imagine a hundred years ago, fifty, even ten – that would've been a gargantuan struggle. Sure, people's backgrounds and circumstances could still make it pretty difficult – I hadn't found it such a breeze – but overall it was getting easier. In a way, you owed it to others as much as to yourself to be out.

I put some of this to Joe. Joe was looking at a guy and girl skating hand in hand. He finally looked at me.

'It's simpler than that with me, Sam; I just don't want to be gay.'

'Well, why not?' I asked, exasperated. I was sick of asking 'why?' I now just wanted to know 'how'.

'Because, Sam … because I don't want to go to hell.'

It took me a bit to clear up that Joe really, actually, honestly meant hell, as in the fiery infinity. He took the Bible literally, as the unquestionable word of God, and in it apparently homosexuals aren't viewed favourably.

We made our way through the exit. That Shane-guy hurried over, telling Joe one of the boys had gotten the cafeteria girl's number. While he told it, he stared at me. 'Who is this guy,' he must've been thinking, 'to have had Joe's ear for so long?'

Eventually, Shane broke off staring and gazed down at Joe, a little too down for eye contact. I had my hand on my hip so I waved it across Joe's belt. Shane's eyes shot up at me. Smiling, I watched his face turn red, and not just red with anger.

The stupid sheep shut me out of the pen after that, using himself and Joe as the gates. He rabbited on to Joe about how the group was dwindling – more and more members proclaiming their homosexuality was innate and natural as opposed to sinful and environmental. Well, that should've woken them up. Shane was telling Joe 'one had to be ever more vigilant in consequence'. Joe swallowed and nodded – firmly. When he looked up it was at Kelly, standing by the Coke machine.

I didn't know what to do: stay or find my own way home? I went to the cafeteria and bought another crap coffee for the privilege of sitting down.

They were playing this country and western thing over the PA, sung in a real sad way by some woman. Made me so lonesome. Made me think how quickly you can get out of touch with people. Cinders for one. She *had* been a friend – of sorts. I mean, you don't ring someone and next thing you know a month's passed. Not much holds us together …

But what I was thinking was, there's something so sad about certain places. Take roadhouses. I find roadhouses really sad. Couldn't stand working in one. There *you* are, stock-still, and yet there *they* are, all those people passing through, going somewhere. Or maybe going nowhere, but at least they're moving. I'd moved, but now I wanted to get somewhere.

In Melbourne, I'd get to a tram stop, look up the road, and if I didn't see one coming, I'd get itchy. My feet would want to move. So I'd walk to the next stop. Just standing still, waiting, I hated it. I was missing the tram a lot that way.

That's why I took over an hour to walk to Joe's that morning; I had meant to tram it.

I looked out the one window in the cafeteria. It had a grille over it so I could hardly see but I knew there'd be nothing familiar outside anyway. Was there even public transport this far out? I saw I'd have to wait and leave with Joe. I looked back to the rink. If I had to keep skating, I at least wanted to change my skates. They were a bit loose and my ankles kept splaying out.

There were more of Joe's Christian friends (they were everywhere!) sitting on the seat where you tried on skates, and this other girl next to them putting on an extra pair of socks. She looked bookish but interesting. She looked up at me.

'How are you finding it?' she asked.

She had these lovely glasses with blue rims, a loose blue shirt and sapling legs. Her black hair was tied back. Anyway, I just said, pretty uninterested-like (not putting on an act at all – I was just tired): 'Yeah, not bad. I'm staying on my feet more.'

'You're getting better,' she said.

I sat next to her and started putting on my replacement skates. She looked like a teacher. But a nice one. The one you form a first crush on. The librarian. Anyway, I didn't even know why I liked her. Like I said, with this girl sitting next to Joe's friends, I thought – I didn't even think it – I just took her for a friend of theirs.

So I walked onto the rink. Halfway out, I looked back at her and she looked sad, disappointed kind of. Don't know what. Wondered what she could've expected.

I caught up with Joe. He'd left Shane behind. The girl sped past us. She looked good from the back. I'd seen her from the front, and I'd probably seen her on the rink before, but people look more attractive the better you know them. Even if you only know them a little. They're not just a face, then.

Joe wasn't keeping pace with me but racing ahead. I asked him how he knew her – I practically had to yell.

'I don't,' he said.

I almost lost my balance.

'Isn't she one of your friends?' I shouted. 'She was sitting with them!'

I was at a corner, with Joe now well ahead and on the straight. He swivelled so that he was zooming backwards and yelled at me, 'No, I don't know her at all!'

I crashed into the barrier. My knees wouldn't take much more of this.

I thought over the conversation. She said I was getting better. She must've been watching us. Watching *me*. Maybe she'd heard a bit of what I'd said to Joe, and liked it. The feeling behind it, I mean. Maybe I wasn't just a face to her. She'd worked up the courage and I'd snubbed her. Not even that, I'd just … well … I was tired before she spoke.

I almost wanted to hit Joe.

Look, I didn't even know why I liked her. I thought I'd, well, finally settled on a path, so to speak.

Joe was lapping me. I yelled out. He stopped.

'Take me home,' I told him.

In the car on the way home, Joe was driving fast, which I gathered from Kelly, and from the journey *to* the rink, was normal for him. I was next to him and Kelly was in the back. The wind was coming in, cooling us off. Kelly started to speak, voice all girly. I thought of that other girl's voice: free-flowing, liquid, clear.

'Hey, guys, look, you can answer me truthfully here – I want your honest opinion – do you think I've got what it takes to be a model?'

Kelly flicked her red hair. Joe looked her up and down in the rear-view mirror. I thought that was for seeing out the back window.

'You sure do,' said Joe, sticking his tongue out.

'Sorry?' I asked.

Then I remembered he wasn't even talking to me. But he was looking at me hard enough. He and Kelly seemed to be waiting for something.

'Well, Sam?'

The sound of the wind got louder.

'What, Joe?'

Joe slapped the wheel, which looked like a metal backbone turned in on itself.

'You think Kelly could be a model, don't you?' yelled Joe.

I turned to look back at Kelly and she uncrossed her legs.

'Yeah, sure thing, Kelly,' I said.

Joe smiled. Put on a proud-father look and everything. They went into the logistics of it after that. Joe would be her agent, how to avoid sleazy photographers, stuff like that. Now and then I'd listen for a few lines then say something – something relevant I hoped. But I just wanted to nod off, mostly.

The only boon about the whole car ride was the clear view of the scenery, me being in front and all. All those concrete retaining walls along the highway – I could believe I had space. I wasn't just stuck in a car. Nothing could touch me. But then I thought of that girl with the blue-rimmed glasses: sometimes you don't want your space.

Joe and Kelly kept play-acting while I was jet-skiing on the make-believe. Kelly kept tickling Joe's neck through the letterboxing in the headrest. I found it hard looking ahead, at that ever-widening triangle of road. Joe grabbed Kelly's fingers. Christ, how old were they? Kelly breathed on Joe's neck. He turned around for the umpteenth time and the car veered into the next lane. Both my shout and a motorist's frantic horn finally got Joe slowing down and concentrating on the road ahead.

We passed under a footbridge. There was this kid up there, a girl, peering over. I thought how I'd stood on a bridge myself after Arny left and after my horrible night at Dirk's. No, Sam, wait, I told myself, hang around. In no time at all, things will be better, you'll see. And I saw myself go under my feet, on that highway, in a car travelling with two kids tickling each other through a rectangular hole in a headrest. Hang around. Wait.

What was I waiting for?

I'd missed my ride: Arny …

Kelly was running a hand like an amputee spider over Joe's shoulder. Joe was pretending not to see. But he was looking at her through the rear-view mirror, really looking at her, looking with his hands and tongue. Well, maybe ... maybe ... I mean, that girl *had* looked at me, hadn't she?

Maybe it *was* a phase.

Hey, there was something I hadn't taken in at the time: she'd almost crashed into me when we were on the rink. She was going fast, one leg coming level with the other and pushing out in succession. I know what I would've said if she had, now. If she'd crashed into me, I mean. I'd have said, both of us sprawled out there, bums wet on the ice – I had it all worked out – I'd have said, 'That's an interesting way to meet someone.' She'd have laughed, I'd have laughed. Then we'd have helped each other up. Me with my washed-out blue jeans navy blue in the seat, her in those grey slacks with dark grey padding, like jockeys wear. We'd laugh, look at our behinds ... feel their wetness and ... and ... well ...

Nothing probably.

Not a thing. Or nothing sexual anyway.

No, I was gay. I knew that finally. Well, as much as you can know anything without testing it, I guess. The real reason I kept ruminating over that girl was because I'd missed an opportunity to make friends with Arny and I was worried I was making a habit of it. I actually *knew* why that girl said hello. She'd been leaning against the barrier behind Joe while I told him the hard part was coming out. She'd heard it. And it touched her. That's why she wanted to talk to me.

A friend I'd missed out on.

Joe dropped Kelly off first. I hardly answered a word he said to me once Kelly was out of the car. His pretence of helping me get a social life was really about him getting a convert. Prick.

Next training session in the nets, I was going to ask Tubby if he and the guys knew Joe was gay. But Joe watched me with such a pleading look, I said nothing. Instead, I asked Tubby if he had any gay friends. And none of them *ex*-gay, thank you very much.

'Not apart from you,' answered Tubby.

We were packing the gear into two polo bags. Everyone else had gone home, Joe the earliest; I'd ignored him all day. As I tracked down and located the last bail, a thought occurred to me.

'What about Beth?' I asked Tubby. 'Would *she* know anyone?'

'I'll ask,' grunted Tubby as he lifted one of the bags to his shoulder. I hoisted the other bag onto mine. He was lagging behind me on our trek across the oval to the clubhouse. I swung round. Tubby had stopped.

'Man, I'm even pimping for you now!' he laughed. 'You can't catch gay, can you?' he added a second later, half-seriously.

I thought about this.

'No, nor straight neither,' I laughed back.

When I got back to the pub, Wally relayed a message for me. It was from Tubby. That was quick.

'Apparently his girlfriend's got a friend who's got a friend who's friend's friend is gay.'

'Yeah, thanks, Wally.'

Wally poured us a couple of half-mast soapy beers and we took a swig. He let the froth coat his moustache ('for later'); I made sure to lick my top lip. Wally leaned across the carpeted bar.

'Look, mate, why don't you just go to a pub,' he said and then looked around at his regulars before whispering, 'and not *this* bloody one.'

He was right.

At the library, I sussed out this queer event from a gay magazine I leafed through on the sly. Not sure why I was leafing through it on the sly! Anyway, what grabbed me first was this 'Q&A Night'. In this case, Q&A didn't stand for Questions & Answers but Queer & Alternative and it was held on a Thursday night at the Builders' Arms Hotel. It happened to be Thursday afternoon.

When I moseyed back to the pub in order to get ready, Wally shook a snowstorm of dandruff at the corner of the room – to the couch he was too sentimental to put down – and to some guy sitting there. No, not *some* guy; I knew that mop of blonde even from the back.

'Joe.'

'It's a nice room, Sam.'

'No, it isn't.'

I'd taken Joe upstairs and he was sitting cross-legged on the end of my mattress (I hadn't got myself a raised bed yet), staring at me. He *did* owe me one; he was right.

'Look, if you really wanna make it up to me, Joe,' I put to him, 'you can come with me to this Q&A Night.'

Joe rocked forward. When he rocked back, it was onto his hands.

'I'm … I'm not sure, Sam.'

'Come on, Joe, you can be my guy magnet. Just hang around till someone gets talking to me.'

Somehow we never made it, stopping off downstairs to purchase alcoholic courage, saying we'd skol it on the way. We did get halfway, but that was to a park. I sat down one side of a bench, Joe the other. Wally was on the ball when he insisted we take paper bags to wrap our bottles; the police wafted past but didn't stop. Joe drank his lone stubbie of light beer like it was poison – which isn't far wrong. I tore through a six-pack of the full-strength stuff, enjoying it – enjoying beer for the first time. I was learning to let my guard down.

Looking at Joe in the dappled light, with the shadows from the leaves above forming a wreath in his hair, I thought of the book *1984*. Not sure why that, particularly. Maybe 'cause I was trying to suss Joe out, and in *1984* Winston does a lot of 'sussing out' himself.

That's what I like best about the book. A lot of the political stuff goes over my head; I've never been that bright. But I love all that stuff about Winston trying to pick out others 'like him'. It's so subtle. He can't let on he's looking. He can't just scream 'Hey you!' He has to try to tell if they're on the same wavelength from a gesture, a smile. The blankest look. Something so – you know, practically invisible. He's always on the lookout for this sign, this Winston. Wherever he is: out walking, on the train, in a crowd, looking for this sign. Poor old twat.

I tried to read *1984* in 1994 because I thought if I left it much longer, it would be too far out of date. I told a teacher I'd read it – Mr Caton – and he drilled me so horribly. In the end, he reckoned if I had read it, I'd gotten nothing out of it. And I know I was wrong on one score: it wasn't about one time, but all time. Joe reckoned the same went for the Bible. Just 'cause it was written all those years ago – two thousand he put it at – doesn't take a thing from what it has to say today. Not only does it speak the truth, he'd say, but the literal truth at that.

I got through my last stubbie, stood up and deposited the empties in a bin. We rolled over to the kiddies' playground near the new museum (old museum now), which wasn't far from our bench.

'What if the Bible *is* all true, Joe? What then?'

Joe and I were hanging upside down, the blood pooling to our heads. (This was the closest Joe got to getting drunk!)

'What do you mean?' he asked.

'Well, what would there be left to argue about?'

Joe's shirt had untucked and fallen over his head. I saw a single tyre-tread of hair skidding down his middle, braking at the belt.

'Nothing, I guess.'

I pulled myself up, so I could think better.

'We'd just have that one book,' I said, face still plum. 'All the answers in that.'

Joe put his hands flat on the woodchip ground, then cart-wheeled sunny side up.

'We could still make scientific discoveries, Sam. Work out how God made the universe.'

I tried cartwheeling down myself, but I didn't land sunny side up –only scrambled.

'Great!' I said, pulling chips out of my hair. 'That'd be like setting off to discover Australia today, not in Cook's era.'

Joe ran up the slide.

'Well, the Aborigines were here first.'

'You know what I mean!'

I got up the slide the normal way, climbing the yellow ladder.

'Nope, I reckon if the Bible's right,' I argued, 'we've got nowhere to go, nothing to question. That's it. End of learning.'

Joe looked back, chin on shoulder.

'People will never follow the Bible properly, though, Sam. That's why there's been all this trouble with religion.'

'I reckon it's 'cause they *have* tried to follow it,' I said, giving him what I hoped was a pointed look.

But Joe went slippering down the slide.

'Head rush!' he yelled when he got to the bottom, then he turned back to stare at me. 'Shall we … ah, um, get more beer, Sam?'

And that began my time with Joe. For the next two months, we hung out practically all the time, even on those days we weren't already thrown together at training and Saturday matches. Although I can't say it was a totally happy time. I guess I wanted more than a friend. Arny came up quite a bit in my thoughts; my stupidity with all that really got to me. What if he'd been the one – the right one for me? I believed in 'the one'. It occurred to me that I'd always believed in 'the one'. I'm not sure if I arrived at that belief through books or my schooling or the views around me but it held firm. Someone to meet and then to spend the rest of my life with – that's what I desired more than anything. The only part of my beliefs I'd changed was in swapping 'the one' from a girl to a guy. How many more times would I have to alter my dream till it shaped itself to reality?

What Joe and I did in our time together basically consisted of hitting the ball in the park, then a few beers in the pub. Joe and Kelly were still together, still dating, so nights were reserved for them.

One time in the pub, it suddenly got to me, this wrong step I'd taken with Joe. Not just a wrong step, but a step backwards. And that's how I still viewed it. With Joe, I'd merely found someone to avoid life *with*. I was still stuck in kidland, home every night before dark.

'You know, Joe, we've got the same routine,' I said, flicking the plastic ashtray off the table. 'Why don't we really get drunk this time? So we can't walk straight.'

I was taking a real shining to drinking. Because when you were drunk, you felt you might more easily work up the courage to jump at life's possibilities. But hard drinking – and jumping at life – isn't such fun on your own.

'Come on, Joe?'

Joe turned from two dolled-up women on a nearby table who were gasping over him. 'No, Sam.'

I looked down at that ashtray I'd flicked off: man overboard. The wood table rocked beneath my hands. The stupid thing had no sea-legs. My mouth suddenly felt like it had a ruler's edge.

'Joe, your parents are miles away – in the bloody sticks.'

Joe looked at me sharply. We'd discovered we both grew up in the country, not far from each other; in rural distances, that is.

'What did you say that for, Sam? Why did you say that?'

'You know, Joe, Tubby asked about us today at training.'

'Us?' he asked, alarmed.

He was right. There was no us.

'I meant, about all the time you're spending with a gay guy.'

Joe looked panicked.

'Oh, well, what did you …? I mean, you didn't tell him that I'm …? Sam …?'

I looked away, feeling mean. My little threat was pretty low-down and dirty. I took the two pieces of a cardboard coaster I'd torn and stuck them under a leg of the table. It stopped rocking after that.

Of course I wasn't going to tell Joe's secret.

Our next stop was the park, the same one where we'd hung out on the Q&A night. On the swings, I said it was getting late and one of us would turn into a pumpkin. And besides, weren't Joe's evenings reserved for Kelly? He said she had something on.

The conversation ended up the usual place: how I would go to hell. It amazed me that people still believed this stuff and, worse, that they still taught it.

'No, I'm not planning on going to hell, Joe,' I said firmly as I swung back and forth in the tyre, with its nasty wire hairs where the rubber had rubbed away. 'Me and God,' I continued, 'we've got things to work through. He's got a lot to answer for, that guy. Like why Australia lost to India in the Test match.'

Joe laughed a little, leaning back in the swing. With the sun now well and truly set, everything looked feathery and Joe was alive with moonshine. You could see it in his hair, nestling there. He was looking through his legs at the woodchips, which were practically black in the light, or for lack of the stuff. Actually, I don't know that light's stuff, exactly. I guess Joe could've put me right, being the one with a degree in physics.

Joe started swinging over that black patch. Only a ruler's length swing, mind you, but swinging all the same, all the while looking down. I swung in time with him before grabbing the chain to his tyre.

'It's all right, Joe, we'll tell God off together.'

I put my hand on his knee, the way Arny had put his on mine at that holiday shack. Like me back then, Joe's body stiffened and he moved away.

'Only the perfectly good and virtuous go to heaven, Sam.' Joe stared at me with heartbreaking concern for my soul.

'Then damn it, Joe, I'd rather go to hell and have company.'

And I laughed, but he didn't. Humour doesn't always work.

It was the early hours of the morning when we ended up at his place – only the second time I'd been invited there. I sat next to Joe on his bed and he kind of looked angles at me but I didn't budge; I wasn't sleeping on the floor. Joe put a couple of pillows between us as something of a Great Dividing Range. We got down to boxers and then Joe turned out the light. I was pretty tired, but I couldn't sleep. My hand accidentally touched his shoulder but he shooed it away, mumbling something about getting the flyscreen fixed.

I thought back to that time at the shack when I invited Arny to share the couch bed with me. The current situation with Joe had similarities … disappointing similarities. Sleep came. You know when you're asleep and you haven't realised? Well, like that.

Sleep. Dreams.

And a thousand coconut castanets above.

I went to shoo the horses off the roof but Dad said they might stampede. All that red-righteous clay, clinkering to pieces – Mum wouldn't be happy.

Horses on the roof …?

The sun was teasing the room gold. It'd worked its way under the blinds. I tried to roll away but I'd lain on one side too long; my arm was fizzy. I worked it round bowling-action-style till it went flat. Joe's head popped up over the Great Wall of Pillow, and his face came over grey.

'Sam?' he asked, startled.

'Nothing happened,' I assured him wearily.

'Oh,' and he fell back on his side of the wall.

A bit later, we both woke up properly. The sun had called the room yeller.

Joe reached for an orange book on his side-table and started reading. It was *To Kill a Mockingbird.*

'Is that one of your favourites, too?' I asked.

'Of course,' said Joe.

'Then read it out loud.' I was glad to know Joe read something other than the Bible.

He had a good voice. Very lively. Hopped along the words. Made me think of Mum reading to me, a chapter every night. I'd get into bed early, pull the doona up round my neck, breathing in that ironed smell of clean sheets and my damp hair. Used to shower nights, see, not mornings, and I'd leave my hair wet to take the heat out of my head. Only got three minutes drenching, seeing we lived on a farm and water was scarce. I'd listen real hard. Mum'd finish the chapter and I'd beg for another. And another. I loved those stories. It was like you had two lives: the one you lived, which was pretty crappy, and the one in books – heaps better.

Mum once read *To Kill a Mockingbird*. It inspired me so much, we tried to take after it, with the dares and all, me and … well, my cat Zorro. (I'll get to Zorro later.) I got so into that book that when it came to the end of the last page, I said, 'Right, what happens next?'

'What do you mean?' said Mum.

'Well, what happened after?' I asked, pulling at her shirt.

Mum pulled away.

'What happens to Scout an' Jem an' Boo an' all the rest of 'em? I reckon Scout just had to've become a lawyer. Well, did she?'

Mum put the book down on my side-table and got up.

'Sam, you know about this.'

'But, Mum,' I said. I'd half crawled out of the sheets.

'Sam, stop playing.'

'I'm not.'

'She's fictitious.'

'What's that mean?'

'Made up.'

Now I'd known what 'made up' was, all right. Everyday, I'd make up something: that I'd done my homework, brushed my teeth, washed my face. But seriously, I'd make up other stuff. Those rocks – shaped like chairs – they were the Monument; that stand of blackberry bushes, that was the Amazon; and that old settler's house, over the other side of the creek, next to the Chandlers' – that was the Castle. But *To Kill a Mockingbird* wasn't made up, none of it. It was more real, somehow, than what *was*. And to think Scout and Jem and Boo and the rest of them were fictitious ... I ask you!

Mum insisted.

'It's just a story, Sam. When a story's over, nothing happens next.'

To Kill a Mockingbird was the last story Mum ever read to me. Said I was old enough to read on my own after that. I hated her for ages. Reckoned she'd all but killed Scout just by getting to the end of that book. Scout couldn't be dead – she couldn't. I had gotten to know her – like she was a friend – and now she'd died. Mum had killed her.

'You've killed her, Mummy! You've killed her!'

Dad came in. He and Mum looked at each other. Mum shrugged. I couldn't stop saying it. Dad told me to stop yelling. 'Do I have to take my belt off, son?' – that kind of thing. He told me to lie down (I was sitting up) – to lie down and turn off my light. I wished he hadn't told me to do something, because then I knew I wouldn't. Dad stepped forward.

'I won't ask again.'

Mum stepped in. 'Let's just leave him, darling.'

'I won't ask again, Sam.' And he didn't – he backhanded me one. I lay down after that, the force kind of made me. They turned off my light and shut the door.

Only then did I cry. And cried and cried. Were you like that as a kid? I reckon I cried just about every night. Don't know why. Must've been crying over something, I guess. Actually, I *can* remember some of it. Like, I'd cry over stupid stuff. Not even things that were real. Like I'd imagine Mum and Dad were dead. And I'd see myself at the funeral, and I'd be in black, but not crying, with all the teachers and kids looking at me different, somehow. Like I was strange, and the kids waiting till I'd found my seat in the classroom before they took theirs. And all this time I was make-believing, tears would tease their way out. There I was, under the blankets, with eyes shut like nail marks on your palms. I didn't make a sound. Never have. And I always hoped Mum or Dad would come in one time and see. 'Cause that was about the only time I cried ever: nights. Not much good, then, I know. I don't know why, but I couldn't cry in front of anyone. Never. I just felt like … well, it'd be easier getting caught starkers. Besides, I didn't want to be known as a sissy.

The one time one of 'em did come in – to close the window, I think (must've been raining) – I wiped my eyes so well they didn't see. *He* didn't see – Dad. Guess I knew I couldn't explain it. The crying. That's why I wiped the tears away. Hell, couldn't explain them – then or now. Just wondered if any of you were like that, that's all. Forget it.

But I got over Scout. Got over her enough to read that book again much later. *To Kill a Mockingbird*, I'm talking about now. Only, I had a bit of a problem with Atticus. For quite a long time, too. He annoyed me somehow. All right, I'll be honest: he annoyed me something shocking, though I couldn't see why. No one could. 'But he's so nice,' they'd say. I almost felt bad for hating him. I couldn't work it out for a long time, either, so I read the book again, wanting to like him, and finally saw something in him I could.

All the way through the book, Atticus does everything right. He's the father of Jem and Scout and they live in this old American town. God knows where but it's dusty, with swinging chairs on the front porches, guys with guns split over their knees like broken branches, that sort of thing. Anyhow, he's just so right about everything, this Atticus. Like, there's this time when a friend of Scout's asks for treacle to put over his peas and beans. Well, that's a pretty daft thing to do and Scout makes fun of it. Their housemaid, Calpurnia, tells her off after, and says the boy was her guest, don't be rude, and if he wants to put treacle on savoury food then that his biz. When Scout complains to Atticus, Atticus backs up Calpurnia, one hundred per cent. Well, Atticus was right of course to do that. But that's just what makes it all so sickening. I mean, he's *always* right. And so-o-o nice. I mean, no one's this nice, ever.

But the man's saved, 'cause there's this bit at the end where this guy's killed. Mr Ewell, his name is. Real nasty piece of work: hates blacks, women; you name it.

Hell, I'm sure you all know the book inside out on account of everyone having to study it at school.

But just in case, maybe you live on Mars or something, I'll continue. This Mr Ewell tries to attack Jem and Scout 'cause Atticus makes him look like dirt in court. Atticus shows it was Mr Ewell who raped his *own* daughter, not the black guy, not Tom. Atticus defends this innocent Tom guy but Tom gets convicted all the same – I don't know, townsfolk soft in the head or something. Anyhow, even though this Mr Ewell gets off in court everyone still knows he's really to blame. So that's why Mr Ewell tries to kill Atticus' kids – he has to get back at someone.

But there's this other kid, Boo, who's a bit of a mushroom on account of his never having seen the light and soft in the head like one too. And Boo saves the day by killing Mr Ewell with a knife. Up under Mr Ewell's ribcage it goes, kaput.

So now this Boo guy, who's really no more a nuisance than a mockingbird, will be up for murder.

Atticus starts going off: 'I'll defend him, won't be easy, we can plead this, plead that, Defence Article three-two-seven' – you get the idea. But the sheriff just says, 'No, Atticus, Mr Ewell fell on his own knife.'

'No, he didn't.'

'Yes, he did,' says the sheriff. 'He fell on his own knife.'

Atticus hadn't managed to save Tom, not by the law, and finally he sees he might not save Boo, not by the law anyhow. And that's where I liked him, truly, for the first time. 'Cause he saw something. He saw you can't do everything by the book.

Joe looked at me for a long time. His leg was on mine, half over it in fact. Somehow the great wall of pillow had been razed. He put down *To Kill A Mockingbird*.

'For the first time, Sam,' he said, 'I feel … I feel passion! Such passion and desire!'

I was back in that room with a jolt, staring at Joe and nervous as hell. I somehow found courage to take his hand in mine, but half expected him to snatch it away. Instead, he blushed and laughed in about equal measure and got out of bed.

'I should make us breakfast,' he said.

Joe didn't come back. Guess he expected me to eat breakfast at the table, but what about that talk of feeling lust for the first time? My stomach was in a flutter. Did he mean it? And if he did, did I return the feeling? I wrapped Joe's dressing gown round me. Lydia was in the kitchen, cutting up carrots for juice. I said hello. She stared at me, then even harder at Joe's dressing gown. Embarrassed, I asked if she'd gotten a good sleep. She asked me back, quite pointedly.

'Didn't get to sleep till six,' I said.

Lydia stared at me. 'What time did you get in?' she asked.

'Oh, ever so late. 5 o'clock maybe.'

Lydia eyeballed me. 'I heard you come in at four.'

'Oh.'

We both just stood there.

Well, I'd added on an hour. You know how you do. A night out, you always beef it up. But I reckon it *was* that by the time we'd gotten home from the park and gone to sleep.

Lydia looked at Joe's bedroom door where I'd just come from and then at me.

'You're obviously not one of Joe's "cured" friends,' she said.

She was sure sounding jealous. Then I remembered: at the ice-skating rink, Joe said Lydia had 'a thing' for him too. Too! Did *I* have a 'thing' for Joe? Lydia averted her face then turned on the blender. The sound cut up the room, piecemeal. Noise is a weapon.

Joe was in the backyard, sitting in a wicker chair, looking happy. I sat next to him in a chair that had the bum worn out of it. Joe turned to me. I was still in a torment over this new 'passion' he felt, but Joe had something else on his mind.

That 'something' emerged through the side gate, red hair right royal.

'I invited Kelly over, Sam, this morning when you were … ah, um, before you got here.'

I didn't correct his lie. He must've rung Kelly while I was waiting for that breakfast. 'Passion' and he rings Kelly?

'We need a drink,' said Joe.

Unlike at the pub, he didn't mean the alcoholic kind.

When we went into the kitchen, Lydia was waiting at the fridge like a cat. She said she was taking a permanent break from working on *Untitled Number 372* to fix herself a cuppa. That meant we were all four crowded into the kitchen, trying to fix ourselves drinks: Joe and Kelly their hot chocolates, me a strong coffee and Lydia some exotic herbal tea. Then it was musical chairs for young and … well, young. Me and Lydia went to sit next to Joe on the two-seater, but Kelly got in first and trumped us both. I could see Lydia straighten her neck, emu-like, at this – probably as confused as I was. First she thought Joe and I

71

were getting it on, now it looked like it would be Joe and Kelly.

That was certainly looking pretty likely, with Kelly rubbing against Joe on the two-seater. Somehow, it made me think of our old goat back on the farm, rubbing against the barbwire fence to alleviate an itch. At his favourite spot for that, the fence ended up a bit of a clothesline with all these mini wool jumpers hanging from it, pegged at intervals.

I guess all animals are enterprising creatures, no matter the species.

We each sipped in slurpitude.

Joe sprang that it was time for Bible studies. Lydia huffed but Kelly leapt off the two-seater, saying she'd join him. Joe looked surprised and happy. Obviously it was the first time she'd offered. That Kelly was pretty damn committed to the cause. I could tell even Lydia was impressed in her own, grudging way.

'Can we tempt you as well, Sam?' asked Joe, beaming.

After all, he now had a convert to his name. I wasn't about to give him a second.

'Prob'ly burn in my hands, Joe.'

The two disappeared into Joe's room to get ready. The two-seater was now empty but neither Lydia nor I sat down. I noticed her cup. In bold black: 'Don't be a mug – pray to Jesus'. Lydia blew so hard on her herbal tea it would cool in no time. Geez, she was taking it hard.

'Hey, Lydia – '

'Quiet!' she hissed.

Joe and Kelly were making funny noises in Joe's room. Eventually, they put on the radio. Lydia and I stared at each other. I'm sure my expression was as strange as hers. I kept telling myself to leave. Too late, Joe and Kelly emerged from their room, flushed and sweaty. They were standing close. Very close.

So *that* was the outcome of his feeling, for the first time, 'such passion and desire'.

'Good news, Sam, Lydia,' said Joe.

'What?' asked Lydia tartly.

'Kelly and I are getting married.'

'True love has stopped waiting!' shouted Kelly.

She and Joe certainly *looked* happy. I felt tricked – again! Lydia told them they were too young, but I simply congratulated them. Joe took my hand heartily enough but didn't quite look me in the eye. Again, I thought of Winston from *1984*, trying to pick out others 'like him'. Joe wasn't 'like me'. I hurried home to my room over the pub.

I'm ashamed to say I became almost bedridden for the next few weeks. My ventures into society in Melbourne had been fairly disastrous. Cabin fever eventually forced me out of one enclosure, my room, and into another, the library. There, at least, I could read up on my new life. Trying to sandwich about ten gay-themed books between a John Grisham and a Thomas Harris, I approached the loans desk.

My librarian was onto me.

'Do you really want *these* two?' she asked.

Her name was Jen. Sussed that out from her nametag. She called me Sam, obviously from my card. Quite spontaneously, I told Jen I was gay.

'I know,' she said.

There was something familiar about those blue-rimmed glasses.

'Hey, haven't we met somewhere before?'

As soon as I said it, it sounded like the worst pick-up line ever. Sending mixed messages! What was I doing? But Jen didn't take it the wrong way.

'Yes, Sam,' she said, 'we *have* met before. At the ice-skating rink.'

She was having a pretty quiet day, she said, so we ended up having a good talk about places she'd hang. Turned out she was single and looking for the right gal. That made me think: I was single and looking for the right guy. But she beat me to it.

'Maybe we could hit the clubs together,' she suggested.

Life was starting!

Chapter Three

My brother Ashleigh rang, laying guilt on me about Mum and Dad. He'd called the pub direct.

'Hey, Sam, come back. You can stay with me and Tarlia if you want.'

Wally was watching from behind the counter. I told Ashleigh about that night at Dirk's, but in whispers, half-twisting the phone cord around myself to get some privacy from Wally, who eventually got the hint. Then he started collecting bottles, adding another distraction.

'Yeah, well, Dirk can be like that,' I heard Ashleigh say between clinks. 'But, Sam, that's Dirk's life, telling jokes. We had it harder than you. By the time you'd come along and wanted to be a batsman, Mum and Dad didn't say a word about a "sensible" career.'

Dirk had been a good wicketkeeper, but Dad insisted he finish his mechanic's apprenticeship. Dirk still listened to the cricket, working under the cars.

'And what about me? I can't even catch,' laughed Ashleigh.

Ashleigh was as crap in the field as on the pitch. He'd lucked out there.

'Mum and Dad are coming round. People get worn down by life, Sam.'

Perhaps being worn down was a good thing. It made you rounder, smoother. Wally walked back in, dumped the bin, and resumed his place behind the counter. He made a show of busying himself with checking the levels of the spirits.

'Tarlia's made up the bed in the spare room for you, Sam. I know what it's like staying with your parents once you've moved out.'

Ashleigh had moved in and out of Mum and Dad's quite a number of times; finding a job was tough.

'Thanks, Ash,' I said, moved by how supportive he was being. 'But I need to make my own way for a while.'

Tarlia came on the line.

'Next time we come down to Melbourne, Sam,' she said, 'we could go to a gay bar. It's so nice to dance without being hit on.'

We wrapped up the conversation and I handed the phone back to Wally.

'Who's coming down?' he asked.

I dropped by the library. In the past weeks, Jen and I had become good friends, planning our assault on the town. When Jen got a break from helping customers, she came over to the seat where I was reading. She was wearing a suit. Instead of the blue glasses, black.

'Guess what?'

I shrugged.

'I've got you a date for Friday.'

I grinned.

'If it doesn't work out romantically, Sam, you can still be friends.'

I didn't hear her. Friends? To me, it was a date. Couldn't stay cut up over Arny. And Joe? He'd made his choice. This time I wouldn't miss *my* chance.

On the Thursday, Jen got me to try on about a zillion outfits up and down Chapel Street. Had to spruce up, she said. No more tracksuit dagginess, baggy green caps, any of that cricket casualness. Nup. Tight-fitting stuff from now on. Sleeves cut off just past your shoulders, not billowing out like dresses over your elbows. That's all right if you've got muscle to give your shirt shape, not ribs like me, your skin pushing against them like sails. I felt like a bit of a nong at first, staring into the shop mirrors. Afterwards, I even had my hair cut. Short's the go in this scene, too, apparently.

'What about a piercing, Sam?'

I baulked at that.

'Through the eyebrow?'

'Nah.'

'The ear?'

'Nah.'

'A bolt …?'

'Oh all right,' I said. Bloody hurt but it was cool, I guess. Jen said so.

So that was me decked out.

A date!

Now I know you're going to think me pretty daft, but all the way to the restaurant the next day, off to meet my blind date, I kept thinking over the night. The night to go, I should point out. Yeah, I know, pretty dumb. I mean, you can't think over a night till it's happened but some of us are daft enough to try. Maybe you've done the same so you won't be judging me too harshly. I'd seen how me and my date just sat and talked, the deepest stuff, for ever so

77

long. Oh, I don't know, but on and on, the candle lights linking together in streamers. Then the walk home, the goodbyes outside the door, and the kiss, lips polishing lips. The only boy I'd ever kissed before was Arny … But I had to put him out of my head.

No, the new guy – he was 'the one'.

I was getting pretty mushy on this sop when I got to the door of the restaurant. When I walked in, there he was, sitting by the window like Jen had said he'd be.

'Sam …?'

And he put out his hand.

Hello, I thought, you'd go down like a good claret.

And he said his name Jen had already told me.

'Zane.'

Zane ordered from a woman who, from the looks of it, moved on tracks. She just seemed to glide by.

'That was the *maitre d*',' said Zane. 'I call her The Stopwatch. She times just how long you take to give your order. Sammy, you were taking far – *far* – too long. If I hadn't jumped in there and saved you, darling … well, you never know what. She might've ticked you off.'

And he tucked his great big serviette into his collar.

I was a bit taken aback by the flamboyance. I almost wanted to leave, but stopped myself. I couldn't run again. Besides, his manliness, or lack of it, didn't reflect on me now, did it?

I decided to be chuffed with his talk, the use of 'darling' – okay, maybe he said that to everyone – but the overall chumminess, anyhow. And he called me Sammy, too, which I'd never liked till Arny had called me Sammy. Yes, everything was as it should be, 'cept there weren't any candles, of course, still being daylight and all. Hell, I wasn't going to let myself get too fussy.

Out came our meals and we got stuck into them. Zane had ordered us a treat – eye fillet, medium rare.

I kept looking at Zane, tearing and munching the meat, the blood making his teeth pink. I must say, he looked at his food almost lovingly, which was fair enough – meat's meat – but boy, was Zane something to look at himself. He had the longest lashes, black like a match gets after the flame's gone out, skin browner than barley sugar and … and twice as sweet, I'd say. You wouldn't say he was tubby but he was, well, thick. His arms were thick, his hands were thick, even his fingers were thick, right down to the tips. Hell, thick elsewhere too, I guess.

So nice not to have to curb a thought.

All that closeness with Joe, our time together, that night sharing a bed – in truth, I didn't have any other thought.

Zane must have known I was watching 'cause he looked up, trying to chew down a mouthful too big, pushing a boomerang of onion all the way in with the back of his knife, so he cold get his words out.

'I'm just a tubby bitch, that's all I am, Sammy.'

I was a bit shocked. I was about to say, no, I wasn't looking at you … I mean, I was, but not at you eating specifically … I just meant …' when he jumped in first.

'Sammy,' he said, leaning forward, cleaning the corners of his mouth with the napkin, 'on weekdays I'm nothing. At work, I'm ambiguity itself. Meek as a mouse. But on weekends? On weekends I'm a faggot. Ferociously.'

Hell, how would I catch up? Zane was way out in front in this game. He even wore a shimmering chain round his neck. Couldn't pick its origin, but it was pretty flash. Sexy as hell. I felt round *my* neck. Just skin. I'd never worn a necklace. Bugger that. I mean, they were for … for …

Well, 'poofters'.

So all in all, with Zane sitting there, groomed more immaculately than a dog at a doggy sideshow, I felt pretty normal all up – downright conventional, 'one of the guys'.

'Conventional?' screamed Zane when I put this to him. 'Darling, I hate to lift the bridal veil from your eyes, but you're homa-sex-u-arl. There's nothing conventional about being gay.'

I smiled. Homa-sex-u-arl – he even gave that word a tasty tang.

A clatter at the door – a woman was trying to get her pram through. I got up to help when the *maitre d'* cut me off with her sawtooth hair.

'Breeders,' said Zane, pouring the wine. 'Can't they fuck off? This is a *gay* restaurant.'

'What?' I asked.

'Breeders,' said Zane. 'Hetero trash.'

I looked over to the woman with the pram. She was trying to wheel it to a table. No one moved out of the way. I thought of Ashleigh and his fiancée, Tarlia, soon to have a kid, and … well …

'Don't you have straight friends?' I asked Zane.

'In orientation, yes. Not in outlook. Like I said, I'm only straight during the week. At work.'

I looked around. How could a restaurant be gay? I mean, that's like saying 'gay tyre' or 'gay pencil sharpener'.

I put some of this to Zane, not so well as all that (or as badly, you're probably thinking) but this is what he answered: 'You really are a novice, Sammy. I'll have fun breaking you in,' and he took a slurp of the red. I spluttered mine, that echidna in my stomach unfurling. This wasn't Arny, or even Joe, but I'd stick with it.

Zane went on to talk about how everything he did was gay in *some* way. 'Except work, of course.' He kept throwing that in.

Well, I'm not too bright. Abstract stuff – I'm no good at it. So I asked him to give me an example.

'All right, my wuff twade,' he laughed, 'I'll outline my day for you.'

And he went on to tell how in the mornings he'd nip over to the Prahran Pool – notoriously gay (that was his word) for a dip and a squiz. Then it would be the whole big breakfast thing: eggs, bacon, tomatoes, at Fresh, the gayest gay eatery in town. Then work. That word again, which he'd always lip-synch. (I'd have to sing it in my head to hear it at all). For lunch, he'd duck out to feast maybe at Geralto's, run by the Gay Supremo, Costa, or even the place where we were now, Settee, with the StopWatch, a biker dyke if you've ever seen one. I gave her a look. Hell, I hadn't even picked she was a dyke let alone what brand. This Zane was in. The In Zane, as he said it. He went on to talk about his gay gym after work, then the men's bars, the gay nightclubs. Hell, you could spend all your life in a gay world.

It was kind of entertaining and all, and nice of Zane to fill me in, though I reckon he enjoyed it something shocking, but it was also a bit sad somehow, like an old lady dancing with a teddy bear. I didn't know why, exactly. It just was, that's all.

And I wondered if it made me sad because I was worried this was to be my life.

Zane slurped his wine. When a bit sortied his shirt, he said sorry but he just *had* to refuel after all that gasbagging. Then *I* said something – something I didn't mean to – but it just popped out.

'I don't wanna be gay all the time.'

Zane looked up.

'Sorry, darling?'

'Well, I mean ...'

'I hate to shatter your illusions, girly, but you *are* gay, now and always. Well, not unless Jen's given me a bum steer.'

I shook my head. I could see him looking around, trying to locate the waitress. Hell, maybe I'd gone on a bit too much with all this. I'd said enough, and now I was boring him. Sam, Sam, you're spoiling it, I thought, but ... well ... So I said, 'Zane, sometimes I'm Sam just riding a bike, or Sam playing cricket.'

Zane stopped waving for the waitress and turned around to face me.

'Oh yes, but you're always *gay*, darling,' he said. '*They* don't forget that.'

And I saw what he meant. But at the same time, I sort of also *didn't* see. If you can do both, that is. I was just going to be Sam, who also happened to be gay. You know, the way straight people might also happen to be hydro-geologists.

But was being gay more than just who you wanted to have sex with? One of the books Jen put me onto at the library was by a celibate priest who still felt the need to out himself.

I tried to order. The *maitre d'* looked away.

'Don't fret, Sammy,' said Zane. 'The Stopwatch will notice *me*. Everyone notices *me*. Here, watch this. She'll give *me* service, darling. The royal treatment.'

The waitress walked over to a bald man.

'Oh, look at that fat queen,' cried Zane. 'Probably, secretly, a leather man. Oh baby, baby, beat me, I've been baaaad!'

And he accentuated the 'a' in bad, dragged it like a sack along a highway.

'I don't think people notice *me* much,' I said as the waitress finally looked over in a seagull sort of way.

'Oh, come now, darling,' said Zane, 'you're not that bad-looking,' and he scanned for the waitress.

Just great! There I was, self-deprecation. No one gets off on modesty. So I thought, I'll make it into a joke. I kind of had to tap the table a bit before he stopped looking around for the waitress. Then I hosed my throat with the red.

'Zane,' I said, 'people *really* don't notice me. I mean, people have sat down and said, "Oh sorry, I didn't know you were there." '

Zane said nothing.

Shit.

Fuck.

I'd done it again! Could've hit myself. Self-deprecation a second time! I'm such a moron, I know it. But then the impossible happened. The joke got through. Zane actually laughed.

At least he knew I had a sense of humour, even if it was lame. Before, he must've wondered if I wasn't as sharp as a sponge.

Keep with it, Sam.

'That's Sammy's street sculpture,' said Zane, re-tucking his napkin. 'Living sculpture at the tram stop. You pretend to be a seat. "Come sit on me, come sit, come sit awaaay." '

Hell, he was even going with it now, adding his own twist.

'We know how you get your jollies,' he added.

We both laughed. The other customers smiled. Zane's laugh came out like a dessert wine, mine a breathless whisky. But then Zane stopped, mid-guffaw.

'You're very heterosexual, Sammy.'

'What …?' I'd stopped too.

The way you carry yourself … laugh,' said Zane. 'You've got to suppress those heterosexual urges.'

'What …? I …?'

And I groped about. Like the only light on the moors had gone off. A house snuffed into darkness.

Zane must have sensed it, 'cause he said, 'Oh, Sam, don't listen to me,' and he leant across and patted my hand. 'I'm just a silly Sally, Sam. Aren't I a silly Sally?'

And he smiled. He'd found a torch, spotlighted the way. I guess I was proud of being a regular guy, but did being a regular guy make me a bore? Jen had completely altered my wardrobe and hinted that my old outfits were pretty daggy.

Zane had let his hand rest on mine. Here I was, doing something I'd put out of my mind for so long. Hadn't even acknowledged, except in dreams, and you can't help those. But now here it was, for real. I was out, on a date, with a man! I wanted to say something to Zane, tell him thanks, what it meant, and I was just about to, honest, when … well … his hand shot away.

'Look at that!' he cried.

'What?'

I looked about. I couldn't see anything.

'My God, I'm going to be sick.'

'What?'

Zane stared at me.

'That bitch's hair, that's what.'

'Who?'

'The breeder with the baby.'

She was now visible through the gap the leather queen had made.

'Really,' said Zane, 'the blow-wave look. That went out with Tina Turner. Hideous.'

And he picked at his tongue, like he'd half-swallowed a hair.

After the bill had been asked for and paid, we sallied on over to Zane's joint. It was the swankest apartment you ever saw. Real precise and geometric like the insides of a computer. I couldn't see a single sock lying about or even a plate left unwashed. Zane buzzed about this metallic vase on his mantelpiece for ages. Muttering something about how harmless I looked, he finally reached into the vase and pulled out a letter. Pretty odd place to store correspondence, I thought, but then he said: 'Want some Charlie?'

For a sec, I thought he meant Charles Acton-Heath. But he couldn't. I hadn't mentioned him to Jen, and she was the only connection. I decided to play it safe.

'Who's he?' I asked.

Zane laughed, patting the envelope.

'Darling, you really are a novice.'

Charlie *was* the envelope? Or in it? Zane pointed to the stereo. When I did nothing, he pointed twice. It took me a bit to get his meaning, but finally I sauntered on over. He had a stereo like the cockpit of the USS Enterprise, it was that flashy. He told me to put on some easy beats: the soft-serve sounds of Air. It was like nothing I'd heard before. 'Loungey' was Zane's word for it. After all that pub rock back home, this was a revelation – liquid beauty steamed into sound.

Zane slapped a porcelain ashtray in the microwave.

He showed me what was in the envelope, and who this Charlie feller was.

'He's A-Grade stuff, Sam,' said Zane. 'Two-twenty a g, darling. Mates rates.'

That fairly blew me. I mean, I knew what a g of dope went for (through Cinders, of course), but this was off the scale. I looked in my pockets for cash. Zane waved me away. He'd done the same over dinner.

He set the microwave: half a min'. When it lit up, it was like there was this room within a room all of a sudden. Then it beeped out, leaving us in the half-light. Zane didn't wait the five secs', but flicked the door open, clanking the ashtray down on the marble bench, then dump-trucked the Charlie. It made a snowdrift.

He must've seen I was watching edgeways 'cause then he said, 'Easier to spread, darling, if the dish is warm.'

He cut the powder with a razor blade – tiny guillotine slices.

'Good for twenty-four lines that,' said Zane. 'Twelve each.'

He opened his wallet. Plastic popped out, concertina-style. Zane half slipped out his Visa, but stopped and laughed, sliding it back into its sleeve, divvying the powder with the blade instead. But he went that other cliché, rolling up a five-buck note. Zane did the first line, then held up the fiver to me.

Oh well, here goes.

And I did the second.

Then it hit.

A vanilla essence tang, shooting up my nose like I'd pin-dropped into ice-cream, a creeping down the back of the throat, a Snuffalufagus snorting, but *in* instead of out. We fingered the paper envelope and rubbed the last of the piss-yellow specks on our gums, getting a numb-gum dentist feel, lips like a horse's, but with a vibrato buzz.

Tasted like a punch in the nose. Metallic nasty.

'Now, Sam,' said Zane, splashing the finest crystal water on his face, fooling into the bevel-edge mirror, 'time for an E.'

'E?'

'Ecstasy.'

Ecstasy? Hell, I hadn't tried drugs before. The odd beer. More than the odd beer lately. But now an E on top of coke? Zane whisked out a white pill.

'Swallow,' and he gave me a brandy chaser to wash it down.

I asked what was in it.

'Ketamine. Good for stallions. Good for you.'

I slapped down into this black couch, which was having its own pillow fight, it had that many cushions, and cased the place from comfort. Something was odd, only it took me a bit to work it out. Then it clicked. There wasn't a single photo in the whole place. Not one. All this artwork, yeah, but no photos. Jen said Zane was from New Zealand, so you'd think he'd have brought something with him. Maybe even some trashy picture of a peak in Wellington. But nope, not a thing.

He'd done well to hide his accent. I wondered if that was something he'd had to work at, or whether it fell away naturally.

I don't know why, but I tried to ask him about his parents (guess my own were figuring on my mind), but he said he didn't have any. Hell, everyone does. He grabbed my arms, lifting me up to dance. But I wanted to nail this New Zealand thing. Zane muttered something about the type that gets talkative on E's. Just his luck.

I fell on his bed and pulled a pillow under my head. There was so much, shaken beer-like, I had to say. Zane changed the beats to WagonChrist, another education in sound. The mood flipped, but I couldn't stop thinking about Zane's parents. There I go again, you see. Like thinking over this night before it happened, I was thinking about Zane's folks without ever having met them. But I was thinking about them all the same, wondering if somewhere over there, in their house, they had a picture of Zane, on a dresser, maybe. And even things lying about: unpaid bills magnetised to the fridge, washing up undone … All I knew was that I had to express myself somehow … To talk. More than I'd ever wanted to before. Was it the coke, the E, both?

'Zane,' I said, 'don't you think it makes you care more?'

Zane stopped dancing.

'What?'

I sat up on his bed.

'I mean, all this time in the closet, you're hearing stuff that's hurting you. Even if you don't know why exactly, it makes you think about what you say, and how it might hurt others.'

All those times hanging out with Dirk and his mates, rubbishing homosexuals, even though I hadn't even considered myself gay, I never joined in. Well, except for that day at school, teasing Carl.

I could see Zane staring out the window, sipping some banana smoothie cocktail he'd fixed for himself. I tried again.

'It does make you care more … don't you think … Zane, please?'

Zane licked away his pencil-thin mo of foam and leaned forward.

'That might have been the case for *you*, Sammy boy, but not for everyone. Gay people come out when they no longer care. While they do care, they can't. Not caring is the stage they have to reach. They don't care about themselves, they don't care about their parents, their friends, society. Every gay person starts their gay life not caring. And why the fuck should they?'

'Yes, but – '

Zane cut me off.

'You sure you're out?'

The mood passed. I forgot what I was thinking about. All I could see was that I was spoiling things. Get this moment, Sam, *this* – while it's happening. Zane's actually angry, idiot!

'Sammy, darling, enjoy your sexuality while it's still novel. In only a few years, there'll be shows on those commercial channels where the aim is to pick "straights" from "gays".'

'No way!' I spluttered.

'Capitalism was always going to ensure our liberation. There is money in the pink dollar.'

Zane proffered a hand.

Dancing scared me but I took his arm. Go with it, Sam. Get dancing.

So I stood up. Zane got in close, moving to the beat with me, but I was out of step. I couldn't – could never – get any rhythm. Zane turned off the music and went back to the window.

'What are you doing?' I asked.

'I'm just going to hang my cock out the window. Let's face it, it's the only way I'll get some action.'

I moved to the door. Did he have to move so fast?

'Relax,' said Zane, 'I'll pack a cone. Want one?'

Dope on top of coke and an E? He pulled an envelope from another vase, this one filled with bud. (I could tell marijuana when I saw it from watching Cinders roll countless joints.) As Zane chopped the leaf, mixing it with tobacco, I started to see his hands as Arny's hands, his arms as Arny's arms, Arny's face as his. Then Arny, in full, by the fire, toasting the sides of the burger with a fork.

Which he'd toasted to perfection, if I remember right. Pretty good, that, considering what he had to work with. A crackling fire and a bent fork. He'd rolled it round, making sure it was just right.

I remembered how I couldn't do anything but eat it. Even with those cricket mates sitting around, their noses in the air like they'd sniffed something was up. And how it was actually really good. I could see the others looking at me. *He* was looking at me: Arny. Rather than lean back, he leant forward, head tilted up.

And then those words later, the two of us alone, in the shed, where the light pierced the boards.

'Nobody's Sam, don't you want to be *somebody's* Sam?' he asked.

And then the killer.

'Maybe even … Arny's Sam?'

'Arny,' I yelled, 'you've got it wrong, I'm not a … I'm not …'

But I am. And that thing I'd wanted to say. 'Yes, I do! Sam's Arny, yes I do.'

'Sam.'
'Yes!'
'Sam!'

'What?' I looked about. Zane had finished packing the bong.

'Toke this.'

And he passed me a bong shaped like a cock. He laughed when I tried to draw it in and nothing happened. He showed me where to put my thumb over the hole. I sucked till my mind condensed to white.

Outside, we went pounding the streets. Zane said we had to dance. So I guessed that meant he was dragging me to a nightclub.

I was scuffing the pavement as I walked. People were looking at me funny. Zane pointed to his nose then at mine. I felt it out for size. When I pulled my fingers away, they were red. My nostril was bleeding, the one I'd snorted with. Zane handed me a handkerchief.

'Blow into that.'

When I pulled the handkerchief away, there was this Rorschach pattern. Saw something straight away, relating to my childhood reading. This boy and his girl – it was always a girl, then – walking in a desert, something harking back to a pulp novel when D-day stories were hip. Boys living in a nuclear wasteland, that kind of thing. Blood noses were the first sign of the end: death from radiation poisoning. I'd seen myself as a survivor – eking out my days in *Mad Max* romance.

Zane wasn't looking in, but out.

'Oh, breeders,' he said, 'we don't want them. Go! Go away! Shoo! Look at that rubbish. That's what you get with breeders, Sammy. Rubbish everywhere. Ever seen a homa-sex-u-arl eating while they walk? 'Course not. Ugh, breeders, the way they parade about. Showing off their sexuality. No shame.'

I looked over at a guy with black curls, and a gait like he was balancing a rake on his nose, and saw him as Arny ... Arny's Arny, forever. Zane saw where I was looking and snorted.

'Let's face it, deary, all men look the same from behind. Unless they've shaved your name in their bum fuzz. How touching.'

Zane looked me in the eyes.

'You're flying, Sam. You're flying.'

Then The Saloon.

For those who aren't in the know, and I certainly wasn't, The Saloon is a dyke bar. The female security weren't going to let us in at the door but Zane said something about his friend Tash and that did the trick. They waved us through. Zane could even get into girl bars.

Inside, Zane picked out Tash. Had a cowlick you could surf along before riding to the crest, a mean-looking collar about her neck with nasty studs, and a tight comic-book top. Dark features and gelatine eyes. She was sitting with a whole bunch of girls, and straightaway I saw Jen was one of them. She looked pretty out-there, too, free of her library gear. She'd swapped her black-rimmed glasses for ones with webs at the edges. Her pupils were trapped insects. Tash sighed at the gathering before standing up. Zane waltzed over to her, arms out stiff, mummy-like.

'You know, I think I'm going to hug you, darling,' he screamed. 'I'm in that kind of mood. Don't mind the man-sweat. Don't we dykes hate that?' And then, firing his tongue in and out, 'la-la-la-la-la.'

After hugging her half to death, he pulled her over into a corner, and then, with the two staring at me, nattered on. No one introduced themselves. The other girls were looking at me as they talked, too. Jen found me a stool so I could sit down next to her.

'How's it going, Sam?' she asked.

'Zane seems to have forgotten me.'

'Hey, Sam, don't mind Zane. He's actually really nice. He just gets like this.'

Jen told me that Zane and Tash had been friends for yonks, and that Tash was also a Kiwi – they'd flown over together. I asked Jen how well she knew them. Jen said she knew Zane fairly well – a day or so after he'd touched down in Melbourne, in fact. But she didn't know Tash well at all. Basically, I gathered, 'cause Tash had found a girlfriend pretty much the moment she arrived in Australia and the two had disappeared into honeymoon hibernation.

I kept watching Zane and Tash talking about me. I guess Jen and I were talking about them. So I tried to say a few things their way but they ignored me. Suddenly jack of it, I got up to go.

'Don't fret, Sammy,' Zane called out. 'We're talking about Tash's ex. It's at the bar.'

'Sam, look at that bitch she's with,' said Tash, for the first time addressing me. 'Tell me you'd take that bitch over me.'

I looked across at the new coupling through the breaks in the carriages. She seemed okay to me, not that you can really tell much from looking at someone through bar fog and beer. But that hand wasn't backed onto breast or backside. It was parked snug in the crook of an arm. And that seemed sort of nice. I mean, it's nice when you can touch like that. I reckoned I must've dithered too long, smiled too wide and too softly, 'cause Tash ups and snorts, 'Ha!'

'Sorry?'

'You know, Sam,' continued Tash, 'I could tell you were a faggot from the moment you walked in. Zane tells me he wasn't so sure at first sight, but I was.'

'Leave him alone,' said Jen. 'Sammy and I are friends, aren't we, Sammy?' and she looped her purple-robed arm round my neck. It was pretty nice, her doing that, and I wanted to hug her back, but I didn't straightaway and, well, the longer you leave these things, the harder they are to get started – I don't know why. I must've looked a right Rambo, 'cause Jen just lassoed higher, playing with the down on my neck. Her fingers felt new at the ends, as if she'd cut her nails.

'They're actually really nice people, Sam,' she said.

Zane beamed prayers to the ceiling.

'Oh God, Jen darling!' he yelled, fanning his chest. 'You're the only person I'd call nice without meaning to be insulting. And as for you, Sammy, you need to go to a sauna. There'll you'll find some real nasties. That'll fuck you up. In more ways than one!'

Zane and Tash squealed.

'Don't mind them, Sammy,' said Jen, playing with my ear now. She looked round to the lights that got through the grey, into the darkness and beyond where, amid the mostly girl crowd, the occasional boy in tight shirt and trousers bent and bubbled to the beat. 'I feel sorry for the nice gay guys,' she said. 'It's such a meat market.' Jen turned back to me. 'You'll get hurt, Sam.'

My hands choked my beer. Where was that other hand, snug in the crook of an arm? I couldn't see it. Not a sign. Then I saw this feller, built to withstand an earthquake. He must've thought I was looking at him, 'cause he nodded at me and then to the toilets. Zane roared.

'Go on, Sammy! There's your date.'

I reckon I've never looked away so fast. Couldn't believe it. These things really went on! Zane and Tash told me to get moving, go for it. Jen held me tighter. Their talk burst like bubbles under a wave. I thought of that other nod, of Arny's, not to a cubicle but to a crest, the crest of that hill, and how I'd followed him, while the others went their own way, noses to the ground.

And then Arny staying at the top of the hill when the others kicked the footy off and were racing down after it. Just Arny, standing, watching the sun, as it melted into the troughs and dips of the valleys, ran in rivulets into the earth and was gone. 'Don't you want to watch the sunset, Sam?' he'd said. Arny had said. And what had I done but turn – turn from the yellow into a silhouette, muttering something about chasing after the ball with the others?

Zane, Jen and Tash were before me again, like I'd opened my eyes and ears. I looked at them. Slowly their words made a dent.

'I want romance,' I said, and they shut up for a moment. Even the music took breaths between tracks. Zane and Tash looked down on me, as from an observation deck. They seemed to be waiting. So I went on. 'Holding hands … A peck on the cheek … Flowers – '

'Flowers! Darling, you're not serious?'

'Yes, he is, Zane,' said Jen. 'Have you ever given a guy flowers?'

'I've given a man a deep-dicking, darling, but never flowers.'

'Well, maybe you should.'

Zane yawned to the walls. 'Oh, it's all very ho-hum, leave 'em laid out an' bleedin' … Oh God, cover my eyes!'

'What?' cried Tash.

Zane practically jumped into Tash's arms.

'Tash, Tash, a newbie! Save me!'

Jen turned to me and smiled, shaking her head.

A newbie? Didn't know what one was. All I saw was a girl, looking lost but hopeful. But then I saw something else: a Chinese whisper, weathering its way through the girls, from bar-end to dance floor and back. Then it clicked. A fresh dyke had arrived.

'Hair too long,' snapped Tash.

'Too long?' I asked.

Tash turned to me. 'Hel-lo, girrrlfriend, it's past her ears.'

'And look at those shoes,' chimed Zane. 'Sandals, for Sally's sake. How's a bitch to bop in those?'

Tash smiled back.

'Fuck!' she screamed.

'Fuck, darling, what have you seen?' asked Zane.

'Those fingernails.'

I couldn't see what was wrong with them. They were long, well kept and lacquered red. I looked at Zane.

'Oh please, file away!'

'Leave her alone, you two,' said Jen. 'She can hear.'

Zane collapsed like a log onto the table, till he was in Jen's face.

'Then why don't you go over and save her, Jen darling?'

'Well, Zane, I just *might*.' And Jen half got up when Tash called out.

'But just remember, pet,' said Tash, and Jen paused, '*you'll* have to do the fingering.'

Zane and Tash vomited more laughter.

Jen sat down again, then turned to me, putting her arms around me.

'Don't listen to them, Sammy,' she said. 'They're not that bad, really. Just when they're together.'

And I wanted, just once, to hug her.

Jen and I talked amongst ourselves again. Not about anything much, at first. But then Jen asked if I thought she was in with a chance now Tash was single. I must say, that surprised me. Without thinking, I looked across at Tash. Jen practically pulled my head back so I wouldn't give her away. Somewhere in my foggy mind I thought we were all very much like separate clutches of schoolkids whispering about crushes in the yard at recess. I'd also felt like a kid hanging out with Joe, and I didn't like the repeat picture. 'Cause I wanted – I very much wanted – to grow up and enter the adult world. I tried to share this with Jen but my words blurred. Jen held my chin again and looked hard at me. 'You surprise me, Sam.' She then looked hard at Zane, shaking her head and clucking. 'Zane, his pupils are like dinner plates.'

Zane sighed, got up and grabbed my arm.

'Come on, my incurable romantic, you need to dance,' and he drew me onto the floor.

I'd always avoided dancing because it put my awkwardness into sharp relief – but upon that dance floor, my life changed. I fell into a rhythm I'd never known, becoming one with the other dancers, a single, throbbing beat. I was remade and undone. Mistakes put the breaks on chances we take, but I wouldn't hold back, or back-track. My arms and legs stacked and sorted space in beautiful, abstract shapes. Trusting to a deeper instinct, I saw we are far from who we are. Alive because I wasn't sober, walls swayed and dancers stayed still. It's reality that kills.

That moment atop the hill – that moment with Arny – was there a pill, a pill for *that*? That feeling, that reeling? Could I feel alive *all the time*? Could I capture it again? Not 'now and then' but ever – forever? Why is life ordinary? Why can't it be the inverse, exceptional with the odd bland bit thrown in?

I had to tell someone, to tell them, to explain this revelation, someone …

Jen – where had she gone?

I had to tell her. I had to tell her I …

This feeling, so strong …

That there was something …

But where was she? Where?

'Where what, Sammy Headcase?'

Zane was shaking me.

'Where's Jen?'

Zane fell back against the bar.

'Gone off with Tash, lucky bitch. Probably carpet-munching as we speak. Just Tash's luck. Come on, this place is dead.'

So Jen was a fast mover like Zane? Could I keep to their pace?

We fell outside into the aqua daiquiri dawn.

But I didn't know what to do next. This was it. Courage, Sam, courage. My palms were sweating. Get his number. You could meet up. Would I know what to do?

Zane did a few loops, half wandering down the road then coming back again after a singing-in-the-rain loop around the telegraph pole. He stopped, at last, in front of me, with hands in pockets.

'So, Sammy,' he said, staring me in the face, 'you like dick or what?'

I just about fell over. Would've choked if I was mid-sip through beer but I just spluttered on air.

'Sorry?' I said at last.

Zane threw a thumb in the direction of his neighbourhood.

'Your arse or mine?'

'What?'

'We'll make it my place.'

I looked about. The street was losing its bruises.

'Zane,' I said, 'maybe we could see a film tomorrow. Throw a ball in the – '

'Sammy, I can talk lattés with my lady friends. Do you wanna suck and fuck or what, darling? Ting! I've got the metre running.'

I could see him pulling away from the kerb any second. Already, he was in first. Here's your chance, Sam. Don't blow it like you did with Arny. There! Resolve – at last. Plus, how – how I wanted it! I looked at Zane and nodded. Zane smiled, pulling me in with those pincer arms.

'The cock wins out in the end, Sammy,' he said. And he dived, tongue-first, straight into my mouth, but not before he had time to add: 'When those balls kick in.'

When we got to his pad, my heart was hiccupping. Sweat beads picketed my neck. I didn't know if I could do it. I didn't feel too sexy; I was hot and sticky, and breathed beer and drugs.

'Have you, um … have you got a spare toothbrush?' I asked as Zane unzipped my trousers.

'It's a bit soon to be moving in!' whooped Zane.

I backtracked. 'I just mean … um, my breath's not so good.'

Immediately Zane's hand stopped.

'You don't know about not brushing your teeth before oral sex?'

I must've imitated a wall supremely well because he promptly explained.

'You don't want those gums bleeding now, do you?'

And I saw the danger of it: human contact.

I *did* know what to do. I knew 'cause I'd done it a million times in my dreams. Halfway through, Zane stopped me with his hand.

'Uh-uh, Sammy: condoms. I treat everyone as HIV positive, even myself.'

And with a minimum of fumbling, we were back in business.

Afterwards, I sat back against the headrest, trying to get my breath. Zane rolled onto his side, the side away from me. I looked up from him and out the window. Already, there was this yellow fuzz on the lip of the sky. It matured into the sun. Soon the sun rose behind the venetian blind like cheese up a grater, sending spirals of light into the room. I slid behind Zane till we were spooning. Zane popped a few pills to help him sleep.

His shoulder was coffee coloured in the light. I felt sort of thrilled. After all, here was this live human, right next to me, living, breathing, not pretend, but real. Not like that eyeless teddy you had as a kid. This toy lived, breathed, had a smell all its own. *He* had a smell all his own. Zane. Things could work out between us. I mean, he wasn't so bad on his own. On his own …

I smelt his smoked hair then sneaked an arm round his waist, feeling the baubles of hair on his stomach. Zane's face popped up, a damp soap in the dark. He looked at me then down at my arm.

'You still here?'

'What …? I …?'

Zane sighed then unhinged my arm at the elbow, swinging the gate closed.

'Sammy,' he said, turning away again, talking into his pillow, 'I don't know about you but this bitch needs her beauty sleep.'

He promptly began to snore.

100

Chapter Four

Zane cooked up a confection of scrambled eggs and coffee. He was wearing an old-fashioned, diamond-patterned dressing gown with a purple, insect sheen. I asked him where we went from here.

'One night or six weeks, darling. Isn't that the gay way?'

The words Mum spoke over the phone, repeated on me.

'How can you be happy with this … this lonely lifestyle choice?'

Lifestyle choice! Who would choose a gay life? Fuck those who said it was a lifestyle choice. Who would choose this? Fuck that, fuck them, fuck – !

Zane tapped me on the shoulder. He dipped his caterpillar eyebrows at me, each hunching at the middle before dragging their back ends forward in a frown.

'Sammy,' he said, 'this girl can't be chained to one ball. Especially not now.'

I dropped my spoon into my cereal.

'Why not now?' I yelled, milk dripping down my chin.

Zane threw up his arms.

'Oh, you really are out of it, Sammy. It's Flirt in one week!'

And I saw Zane bedding a different boy every night, all that fumbling, get-what-you-can-out-of-it sex. You suck me off, no you suck me.

'Don't you think, Zane,' I said, not wanting him to think he was my first, 'the better you get to know someone – I mean, the more you trust them – the better the sex gets?'

'The more boring it gets, you mean. Look, Sammy, even though I'm a civil servant, less is more is not my dictum when it comes to boys. It's more like everything is not enough.'

Zane was about to continue when he saw the time on his watch. He quickly drank his coffee down to the dregs, wiped his mouth with his napkin and stood up.

'Talking of work, Sammy, I'd better get this girl dressed. All right,' he said, patting me on the head, 'let's put the dog outside.'

Me? Surely not!

Zane grabbed me by the shoulders, laughing. 'You can take *yourself* for walkies, I assume?' And he led me outside.

Zane's metal door clicked behind me. The outside world was bright, too bright. Already, the chill crisp of morning was thawing into tepid heat. I walked down the concrete stairs, their balustrades sanded down to a blue-flint patterning, and reached street level. I made my way through the park towards home. We'd just had a week of leaves and I felt every one crunching under my feet.

That afternoon, Jen and I moved into a rental we'd found. Luckily she had furniture from her old place. Plus fridge, washing machine, you name it. Once we'd moved it all in, and my few things into my room, Jen put up some posters to make it look more homely (even if they were only posters for the latest books she'd grabbed from the library). Then she pulled out the champers and we toasted with two ceramic mugs. I felt pretty mean and all about that. I mean, I wished I'd thought to buy the champers myself, or even glasses. Something.

Next time, hey …?

There's always a next time.

Until one day there isn't.

It wasn't too bad a place. It sure beat my room above the pub. The house was in Canning Street, Carlton, with all the terraced houses sharing walls with the ones next to them. Made me think of times I'd been cheated out of both armrests at a cinema.

Time doled out days and as quickly took them away. I rang Mum and Dad, giving them my new landline, plus the mobile I'd bought and was already addicted to. They were worried about me. Dad wanted to know how many people 'I'd told about myself'. He wanted it hushed because there were 'people I could see who might help'.

'Let's ascertain the facts, first.'

I didn't want it hushed. I remembered Mum's brother, Uncle John, whose whole life was hushed. Uncle John who never got married and stayed at home to look after his mum after all the other kids moved away, married and started families. The fifty-year-old Uncle John. The one with a weak smile.

The cricket season had ended in March, leaving me without an income. I was struggling a bit, but there was the dole, and some cash-in-hand work sorting shelves at Jen's library. It was pleasant but there were still days between days. Tubby and the other cricketers were planning on taking up winter sports to maintain their fitness. We'd caught up socially a few times but they all had partners and I didn't see how *I* would meet anyone, hanging out with couples in their backyards. Jen was no longer interested in going out now that she and Tash were an item, and I was too shy, or maybe just plain cowardly, to hit the gay clubs on my own.

Even though Jen had found someone, she didn't look very happy to me. Tash would call then not call. Stay over every night for a week then stay away for two weeks running. Jen said it was better than not being with anyone. That sort of hit me hard, although I know Jen didn't say it to remind me of my single status.

On the nights Tash came over she asked me where Zane was. Why wasn't I with him? The first time it really threw me. Didn't know what she meant at all. Tried to puzzle it out with her. Tash just threw her head like I was the dumbest thing alive. But she asked it the next night, and the next, and it dawned on me. The question wasn't, 'Where was Zane?' 'cause Jen told me that Zane and Tash breakfasted every morning, so Tash knew what he was up to; no, the question was stranger than that: it was why hadn't *I* rung him?

I couldn't get the protocol at all. Besides, why would I ring Zane?

Well, I did want to meet up with Zane for one reason. I couldn't remember that girl bar too well, but I could recall being on the dance floor, and how I'd fallen into step with a different reality, a reality that was unreal for being so heightened. Just as I could now appreciate a drink, I felt I might also appreciate the odd pill or puff of weed. All those ads warning you off drugs – they were obviously made by wowsers. I mean, my increased drinking wasn't doing me any harm.

I was sitting in our lounge-room, trying to 'read something written in the last fifty years' – Jen's suggestion – but my mind was filled with my own life, not the lives of the characters on the page. Also, terrace houses may look nice, but they don't have much light. In fact, it wasn't the most hospitable place. Cracks abounded in the ceilings, the floor sagged, walls and furniture leaned, and it was damp. The days were getting shorter and the weather colder. It was, after all, nearly July.

I needed to get out.

Jen walked in from the kitchen and threw a gay magazine on the coffee table. She noted the drink in my hand.

'It's not midday yet, Sam.'

I laughed. But she didn't, and went back to the kitchen. Wowser. I picked up the magazine. It was called *Stud*. Subtle. I leafed through it all the same. Not much else to do. Page One: a practically naked guy, hugging a pole. Page two: two practically naked guys, straddling a fence. Page three: three semi-naked guys, playing mixed-up tennis doubles. Page four, you can imagine. Page five, six, seven and all the way to the end, you guessed it – more of the same.

I tried reading the articles.

'Not Just Good Behind the Wheel' about a racing car stud who can do a gear-stick shift in two seconds; 'Heads Down' about studying hard and staying in shape at the same time; and, finally, 'Hands On' about a wankers club. Yeah, you read right, Wankers Club. That one kind of took me by alarm as well. Picture about forty men in a room, tarps on the floor, the 'no lips below hips' rule and plenty of baby oil. Talk about everything not being enough. That just about amounted to anything being the go.

I expressed my distaste to Jen.

'Sam, aren't you being a prude? You're out – time to enjoy your sexuality.'

I stopped reading to her, but looked through the ads.

Lots of upcoming dance parties; raves, with ads telling you how to prepare; gyms, to tone those abs; laser hair removal, for those stubborn follicles; and, if you were really committed, the back, sack and crack wax for the full deal. Then it was ads for the party after the after-party: condoms, lubricants, sex toys, dildos, butt plugs, Viagra, penis extensions. Then the ads for the day after; the gay drug support groups, the AIDS support groups, the life support groups, the coming down, the low. Then the personals: male ISOs (In Search Ofs) in search of commitment, in search of non-scene men, men in search of not other men, but The One Man. And finally, ads for depression, counselling for neurosis, dabblings in death.

Only joking about the death. They didn't advertise that.

I put the paper down.

'I fucking hate faggots!'

Jen peeked round the door.

'Sam, I haven't heard you use that word before.'

I had. When I pushed Arny away. Hell, I didn't feel cut out to be gay. Not at all. I didn't even *feel* gay, except for the lust bit, and that seemed such a small part. I thought after that stuff with him, with Arny, the whole coming out-thing, it would be easy. But that was just the beginning. That was like the flight from the war-torn mother country to the land of so-called freedom. And here I was, trying to learn a whole new language, trying to understand a whole new culture I hadn't been brought up in, hadn't been brought up for, and it was killing me, doing my head in. I didn't fit in, in either set. Talk about culture shock.

'Who'd be gay?' I asked as Jen walked up to me.

'Gay but not happy …' she said, a strange squint in her eye. She tousled my hair – very touchy-feely, Jen.

'I wouldn't want to be any other way, Sam,' she said at length, looking me direct in the eyes. I pulled away, pretending to be engrossed in the magazine once more.

'You must need a coffee, Sam,' she said after a quick glance at the empty beers on the table, and at my drowsy head, probably. She headed for the kitchen.

I threw the magazine under the coffee table – luckily no glass top so the damned magazine couldn't stare at me.

'Where are the regular gay guys?' I hollered.

Jen appeared, coffee plunger in hand.

'Probably sitting at home asking the same thing. I tell you one thing, I bet they aren't on chemicals at dance parties.'

That made me pause. Was that a snide reference to my drug-taking with Zane?

'What other sort are there?' I asked half pleading, half narky.

Jen winked. 'Let's have our own party.'

The party idea got me pretty excited. For a brief bit, I thought about asking Tubby and Beth. But whichever way I figured it, I couldn't see them fitting in. Jen asked all the gay guys she knew, telling them to bring along some down-to-earth gay friends of theirs, too. It gave me a bit of hope. I told Jen she should ask some lesbians as well. She gave me a look. I knew she was dating Tash and all, but … well … Jen said all the lesbians she knew had all dated each other at one time or another, and there was nothing more despicable in a dyke's life than the last ex.

Jen got good responses. Lots of RSVP's. She said they were all excited by someone new in the loop. Like getting a stranger in a country town but without the suspicion. I asked her if we shouldn't have some straight people, just to show we weren't discriminating (I still had Tubby and Beth vaguely in mind).

She said there'd be only one straight guy there.

The night of the party came. Jen and I split 50/50 on buying the alcohol. The cost made me cringe, but what the hell! I downed a six-pack to get in the mood. By ten, the party was two pins standing. Not quite a full strike, but bowling along.

Zane and Tash didn't talk to me, but every time I said I was Sam, these girls I didn't know would go, 'Oh, *you're* Sam? Where's Zane, then?'

It made me feel pretty uncomfortable, I can tell you.

Jen introduced me to this colleague of hers at the library, Astrid. I'd seen her there plenty of times but never really spoken to her.

'Are you all gay?' she asked. 'Oh my God, oh my God, oh my God! Re-ea-lly? Wow. That's so good. That's so exciting. Is Jen gay too?'

I told Astrid she'd have to ask Jen that question, if she really needed to. Astrid took my answer for a yes.

'Oh my God!'

Astrid's hair flew in the air. She had it in a million tiny braids, so it was like some sort of leather tassel thing, blonde. She had the whole Nordic thing happening; white skin, fine features. She grabbed my arm and didn't let go.

'I now know a lesbian,' she said in a stage whisper. 'I feel I can say I know you too, can't I, Sam?' She now had two homosexuals to her belt.

We were standing by the stereo and her words weren't dodging the beats too well. She kept fixing herself vodkas and lemonades. Her arms didn't leave mine. Soon she'd done an upshirt on me, saying she loved my snail trail and all. I didn't know about that. I pulled my shirt back down.

The house continued to fill.

I checked out the fellows as each one arrived. Studs, all very beautiful and knowing it – completely out of my league. So much for 'down to earth'. The two prettiest guys found each other straight away and left together not long after. All the rest seemed to be grouping with ease. I might have been the 'someone new in the loop' but I wasn't doing much of a job generating excitement. I went out back to shoot myself. Jen and Tash had filled the yard with candles, and their flames moved like belly dancers in the night breeze. I was looking for a spot to sit that wasn't taken up with a candle, when I saw this guy. He was standing, cigarette between teeth, under the Hills hoist that filled our concrete back yard with clothing. That morning, I'd gone to take my washing down but Jen had shaken her head. 'No pretence,' she'd said. 'He's got to love you *and* your laundry.' And I'd let it hang, y-fronts and all. But now I wished I'd taken it down, even if to retain a little class.

'This yours?' he asked, nodding at some jeans I'm sad to say I owned. Girl jeans with little pleats on them. Emergency wear, basically. But I lied.

'They're for the gardening,' I said.

He looked down at the concrete yard, then at me.

'I'm Luke,' he said. 'And you're either very cold or incredibly nervous.'

'I … I …'

It was … It was such a bold thing to say. At least a minute passed. I had to say *something* back. Jen was tapping on the kitchen window. Geez, couldn't she see I was working it?

'*You're* not shivering,' I said.

'I'm a smoker,' he volleyed, and gave me a ciggy to light me up.

I sucked in. The smoke gave me a head spin. I couldn't believe it – a guy as good looking as Luke was, dressed in the same kind of daggy gear I used to wear before Jen's makeover. And hanging out here on his own, not even a beer for courage. How had I missed him arriving?

I took another puff, letting the smoke fill up my mouth like water in a dam before overflowing, spilling into my throat and lungs. Quite a rush. Sad how the best things are bad for you.

The end of Luke's ciggy glowed brightly. For a moment, everything round it seemed darker.

Luke hung a curtain of his golden retriever hair over one ear, and gave me a round-house punch in the shoulder – but soft.

'Tell me about this cricket thing, Sam,' he said. 'Jen says you're pretty handy with a bat.'

'Well, I …' and I sort of ummed and ahhed about the whole thing. I didn't want to go the modesty angle too much, but then I didn't want to slide too far the other way. And I never was too comfortable talking myself up anyway. Luke seemed rapt with everything I said. His eyes never left mine. But half way through, Jen came out with this plate of red capsicum dainties, telling me how some of them were straight, but the ones that curled, the bent ones, were better. She kept trying to push the straight ones onto Luke (more his 'sort') and the 'bent' ones onto me. Finally, she just huffed and went back inside.

I was too excited talking to Luke, and probably too drunk, to take much notice of her. He was so normal, so down to earth. And cute, with that ridiculous shaggy hair.

Luke said he'd heard how I was good enough to pick out targets with the ball – live targets. That impressed everyone, it seemed.

'Geez. Now look, man, you know I can't go home till you've told me all about it.'

I tried but halfway through my tale wagged out. I was feeling too nervous to continue.

'Just off to milk the snake,' I said.

It was only when I was in the can frothing up the toilet water good enough for a schooner, that I registered the look Luke'd given me. Milking the snake? Yeah, that was pretty raw. Alcoholic courage turned to crudity.

I washed my hands and was about to step into the yard when I saw something I couldn't believe: Zane talking to Luke! Zane moving in on my target! But I wasn't worried. Zane wouldn't be Luke's type, no way. Zane was too prissy.

Luke looked over Zane's shoulder, tilting his head at me. That was pretty sweet. Zane noticed, and asked Luke how he knew me. Luke explained that he didn't but that we'd hit it off almost immediately. From the way Zane screwed up his face at that, you'd think I was someone special he was worried about losing! Strange how that works.

But it was promising – what Luke said was promising. And Zane asking how long we'd known each other, just from observing the nod Luke gave me … Well, did we look like a couple already? My heart beat double time. I stepped down the concrete step onto the concrete slab, and joined in.

'Sammy?' said Zane, putting his arm on my shoulder. 'You're back. Off to be bad, were you?'

He turned back to Luke.

'Luke, you should know something,' said Zane, and he leaned into Luke's ear. 'Sam's the sort of guy who would bend you over and fuck you dry.'

'Whoah!' said Luke, retying a drape of curls that had come unstuck.

I couldn't think what to say or do.

Tash and Jen stepped into the backyard. Tash held up one of those stupid capsicum garnishes with the 'straight' filling, and waggled it in Zane's face. He looked from the finger food to Luke and mouthed a big 'Oh'.

'My dykes? My dykes!' he screamed. 'I'm a little girl lost without my lesbians. Lukey, that's how Sammy and *I* met. *His* lesbians talked to *my* lesbians. I think I'll go join them.'

Then he turned to me. 'Good luck, tiger.' I went redder than blood in the light.

Luke watched Zane skip over to 'his' lesbians, then turned back to face me. I couldn't imagine what he was thinking. I could only think of one thing to say.

'Zane's insane'.

Luke smiled. That made me breathe easier. Some people have the winsome-est smiles, don't they? Comforting. A perfect letter with little quotation marks either side. And that letter's 'u', I guess. In this case u meaning me. Me, Sam. I looked over at Zane, Jen and Tash, and thought of those hints that Luke was straight. Luke was back on the topic of cricket, pushing that impossible hair out of his eyes.

'Hey, Sam, you know I'm gonna haunt you all night,' he said.

Straight?

The rest of the night I don't remember very well, what with the beers I was drinking. Luke was about the only one there I wanted to talk to, but I didn't think I should appear too keen in case he *was* straight after all. Besides, if you're too keen that's off-putting to the person you're keen on 'cause you look desperate. But then again you can't be too cool, can you? Oh I don't know.

Anyway, when Luke and I went back inside, he got caught up with one group of guys in the lounge while I got caught up with another group in the kitchen. Jen wafted past me at one point, looked at the three guys I was talking to, then smiled encouragingly.

All I could think about was the look of disappointment on Luke's face when I slipped away. I excused myself from the trio, hoping to track Jen down and get some answers on Luke. But Astrid got me on the dance floor, which was the space between the kitchen bench and the pushed-back dining table. She was already bendy as overcooked asparagus. Me, I was more refrigerated celery. When Luke walked past, she said, 'Oh, I know him.' Well, that was a boon. I wanted to find out just how well but she started putting her hands all over me. I didn't know how to stop her. Then I started feeling her up in return. That worked. She took a seat between songs and stayed there.

I was trying to drum up courage to circulate some more, when Luke found me, saying he was leaving. Then he hugged me. Hugged me! Like before when he said I was either incredibly cold or very nervous, I was stunned. Couldn't say anything. Again, it was so forward.

I decided I must like people who are forward. But forward in a friendly style. Arny was like that. I still remember that first time we spoke, at the lockers, when he'd put his hand on my back and left it there. And then, at the shack, when the others were planning on climbing the hill, 'You'll come, won't you, Sammy?' he said. It was phrased like a question but it wasn't. I was won over the moment he said it.

113

'Hey, um, Sam, maybe we should meet up,' said Luke. 'Show me how to bat.'

He gave me his card and said he'd added his home number for me. I looked at the card in my hands: Veterinary Surgeon. Animals, pets – it was a good sign.

When I looked up, Luke was fishing out a second card, that he got me to write my name and number on for him. Another good sign. Then he was gone.

Thankfully, the others piled out soon after. As Zane left, he muttered something about good luck with Goldilocks. I could've hit him.

When the house was back to just mine and Jen's again, and some of the balloons were giving up their grip on the ceiling, Jen cornered me.

'So, Sam, how did you go with Lochy, Aaron and Matt?'

'I got his number, Jen.'

'Which guy?'

I handed across the card.

Jen stopped what she was about to say, did a double-take and asked: 'Luke? *He* gave you his number?'

'Yes.'

'Sam, I thought you got my hints! Plus I told you there'd be one straight guy at our party – that was Luke.'

I told her about Luke saying I must be either very cold or incredibly nervous. Nervous! What else would I have to be nervous about if he didn't mean himself? And then I mentioned the hug when he was leaving.

Jen did a second double-take, removed her glasses and rubbed her eyes. She put them back on, removed them, cleaned them on her shirt and put them back on again.

'Sam, I'm … pretty sure he's not gay.'

I said goodnight, went to bed and tried to sleep. But I couldn't get Luke out of my head. I wanted to clear up whether he was gay but I wouldn't ask Jen to investigate. Later, going to the toilet, I passed the empty vodka bottle on the dresser. It made me think of Astrid, and how she said she knew Luke.

Next morning I gave her a call after scrolling through Jen's mobile on the sly. Astrid was obviously a big phone chatter but I'm not. I asked could we meet and suggested the place Zane had taken me to. Couldn't think where else. So we hooked up at Settee.

Astrid ordered something delicate, me something cheap. She ate like a mouse at a tea party.

I put the question.

'Luke? Oh, I know Luke. Through Peter and Audrey, Mike's friends from – oh, doesn't matter. Why are you asking about him?'

Without meaning to, I smiled like a little boy. Astrid almost screamed.

'You like him? Oh my God!'

The Stopwatch shot us a look.

'You like him, don't you?' continued Astrid, not much softer. 'Don't you? You know you can tell me, Sam. Don't you know you can tell me?'

I couldn't tell her anything. And she couldn't tell me much at first either, just: 'He's very neat. You know I don't mean that to be insulting but he's just too neat. He hasn't had many girlfriends even though he's so good-looking. Don't you find that suspicious?'

I didn't know what to think. If neatness meant you were gay, then the state of my room meant I was straight. And the word 'neat' didn't come to mind so easily when I thought of Luke, either. But then Astrid gave me real hope.

'You know, Sam, you've made me see that I've had my suspicions about Luke as well. He and Mike spent every day together practically for a year. Now they hardly talk to each other. What happened there? Mike's never adequately explained that one to me.'

Astrid put a tiny morsel of food in her mouth, chewed it quickly and then resumed.

'Look, you'll have to come to my party, Sam. Well, launch. Same dif'. You've got to come. I'll make sure Luke's invited. Oh my God, this is so exciting! You two will make such a lovely couple. It's not fair, it's not fair!'

I got Astrid to calm down – not an easy job! – and promise me a few things. It was looking hopeful, but if Luke was gay he obviously wasn't out. And I didn't want him being scared off.

'So don't say anything, Astrid,' I told her.

'Oh, all right, but this is just so exciting!'

Astrid rang.

'Sam! Sam! He's coming. It's all organised.'

My stomach missed a step and tripped three floors.

'Let's meet for lunch,' I suggested quickly.

And we did – her house. I knocked on her door.

'Sam! Can you wait? This thing's boiling.' I had to half run to catch up with her in her kitchen which was so white you needed to keep tapping on things to make sure it was there. Or you were. One of the two.

'Sam, I'm just on such an emotional rollercoaster. Ever since Dale, and you didn't know him, all this shit's going on.'

'What shit?' I asked, dodging the wooden spoon in her hand. I wanted to show I cared about her love life. That I wasn't just interested in her for what she could do for mine. And I liked her – the way she'd befriended me so quickly.

116

'Well …' she said, dipping the wooden spoon back into the pot again (which made me feel safer), 'you know when you know it isn't right? I'm so sick of duds, I don't want anyone. But I've met someone new: Jeff. So I'm trying to see him as a friend. I truly believe you have to fix yourself up first. Be strong before you move on. Do you get offended?'

'Sorry?'

It was a bit left of centre, her question. She stopped stirring the sauce.

'Have you seen that ad with that gay hairdresser? Well, he's obviously gay. But it's hilarious. Hil – lar – i – ous!'

I must've looked a bit glum. Astrid lifted up the wooden spoon and blew on the red sauce.

'I can tell you're offended. Well, loser, get over it! I hate that. Anyway, this guy – it's too soon to *know* know; it's the lovey-dovey stage. But we went to Shaun O'Casey's and it was such a good night. This guy was the best dancer I've ever seen. He was a divine dancer. And he proposed to me. Oh my gosh, this is so exciting. Aw, Sam, you know it was really weird. We're, like, downstairs, right, and we're thinking, oh no, and then we get up there. He would lift you up in the air. He was so-o-o strong. Oh my gosh. Oh, come on there,' she said, slapping my arm and spilling some sauce, 'guys just don't know how to communicate. But don't you think, like, you've got heaps to say? Heaps. I mean, if you like someone? Guys go out fishing, they say nothing all day, and they come back thinking they've had a good time. I wanted to say to him, "You don't know me. You don't really know me." But even, like, I don't really. So, as I said, I'm seeing Jeff as a friend for now.'

I'd love a guy I could go out fishing with, say nothing to all day, and feel like we'd talked a world away.

Just as I was walking out the door, I finally got to ask the question I came to ask. Was I going to be the only gay person at her party? After fighting for acceptance among the cricketers, I didn't feel like doing the same in other groups. So if Astrid already had a few gay members in her troupe, I would fit in without comment. I guess I was nervous on this question because Astrid seemed so excited that Jen and I were gay.

'Well?' I asked again after she'd blinked several times.

'No,' she answered.

'Oh good.'

'There's Jen as well, loser.'

Jen wasn't too happy about that either. But she came with me on the night – even drove us there – and stood outside with me for a bit before we went in. All the guys had black shoes and trousers. Their only concession to trendiness was having the top buttons of their shirts undone. The girls were nearly all in dark dresses and high heels. Standing on a slope all night, was how Jen described that particular torture. Jen and I looked down at her flat heels, then up the length of her pants to her tight top. Our eyes then floated over to my tight top, down my homey jeans and finally hit my skater shoes.

And talk about prosthetics: I reckon every guy there had a beer at the end of one arm, and every girl a purse.

This was going to be a ball.

Before we knew it, Jen and I were separated – she by some library colleagues of hers and Astrid's at the library, and me by Astrid herself. She'd speared me with an arm and was lifting me at bends-speed above water.

'This is my special friend, Sammy,' she said to one particular group. 'Isn't he gorgeous? I wanted Sammy the moment I met him. I don't know why, but it hasn't worked out. Can you guess why not? Can you guess?'

I couldn't believe it. I thought of Zane's reference to game shows of the near-future: Spot the Gay Man. I reckon the others in Astrid's circle didn't know what to say either. Well, leastways they said nothing.

Astrid was unstoppable.

'Come on, can't one of you guess why it hasn't worked out between us?'

One girl tried to be helpful. 'Well, I guess it does all come down to chemistry, Az.'

'Oh, yes Celeste,' said Astrid, 'but look at me, I've got my hands all over him. Feel that snail trail. There's just one thing stopping us. Can you guess? Can I tell them, Sammy? Can I tell them?'

I tried to bring my beer to my mouth but it shook too much. I couldn't answer. Astrid huffed.

'Well then,' she said, 'I'll just have to tell you.'

Her hands went from her hips to opened-out palms.

'He's a gay.'

A gay …?

I felt like a headless clown, mouth open. I gawped at every face in that semi-circle and they all tried to smile back.

'You'd never tell,' said Astrid.

Celeste looked me up and down. 'Well, Az, he *is* clean.'

Hard to tell if she was being ironic. The rest nodded. I never felt so dirty.

'I now have a gay man to talk hair and makeup,' said Astrid.

I'd never worn makeup in my life.

Somehow I got away by asking Astrid to point the way to the bathroom. On the way, I did the periscope since I was taller than most people there.

Luke still hadn't shown.

'Don't despair, Sam,' said Astrid (she'd decided to accompany me, arm looped through mine). 'Guess what, I met another gay guy the other day. That's two in one week! And he's just arrived. You'll have to meet him, you'll have to meet him! I'm pairing you up.'

Astrid escorted me through the house, the guys parted with smirks, and there, at the front door, Astrid brought me up to a feller at least twice my age, maybe more, two-thirds my height, maybe less, and ten times as hairy, possibly more.

'I'll leave you two alone, shall I?' And Astrid was gone with a wink.

'Grover' started on about the cricket thing straight away. Seemed everyone knew about that. He stood too close. He was maybe forty but he looked sixty. From a lifetime of smoking, I'd say. It certainly smelt that way. His face was a cracked and glazed earthenware pot. Astrid kept tooting her champagne glass at me and then, when I looked away, Grover would look over his shoulder to see where I'd been looking.

Grover told me how swell Astrid was. Did I realise just what an up-and-coming poet she was? She'd just won the Prue Forsyth Female Poets Scholarship Prize. This night was a launch for her first limited edition collection of poems called *Soul Whisperings*.

A few clinks with a knife on a champagne glass and the crowd hushed as she read one out:

I smelt hyacinths in your hair – Tuesday.
Thursday, the salt of Wednesday.
Friday, the taste of the weekend.
I reach for the breath of God.
Even the pebbles rejoice
At the foot of the water lilies.

Yellow, blue, white, pink
… you.

My mobile beeped. It was Jen. A few people in my blast radius turned and gave me a missing-limb look. I saw Jen through the casualties. She smiled. So *she* was the terrorist, with her text message.

> It's easy 2 b nice
> if you're happy,
> it's a cinch 2 b
> generous if
> you're rich, & it's
> quite ok 2 b
> lesbian or gay, if
> u really couldn't
> care, give a shit.

I looked up at the fêted poet, Astrid. Some guy stood beside her and said, 'Right, let's hear a round of applause.'

Grover started clapping in a circular motion next to my ear. All I could do was pretend I was too immersed in the general proceedings up front to notice. If I looked at him, I'd have to force a laugh. I reckon Grover kept doing his circular clapping, his 'round of applause', a full five seconds after everyone else had stopped. People were staring at us.

When Astrid came past finally, I grabbed her and said I was going.

'Well, I'm sure Grover will walk you to your car.'

'Oh no, well, Jen drove me.'

'I'll tell Jen you're leaving. Off you go with Grover.'

'No, look, I …'

But I couldn't finish my sentence. Something had caught my eye. Astrid and Grover turned to where I was looking – at Luke, parting the crowd like he was searching through dog fur for fleas. He was wobbling a little. Maybe he'd come from another party.

'Hey, Sam! Good to see you.'

He gave me a hearty handshake. Yeah, party-hopping for sure. When he put an arm round my shoulder, I couldn't help but scope the crowd. Sure enough, one guy with a devil's peak gave a sharp snort, then had a sharper word to his friends. But hey, this Luke was so forward. It was so lovely. He was so brave with his affections. Braver than me. I was nervous about hanging out with straight people. If only I had more courage.

'You look like you need a beer,' he said in my ear. It was like he'd read my thoughts. Beer was my courage until I could brew my own.

'Yes,' I answered.

'No.'

'What?'

I looked around.

'No, excuse us, Sam's just leaving.'

It was Grover. Luke looked at the human walnut, with his car keys already out of his pocket, then at me, the poor sod next to him. The best I could manage was a shrug and what I hoped was a wry smile.

'Well, hey, there's this film I wanna catch with you, Sam. Give us a call.'

I was drawn backwards and away from the launch. The last I saw was the guy with the devil's peak hurriedly leaning over and whispering in Luke's ear.

I forced myself to wait almost thirty-six hours before sitting down in my room and preparing to ring Luke on my mobile. The landline in the lounge would be cheaper, but this way the call would be private.

I was nervous but at least had a substantial excuse to ring, an excuse provided by Luke himself – this film he wanted to see with me. I knew the one he meant. It was about cricket. Called *Shining the Ball* or something. Luke talked about cricket a lot. Actually, I'm not that fussed with sport talk. I like playin' it, hell yes, and watching a good game, but it's in-the-moment stuff. All that off-field banter, post-game assessment – 'next time we'll do harder, we really took it to them, the ball was turning' – well I don't care for it much. If ever I get to play for Australia, and I'm giving my man-of-the-match speech, I won't sling any of that bullshit – how I held up well considering the groin injury and all, I'm seeing the ball better off the pitch, the other team played well, just made a few costly mistakes and all. Hell no, I'm just gonna say something like … like … well, what *can* you say, really?

But right then I didn't want to be reminded of cricket. Back home, as a kid I drove my family mad getting them to throw cricket balls for me the way some dogs drive you mad getting you to throw tennis balls for them. In the end, to stop harassing everyone, I'd trained the Bradman way, hitting the ball against a corrugated tin tank. The ball bounced back every which way. My bowling's a bit the same, so I really was playing against myself. Since picking up a bat as a kid, I'd rarely put it down. But with the cricket season over, I hadn't touched it. Tubby occasionally called to say the guys were practising in the nets but I somehow never managed to make it. I wasn't doing anything to keep up my fitness or skills.

It narked me that I wasn't, but there were too many other things going on.

I went into the lounge and picked up the paper which was sitting on the coffee table. I leafed through it for the session times for this film Luke suggested, then rang on the landline the nearest cinema just to make sure. I could see Jen and Tash in the backyard, trying to catch some sun. But, just in case they came in, I returned to my room and picked up my mobile. Finally I rang Luke.

That voice again, almost ocker but not a word of strine. Beautiful.

'Oh, right, Sam. Yes, wow, you rang. I didn't think you'd ring. You know, I was very drunk at Astrid's launch. I couldn't remember much. Wow, right. We said we were going to catch up. Cool.'

'Yes, that film. So, um, tomorrow? 6:30, Nova?'

'Yeah, right. Cool. Look, I'd love to talk all day, but I should be getting back to work. But hey, great launch, wasn't it? Can't remember much.'

I turned up to the Nova at 5.45. Can you believe, 5:45 for a 6:30 date? That's me, either bloody early or as tardy as all hell. Never on time. It was pretty cold standing in the foyer. The doors kept opening as the people came in. I was wishing we'd said we'd meet over the road, in *Readings*. That way, I could've read, not that I would've seen the pages for his face. Hopeless case, aren't I?

6:30.

Sunlight almost faded.

6:35. Okay, so he wasn't an on-time sort of guy. I liked that, that was good.

6:45. The film was starting at 7:00. I wanted just a little time to chat before we were in the dark.

6:50. If ever you've got to wait outside somewhere, at night, it's bloody cold. There were these two other people waiting, a girl with a white jumper, stockings, fairy-floss hair and lipstick, plus this feller with Elvis sideburns and overall retro look. Now and then me and the girl would smile at each other after we'd both looked up and down the street. Both waiting for dates. That was our connection. The Elvis wannabee was obviously too cool for school. He wasn't looking anywhere but at his watch – 6:55. The film was starting in 5 minutes. Seemed it was pretty popular, too. The usher called out, last chance to buy tickets. I didn't know whether to. People kept coming in all the time. I thought, if I didn't, Luke would turn up and we wouldn't get in. I didn't really know what else to do, so I bought two.

'Concession?'

'Um … well, yes … please.'

'Cards?'

'What?'

'Your concession cards?'

'Um, not on me. My lov– … um, my friend's got them.'

'Adults then. Thirteen bucks each.'

'Fuck.'

And I bought them just as Mr Retro came in with his retro girlfriend, the two of them arguing. As I stepped out, the lady's date turned up also, a feller with hair dry as a delicate fungus. He didn't even say sorry, just threw his arm out wide – dragnet fishing. She got entangled and was hauled up. I tried to smile at her as the doors closed but she wasn't looking my way. We weren't soul mates anymore.

I waited another half-hour, sitting on the green seat out on the footpath, and was about to go home when guess who turns up? Zane. The In Zane, as he'd say it. Plus Tash. It couldn't get worse.

I didn't want to run into Zane and the others, not like this.

'Where's your date, Sammy?'

'He's sitting on it,' said Tash.

Zane and Tash laughed. A tear got out my eye. I could've hit myself. Zane punched me lightly.

'These straight abusers, Sammy, fuck them.'

'They love the attention,' said Tash.

Zane went on to rubbish Luke to the ground. I didn't want to hear that, any of it.

'Fuck straight people,' said Tash.

'Pick up at gay bars,' said Zane.

'Why don't you come with me to Trade Bar?' he went on. 'I don't have anyone to go to boy bars with. I've only got my dykes. It'd be nice to have a faggot friend. We can score some girl cock together.'

I looked up and down Lygon, still vaguely hopeful. Zane leaned over and gave my shoulder a little swish with his fingers.

'Don't mind his sort, Sammy, they're *try*-sexuals. They're not gay, they're not straight, they're not bi, they're try. Trying very fucking hard.'

Zane and Tash laughed. The crowd from the last film was starting to regurgitate between the columns of the cinema. They'd all either turned on, or were turning on, their mobiles. A symphony of beeps. They didn't exist unless they were missed. A couple jostled Tash.

'Breeders? Can't they fuck off,' she screeched. 'I'm off to a *gay* zone while there are still some left.'

Zane shielded her with an arm then turned to me.

'Sammy, see this fist? That's been up some boy pussy. Don't look like that. The girl was gagging for it. Look at those soft hands. Tempted?'

I wasn't in the least. But all I said was, 'Zane, I normally start with a kiss.'

'A kiss, darling? Snogging, what's the point in that?'

'You snogged me,' I said.

'Only because you're special, darling.'

126

Tash pitched in. 'Zane's rule is no lips *above* hips.'

Zane found that hilarious. The two laughed for ages. You hear about prostitutes doing pretty much everything *but* kissing, and I understand that, I really do. Kissing's pretty intimate. It's face to face. It's direct speech. Quote unquote. It's language of taste and touch.

Zane dragged me to my feet.

Tash excused herself. Off to see Jen. They might have some raunchy sex with me out of the house for a change.

'Let's get some pills, Sammy,' said Zane as he watched Tash scissoring towards Elgin. I didn't need persuading. I'd been wanting another look at what I saw that night with Zane.

I wondered where we might score. Zane wasn't hopping down any side alleys but going straight up Lygon. He then cut down to Rathdowne. Suddenly he was stopping at the Video Highlights store. Videos? I didn't want to watch films. I mean, I reckon videos or TV's what you watch if you're bored or sick. And if you're bored, it's just going to make you more bored. Not that I mind a good film. I don't. I just think you have to go out to see them. Otherwise you're stopping the tape every ten seconds for some toilet or munchy break. If you know you're not going to be able to piss for an hour and a half, suddenly you'll panic. I had this relative, and every time it was Mum and Dad's turn to go somewhere with her, we'd drive to the weir. But every time we got in the car, it was when is the next toilet? It was toilet stopping, all the way. But maybe she had a weak bladder and I'm being mean. I mean, you don't really know about people – ever.

Inside Video Highlights, there was this guy behind the counter, smiling at us. He was big as in fat. He was decked out in a red baseball cap, and a sloppy shirt with a screaming tyrannosaurus on it, a comet hitting the earth in the background. The caption read 'Dinosaurs Died For Our Sins'.

Zane laughed and pointed at the bloke's card, safety-pinned to his shirt.

'What's that?' asked Zane.

The guy looked down at the card.

'That's me card: L L Filter, Video Guru.'

Zane giggled. The two obviously knew each other.

'How'd you get that, Filter?'

'The honchos at *Video Highlights* headquarters. So I say, right, here's this card you've given me. With me certificate. Noice. Hello? The other side's blank. Could always use it for notepaper, I says. And it's as easy as that. So, what you want: clarky cats, dexters, triple sods, amyl nitrate for the ladies?'

Filter looked at some customers walking in the door.

'Hello? More NAVS.'

I whispered into Zane's ear: 'Oi, what's a NAV?'

'Non Anal Virgin, darling.'

What else!

Filter stared at them gathering around the cult section, the yellow shelves even more garish in the fluorescent light.

'What's this?' he asked to the general room. 'Hoola-hoop city. Doing the pogo stick, are we?'

Then he looked at me.

''Ello, Zane? This your latest? Doesn't look like one of your team.'

'Straight-acting – don't you love it? Sammy's my wuff twade.'

I wasn't Zane's anything but I let it slide.

'Now you point it out, Zanwar, clear as buggery. Lip-definition. Always a give-away. Same thing for Christians, mate.'

128

Zane asked Filter what he had. It took me a bit to realise the two weren't discussing the latest releases. Zane then quizzed Filter on whether he'd tried his own wares.

'I know you, Filter.'

Filter grinned.

'My GP asked that and all. The doctor said, Do I substance abuse? Do I what? Substance abuse? How you like that? Know wot 'e asked me next? Just flick your feller out, would you, he said. Swing that chappy. Come on, make it snappy. Nice weight. I tell 'im, I'm sucking up to Mother Nature. Crawling back into the womb.'

Filter looked me square on. 'I've got a big head, Sam. Yeah, mother complained about it and all.'

And he slapped the counter.

'Tell you what, I knock off in a minute. If you two hang about while I balance the till, we can trip together,' and Filter turned off the main lights, leaving the last customers to find their way out of the romance section with the display lights only.

My stomach stymied for a second. Did I truly want to take this path? I mean, go further down it than I already had with Zane? But then, my resolution was to embrace life, and what was life but experiences?

Yes, I would do it.

We trundled our way to the Carlton Gardens via a bottle shop. Filter had quite a brisk walk, for all the baggage he carried. Actually, he was quite a smart dresser. The latest engineered sneakers, latest engineered jeans, latest designer shoes. Certainly not all bought on a video store wage, that's for sure.

At the park, we found a bench. Filter took one side, me and Zane the other. We'd bought a six-pack each on the way. I remembered when I sat with Joe at a park bench, maybe the same one, he drinking his light beer, me the full strength stuff. Then, I was wondering if I shouldn't be someplace else. Now, I was perhaps still in the same place, but was I with the 'right' people?

We got through our beers quickly, then Filter brought out his stash: magic mushrooms. I felt sick with worry taking them (heard some horror stories back home) but I was also excited. They smelt a bit rank, and the taste was ten times worse, but I managed to chew three down.

Forty minutes later and I felt a bit odd.

'Time for you to wake up, Sammy,' laughed Filter.

Wake up? To what?

My world unhinged.

Everything came unstuck and floated. Trees, cars, people – distinct and vital.

'Walkies,' said Zane and the three of us rose from the bench and floated towards the giant Rubix Cube, part of the new museum. In the darkness, it was like we were walking through paintings, pop-up book places, shooting galleries, with us the targets. Background, middleground and foreground came unstuck and travelled different directions.

'Wow,' I said. 'Wow!'

A playground, suddenly daylight divined. We were … it was so clear …

'For the first time …'

'What Samster?' asked Filter, the three of us clambering up the kiddie's fort.

'Suffering beautiful children can make passionate people, by pooling millions of moments, uniting strands in time.'

Filter and Zane looked at each other. Then at me.

'Wait … please … if we can be awake to this world then, occasionally, this world can flood over, seep into ours. I hear the heard of words.'

'What you say, Samster?' asked Filter, popping a head through a tyre.

'Shearing the herd of words, the words heard.'

'Get a load of this, Zane,' laughed Filter, half stuck in a metal tube.

Looking over the park, the tree trunks spread like pillars of chocolate sauce poured into an olden bowl long ago – till I saw the forest extend without end. The three of us hid behind fingers, circling each other atop the fort. I took the yellow tongue slide down to the ground.

'We can't be gagged and bound,' I shouted. 'We won't be down, at least not in the here-now, the now is forever.'

That seemed wrong, somehow. 'Forever? No, Sam, the "now" is never.'

Filter slid down behind me, bumping me to standing position.

'He's talking to himself now,' he laughed.

Next, Zane bumped Filter out of the way.

'Stop!' I yelled, seeing the other side, knowing I was right, 'The "here" disappears?' I asked, contemptuous. 'Why, the "here" is here!'

'Too right!' shouted Zane and Filter, taking one of my hands each, and spinning me on a spinning wheel.

'We are writing our names in this time, bleeding through to the page underneath!'

Zane braked the wheel.

'Sammy, you're turning a new leaf!' he squealed.

The lines were coming back, the signs of industry, the poles, the holes. I could hear the fences crying, every creak and squeak a moan. I saw a billboard boy, with a smart suit.

I hopped off the wheel, still reeling, and pointed at him.

'Do you know if what you want is what you need?' I asked.

Filter and Zane beside me, looking at Mr Billboard.

'We're prey to the desire capitalists,' sighed Zane.

'What is our asking passport price?' I wanted to know.

I shouted at the billboard, at his slide-on scuff accessories, his home-ware appliances.

'I'm in another world, your world's in mine. I'm feeling stupid, you're feeling fine.'

'Oh well, whatever, never mind,' sang Filter.

'But he's cute,' I told them.

'You're no longer wearing shades on desire, Sammy,' said Zane. That's right, 'cause I was diving gently into this new world, climbing softly out of everyday ours. Meeting people with the possibility of being held and understood. I was connecting lightly with their worlds, bringing back a little piece into mine. Holding over something from sleep.

Something from sleep …?

That was it!

'Zane, Filter!'

They turned from the billboard to me.

'What, Sammy?'

'This is the daydream beautiful. We have to hold over something from sleep. For once we have to bring a little bit of this magical world into the everyday, we have to hold over something from sleep!'

'That's right, Sammy,' laughed Filter, gently pushing me over before hauling himself up the slide. Zane took the ladder but I followed Filter.

'We must be awake to *this* world, so many convergences, so many moments, brought in on time.'

'Our lives, filled with utensils,' moaned Zane, his arm around my shoulder.

'Are they … are …'

'What you saying, Samster?' asked Filter, sitting down to get his breath.

'Come on, come tease this dear nature!' I shouted.

'Come on, Sam, come wake up their world, let's pull a bit of it into ours!' shouted Zane.

The two of us holding hands, ring-a-ring-a-posey, pocket full of time, precariously atop the fort.

'I see, I see,' I said. And I saw. 'We have to be ready to resurrect! At any time.'

'Wake up to our nation,' bellowed Filter, swaying dangerously atop the yellow tongue. 'See this beautiful carnation, Sammy?' he asked, pulling a damaged thing from his pocket. 'Sing this beautiful carnation.'

Don't partake of dutiful silence …? That was it!

'Filter, Zane! We have to put this sleeping world's finger into cold water.'

'Too fookin' right,' and Filter pissed down the slippery slide.

But not that way, hey …

The kiddies' playground. Kiddies …

Drop out.

Level.

The same kiddies' playground where, a few months earlier, I'd been swinging with Joe. Joe who I could see clearly now, smiling at me.

I felt sick. Maybe time wasn't just a one-way ticket.

When I get back to the top of the slide,

And I turn,

Helter – helter shelter. Pitter-patter, just a smattering of rain.

'Come on, Samster,' yelled Filter, taking the fire pole elevator, then tugging my feet, and Zane's also, with us following, then dragging us under the giant veranda of the new museum, Zane flicking water from his hair, every bead a bubble, a world achingly breaking apart.

'Zane, Filter, we are bringing from stubbornness a bit of excitement. We are making the trees sit up for once, we are bringing a bit of magic into the world.'

'Don't go over, Sam,' warned Filter.

Go over?

'I'm … I'm …'

'Yeah?' he asked.

'I'm … I'm …'

'You're a testified winner!'

And Zane and Filter high-fived. I was slipping deliciously into this new world, zoning quietly, quite contentedly out of ours. Climbing into a whirlpool, let loose in drunkenness.

'Sammy, lately you've been aching,' said Zane.

'Lately I've been waking up to this world.'

'Lately, Samster,' added Filter, 'you are waking, aching beautifully into ours.'

We wandered up the veranda, and were wet right through with dew and rain. I started to shiver.

'Eleven o'clock, Samster. Not much longer to go,' comforted Filter, oven-glove hand on my back.

Binding into wonderful, let loose in drunkenness.

Huddled together out of the rain.

Sounds succinct as breaths.

Words succinct as breaths.

Aching, breaking into wonderfulness.

Leaving behind what's left behind.

A few seconds to go.

In mind.

'Sammy!' yelled Filter. 'When you come out of the water, have you worked out your opening gasp?'

'The winter warmth at your feet?' added Zane.

And I had.

'Luke!'

But can a dream survive waking?

I woke up on my mattress, fog clearing from my head with a rush of thoughts. Through the window I could see it was grey outside, but definitely day. Rubbing my head, I vaguely remembered Zane escorting me home.

In the kitchen, I fixed myself a coffee. Taking it into the lounge room, I eased down into the couch.

'What a night!'

I spilt coffee on my knee, scalding it a little. Putting the mug down, I began pacing. Jen and Tash didn't appear to be about – bonus. I could think – think! And what thoughts I had.

Those magic mushrooms had felt like the profoundest thing ever. I was so grateful to Zane and Filter. We were all locked on the same wavelength, completely. The whole night had been momentous. It was the first full-on trip I'd had, and Filter was right, it *was* like I'd woken up. My whole obsession with books was clear to me at last. As a kid, it was like I had two lives: the everyday one, which was crappy and shallow, and the one in books, which seemed deeper, closer to something … something more meaningful, alive. For the first time, maybe my life was going as deep as those books I'd read at night, in the morning, to school, from school, all the time.

On the coffee table was the book Jen had suggested I read, with the bookmark at the halfway mark, where it had been for weeks. Maybe I couldn't get into it because I was getting more into my life.

I saw how authors organised life into coherent structures. Life is pretty shabby, pointless, rambling. But that's what authors do – the best ones – they give it shape. But maybe life itself didn't need such big love handles. Just maybe, like a composer organising the perfect string of notes to make the most beautiful melody, I could arrange the most beautiful string of 'moments'. Perhaps I could actually be good at life. Maybe life was worth an 'A', after all! An 'A triple plus', even. I'd almost scored a high distinction with Arny, hadn't I? Everything was right, the setting, the lighting (the sunlight seeping into the hills like a vintage port, wasted). I'd just … well, I'd just stuffed up the critical part, that's all.

Out with literature! My life was going to read like a book.

And Luke would be the denouement.

At least for this chapter.

Chapter Five

I rang Astrid. She said to come over. She was just doing some 'signing'. When I got there, she had about a million copies of her book, *Soul Whisperings*, step-pyramid-shape on her dining room table. I picked one up, and thumbed it open at the first page. It was 'dedicated to the original peoples of Australia who taught me to hear between the spaces, to know this land's *her*story, the language of M/other Nature, the red clay insights of the Earth'. I couldn't remember any blackfellas at her party.

I asked Astrid about her feller before I got to mine. Astrid stopped signing her books.

'You mean Jeff? Oh my gosh, Sam, I've got the ending. I've got it! This is the thing that freaks me out. I get messages with guys. This is why I'm shitted with myself. I should've pissed him off, right. He stayed over one night, okay. I swear to this: during the night I was, like, I was so-o-o scared. I just woke up. He freaked me out. It was just this vibe. That's why I totally got scared. This is why I believe in God, in saints. They warn you about this stuff.'

So far this wasn't too literary.

Astrid jumped round to my side of the table.

'I'm talking to his ex-girlfriend, I find out stuff about him. Not like I hate him. He's just this psycho with a passion. But it's really dodgy 'cause, like, I'm upset that there can be dodgy people. I mean, look, I don't care. Here I am, thinking, oooh, there's something dark and scary about you. Things are just suss with him. I think he's got issues with girls, whatever. I'm just getting all the – you know when you know – someone's just dodge.'

I kept nodding but my mind was wandering. Drugs, that's what the conversation with Astrid needed. But can you be on drugs *all* the time?

'I think,' continued Astrid, 'that people who hide things like that are in some way stupidly open. Yeah, you could send someone crazy, he was just creepy.'

No, you can't take drugs all the time. What I needed was to tap into the place drugs take you, without taking them. At least, once I got the hang of it.

'There are so many complications. Anyway, we'll just be friends, whatever, blah, blah, blah, right. He's a total house cleaner, right. It's nuts. His socks drawer is like a bloody maths equation. He cleans, he cleans, he's a mad cleaner. Hey, don't be offended, but that's pretty gay, isn't it?'

I got Astrid in focus.

'I'm not into cleaning,' I told her.

I looked at Astrid's white eyebrows.

'You're offended now, aren't you? You're offended. Get over it! Please! Look, I don't know, he's just creepy, that's all.'

Astrid shut her last signed book.

'But hey, you know, what do you think? Is he gay? 'Cause you can tell that, can't you?'

The doorbell rang. Astrid smiled as widely as her little mouth could.

She got the door. It was Luke.

'Hi.'

'Hi.'

And he shook my hand.

We started going out after that. I don't mean 'out' out, just out to places, that kind of thing. Luke never mentioned the film and I never brought it up. He was the biggest cricket fan. He kept asking me over to watch the international cricket on Foxtel, but he'd always ask another mate as well, every time. And they were the sort of guys you wouldn't want for friends if you were gay. I didn't see what Luke could see in them. He seemed different to them, more alive somehow, interested in more than girls and getting drunk with the lads at the weekend. I'd ask him about himself but he'd ask *me* questions, mostly about cricket. He was very touchy-feely. He'd sit close, we'd share drinks, meals, even a fork once. It was sending me bonkers. I wanted to know. Eventually I just said, when one of his tag-along mates was in the can, 'I'm gay.' Well, there was a bit of a pause and then he said he'd dressed as a woman a couple of times. I put every damn spin on this one I could, going over it again and again.

When I got home and told Jen, sitting us down in the lounge room, she didn't want me to get excited. She said every footy player dressed as a woman. And anyway, it was in the main a straight thing to do. They got off on it because they got off on girls.

We ran into Zane at a café and we both put the cross-dressing thing to him.

'Ever wanted to dress as a girl, Sammy?' asked Zane, seemingly taking more interest in an insect that had crashed into his coffee.

I had to admit I hadn't.

'What do you see in him, Sammy?' he asked, rescuing the downed bug. 'So, he's good-looking. So what, darling? All men look the same from – '

'Behind. I know.'

I got so I couldn't sleep over old Luke. I couldn't get any sleep because even if I closed my eyes I saw his face.

But all our time together, it was so damn superficial. I started seeing a bit more of Zane and pestered him to organise another drug session. I'd find that place then take Luke to it.

Zane dragged me to this gay nightclub, The Pit. Once in, he gave me the tour. Daddy-long-leg lighting. Fairies dolloped on seats in the chillout room. Guys with exit wound eyes circling the rice cooker. Zane did the rounds for a while then came back to me.

'What about that one, Sammy? He's got the right DNA.'

I looked over but wasn't fussed. I also saw this other guy that Zane had been talking to, who was still checking Zane out.

'Are you going to take him home, Zane?'

'Oh no, it wouldn't be right *now*, Sammy.'

'Why not?'

'He told me his name. Remember, Sammy darling, people suck, and not just each other.'

'Go on, take him home.'

'But that would mean waking up next to him with his pillow hair.'

'That can be cute.'

Zane gave me a look but his eyes slipped off mine and onto someone else's.

'Hello, look at that mesomorph.'

Mesomorph? There was a dark-skinned guy, tight maroon top, staring not at Zane but at me!

No, there was Luke to think of.

Next morning, Jen cornered me in the kitchen. She said if a guy wasn't out then 'for all intents and purposes' he might as well be straight.

'But isn't that making the same assumption that straights make about us?'

'It's being realistic.'

Luke was so close to telling me. I knew it. I just had to get him alone. Retreating to my room, I pulled my mobile out of my pocket and rang him at work, asking him along to a play some out-of-work actors were putting on in the Edinburgh Gardens.

'You'll come?'

'Yep.'

'Just you?'

'Yeah, sure thing, Sam. Where to?'

I'd seen a notice for the play and thought it sounded good. Pretty cheap. Just a gold coin donation. During the day, too, one o'clock. I wanted to do anything but watch cricket in Luke's pad. Besides, all that cricket was making me feel guilty about my own game. Tubby and the coach had been ringing regarding some off-season workouts. But cricket and books had dominated my life long enough. All the while, around me guys and girls my age flirted, dated, made love and married. It was my turn.

So I got to the park. Early again. I'd brought a blanket and put it on the grass next to some other people, but straightaway I wished I'd thought to bring some food. Sometimes I'm so daft. I waited and waited, watching the people nibbling on their cheese and biscuits between sips of red wine. The cloudy sky bulged like an old mattress that had been thrown up on invisible netting. Luckily the netting held. The actors came to the stage (basically the space between two trees) and froze in their starting positions. Luke still wasn't there. Then I saw him, hurrying up the tree-lined path. I could see he had a rug and picnic bag – both. Glad someone was thinking. But then I saw he had more than that. There was a figure running alongside him – a girl, carrying a bottle of wine. Luke smiled at me sheepishly as he plonked down his stuff then laid out the blanket. The girl, a blonde thing, sat down demurely on it and looked me up and down about as indiscreetly as a four-year-old. Luke was about to say something, maybe introduce us, when the first line of the play was spoken.

Why do you always wear black?

I turned my head to the actress up front, but my eyes were still on the girl beside me. Who was she? A friend? A sister? (Couples who look like siblings are wrong!) She was certainly attractive enough to be his sister. The play went on.

I am in mourning for my life. I am unhappy.

Why?

The girl put an arm round Luke.

I don't understand ...

Then her chin on his shoulder.

You are in good health.

And started kissing his neck as she looked at me. Luke tried to glance sideways at me but his smile caved in at the sides and became another look altogether. Finally, the girl turned his mouth to hers, and the two breathed the same air.

They are in love with each other ...

I tried watching the play.

... and today their souls will be merged in the desire to create a single artistic image ...

I saw blonde Adonis and blonde Aphrodite – cardboard cut-out smiles and pretty little lips, red and perfect – and how nothing mattered or ever happened except it hurt. I got up saying something about finding a toilet and never made it back.

That night, Jen and Tash drank half a bottle of vodka with me in our damp, dingy lounge room. Jen had a story about Luke she'd heard through Astrid, of course. Apparently, no one at Luke's work knew about his girlfriend either. There was this nurse there who used to bring him lunch every day at the surgery. Then one night the whole staff went out for drinks and, for the first time, the girlfriend came along. The nurse with the crush on Luke ran off crying and quit the next day.

The vodka put me to sleep.

It's hard to be alone in the city. Zane and Filter tried to call during the next week but I let my mobile ring out to Message Bank. Tubby tried too, then stopped. Jen and

Tash gave me space in the day, but I stayed out mostly anyway, hanging out in stormwater drains and the like. In certain places, at certain hours, between about two and four in the afternoon, when people are back from lunch but not yet ready to leave for home, it's almost possible to imagine everyone is dead. But then the rush hour hits.

I was sitting under a bridge, hearing the traffic scuttling overhead, feeling such a nong about the whole Luke thing. How could I be so dumb? When I thought back on the affair (not that that's the right word), I realised he hadn't once done or said a single thing to warrant me assuming he was gay. I'd been a right tosser from the start.

But what about that trip, the mushroom experience? It seemed magical at least. Then I remembered my last thought coming out of it, the one I'd pushed back.

Can a dream survive waking?

I climbed up to the road above, hauling myself over the railing, and began the walk home, passing through the back streets where every road was either one-way or full of road bumps to deter the traffic. I was nearly home when my mobile beeped. Astrid. I read the message.

> Guess what
> loser? luke's
> single! he & his
> girlfriend broke
> up!

That kind of stopped me right there, in the shadow part of the lane, still a good two blocks from my front door. That hadn't lasted long, had it? But then again, how long had it been going? Maybe … maybe …?

I'd just got it out of my head that Luke was gay and here was Astrid, getting me thinking again. I'd text her back. I needed a joint, that's what. And I could at least fix that need. Zane had rolled a few for me after that night at The Pit. There was a car-width alley to my right, lined with bluestone smoothed from traffic. I ducked down it and into a bit of a recess where I could lean against a graffittied garage door. I took the joint out of my pocket and lit up. With it dangling from my lips, I fished out my mobile.

> Why'd u have 2
> tell me Luke's
> broken up with
> his girlfriend?

The message flew off. I drew deeply on the joint. The shadow in the street had reached the bottom of the wall on the other side. It was getting cooler but I couldn't move. Already my legs were filling up like I was a hulled galley. At last my mobile beeped. It was from Astrid again. I breathed out like a dragon that was all smoke and no fire.

> sorry loser did i
> also tell u hes
> cum out as well?

I felt the biggest rush ever. It threatened to lift me off my feet, whip me on the breeze and send me over the rusted rooftops in endless spirals. What to do next? What to do next!

I wanted to ring Luke, ring him straightaway. Wait, Sam, wait. You don't want it to seem like a come-on. As though I was jumping in for the first bite. But how good was it!

145

That other night *was* real! Of course I could make reality as good as daydream. For once, reality would relent.

This was going to be great. Someone to discover a world with – so nice! Everything's much easier with someone beside you. Someone where you're at.

I knew I should talk to Astrid first. Get some details before I went storming in. I started texting but stopped. Too slow. I rang but the call went to Message Bank. I practically yelled.

'Astrid, you can't tell me something like that and then turn your mobile off!'

I was furious. Maybe she was on another call. Anyway, it was Luke I had to talk to.

My hands were sweaty, my neck was sweaty. So nervous. I didn't have reason to be nervous any more. I started jabbing letters.

Hey Luke, heard
you've come out.
Way 2 go!
Anytime u wanna
hang with me &
Jen & c the gay
world, give us a call!

I read over the message. Read it again. Too many exclamation marks. I took out the second, saved it, deleted it, went to Outbox and retrieved it again.

What was I thinking! I deleted the message properly, scrolled down to Luke's number and rang. A mobile calling a mobile? Nearly 5 pm? Well, just this time.

I thought the call was about to ring out, and I hadn't got a message prepared, but then there was Luke's voice in my ear.

'Hello, Luke,' I said.

A pause then: 'Sam? Hey, how's it going?'

He sounded so casual. Not a bit shook up. So confident. The guy was incredible. I was a wreck when I came out. Crying in front of that old lady I didn't even know, the one with the green scarf. I went to say more but Luke beat me to it.

'So, how can I help you, mate?' he asked.

That kind've derailed me a bit. I mean, it was a bit funny. He must've known why I was ringing and all. He was being too casual. He'd have to start being more open. There was lots of noise in the background. Maybe he was in a car.

'Well … I just wanted to say congrats.'

'Congrats …?'

'I know how hard it is. I was just saying (well, not to anyone, actually, I'm quite alone), that you can come out with me and Jen any time – I don't mean "come out" come out – *again*, of course. You know what I mean.'

There was a bit of a pause.

'Hey, Sam, you're not on the drugs again, are you?'

I might as well have been. What was I saying? The joint had burnt down to the fingers on my free hand. My head was swimming, the picture blurring. Filter said the mushrooms would stay in my system a few weeks. If I was susceptible, I might even have flashbacks. A joint could bring it on.

'Look, Luke, I just… You're not making this any easier.'

He started to say something back but my phone creaked. Incoming message. A second later it beeped. Message Received.

'Hey, Sam, this isn't a good time. I'm – '

147

'Look,' I said. (Why couldn't he make it easy on me? I thought maybe there'd be a tear or something.) 'Look, Luke, I just wanted to say it's not so bad.'

'Hey, Sam, the phone's cutting out.'

'Being gay, I mean.'

There was quite a pause after this. A long pause.

'What did you say?'

'Well,' I said, the wall opposite practically dripping (don't flashback now, Sam), 'it's great you've come out.'

He killed the call. I dropped the mobile. My whole body trembled. Sweat squeezed from my pores. Luckily I was sitting by that time, on what little kerb the alley boasted. If I could just get the alley to sit still. Sit still. Sit!

I got the cornice of the building opposite to stop. The rest stretched away but then slowly pulled back. It was okay. Bolognese in my throat. Quiet. On the main street, cars going past at timed intervals, faintly, deliberately.

It was okay. My heart was slowing down. I didn't know what to do next. I had no idea. I wasn't sure I could even remember how to use my legs. The message box on my mobile caught my eye. Message Received, it flashed. That message that had interrupted me talking to … well, him.

Astrid.

Well loser did i
also tell u i hav
a naughty sense
of humour? Get
over it!

The building opposite bubbled into a skyscraper and I almost screamed.

Next day, I was wandering near Video Highlights so I thought about dropping in, seeing if Filter was working. Filter was Zane's friend, not mine. I'd only met him that one night we did mushrooms, but I figured it would be okay. When I went in, Filter was doing a lone shift but there was a second stool behind the counter which he told me to take. He didn't act like my showing up was unexpected or odd. He merely said I looked down. I nodded.

'What you need, Sam, you need a bit of fun,' said Filter. 'See that video in my bag. That's it. Crap Movie 2. That's it, open it up.'

So I grabbed the video Filter had pointed out. I opened it up and there were all these little plastic packages inside. Weed. I quickly zipped it in his bag; a customer was asking for films.

'Excuse me. Have you seen this film?'

'Which one?' snapped Filter.

The moustache held it up.

'I haven't got me glasses.'

'*All The Pretty Horses.*'

'No,' said Filter.

'What about *Miss Congeniality*?'

'No.'

'*Two If By Sea*?'

'No.'

'Look, I'm always asking you about the latest films. You don't watch them, do you?'

'Does a smack dealer inject?'

The mo nearly screamed.

'Listen, mate. Five new films come in here a week. On average. Get that? Five. That's about a whole extra shift of movie watching. Now I ask my boss, you wanna pay me

149

an extra day just to watch movies? What you think he says to that, eh?'

The customer got his videos and left.

The question was pretty forward, but I asked it anyway. 'Why do you work here, Filter, when you must be pulling it in with the drugs?'

'Got to have a few rocks, Sam. You and I, we're swimming the non-pedestrian current. That's what makes it a fookin' ride, mate, but it also makes it fookin' scary. So you've got to scatter a few rocks in your stream. Somethink to hold onto, now and then. My video store shifts punctuate the week for me. My taste of the pedestrian beat. Don't let that cricket go, my boy.'

Cricket? Had I talked about my game that night on mushrooms? Zane had, I guess. Or had since.

'I don't ask for much, Sam. You know, I've only ever wanted one thing in life. Yeah, my way!'

We both laughed. I had to admit: he was different. I mean, what had Luke talked about? Cricket.

'Hey, Sam, you look a bit thin,' said Filter. 'Why not nip over the road and get yourself a pizza.'

Pretty thoughtful too.

'Okay,' I said, 'I *am* a bit hungry.'

'Hey, if you're going anyway, mind if you get me a medium Mexicana? Actually, make that a large.'

And that sort of began my time with Filter. Next day he got me a position at the store. My first real customer service job. With that, and sorting shelves at Jen's library, I'd be pulling it in. Well, relatively speaking.

It was now well into August, over half the year gone. Not everything had gone right since coming to Melbourne but a lot had. A good friend and housemate in Jen; an unexpected friend in Zane. What would come next?

150

Filter had a few rules regarding the clientele. One customer that used to come in, a guy with black hair like a bird's nest, with one big egg in it, his bald crown, was a favourite of Filter's for demonstrating protocol. Now, mostly you just asked the customer what their home number was, to confirm their membership, but Filter asked this guy his surname.

'Why do you always ask me that? You have it there.'

'We ask everyone, mate. Procedure.'

And the guy would be forced to say it.

'Vagiatis.'

'Mind spelling that, mate?'

Bird's Nest would nearly scream.

'Don't bovver yourself,' and Filter would scan the guy's videos through.

Every day we averaged forty people we had to call about late videos. Yeah, it's a lot. The first introduction to phone etiquette, I tried to manoeuvre behind Filter to turn down the stereo. He nearly slapped my hand, his CT's (Chicken Tits, as in Kentucky Fried) shaking under his T-shirt.

'Rule number 8, Samster,' and he called up a screen with rule number 8.

8. When ringing the customer regarding overdue videos make sure to turn up the music as loudly as possible and shout down the phone. That way, they can hear you, but you can't hear them.

There were other rules too. Like for instance, number two, one of the most important.

2. The customer is always wrong.

And number three, nearly as important.

3. The customer is never right.

I reckoned this one was pretty much the same as number two but Filter went on for ever so long about the subtle 'differences and delineations' in meaning that I let it rest. Might as well give you the rest of his rules 'for dealing with the customer', though.

4. The customer is not your friend.

5. The customer is your enemy.

(I must say I thought these two trod the same ground as well, but Filter was adamant.)

6. Never feed the customer.

'What?'
'You grew up on a farm, Samster?'
'Yes.'
'Well, if you've got to feed the customer, remember the way you feed a horse?'
And I did. Palm flat, so the horse didn't nibble off your fingers with the apple.

7. Never accept food from the customer.

Rule Number 8 you already know.

9. Never acknowledge the customer outside the video store; barely acknowledge the customer within the video store.

One day Filter reckoned I made the worst mistake you could with the customer. After this hottie walked out, I turned to Filter and said, 'Hey, he's cute,' which he was, with his shaved head. (Shaved heads really suit some guys.) But Filter nearly went mad over it. First I thought it was about me eying up a feller, and I didn't want to put up with any homophobic crap from him, but it turns out it wasn't that at all; I'd broken the cardinal rule, numero uno.

1. Never, absolutely ever, anthropomorphise the customer.

I had to look it up my next library shift. That Filter was bright all right, but I reckon he could've put his smarts to better use. I've come across a lot of brains about the place since, either stacking supermarket shelves in superstring patterns or filing parking tickets according to Mandelbrot theory. Staying interested, as Filter put it. But one by one they get 'real' jobs (in other words, careers). Used to annoy Filter something shocking as he saw his mates dissing the homey gear for corporate suits. Falling asleep was how he liked to put it. Ever seen *Invasion of the Body Snatchers*, the 1950s version? Don't bother with the remakes. Well, there's this town in the film that's slowly getting taken over by aliens. When you fell asleep, they stole your body. So you basically had to stay awake as long as you could. Otherwise, you'd wake up as one of them, living out in Legoland with your common-law wife. But staying awake's pretty hard itself. Soon you become another sort of zombie, just as comatose.

But the most important rule of all, apparently, was rule number ten. Filter said he'd tell me what it was one day. I wanted to know why he couldn't now.

After a rare Friday night out with Jen and Tash, I left them to drop by the video store; I knew from the roster that Filter was on. He was more than usually glad to see me. He'd had a pretty big blow-up with a customer earlier.

(The guy wanted to join up, his only ID being a handkerchief with his initials monogrammed into a corner). But nothing happened when we locked up.

Filter slipped his plastic into the ATM across the road then checked the money it coughed up.

'Making sure the fooker hasn't short-changed me,' he explained.

Then off to a restaurant, a little Thai place on Victoria Street. We had to slip our shoes off at the door and carry them with us to our table in the plastic bags provided. You sat in these baby-pool-sized depressions. The table was floor-height. I tried to toast with some wine we'd bought, but Filter had already tucked into his food, which was this calamari and lemongrass dish that overlapped the side of the plate. But not before he took a digital photo. He'd burned about ten CDs worth of food footage, he told me. His new porn.

The waitresses giggled. They gathered round Filter, handing me the camera to take the group photo.

'Smile.'

And they did, Filter the most broadly.

'Best bloody Thai joint in Melbourne, Sam!' he shouted. The waitresses departed and we were alone again.

He started talking about the Friday and Saturday evening shifts at the video store, the only time the boss put on more than one person, 'cause it would get so busy and all.

'I'm at work, right, with these two sheilas, right, and what do they talk about? "Ooh, Doris, I was in the shower last night, and would you believe, but Teddy popped in, quite unexpected." They're saying all this right there in front of me, like I'm one of the girls or somethink. How you like that? They think they can shoot off about their men's dick tricks with me. I'm that much of a puppy, am

154

I? Put me on the cover of *Non-threatening Male of the Year*, would you? Talk about the fag-confidante who ain't a fag. Fook me.'

Filter slurped in a good dose of Tom Yum soup. He looked up to see me looking.

'Man, that shit you spurted the other night, on 'shrooms, that was real inspiring. Made me rethink my whole approach to music.'

I'd been trying not to think about that night, how wonderful it seemed, how alive. It was like being a kid, or a visitor to Earth. Everything was amazing, even simple stuff like flowers, and that carnation, and those raindrops shaken out of Zane's hair. But now everything seemed so solid. Nothing went deeper.

Filter burped, gripping his stomach.

'Call me Too Big, Sam. Here I am, fat as an American. Least you're a slim bastard. Being gay, you've got to like it. I love my lard. Even give it a name: Pudgy. Oi, Pudgy, fancy a bite down the pub, do ya? We might even 'ave a kip later. Wot you say to that? A nice snooze after our feast? Just so we don't work it off, eh? Wouldn't want to do that. Tumble, grumble. He's up for it.'

This was *so* reminding me of my first dinner with Zane, and how he went on about his weight as well. Not that Zane had any lard. Maybe fat is a state of mind.

Filter stopped rearranging his beanbag belly. Our waitress tweaked over.

'You like, Mr Filter? You full?'

'Listen, lady, do an ultrasound on this baby' – rubbing his stomach – 'I've got *two* people to feed here, I 'ave. How's about a second helping, love?'

'Naughty, naughty,' said the waitress, shaking a finger. Then she turned to me: 'Your friend is very bad.'

'Sure is,' I laughed.

Filter daubed his lips with his serviette. I was practically crying from the spiciness of the food. But it was pretty damn tasty.

More dishes arrived by the later train. Filter asked how Zane and I were getting on. We'd got the fucking behind us, which was good. 'Just 'cause you've got a prick, doesn't mean you *are* one,' he added for good measure, not that that really followed.

'He's a good bloke, Zane,' continued Filter. 'We've come a long way, us two. We decided where we had to get to, and went for it. You should see our passport photos, mate. Like a pair of Jehovah's bloody Witnesses!'

Filter pulled out a little photo.

'See the change. Just got knocked up along the way, that's all. I only ever wanted to find snatch so I could get fat. Only fookin' problem is, I got fat first. Fook' me.'

Filter grabbed the passport photo. Maybe I'd panned between him and the photo one too many times.

'Get Zane to show you *his* some time. You'll piss yourself. So what's *your* journey, Sam? From country bumpkin to …?'

To …? To what? I'd never much thought of life as a journey before. It sounded so wanky. Like something off crap TV. But in hindsight, maybe I was … What had Zane said during the mushies? Turning a new leaf? I gave it a shot.

'Well,' I said, 'I guess I want to …' and I trickled out. After the mushroom episode, I would've said I wanted to live the life of books, to find a boyfriend as real as the best drawn characters of fiction, but that hadn't panned out so well.

So what did I want now? I guess I just wanted to meet a normal, down-to-earth guy and the next minute we'd be going out together, life partners. I put this to Filter.

'For starters, you've got to work out your type, mate.'

Straightaway, I saw how profound that was. Your type! Maybe I'd been pissing skyward. Luke seemed to be my type all right, except the straight bit. But then again … Well, that guy who'd come into the video store with the shaved head, the one Filter had gotten angry about when I said he was cute. Justin his name was (I looked it up on our computer). Maybe *he* was my type. Never thought I'd go for a guy with a shaved head before. But I guess that just made him look even *more* manly. Come to think of it, Luke with his lady-locks was a bit of a girl. I was into guys because they were guys. So why would I want a girly guy? Defeats the purpose.

The waitress brought us extra rice and naan bread (on the house) to fill out the meal for Filter. While we resumed stuffing, Filter went on about the detailing in the place, sitting down on cushions to eat, that sort of thing. We'd eaten so much at Filter's insistence, it was a struggle to stand when we were done.

'You've done a damn good job,' he said to the waitress and cooking staff afterwards in the doorway of the fogged-up kitchen.

'Thank you, sir, thank you.'

'You're trying,' shouted Filter. He was pretty tanked. 'That's more than I can say for half the shops down this street.'

'Come on, Filter,' I said. I wanted to get outside, in the cool. Something made me remember Filter hadn't told me rule number ten for dealing with the customer. Our waitress escorted us to the door. On the way, Filter told her to get rid of the few tables and chairs they'd still kept. If those pedestrians couldn't sit on the floor to eat their authentic Thai meal, then they should get their cardboard quick fixes with the rest of the Dearly Disappointed over in KnifePoint.

At the door, Filter had to compliment our waitress a few more times.

'Your friend – he is old-fashioned gentleman,' she said to me.

She knocked me with an elbow, laughing at the same time. 'Make excellent husband, no!'

Filter was beaming. Eyes closed like two arrows pointing at his nose. He was lapping it up.

'He is very nice.'

Filter stopped smiling. He opened his eyes. The arrows hit their target.

'I'm nice? You think I'm nice?'

The waitress nodded, but not so sure now.

'Shit!' yelled Filter. 'That means you won't fook me now.'

She backed in through the door. It shut behind her. I was about to run back and say Filter hadn't meant what he said, when he grabbed me to race after a tram.

We popped on the 86 up to Zane's, holding onto the horse stirrups for support. The tram took off with a John Wayne stagger, giving an excuse to the frottage from the suit behind. I motioned to Filter, and we made our way to the back. It was pretty packed, so everyone was more or less travelling cattle class.

'You're too fookin' right, Sam,' said Filter suddenly. I wondered what I was right about.

The poor sod was looking suddenly morose. His jowls were hanging past his chin.

'You're not the only one with talent, Sam. *I'm* a muso. Zane told you that?'

I shook my head.

'Another fookin' demo sent back this week,' he said, searching through the window for our stop. 'The flossers probably didn't even listen to it. I'm not much younger than Richard James, Luke Vibert and Tom Jenkinson. And they're millionaires now. You know, *I* introduced The Avalanches to Dr Octagon's beats. I was at that party on Canning Street, where you are now, where the The Avalanches got their first record deal. Tried to talk to Dexter at the New Buffalo concert – think he remembered me? Mate, I work to create the fattest beats, the – what did you say, "perfect string of moments" – but look at me fookin' life, it's shite.'

Filter couldn't get a break, it seemed. His music was too 'out there' or something. Had a pretty high opinion of himself. His next sentence confirmed it.

'I never asked to be a genius, Sam. All I ask is that me genius be fookin' acknowledged. Living with the pain, that's what I'm doing. Mozart's genius was recognised at six. I'm nearly *five* times that age. Mate, I tell you, I can't cope with obscurity any more. I live with it every day of me life.'

I didn't know whether he was joking or not. A few ladies near us were trying not to start each other laughing. Luckily they were behind Filter, so he couldn't see. Taking another census of Filter's face, I decided on high seriousness, but the ladies finally dropped plates of laughter.

Filter looked at them and then away, staring morosely through the crook of his arm that was hanging onto the horse stirrup.

'Man, Zane says you were being groomed for the state team, Sam, and now what are you doing? Getting fat with us.'

I had to turn away quickly.

Getting the answer to rule number ten could wait.

Me and Filter bouldered into Settee. We saw Zane in the spot where he and I first dined together. Seemed like years ago but it couldn't have been more than a couple of months. Filter and I sat down next to him. The waiter, a guy (No Stopwatch today) came over to inquire whether we were eating or just drinking. 'Neither,' snapped Filter, and the waiter gave us the dirtiest look. First time he'd actually looked at us, so I guess it was an improvement.

'He's so arrogant,' I said.

'Well, Sammy, he's a waiter at Settee,' laughed Zane. 'But the thing about that is, even though you may be a waiter at Settee, you're still a waiter.'

Filter smiled, then asked me to grab us some beers. Pints. *He'd* go the next round. I'd gotten out my ten-dollar note when he grabbed it, saying not to worry, he'd make up the rest. Zane shook his head as Filter wombled to the bar.

Zane put aside the magazine he was half-reading, *Inches*, and stared at me.

'How you liking our friend, Samikins?'

Filter wanted my opinion on Zane, too. The whole thing felt like a game. When I faltered, Zane changed subjects to Luke.

'Yeah, I'm over him.'

'I don't think you are, Sammy, but I'll leave it at that.'

Zane tucked his serviette into his Esprit shirt with microsurgery precision and, it can only be said, made love to his meal. Was that all life really came down to: good food?

A last strand of spaghetti disappeared down Zane's mouth. The slurp turned my attention from what I'd been staring at: a young couple with a baby in a pram. Pretty late to still have a kid out.

'I must confide in you, Sammy, I'm not in a good mental state,' Zane offered, dabbing his lips with all four corners of his serviette. 'Really, I'm not. For the first time I can understand this having babies thing, I really can. It finally takes the emphasis off yourself. Breeders are onto something there.'

Filter slapped down to my left. The chair nearly exploded. Filter didn't have a pint on him. I was angry, but he showed me under his jacket that he'd got us four Guinnesses in cans, much cheaper, from the bottle-o across the road. The turntable revolved.

'Oi, what's this? Kylie?' asked Filter, looking up at the speaker nearest us. 'Where would I be if I had a tush like hers …? Hey, aren't you two screaming benders meant to be into Kylie?'

There was the answer: no way. I wasn't going to subscribe to *any* stereotype.

After we downed the last of our stouts at a table in the park, Filter drinking the fourth 'cause that was his bit he put in, he flipped us an E each. Blue Batmans. I hadn't had an E since that date with Zane. Zane swallowed his with the last of his Guinness. I was about to do the same when Filter said 'forty-five bucks'.

'Filter, you can get them for thirty-five,' said Zane, and he handed across a fifty and a twenty with a wave of the hand when I started to protest.

I swallowed the pill. Filter looked at the kiddies' fort, then across to the road, with its now stationary/now passing cars. The lamps in the park and the street lights glowed orange, like decoration on a giant Christmas tree knocked flat. Possums scooted down trees, across the grass and up neighbouring trunks in a dance sequence only they could choreograph.

Filter slapped the wooden table.

'Right, change of scene. An E calls for a water backdrop.'

Zane smiled, obviously used to Filter's moments of inspiration. We got up on our feet and Filter led the way. He had a gift, even in the heart of the city, of going the most private route, taking the shadowy side of the street, cutting across demolished lots, ducking down restricted roads.

I smoked the last joint I'd saved. Zane and Filter looked at me but I wanted to maximise the night.

We stopped at what seemed like the edge of another park, dark pockets of sweat under Filter's arms, smaller ones under mine and Zane's. Zane looked at his watch.

'The forty-five minutes are almost up. It should hit any minute.'

'Perfect fookin' timing, then,' ripped Filter. He led us along a path into the scrub.

Waiting, I was waiting, the way you wait for sleep, then don't remember exactly when it happens.

And it happened, but I didn't know it. Not until …

My world was sliced like bread. My life – so many layers. Ankle-height, waist-height, which one tonight? Yes, yes, yes!

'Thanks, guys, thanks, Zane, thanks for this.'

We stopped amid the undergrowth, barely able to see with the city's lights blocked by the trees' canopies.

'Hey, man,' said Filter, 'this night's for you. This is all for you. I'm fookin' happy to be your drug buddy, your euphoric guide.' And he slapped me moving.

'It's so beautiful,' laughed Zane appreciatively, as we made our way down the steps to the Yarra. I was in the middle, so they wouldn't lose me.

We came down to the Yarra River brown. And I found ... How I found ...

But all I could say was, 'I've been so unhappy, Filter, Zane. I'm so lonely. Can I say that?'

'Yeah, you can fookin' say that.'

'I was so ... so ... I was ...'

'What you saying?' asked Zane.

'That I ... I ...'

'Don't try so hard, mate. The harder you think, the harder it comes on.'

Schlepping along the path, trees bent towards us in reverence. Colours announced themselves like never before. The path rolled back like a dog's back brushed the wrong way, taking us forward seemingly forever, but never really getting anywhere.

'I was so ... so ... so worried I wouldn't live a ... a normal life. Hang out with normal – with normal people.'

Zane and Filter turned from the trees, the grass, the rocks, everything wondrous again, to me, wondrous for the first time.

'Sammy darling, I hate to break it to you, but Filter and I aren't exactly normal and this ain't exactly normal behaviour.'

Filter gave Zane a soft backhander on the shoulder.

'Man, you're a brave guy, Sam. You're the bravest guy I know.'

Bopping along, in rubber-plant gyrations, telling Filter how hard it was.

'What's this? You should do an exposé, Sam. I can see the headline now. Anal Sex – The Inside Story. You got a big heart, you see. That's your problem. All these people –

Zane, your friend Jen – they've got big hearts. No use in that. Phar Lap had a big heart – wot they do? They poisoned the trotter.'

I stopped. It was all too bright. The sunniest day was overcast next to this night. Zane and Filter braked a few staggers ahead and turned around.

'Was it …? Is it …?'

'What, Sammy?' asked Zane.

'Is it real?'

Filter laughed. 'This ain't dope revelations, man. This is real.'

Wandering along the path that spooned the Yarra, taking it all in. How to begin? Where to go? Our dog-trot, jog-trot, foot pace, a crawl.

Asking if this was real, and waking life wasn't …? If this dream were the cream, and the wide-awake world a mean substitute …? It just didn't compute. Where are memories made? Living every permutation. Taking the easy path through *my* life. Making the world over. Getting to the end of the past, stepping up into light. This time, things were going to be all right. Good-bye black days. We'd come so far.

'I've … we've … I've come so far.'

Sneaking past the backs of factories. Brick-a-brack walls. Feeling the force. The bricks a Rubix Cube, switching through every configuration.

'Sammy,' shouted Zane, 'didn't you know, darling? Gay people really *are* lucky. We *choose* who we want to be. That's because we're forced to think about it.'

Filter on a green bench standing. Filter screaming.

'So who do *you* wanna be, Samster? Who do *you* wanna be!'

Streams, crying beads, rivers from each, our eyes. So beautiful, the city so alive. Building blocks – the stars in stacks so high. How'd they ever stack the stars so tall? What was … what was … the something of it all …?

I was climbing out of the pit of my past into this new world, standing on the shoulders of sheep – woof woof!

I was – we were – for once, not just a line through life, but a bubble spreading out. Passing through people's wakes. Awake in Filter and Zane's jet streams. Knowing everything they'd come through to come thus far. Failing to be angry. Beyond hate or forgiveness. Complete understanding. Them making it easier for me, by me travelling in their jetstream, since they'd moved on in time. Since they'd broken the toughest of the Brylcream waves and – our mothers and fathers before us – the fifties curls, the whorls upon worlds.

'If you stand in other people's shoes ...'

'Yes, Sammy darling?'

'… you can't shoot them.'

This got a laugh. Zane and Filter laughing, both atop the bench.

'But it's true,' added Filter. 'Too fookin' right, mate. Must remember …'

But he'd forget.

'Anchoring your boat in the present,' I began, 'spreading out in ripples through space. Feeling through everyone's history. Knowing how hard it was for you, Filter, for you, Zane, for the three of us to be where we are, to have made it this far, on time.'

'Oi, Samster! Don't go too fookin' deep, mate!' shouted Filter, jumping off the bench and grabbing my shoulders.

Too deep? Don't spread too far in this lake of time. Who was saying this? Who? Already, I was in Jen's head, sensing a tender moment with Tash, 'While it lasts' on their lips. Let go, Sam. Get shunted ahead. Before the spray becomes molecules. Before you can't pull it back in. Jumpcutting to the next moment ahead in time, reduced to a point, a line. Dropouts in memory. The fading away of the high. Being brought back down to this world. Standing on ground. Feet on the earth.

'Just keep walking, Sam,' chanted Filter. 'Just keep walking,' chanted Zane, whisking me back into movement.

Our dog-trot, ambling, snail's pace, a crawl.

'Live life,' I sighed, 'just for a moment. For one time, the economy of books. In this night, everything beaming. Every moment momentous, packed with meaning.'

We stopped by a lookout. We looked out, not wanting to pass the baton, seeing the river stretched so lowly.

'Write your life as an edge-of-the-seat romance!' I shouted. 'No filler, Filter. No filler, Zane. No airport-lounge, doorstop, non-stop, comfy chiller. No steady state, no filler. Because we *are* fil-a-ment. We burn in the firmament. We shine. Come on, Duke Apparel, I crown me Duke Apparel. And I ask you, does the day have to be this way? A hundred ways to fall. So many choices, all real till decided, all waiting to be divined. Just for a moment, keep everything in mind.'

'Just for a moment, Sam …' sighed Zane.

'For a moment, Sam,' sighed Filter.

The moment passed.

We lumbered, heads befogged, along the byways and highways to Filter's flat, slower now, heavier. His flat was behind a house, down an alley and up a metal stair. Filter unlocked ten locks on the door with as many keys and we were inside. He flicked on a switch which turned on every light in the room. But it wasn't overbearing because the lights were subtle, shaded, dim. Filter's place couldn't have been more of a contrast to Zane's pad. Imagine every conceivable space taken up with props and costumes from the drama of Filter's life, most of them of a musical nature.

Filter eased down onto his vast, black-quilted bed. He was obviously pained from all the walking. He said we should smooth out the come-down with a few 'parachutes', but of a domestic, sleeping pill, kind. In Zane's words, 'housewife drugs'.

Zane prepared the mix while I took a seat on the hard-rubbish couch – a pensioner-age, leather one.

And had a think.

I'd got the whole friends thing figured wrong. My searching for a gang? Well, your friends actually find *you*. Back home, Mum and Dad tried to get my brothers to take me out with *their* friends. But they weren't my friends – they were my brothers' mates. Off my own bat, I tried to join Cinders' posse but only succeeded in befriending Cinders. In Melbourne, I wanted to fit in with the cricket crowd at first, but I guess my avoiding their functions showed they weren't quite where I was at. Next it was Joe, who was going his own direction. Then I thought I'd get sophisticated with Astrid and Luke but that had all turned out pretty badly, as I've recounted. Even though Zane and Filter were pretty rough, I hadn't had such a night in all the outings with Luke, had I? Zane and Filter took me in, unreservedly. I was seeing things went deeper. I'd wanted to be a surface-dweller, but maybe a deep-sea fish was … well, a damn sight uglier, but more interesting somehow.

It's something to think about. I mean … well … maybe friends are like books. Not only have you got to come across them in the first place but also at the right time. Zane and Filter were right for me right now. A year earlier, I would've totally sidestepped them as being 'too weird'. That can also happen with books. With *Catcher In The Rye*, I tried reading it too young. Couldn't relate to it. Tried it again a few years later. By then I was past it. The friends you miss out on.

Guess you could say Arny was my *Catcher In The Rye*. If only I'd taken him off the shelf a month later. But it wasn't all doom. I'd put Arny out of my head, filling it instead with Joe and then Luke, guys who didn't matter when Arny was the one, wasn't he? He'd be back by the end of the year. Would the magic still be there between us? Hopefully the end of the year wouldn't be too late to recapture those few moments we'd had. There's only a very short window of opportunity, as they say.

And that's the other sad thing, when you think about it. A new discovery doesn't stay new for long. I remember when me and Cinders would hang out all the time. Now it never happened, with me moving to Melbourne and not visiting home on Sundays and Mondays like I used to. It would probably go that way with Zane and Filter. Must look to books, but. I mean, you can pick up a past fave any time, can't you? Take *To Kill A Mockingbird*. A few pages in and it's old times again. Hopefully, that would be the same for me and my friends down the track, as we each went off to collect different books for our libraries. A few pages in, that's all it will take. It will be okay. Old times.

It was a theme I'd been developing previous times I took drugs, but I took it up again. There was a way books could be even more like life, or life more like books, to be accurate, and I clearly saw how. Half comatose on Filter's couch, but ruminating pretty hard, I saw the answer.

Drugs.

No, don't be sceptical. I'd taken up the thought after my first full-on trip with Zane and Filter, then dropped it after the Luke episode. But I was wrong to. Listen, drugs

168

are the missing tool. Life's pointless, plot-less, a real let-down next to the well-conceived reality of books. No, hear me out. If there's an author to life, then you can be that author, and your writing tool, drugs. I mean, drugs provide every literary device. Compression of the moment, expansion of time. The boring moments are buggered off, while the better ones get rummaged over. Thoroughly. And then there are the flashes of insight. Epiphanies, I think the modernists called them. Hell yes! What you think is a world you couldn't get more sick of, suddenly sprouts anew, just with the way a leaf or flower takes on a new magnificence with the mental light. And to think, it's all in your head. Life can go from one interesting moment to the next. Everything momentous, packed with meaning. Life can *read* like a book.

And every great book is a love story, no matter how mad. Take *Wuthering Heights*. Case in point. Which is something I couldn't get about Filter. The love thing. I mean, he didn't even *seem* to be looking. Zane was at least having a go. Well, kind of.

I opened my eyes on that couch and looked over at Filter. He was leaning back on his low-slung bed, pipe in hand, chuffing on some hash he'd cut from a bar of the stuff. I asked him the question.

'I'm happy with myself right now,' he answered.

'But don't you want someone?'

'Looking won't make it happen, mate.'

I don't think he was even *not* looking.

Zane handed us the cocktail he'd been making. To stop the buzzing. I tried to impart some of what I'd been thinking but Filter said nothing and Zane's response was disappointing.

'Sammy, darling, with that attitude to drugs, never ever record yourself while tripping. We did once and it was the most embarrassing garbage.'

'It's not all garbage, Zane,' said Filter from his prostrate position on his bed.

Zane shrugged. I tried to quiz Filter about the search for love, but he barely returned a word. With neither of the two keen to continue either conversation (love or drugs), I looked about more attentively. Records and CDs; recording equipment; posters for touring bands; about ten instruments, all in various states of undress – the musician's studio. Filter saw me looking and got up slowly. He showed me how he made his music. Pretty interesting, and mostly an electronic affair. Said if he died tomorrow he'd have enough stuff recorded to ensure his immortality already, but he went on creating. He called up on computer the songs that would one day make up his first CD.

This was the tracklist:

Your face, my fist (dedicated to the music industry).

Fuck you where your mouth is (which he hoped would gag the critics).

Hmm, what a wonderful day to be white (about Australia Day 'celebrations').

Lest we remember (about ANZAC Day).

It's not you, it's me in you (for an ex).

Reality made Isabelle sick (for his niece).

How strong is your noise constitution? (mine didn't hold out).

And, finally, the track he wanted to complete now:

Desperation hole.

Which was incidentally the name of the whole album. Filter wanted to record me saying a few things to wash through the unfinished track. When he played back the recordings, I was a bit shocked. My voice sounded so high-camp, like that killer in *Silence of the Lambs*. I thought I had a rough voice.

'What you talking about, Samster? You got a good voice, mate. Bit of range. Wish I had your voice. Might be able to sing a bit better.'

He distorted my vocals some more, put some reverb into it. It was almost listenable. Zane watched on, bemused. Filter dropped my modified voice into the track. Finally, he played the song through. It was just the one line, over and over.

Even if you were dead and turning blue, baby I'd still wanna fuck you.

'That's real love,' said Zane and clinked my glass.

Chapter Six

When I woke on my own mattress at midday, I didn't want to get up. To tell the truth, I was scared. All right, petrified. It just came over me as I looked through the blinds and onto the daylight world. There were no shadows to hide its rawness. I got up and took forever to have breakfast. Jen asked me something and I snapped. Hadn't even heard what she said. I took off outside. I looked at the time on my mobile. Less than an hour since I'd got up. Unlike the night before, now every minute had to be lived through. I looked ahead. The days jammed against each other like cars in heavy traffic, with me impatient to overtake. No, I wouldn't wait. I wouldn't wait on a half-hope with Arny. Filter could wait all his life, but not me. I'd had the one chance – it could be years before the next if I didn't make it happen.

Even the cars crusted on the street were too chirpy, too bright. Looking at their polish stealing bits of light, I felt worse. This morning wasn't like a book at all. I texted Filter.

How does it feel
2 work 9-5? How
does it feel to b

a pedestrian?
How does it feel
2 wake up alone
at night? To
know u could've
been a
contender? 2
not matter?

Filter rang.

'Right there, Samster. That hurt, I must say. It hurt 'cause it's a bit true, I guess. But tell you what, I'm gonna let it go. Know why? We'll just put it down to Tragic Tuesday.'

'But it's Saturday.'

'Just get over to Zane's, mate. We'll ride it out together.'

The slightest movement and some damn car would blink at me.

I got on the train, passing all those sawtooth factories, sitting on the tan seats with their tar patches, mummified chewing gum. I texted Zane for good measure.

If you were a
day, you'd be
Monday. If you
were a flavour,
you'd be plain.
If you were a
position, you'd
be side-saddle.
If you were
dead, you'd be
interesting.

What was happening to me? I hadn't felt this angry since smashing up Charles Acton-Heath & Co. And the night before I was so peaceful, so inspired.

When I knocked on Zane's door he told me straight away he'd deleted my message. Then he added that it was a good thing we were getting together. It was too dangerous for any of us to stay alone like this. Dangerous? He invited me in and we took a seat.

'Drugs can alter your moods sharply, Sammy,' explained Zane.

Would I feel the low as strongly as I felt the high?

Now I was scared.

Zane's mobile beeped. Filter had texted him. It was a full-on roundelay.

Went inta
Maccas. Asked 4
chips. "What?"
she says.
"Chips!" I says.
"You mean fries,
sir," she says.
"Sorry Miss," I
says. "I forgot
this was FUCKING
AMERICA!"

Zane looked out his window, at the Maccas over the road. He took my hand and led me out. We passed under the golden arches. Filter continued his diatribe, still stuffing a Big Mac between his lips.

'What size meal? she says? What size meal? Regular or constipated? The latter, love. That's all you serve up.'

'Too true, Filter, too true,' laughed Zane. And we were out of Corporateville and back on the pavement.

We were hopping through the streets, dodging the pedestrians. A guy came up to us dressed in green.

'Want to support Greenpeace, friend?' asked the leprechaun. Filter turned on him.

'What did you fookin' call me, cunt?

'What? Er … nothing.' The leprechaun backed away.

My muscles knotted with nervousness.

'Friend,' answered Filter for him. 'You called me "friend". You don't *know* me to call me friend, fuckstick.'

Zane grabbed Filter's arm. The pedestrians were passing round us like a stream round a boulder.

'I'll smash your fookin' teeth in with me dick,' shouted Filter. 'Yeah, it's diamond-hard and all, mate.'

Zane went to give the leprechaun a few cigarettes to placate him, and ended up handing across the whole pack.

'I went down on your mum but I could taste *your* cum!' put in Filter as his last word.

I trembled after them till we got to a coffee lounge. The unpredictability, the anger. Filter seemed so nice, and now …? He had a definite dark side, for sure. Was that the drugs? The other side of them? I sipped my cappuccino, shaking. Zane counselled Filter to go easy on the drugs a bit. Maybe that's what it was for all of us. We'd been overdoing them, he added.

Filter got up, saying he had a shift at the video store. He'd catch up with me and Zane later or maybe sooner than later. Work was so boring, he was in danger of strangling his feller behind the counter and getting fired. Zane took me to the Prahran pool and we sat around, swam and generally did nothing for as long as we could. It whiled away the afternoon and kind of helped.

Zane and I went to The Pit that night, after choofing at his place first. This time when I went in and handed over

175

my ten-buck cover charge, I just stood there. They asked me what was wrong. I told them I gave them a twenty-dollar note. They were pretty suss on me, but reopened the till and gave me ten bucks. In short, I didn't pay a cent. Zane said I had the makings of a real gangster.

I went to the bar to buy us a drink. Someone pinched my arse. A guy with a hardware facial, rings and bolts in ear, lip and eyebrow. When I did the frill-neck lizard on him, he pointed above. There was a TV with flickering porn stills. 'What you standing here for then?' asked the guy. I quickly moved away.

How did you ever meet people? The more edgy I looked, the less attractive I'd be. I found Zane watching the dancers in the bullring. I squeezed in next to him and asked him what he was after in a guy.

'Sammy darling, there is only the spoon majoris and spoon minoris. He needs to be shorter than me. I'm the spoon majoris in the relationship, honey.'

Zane could see I wasn't satisfied with that. It wasn't a real answer. He leant in.

'Sammy, you want to know what I look for in a man? He has to be physically tough. If he's physically tough, then he's probably mentally tough. He needs to be able to stick to a regime of exercise. If he's not tough, I'll break him. The bitch needs to stand up to me.'

I looked about. Zane educated me as to all the types: the cubs and bears ('oh, please'), the barebackers ('keep away from them, Sammy'), the size queens ('you'll do well there'), the vanilla boys ('not with your deviant nature').

I got a few looks but didn't know what to do. Men just stared at you like they wanted to mine you dry. The stares were unrelenting too. Not the bashful glance then sidewise look away.

'Oh please,' said Zane, looking at a guy looking at him, 'you're not in my demographic. This just-standing-there-staring-thing, Sammy – I mean, you stare long enough and you reach the point of no return. At least he's genetically correct. But please, edit out the desperation. Oh no, look at his friend smiling at us. He's a year off gay death.'

'Gay death?'

'Gay death at thirty. Seen *Logan's Run*, Sammy? Sci-fi. They killed the poor dears at thirty. More humane. *We* have to live on. Oh God, there's my ex-fuck buddy, Hans. What's more depressing than an ex-fuck buddy? He works at Wet & Slippery. A gay sauna, before you ask. Put that in your black book. But I ask you, getting clothes off before sex? Really. Oh no, see that guy staring at you? Concrete complexion? You should go over and tell him: sorry, I'm gay, not desperate. Oh, these young fairies, Sam. Really, I'm embarrassed to be homosexual these days.'

'But he might offer some companionship,' I said.

Zane looked at me over his isosceles nose.

'To quote my favourite poet from his incomparable collection *As Nice as you Need to Be*: "Add, deduct, fuck & get fucked". That little gem is entitled *Transactions*, before you ask.'

I said the poem was the most depressing thing I'd heard.

'It's an acknowledgement of how life is; that's not necessarily depressing.'

It was all so awful, suddenly. Just the night before, I'd felt so alive I might burst into some other state altogether, like a person feeling dead might tip over into actual deadness, on account of his feeling so corpse-like and all. I know that's pretty convoluted but that's how I felt. But the dead bit this time.

We dripped into the Chill-out Room, with its bubble wrap lighting, popping each sphere in my head. Zane bought me some water. I'd tried to get some in the bathroom but they had hot water running from the cold taps as well. Just that – that meanness – made me almost tip over altogether. Zane sat back next to me on the carpeted block.

When you're depressed, air is water, a plastic bottle a dumbbell. And that staring! If they liked me, why didn't they just come over and say hello. And anyway, what could they see? And why couldn't I go over to *them*? I was out of the closet; what was holding me back?

'We're so miserable,' I said to Zane, my eyes wide with wanting him to shut them. Zane simply locked them with his.

'Never assume anyone feels as you do, Sammy. I'm actually enjoying myself.'

I looked away. So I *was* still alone, even in my opinions?

There'd been some exciting types come into the vid' store, and Filter had shown me how to look up their rental histories. A few *Head Ons* and *Private Idahos* was a good sign. But they were the ones who came in hardly ever. It was the sadsacks that you saw every day and got to know, and parents with kids to switch off.

There was an alternative soundtrack in my head to the one playing.

Can a dream survive waking?

And it did!

'Cause guess who I saw? That hottie who'd come into the video store. The guy with the shaved head. He looked at me, I at him. This was more like it! He'd made his entrance at just the right moment, like the dashing love

178

interest in a book. Perhaps the drugs *were* kicking, kicking into life!

Zane gave him one look and told me he was a player. What rot. I went over.

'Hello, love,' he said.

Love! That was a hell of an opening line!

He told me his name but I already knew it. Justin. But people called him Jussy.

We got talking next to the bullring as one by one the guys around us took off their shirts. All those sweaty backs. You could make a computer game about trying to dodge your way through them without getting slimed. I told Jussy that one and he liked it.

'I've got a hairy chest, too,' he said. 'I mean, I could walk round with my top off, but I'm not going to do that. Want to see my hairy chest? It's part of the Italian in me.'

Jussy was wearing a really low tanktop, which he pulled down lower for my benefit.

'I didn't have any problem with coming out,' he said. 'It was just other people. Such a drag. All this fallout. Everyone upset, my relatives, my girlfriend. But it's all good.'

A few more guys round us disrobed, but they didn't look at me. No pecs, no sex. Jussy asked if I'd seen the film he'd hired out at the video store, and told me to check it out when he returned it.

'I've got good taste,' said Jussy.

The beats were raining down hard. It was a trial finding a spot where you didn't get soaked with their sounds. It wasn't the greatest stuff either. Doof doof, the musical equivalent of driving across the Nullabor Plain. Jussy kept looking out at the dance floor. Finally he turned to me.

'You've got the gay thing happening, love. Spiked hair, tight tops. I'm not really into fashion. Dorian is.'

Before I could ask who Dorian was, he'd slapped onto another subject.

'I just know with people. I knew you were this super guy.'

Meanwhile, Zane had moved over to the other side of the dance floor. He was talking to one of his 'types', a supreme beefcake.

I told Jussy about the cricket thing.

'No way, cricket? You serious? That's the most boring game.'

At first I was offended. Plus I couldn't understand it. Cricket's the best game invented. But then, maybe Luke's interest in me had been solely to do with cricket. In fact, come to think of it, it was a relief Jussy couldn't give a toss about it.

Zane was looking over from time to time.

'Is he your boyfriend?' Jussy asked.

'No,' I said, pretty quick. 'We're just friends.'

'You've got a gay male friend?'

Turned out Jussy didn't.

'Oh, you know, the sexual tension thing.'

The song changed over the speakers. 'Lamb,' he yelled.

'Who?'

'You don't know Lamb! I can't believe I'm standing here with you. You're such a dag. Oh, look at those dancers. They're so affected. I hate mincing faggots.'

Such a dag …? I scoped myself in one of the wall mirrors. Geez, I *was* a dag, wasn't I? But God, he was hot. Features with a soapstone smoothness, a goat's tail of hair under his bottom lip, curling forward and up, and knee-length shorts. No one else was wearing baggy shorts. They were all in their tight jeans; so was I. I saw I was wrong in wanting someone normal like Luke; normal was boring. What I was after was someone with a 'thing'. You know, a

180

certain something. A guy who stood out. Jussy filled the room, but not in a fat way. He had such ease. The bar staff knew him. Everyone. Come to think of it, Luke was a bit of a dork by comparison. He'd bought that whole grunge image, but had ended up more daggy than grungy. Jussy wasn't buying anything. I was pretty chuffed with working out my type. I told Zane when I went to the bar for drinks.

'You're so shallow, Sam,' he said.

That pissed me off. What did he know? It shitted me the way he and Filter had taken me on like some Eliza Doolittle.

I went back over to Jussy. I was feeling pretty bold. Like I was flying. I asked for his number. He stopped bopping for a sec.

'Hey, love, I should tell you, I have a boyfriend.'

I hit the ground. From five kilometres up. Parts of me bounced as much as twenty metres.

'But it's all good,' he added.

The boyfriend, Dorian, was on the way out.

'Hey, you're not really alternative enough for me,' he said. But then he had a change of mind. He'd give me his number anyway. It was 'all good'.

He said it was easier for him if I texted instead of ringing, so I texted him straightaway to make sure he'd have my number as well.

I found Zane at the bar, sipping a whisky and dry. Zane wasn't too impressed with Jussy. He seemed to think the boyfriend bit was bad. He told me to delete the number straight away. That way I wouldn't be tempted. He even tried to take the mobile off me, but I wouldn't let him. Typical that Zane didn't want me to be happy. He said Jussy had a fat head in need of liposuction.

I left Zane to walk home from The Pit alone.

Next morning, I got woken by my mobile beeping.

Got home after Pit
and sort of thought
it cool i had this cool
conversation with
a guy that played
cricket. All good.

I texted Jussy back, saying it was pretty exciting for me too. Then I deleted Luke's number and a text message of his I'd kept. Jussy texted again.

Hey, cum meet me at
work. We can have
cheap beers. Yumm. Fab.

I texted yes, and Jussy texted the details.

We scheduled a lunch date but I was pretty scared what to wear. Jussy was so alternative. He couldn't be pinned down to any look. I saw he wasn't standard issue gay, not like Zane. All the tight T-shirts and stuff that Jen had fitted me out for – well, I saw it wouldn't do the trick.

Jen and Tash stood with me at my cheap aluminium clothes rack.

'Why not that? Or that with that?' Jen kept asking. She and Tash sorted out a 'nice gay-boy look' for me. Even ironed my clothes and everything. I tried telling them it was all wrong. Eventually I had to throw the clothes at their feet.

'But I thought you liked your clothes?' asked Jen.

She didn't know anything. I put on an old shirt I'd brought from home, a black one, pretty retro – only thing old I had – and tore out.

I met Jussy in this bar down the road from where he worked. It was in the modern style – not that I knew about style, but I was learning. You know, wooden venetians hanging from the ceiling at odd places, not just over windows; plastic bladed plants in iron pots, held up by coloured pebbles rather than dirt; long benches and tables with industrial patterns branded onto them. Jussy was so casual-looking. Just a normal top, trousers, sneakers. He told me how everyone's suit at work was worth about a zillion bucks. He wasn't going to pay all that money. The phoneys! A Bonds T-shirt was good enough for him. He asked what I thought of this bar. He told me he knew all the coolest places. But already people were latching onto it so it wouldn't be cool much longer. I wondered how you found the cool places to begin with. Some people just have the knack for life. Others, like me, have got to work at it. This place was so much better than Settee. I saw that straight away. The bar staff here were hip, happening. The Stopwatch and Mr Arrogance at Settee were dags. And Zane saying, 'At least there was no pretence with them' – he could justify anything.

Jussy asked me about my 'search for love'. I told him I had to find someone special, someone worth the effort. I gave him that cricket spiel. It's so hard getting somewhere in the game. You really have to love it to put in the effort but the rewards are ten times better than if you're lukewarm, 'cause then you're only half-arsed about it as well. If you don't try hard you'll never be good. You can then say, well it wasn't worth it anyway, but you don't really know that 'cause you were half-arsed about it to begin with.

'Man, you have this full-on idea about love,' he said. He and Dorian just kind of met. 'But there was all this fall-out. People getting upset, our friends, our boyfriends. I must say, he's not my type sexually. But it's comfortable.'

Comfortable …? Comfortable! I couldn't imagine being with someone just because it was comfortable. I told Jussy that. He laughed.

'You're such a tortured lesbian.'

I was a tad offended. Jussy tried to defend himself. He said Dorian was a friend – his best friend, really. They lived in the same house but they had separate bedrooms. It was easier that way.

'How is it easier?' I asked.

'Oh, you're so nice, you're so nice! I can't do this,' he laughed.

'Do what?'

He stared at me for ten whole seconds. 'You really *are* nice.'

We drank heaps. We got to the tram stop. He asked me how far away I lived. I said when he'd broken up completely with … well, with his feller … Truth is, I couldn't say his name. I got on my tram and went home.

'They live together?' asked Jen in the morning. She sat back on the couch with her big mug of coffee warming her hands. Tash snorted. Jen turned to Zane, asking him what he thought (she'd asked Zane over for brunch).

'Sammy, I don't date guys with boyfriends. If you meet them behind a bush that's one thing, but if you start making "arrangements" that's another. Because at the end of the day, they go home to their man, and you go home alone.'

Zane had to make everything so crass – 'if you meet them behind a bush'. There wasn't a touch of romance in him.

'Well, at least this one's gay,' said Tash.

Zane chuckled. Jen hit him.

It turned out Tash knew Jussy vaguely. 'Yeah, he's hot. And I've seen his boyfriend.'

'What's he like?' I blurted out.

'A real weed. He could do better.'

'Maybe they're in love,' said Jen. 'You like me.'

'Yes, but you're hot.'

My mobile beeped. It was Jussy: Dorian was away and what was I doing that night? Jen told me to text him back that we couldn't be friends right now. Maybe some time down the track.

'Do you think that's too obscure?' I asked.

'No, Sammy,' said Zane. 'He'll know exactly what it means: "Not till you're single".'

I saw they were right and all. It was the only 'honourable' thing to do. But I had to add my own line, right at the end. 'It's going to be hard just being friends.'

During our respective work shifts the next day, we texted each other back and forth. I'll only give you his messages, 'cause mine were pretty sappy and all.

Yeah im thinking
the same. But
Its all good.
Your great fun
to hang out with.

Feel completely
spaced out
though. 6 hours
and counting.

Ha. No comment.
Yes going to Qa.

What does it
Sound like? It
could be cool.
How is the vid
rental market
shaping up this
week? Polymers
sux! Ox

I like bitter and
twisted
personally :) as
long as work gets
me outta bed
before 10 its
always going to
be crap.

I'll bring lamb
cd and some
happy
happy joy joy.
See you there.

Dance like no
one's watching.
Dress like your
life depends on
it. Lose all
sanity. Is the
day over yet? Got
a flatty on my
Treadly. Not
happy jan.

Wow. What a full
on afternoon.
Dying for some
alcohol. See you
tonight. Fab ox

Ah. I found
myself on the
great express way
of the soul. Nice
view, Ox

What did they mean? What did all these text messages mean? All I knew was, you didn't text a guy that many times in a day if you weren't hot for him. It'd only be a matter of time.

Filter dropped by. He took me to a pub. I told him I couldn't stay long. Had to get ready for Q&A. Jussy would be there. He said to relax.

I leant back and looked round at where he'd dragged me – one of those pubs with the TV going. According to Filter, it's not staying home, it's not going out, it's brain-drain amnesia. Light beer living, he called it. We went into the Tabaret part with its easy-listening music, and carrot-vomit lighting.

Filter went crazy. '"Bored by the way you look tonight." "Fucked by the thought of you." What are they playing?' I don't reckon he got the titles right, but he got their ring. Filter raged about the 'fogies' at their poker machines. 'In the time of Leaks and Stoppages. They aren't even giving their wanking hands a work-out,' he said. 'Everything buttons.' Filter gave this one long, exhaustive look round the room, then put on a Shooter's Party voice.

'Bring back euthanasia, I say. Dying slowly's too good for 'em.'

'Filter, shoosh!'

That just made Filter laugh louder.

I wanted to go along with him but it felt pretty mean. You don't know where people are at, how they got there. I

187

remember Jeanie, our neighbour on the farm, saying how tough it was going to the funerals of all her friends. One day she just stopped going. Outlasting the pack isn't always a good thing. Besides, just getting out of the house can be a challenge.

They dished out some actual live entertainment. Well, newly thawed. Some cover band.

Filter called them the Wall-of-Noise band, what with their guitar anthems ending in feedback. Pub rock, Aussie rock – it shitted Filter big time. I didn't mind it so much. I mean, it wasn't really so bad.

'Have a fucking opinion, Sam.'

'What?'

I was taken aback.

'Get angry, bitch.'

Before I could, my mobile beeped. It was Jussy.

Hey you. Me here.
You coming
tonight. (yes yes
yes yes)?

That was so winning, wasn't it? I just *had* to go.

Filter said he'd come. We got to Q&A after nine so there was a bit of a queue, plus it was bloody cold in the wind. Filter went on about the door bitches. The power they have. Girls who can't do anything to get notoriety so they stand on doors to get it that way.

'Hey, do you know who I'm *not*?' said Filter. 'That's right, mate, a fookin' nobody.'

The blondettes were shocked. I was so angry with Filter. At this rate, I wouldn't get in either. But the guy was unstoppable.

'I'm a famous person trapped in the body of an obscure unknown.'

Luckily the muscle head laughed.

'You know what it's like to walk down the street and *not* be recognised, mate?'

The two door bitches and Muscle Head looked at each other. I pulled Filter through the door before he could say more. Being the only fat person there, he beefed all the 'lightweights' out of the ring. The last of his spiel he served to me alone, at the spot he'd cleared by the bar.

'Obscurity in an ordinary person is benign, Sam (so long as you don't give the fooker the Andy Warhol fifteen minutes), but in a genius it's fookin' cancerous. Those star fookers' (the door staff) 'will turn twenty-five one day. Then they'll go back where they belong: yeah, end of the fookin' queue.'

I saw Jussy and rushed up to him. But before I could say anything, he pointed at this guy standing next to him.

'Hey, Sam, this is my boyfriend, Dorian.'

That stopped me dead, looking at this Dorian with his short-sleeved shirt and cut-off leather tie. He had this strange fifties office worker look going on. So different to Jussy. Jussy was almost a harlequin tonight, what with his soccer top and bright knee-length shiny shorts. The boyfriend asked me about a million questions of who I was. Someone else had started chatting to Jussy but I could see he was trying to half listen to what the two of us were saying. I have to admit, the whole situation was pretty horrible. I excused myself, grabbed Filter and got out, beating the fuck-rush.

I was so depressed, so unhappy.

'You're not the only one hard up finding a hole, Sam,' said Filter as we hurried for the warmth of a tram.

He took me back to his joint, where he played me some of his music. He'd watch movies with the sound down. That's how he got his ideas mostly. The images would trigger sounds in his head. You should hear the soundtrack he did for *You've Got Mail*. Tom Hanks was never so creepy.

Filter had to play the right music for the occasion. It just had to fit the mood. He owned about a million CDs plus as many vinyls. Never got the vinyl thing myself. I was born too late to really get into vinyl. CDs were coming in the same time as I was getting into music. They're so much better. You can skip to any track. The best moments. The best music for this occasion was ragtime piano variations on the *Star Wars* soundtracks.

Again, I asked Filter why he wasn't on the prowl like me. Didn't he want to be with someone? I had to push him a bit, then he said he wanted to be happy with himself first. You find someone more easily if you're happy with yourself. Seemed cack-handed to me. You can't help some people.

Zane dropped by. He'd done this complicated knock on Filter's door before Filter smiled and let him in. But when he was about to sit, Filter stopped him.

'Wait.'

Zane raised an eyebrow.

'The other day, I visited my brother and niece in the 'Nong. Well, we couldn't make it an ordinary picnic now, could we? What you two clowns say to this?'

Filter opened his cupboard and pulled out a brown paper bag. Inside were magic mushrooms. Needless to say, we ingested them. Next thing we know, the ceiling started coming down on us like the trash compactor in *Star Wars*. We were stacking cupboards on cupboards to prop it up.

'Ye-e-es! Yeeees! Yeeees!' screamed Filter.

'The door, Sammy, the door,' screamed Zane.

Could I reach it? Just. The ceiling hadn't yet knocked off the handle. A quick shove and we were outside. Saved. It was team stuff, all right.

We went down Johnston Street and got to the lights at Hoddle. 'Are they green, are they red?' the traffic flooding past.

'Pink,' laughed Zane, and we belted across. Beeps and curses abounded and one tiny crash. Down by the Yarra, the trees dancing. I looked at the waterfall. Biggest waterfall I'd ever seen.

'I didn't know there was a waterfall in Melbourne,' I said. 'I thought Melbourne was flat.'

I was seeing the Yarra as vertical, the ground as upside down. Any way was up.

Next we were in a car park surrounded by trees. There were couples making out. Filter cocked his hand like a gun; Zane and I did the same.

'Get out of the car,' yelled Filter. Every headlight switched to high beam. Under attack! We used a park bench for cover, firing our finger-guns over the top in sequence. The war was on. One by one the cars roared off. But I think I shot a few.

We caught another couple coming over the suspension bridge.

'It's okay, it's not loaded.' I giggled and then couldn't stop. They ran back the other way.

It was fun all right, but also disappointing. Nothing like the first two times with Zane and Filter. Those drug dashes were first-rate literature. This time it was more your airport thriller. Entertaining but no subtext. Plus it wasn't fully kicking in. I asked Filter if he had more on him but he was listening to something else.

We heard sirens and made our way up into the houses again. Filter pulled out some starter caps and we set

191

several off. Gunshot blasted. A guy came out of his house in his jocks. Zane started making yelping noises.

'Oi, what's going on?' asked a shaky voice.

'Right, get back into the house,' screamed Filter through the guy's fence. 'This doesn't concern you.' And he set off another cap. Zane kicked over a bin. The guy screamed. Soon the streets were a patchwork of sirens, with helicopters overhead. One shone its light down on us.

Filter stepped in its spotlight. 'Take me,' he cried. 'Take me!'

Filter in the spotlight. Filter, the famed musician. It was all a dream.

Zane coming to his senses, rushing Filter from the light. The three of us making our way onto the main street. 'Just watch the cop cars go by,' said Zane.

We watched. We watched like we didn't know what was happening, as the cop cars and helicopters criss-crossed back and forth. It was exciting, I guess, in a renegade kind of way, but none too poetic. I tried to sink into the moment. When would the magic fully kick in?

Another helicopter light shone down on us.

'Okay, don't run,' said Filter.

And we all three stared up like we were mystified. The helicopter flew on. Suddenly I was up there with it. Yes, engaged!

'I see … from so high … I see …'

Above men …

'What's that, Samster?' asked Filter.

'Above men, at this altitude, seeing them as ants, it is easier to step on them.'

'This one's a card,' laughed Filter.

He might as well have fired an RPG into the helicopter, the way it brought me down. With the tripping over, Filter pushed me and Zane to his place. He and Zane lowered the spare bed resting against the window. I thought of Jussy.

If you could fall in love with me
t'would be
you see
so good for me
and maybe also good for you
I hope that's true
be good for you.

If I could hear what you have seen
what you have seen
and heard
could smell a thought, could taste a word
t'would recompense,
for every sense,
deprived of thee

T'would be, you see
So good for me.
So good for me.
So good.

Zane saw my disappointment. 'The more drugs you take, Sam, the more you have to take to get the same effect.'

He left. Filter locked the door behind him and crashed. Without a pillow, I scrunched up one of Filter's hoodies and used that. Not even Filter's hacksaw snore could keep me from sleeping.

Jussy texted me in the morning. A pattern was emerging: he'd only text me when he was at work, not on weekends or nights. And he never ever called. I woke Filter. In a sleepwalk, he let me out. It was raining, with wet jumper clouds wrung out overhead. I read Jussy's message.

> Forgot to give
> you the CD. Hope
> last night was
> cool and I Wasn't
> to much of an
> arse. Its all
> good. Fab

It was all good for him. Plus 'to' should have been 'too.' That's what happens when you read too much: you become a pedant. I didn't text back. He texted me the next Wednesday while I was in the bath. My joints were sore from dancing too much on speed with Zane at The Pit.

> Hey. Just wanted
> to know if you
> felt like
> catching up it
> would be really
> cool. My beer
> coaster misses
> you :-) fab ox.

That was so winsome, wasn't it? Drying my hands on my towel, I texted something about Q&A the next day and back came a reply:

> Never
> underestimate the
> power of the
> coaster Ill just
> say its rad
> having people
> like you in my

life. Go the
mirror ball! Ox

I went to Q&A with Zane, Jen and Tash. Jussy was there
with his mob, but no boyfriend. He walked over to Jen and
Tash.

'Man, this guy is the coolest,' he said, pointing at me.
'He's got to be the most down-to-earth gay guy I've met.'

He then gave me a present. I unwrapped it: a tiny
kangaroo with a bat. I smiled and winced at the same time.
Cricket. It was spring and training for summer had started.
Not that I'd turned up for any sessions with the fellers yet.

The other three gave me some room.

'Hey, I have to say, I didn't really find you attractive that
night we met,' said Jussy. 'Oh! But that lunch we had, with
you in that tight black top, yeah I did. Hey, would you have
slept with me?'

I think my tongue nearly dropped out.

'Oh yes! I knew it!'

Jussy was wearing black shin-high boots and a tartan kilt.
Talk about brave. He had to buy the kilt to show off his
boots, he explained. Anything else and they'd be half-
covered over. That was his justification. Jussy looked over
my shoulder at some guy.

'Hey, love, that guy's been looking at you. Looks like
his are hard to come by. Ha. I kill myself. This could get
interesting. It's shaping up to be the year of love. Must be
those planets again.'

Jussy went to say something to Zane but Zane gave him
the dirtiest look imaginable. One of Jussy's friends called
out.

'Hey, Thrustin', over here!' And Jussy was gone.

I was so annoyed with Zane for snubbing Jussy. Zane
said he didn't like the guy. If you don't like someone you
should let them know.

195

'Believe me, Sam, it's easier than pretending.'

I turned my back on him and showed Jen and Tash the gift of the kangaroo. It was so romantic.

'Probably to make up for being bad in bed,' said Tash. She and Zane squealed.

'Jen …?' I asked.

'He's got a certain mojo,' was all she could say.

' "Thrustin" has no honour, Sammy,' piped in Zane. 'Remember, life isn't any less pointless if you've got a boyfriend. It's just pointless *with* a boyfriend.'

'But it's that *with* part, Zane.'

Zane nodded over my shoulder at that guy staring at me. I went over.

We had sex at my place. I was sucking his cock. Then he sort of leaned over and adjusted the mirror on my light-stand so he could see me side on.

When he left, I turned on my mobile. Zane had texted.

In hindsight, I
may have been
harsh about your
needs as a woman.
I hope this
malaise passes
soon!! Wash that
man right out of
your hair, 'coz
u'r so much bettr!

I deleted it straight away. Jussy texted me in the morning while I was doing a shift at the video store. On the dot of nine again. Work had started, for both of us. I texted him back that I wanted him to leave me alone for a while. For the first time, there was a delay with the response. But of course it came.

Im cool with what
you want but I
can say that it
sucks. There are
few people this
place that I get
on with, and i
hate losing them.
Dont lose my
number! Ox fab

Filter came in at three to replace me for the afternoon
shift. I hung around a bit, while he went on about how no
one could win in this situation – me, Jussy, the boyfriend.
A customer dropped off videos then walked out the door.
Filter opened their cases. He quickly rang the guy's
mobile.

'None of these videos are rewound. That's all right. I
do the same, mate. Use someone else's toilet – I don't
flush it. Why should I, man? Next feller uses it can flush it
before he goes, can't he? Courtesy. Never heard the word,
mate? Never … Not in your dictionary either? Thought
not.'

And he hung up on him.

'How does the boss feel about that?'

'Used to like it. Shook the difficult customers up a bit.
But had some complaints.'

Complaints? Complaining …

What was I doing? That stuffed toy with the cricket bat
had got me thinking on a number or things. Cricket,
mostly: I had a bit of talent. I should be practising
whenever I could with Tubby and the others. Cricket was
about the only thing I was good at, but here I was ringing
customers about their late fees. I confided this to Filter.

'What you mean, Sam? You got a good life. Out with
us one night, seeing opera with Jen the next. Somethink

new every day. You look at these chumps through their office windows – what you think's going on there, mate? With us, every day it's somethink different. But them? They're on a fookin' learning plateau.'

But I could tell Filter didn't quite think that way about his life. He'd just clocked up his five-year anniversary at the video store. According to his own calendar, he was a multi-millionaire musician living in LA right now, commuting between his villas by limo, a bevy of bra-strapped babes doing some buxom living in each abode.

Filter said to join him and Zane that night for drug-free entertainment. It would be good for us all. I left him with the queuing customers.

Turned out the 'entertainment' was a drag queen that Zane and Filter knew. 'She' was performing at a straight bar so she wanted some queer friendly support.

We waltzed in. It was pretty packed. I'd forgotten what straight bars looked like. It was all pine-stained blonde with sporting memorabilia in glass frames.

'Going to a gay bar and looking for love is no different to guys and girls coming to straight bars like this and looking for love,' said Zane, reading my thoughts. 'There's just a lot less aggro at queer venues.'

He was right. I'd never noticed a bouncer at The Pit. Ever. But every straight joint, they stand out. We found a booth up close to the stage. The MC introduced the talent, Daphne, who straightaway rolled into a number, all mimed.

Christ, what an act, I thought. That lipstick stuck on with lollypop finesse, and powder-puff cheeks. The way he'd tried to pluck his mono brow down to something approaching femininity. Christ, and that prissiness. What a fairy. I was fairly sick.

During the songs, he would banter with Zane and Filter. He was saying to Filter he'd iron his shirts, cook him meals, if ever he wanted someplace to come home to. Filter was lapping it up.

'Look at the legs on this sheila, Samster,' cried Filter. 'Best bloody legs you ever saw, mate.'

And the crowd laughed.

'Give us a lap dance, will you, love,' roared Filter to more whoops from the breeders.

'Oh, you're a devil, Filter,' said Daphne, giving him a whip with 'her' stole.

I looked at the guy's pushed-up puppies. Double-D dungarees (socks basically). I looked round – at the steps, at the thing.

'She's a hotty!' cried Filter.

She? Christ, the guy's tight latex mini had a bulge in it.

The guy saw where I was looking.

'Oh, you're so cruel!'

The cockatoo dipped his eyes at Zane. 'Where'd you find him, honey? On the docks?'

More titters from the breeders, but not so loud now.

'Sam's my wuff twade,' smiled Zane. 'We're educating him.'

'You're not educating me,' I said. The audience hushed. What cheek. Zane nodded to the door. Telling me to leave now? I wasn't going anywhere.

'Uh oh, someone's having a bad life day.'

I looked up at *him*, Daphne.

'Oh man, I is all chubbed up and blue for you,' said the drag queen. 'I can see you're pinballing bad, honey. You need a place to rust.'

'I don't need anything,' I said.

The drag queen tilted his head at me.

'You're right,' he said after a long pause, 'your arse ain't worth cock.'

Zane and Filter squealed. After a pause, the rest of the crowd joined in, half with hands over their mouths. The drag act finally fagged off (half-time), going over to the bar and throwing his boa round the neck of some red-faced guy. I leant over to Zane. I was pretty angry with him. 'Why do you call *him* her?'

'For the same reason I call you *he*.'

'Fuck that. And Filter, all this shit about him being beautiful – fuck, he makes a fucking ugly woman.'

Zane looked at me.

'Why do you hang round us, Sam?'

This fairly shut my trap. Airtight. Had to breathe through my nose for a bit. Again he nodded at the door. Again I couldn't leave.

'See if Astrid and Luke and Dizzy and that lot want you.'

Filter gave Zane a look to say he'd gone too far but Zane turned away. I couldn't help but keep staring at the drag queen. He was still drying the beetroot's neck with his boa. The geezer was wheezing with laughter. Then a girl called out from the other side of the bar.

'Thing.'

I didn't look. None of us did. No one answers to that.

'Thing! In the dead bird.'

The drag queen's eyebrows flapped up. He turned round.

'Yes, you!' screamed the blonde. 'Thing, keep away from my man!'

'Excuse me. Ex-cuuuse me! What did you call me?' asked the cockatoo, hand placed extravagantly on chest.

'I don't know what to call you, thing,' shouted back the blonde, her hand on her bust. 'You're nothing.'

'I'm a woman.'

'I'm the woman, bitch. Feel these.'

Filter pulled a long, half-rusted screwdriver out of his pocket. I stepped back in fright. The husband was trying to get his wife to shoosh. Zane stood up as well, urging Filter to pocket his screwdriver before the bouncers saw.

'Why the screwdriver?' I asked.

'Can always say I'm a fookin' carpenter if the fuzz frisk me,' he whispered. 'Now screw you, lady,' he shouted at the woman.

The blonde backed off, dragging her husband who was still wheezing with laughter. Zane nearly spat in their direction while Filter went over and put an arm round Daphne.

'She had a point,' I said.

Zane turned on me. 'You're a homophobe.'

'What … I …'

Christ, what a thing to say. I nearly hit him. How could he call me a homophobe? I *was* a bloody homo, for Christ's sake. How could I hate them? I mean, us?

Daphne, or whatever his name was, pulled away from Filter, and went to the stage. The show must go on and all that. He started warbling away.

It got all big-time. Filter was up dancing, doing his breaks, Zane his girl moves. Then out rolled that fag standard. You know the one – about 'surviving'. Finally, the bloody tune ended and the two sat either side of me again. Not before a lot of clapping. They nudged me to clap too, but suddenly I was so depressed, so lonesome. That song he'd been singing – well, I thought about the meaning of it.

'Why is the gay anthem about accepting living on your own?' I asked.

'You've missed the point, Sammy,' said Zane. 'It's not about accepting living on your own. It's about deciding not to take any shit.'

I thought about that for a long time.

'I'm sorry,' I told Daphne as we were rolling out. He – *she* – wasn't too gracious about it, but that was understandable.

'I'm not a good person,' I said and then, because I thought I was going to cry, hurried away. Zane and Filter let me be.

I ran into Jussy the next Q&A night. He asked me about the guy I'd walked out with the week before. I smiled more out of reflex than with the memory.

'Oh, yes, yes!' yelled Jussy. 'Man, I knew that's all you needed.'

'All I needed?' I just about shouted. 'How's *your* love life?'

'What?'

'You and your man?'

'Well, it's cool as. It's always been cool.'

His boyfriend, Dorian, quickly walked over and joined us. Jussy put an arm round him. Dorian was wearing a pink-striped, white-sleeved T-shirt and black leather tie, hair coiffed.

'Hey, you still got that cricketing kangaroo?' asked Jussy.

I looked at the boyfriend. The boyfriend smiled back. I couldn't say a word.

'Knew you'd keep it,' said Jussy. 'You're such a tortured lesbian.'

With that, I left before I hit him.

Christ, what was cool about Jussy? Nothing. So, he was good-looking. So what? All men look the same from …

behind. Who said that? Zane. Was I starting to sound like him already? Or *think* like him? But he was right about Jussy. The guy had no honour. And I thought about the boyfriend. He obviously took a lot of shit from Jussy. I wasn't going to be part of that.

'About time you got angry,' said Filter.

We were at work again. Some customer had just told us he'd bought his pass to the 'underground shelter' for when the 'bomb was dropped'. All this conspiracy stuff. Filter asked the guy how much he'd paid for his bunker. The fee was astronomical. Filter got the email address off him, saying he wanted to check it out for himself. He waited for the guy to leave then rang the police (dialling 1831 first to hide the call), then passed on the email address to them. He hadn't made fun of the guy. For a minute, I had thought Filter would whack his nonce. The cop must've asked for a name, 'cause Filter answered 'Anonymous' then killed the call. He then turned to me, quite as if there'd never been that interruption.

I could see that he and Zane had something I was pretty sure I didn't.

But wanted.

Honour.

'Stop looking so hard, Sam. You won't find everything in the one person, mate. People don't stop their lives for you. You'd end up hating them if they did. That's why you have a few friends. You get somethink different out of each of 'em.'

'What do people get out of me, Filter?'

'You're trying, mate. People can see that.'

Mate? Everyone back home overdid the 'mate' thing. I didn't want to be reminded of it.

'Well, why aren't *you* trying?' I asked. 'You're not even on the lookout.'

Filter sat down. 'Mate, I wish people would stop asking when I'm gonna get a root.'

He looked up at me sheepishly, then around at the store to make sure it was empty. 'It's been five years, mate, five. I've … I've gotta get me fuck-legs back.'

He got up painfully, holding his belly.

'I gotta abort this baby, Sam. I can feel it doing me damage. Ripping muscles when I walk.'

He walked over to the DVDs (DVDs were just starting to take over the shelves) and picked up one that a customer had put back in the wrong spot. He put it in its place, then turned to me.

'Stop asking me about finding a girl, mate.'

Filter sat back down again.

'Hey,' he asked, 'will you go to the gym with me?'

'Sure … mate.'

Before we parted outside his Fort Knox door that night, I turned to Filter and asked him the question I kept meaning to get to.

'Filter, what's rule number ten for dealing with the customer?'

It took Filter a few seconds to work out what I was referring to. Then it clicked.

'Rule number 10? We're all fookin' customers.'

It wasn't funny like the others.

Zane asked me about going to the gym with Filter. It was the end of another Pit night. This time I hadn't cheated the door staff, but paid my fee.

'It will be good for you, Sammy, getting a workout. Physical toughness can lead to mental toughness. If you're going to let the cricket go ...'

'Hey, I'm just taking a break.'

Did I ever plan to go back? Maybe he was right. I *was* letting the cricket go. Season nearly ready to start, and I still wasn't turning up for training.

But we hadn't had too bad a night at The Pit. Going in, we'd resolved to actually talk to people, not sit back and despise them. Really, they were all just trying, like us. I saw it was just a whole lotta people, some of them scared, like in a straight pub, wanting to reach out, to connect, to find people who could find them.

So then, because we were laughing and having fun, we were a bit of a magnet. People aren't so bad. Before at The Pit, I'd been so uptight, judgemental, never allowing myself to get into it.

Afterwards, when we walked out, we even made small talk with the door staff.

'Mission successful,' said Zane, shaking my hand.

We were about to separate when Zane asked me to walk with him along Smith Street. That surprised me. I couldn't work out why. Eventually, I got it out of him. Zane was scared, scared of being beaten up. I hadn't ever pictured him scared before.

'Now make sure you want to, Sammy. *You* look straight, but you might not walking alongside me.'

'Well, if you're so worried,' I told him, 'why dress like a ... well, like that?'

Zane looked himself up and down.

'This is how I am, Sammy.'

He reached into his coat pocket and pulled something out. He handed it over. Surprisingly, it was his passport. I remembered Filter showing me his, and telling me to ask to see Zane's.

Carrying your passport out with you to clubs! ID, I guess, since he didn't have a driver's licence.

'Look at the photo.'

I opened it up. At first I didn't recognise the guy in it, but it couldn't have been anyone else. Yes, it was Zane, but Zane looking like a regular guy, looking so ... so 'normal'. For the first time, that word was no longer attractive to me. He had his hair parted to one side, sensible glasses, fawn turtleneck jumper.

I looked at him now: spiked black hair, eyeliner accentuated eyes, tight fitting shirt. Zane pointed at the photo.

'I'm not going back to that,' he said, and took the passport off me. He turned and walked up Hawk to Smith Street. He and Filter weren't the fake ones. In a way, Jussy wasn't pretending to be what he wasn't either. Or his boyfriend. Obviously it was an open relationship and that was the consensus they had come to. No, none of them was fake. *I* was. I was the phoney. And he was right, I *was* homophobic. The homophobic homosexual. I thought fancying the same sex was hard, but imagine if I was female in a guy's body or vice versa. That Daphne, well ... she said to that blonde that she was the real woman ... Pretty brave, that, and true. Normal was what was normal to you. And no one can be truer than that.

And why had I liked Jussy in the first place? Because he was less 'ladylike' than Luke. Why had I liked Luke? Because he wasn't as 'prissy' as Zane. Then the most awful question of all. Why had I – did I *still* – like Arny?

'We're neighbours,' said Arny when we first met at the lockers. He shook my hand. It wasn't too firm a grip, I told myself at the time, and it wasn't 'too limp'.

Ha! There it was again, that Neanderthal obsession with clichéd masculinity.

But I couldn't be phoney right through, could I? My Arny crush was genuine, wasn't it?

It's hard to know what you know. I nearly cried with my stupidity. Maybe one day I would get it, hopefully before I was dead.

I could see Zane disappearing round the corner onto Smith Street.

After a sec, I raced up next to him and walked him all the way to his door. We didn't say anything to each other and no one said anything to us. It wasn't their right to.

Chapter Seven

Cricket's about the only thing that makes me cool. If I'd been an accountant, say, I wouldn't be cool at all. No way. But you *can* have a cool accountant. No, really, I've met one: Arny. So I guess I'm glad of the cricket thing a bit, 'cause if it wasn't for that I'd be ordinary. Totally. I mean, if it wasn't for my batting average, I'd be nothing but a dork.

It was the beginning of October and I caught up with Tubby and Beth. We were sitting around a park bench drinking beers in the middle of the day, and someone said – I think it was Beth – that she was a dork. I said I was too. Soon the whole table said it. We damn near hugged each other, like something off American TV. But for the first time it was okay. We were cool with it. So, yeah, though we still weren't *cool* cool – we were dorks, after all – we were cool about *being* dorks, which kind of made us lukewarm beer. Bearable at a pinch.

And that's when I realised it was okay. There'd be no more trying to be cool for Sam. From now on, what you got was what you'd get.

'Man, I'm so glad cricket's starting again,' said Tubby. 'You're the best bat on the team, Sam.'

'Hear, hear,' added Beth.

'First game tomorrow, hey,' said Tubby. 'Man, you sure you don't wanna get in some practice today?'

'Nah, I'll be right.'

'Welcome back, Big Feller,' said the coach the next morning when I walked into the clubhouse. 'Although I don't know that I can call you that any more.'

The other cricketers laughed. I *was* a bit scrawny from all the high living with Zane and Filter. Compared to the lean beef of those who'd taken up footy in the off-season, I was mutton bone. I took my locker. The one next to it, Joe's – and Arny's before that – was empty. I turned to Tubby

'Where's Joe?'

'He quit,' answered Dizzy, who was standing by the exit, shining a ball on his trousers.

Joe … quit? Was I in any way responsible? I remember telling Joe that Tubby was wondering about him, why he was hanging out with me so much. I'd implied by my tone that I might reveal his secret. Yet as soon as I'd said it, I felt mean and petty. But did I ever make it clear I wouldn't? He'd slept with Kelly after that and I hadn't called him and he hadn't called me. Apparently I was the last one from the club to see him. He'd sent through his resignation via email. That made him the second teammate whose disappearance I was linked to.

I sat down on the bench and gingerly padded up. Tubby slammed his locker and set off another of those landslides in my stomach. He walked over, sat down next to me and started strapping on his pads! With the last Velcro pulled and plastered in place, he looked up, answering the question I didn't want to ask.

'Man, no one else wanted the job. They reckon it's jinxed. I'm your fellow opening batsman.'

Cricketers are a superstitious lot.

The game got under way. Tubby opened. He made ten without me even facing a ball. Then he got out to a bouncer he nicked to the wicketkeeper. 'Cause the ball went up so high, we'd managed to swap ends before it was caught. That meant I finally got to face since there was one more ball to go in the over. The bowler delivered the easiest shot in the book: a full toss. Putting the weight of the willow into my swing, I did the unthinkable and missed. Middle stump cart-wheeled four times.

I was out for a golden duck.

The coach eyed me on my waddle to the stands.

'Probably best not to smash the ball, Big Feller, until you know you can hit it.'

I could see Tubby was worried himself, especially after building me up and all, and his own disgrace at the crease. I guess up till then I'd been cruising on natural talent. To get past this hiccup, would take a fright. And a fright that was. Plus the one thing all people who want to be good at their game need to do: work. I hadn't worked at it, so how did I expect to walk back in at my old level?

The middle order and some of the tail-enders put on a good show and we just made it through the first round. But where was Joe?

I got home and snuck the landline into my room (I was trying to go easy on my mobile), pulling the cord out from behind the cupboards and shelves. Summoning up the courage, I finally made the call.

Joe and Kelly could spare a couple of hours, just. I looked in my door mirror. Already I was taking invisible gloves off my hands, one after the other. Joe and Kelly could manage half an hour with me in a Maccas in Coburg that night, before they hit the road (off to some party). I got to the Maccas first, wondering how long I could wait without buying anything. I needed a slash. Not long since the last one. Maybe nerves. At about that time, Maccas' staff started locking the toilet doors, only handing out the key to patrons. Before then, they were considered public toilets – clean ones. Don't blame the Maccas workers, really.

I bought that syrupy Coke they sell, and got the key for a slash. When I returned, Kelly came in the sliding doors, hair flaming. Joe wasn't like he had been, muscle stacked on muscle, but slim and stem-like.

Kelly and Joe sat down, nudging foreheads on purpose.

'Head butt.'

They'd said it together, in singsong for Christ's sake. I was one side of the table, Kelly and Joe opposite.

Kelly had a tight aqua jumper with little flecks of red. It was like she was a ship on fire and sparks were dropping into the sea. Sizzle, sizzle, hiss. Joe's hair was longer and lankier than ever and a little unwashed, which made it darker. No beach-boy blonde now.

There was a bit of a pause so I asked them what they'd got up to the night before, being Friday and all.

With Kelly, that was like pulling a brick from under the wheel of an old car. She got on a roll, telling how they'd gone to the local. She'd worn her tight leather trousers, tight white T-shirt. Had all sorts of trouble with this old cheese. Crash.

Joe took over the story. His voice had changed like the rest of him. Over the phone, I'd put it down to bad reception. Live, it was unmistakably less smooth, more whiny. It was hard to believe he was the same guy.

'So I told this nuffy,' squealed Joe, 'keep your eyes in your head or they'll be on the ends of my fingers.'

Nuffy?

'This nuffy kept looking at my chest,' said Kelly looking down at her chest, 'saying, please, can't you put them away!'

When a girl's talking about her chest, it's pretty hard not looking at it, even if you're not naturally inclined to those appendages. Joe was looking at me looking and so was Kelly. Pretty raw stuff. Don't judge, Sam, I told myself.

Joe narrated how he stopped the guy staring. ' "Here, does that help," and I put my hands over Kelly's breasts. That made him look twice.'

They both laughed, Joe cupping Kelly's breasts with those external hand bras of his. A gaggle of young girls giggled two tables away.

'Bounce, bounce, bounce,' said Joe and Kelly together.

Maybe it was the Maccas aroma, but I felt pretty sick. Joe had this little pitter-patter laugh – endless. He and Kelly went on about how much they had both had to drink –

Wait!

Stop.

They'd *both* had to drink?

But I'd heard right. Maybe Joe *had* been cured. He was turning into a genuine red-blooded male. Apparently, they'd thrown up ten to the dozen. Technicolour nights. So I thought, if they're gonna go on with these binge stories, I'd mention that I'd downed a whole shit-load of drugs since our parting.

'Grrr, drugs bad,' murmured Kelly, and she and Joe knocked foreheads again.

'Head butt.'

Turns out this head butt routine was alluding to the previous night. They'd been so slaughtered, they'd kept knocking heads.

Joe jumped in. 'Me and my best mate, Dave, kept handballing Kelly.'

His best mate *Dave*?

'I'd take a mark, he'd take a mark. Yeah, Dave scored pretty big,' Joe snorted, pinching Kelly's dimpled cheek.

Kelly looked over at me, laughing at my confusion.

'Yes,' she said, 'me and Dave have to work out our boundaries,' and she zipped up her sparkly purse.

Boundaries? Taking a mark? Didn't make sense. But it soon slipped out. Seems Joe and Dave were both pashing Kelly, taking it in turns, which meant Joe and this Dave guy were slag sisters (in other words, they kissed one person removed).

Kelly killed the catch-up by announcing she and Joe had to be moving on. At first I thought she meant relationship-wise. Turns out, she meant the party Joe'd mentioned: they were meeting up with friends at a pub.

'Everyone will be there.'

Joe gripped the table.

'Guy?'

Kelly smiled. 'Yes, Guy.'

I couldn't believe what happened next. Joe actually growled. 'Grrr.'

Kelly growled back, 'Grrr.' They knocked heads.

'Head butt.'

When they saw my look, Kelly nodded to Joe to explain, so he leaned forward.

'I meet this guy with Kelly, right, and it turns out to be *the* guy.'

A bit of a pause. Joe explained.

'Guy Rogers.'

Not that a name explains much in itself, particularly when you don't know the name to begin with.

Kelly head-butted Joe on the shoulder. 'So what does *this* guy here do?'

I couldn't imagine. I wish I had, 'cause Joe and Kelly took it upon themselves to demonstrate. They both stood up. Joe showed how, still gripping Kelly's hand with his, he rubbed it up and down her crotch.

'Guy Rogers didn't like that,' said Joe, pushing out pellet-sized laughs.

We all nattered on a bit more. Joe and Kelly went easy on the head butt routine, which helped. Soon I couldn't hear their words at all, just a hum.

Joe and I had both been trying to fit our lives to books. Okay, different books, but the same desire. His according to the Bible, mine according to my literature favourites.

Life isn't either. You can't just live the good bits. The rest isn't silence. The rest is padding. But who knows what book Joe was adhering to at present.

Anyway, we said some awkward goodbyes, and they got up to go. When they were halfway to the door, they stopped – from the looks of it, arguing over something. Finally Joe came back to the table.

'You wanna go to the pub, Sam? We're getting there before the others to catch up with Lydia.'

On the way to the pub, we ran into Astrid on a street corner. Her poetry collection, *Soul Whisperings*, was doing well. For poetry. She wanted to hear the latest from me on the man front. She kept nodding at Joe. I kept shaking my head back. Kelly practically growled at the inference. How embarrassing! Eventually I brought up Arny – don't know why – but I wanted to stop Astrid's insinuations. At the mention of Arny's name, Joe looked interested. I always wondered what he thought of the mess between me and Arny since he'd been witness to much of it. (Apart from wanting to introduce me to his 'ex-gay' friends, that is.) I mean, I couldn't help wondering if he was, at any point, jealous.

'Oh no, Sam, you and Arny – this sounds so like with me and Dale,' laughed Astrid. 'All the guys since – don't we know it? – they're just duds.' (Joe pricked his ears like an elf. Did that mean he was cut?) 'But he was the one. We were, like, not just made for each other, we were *destined*. It will happen, I know it will happen, he's just overseas right now. He says he'll come back. That's why I can't ever really commit to anyone else, not when, like, hello, he's my soulmate.'

So Astrid's 'the one' was overseas as well. Yet she still believed they'd get together when he returned. And I was still hoping with Arny. A truck drove by too fast, nudging the air in our path. When the wind backed off, I asked the obvious question.

'How long ago did he leave?'

Astrid watched the truck running a red light at the end of the street then turned back to face me.

'Five years.'

Five years …? Pining over a bloke for five years! Yes, it was silly. 'The one' was silly. If Arny returned and things worked out, that would be great. But in the meantime, I'd be silly to count on it.

The pub was empty. We took a 'grotto', the four of us sitting round a slice of tree. Lydia was looking all Toorak and cream socks, what with her white turtleneck sprogcatcher, and those earrings you could jump a dolphin through. As for Kelly, she let her hair off-leash, dumped her jumper, and was busting out of her tight black shirt with gusto. And Joe? He'd taken off that ridiculous puffer jacket. Underneath, he was wearing that same old stupid white T-shirt. But at least that was more *him*. Did this mean he was stripping back to his old self?

I had a bit of an internal laugh at the three of them. I mean, you couldn't have gotten a more mixed set: the private school snot, Lydia; the suburban firelet, Kelly; and the country yokel, Joe. Then me, of course, done up since the Jen-days in half-arsed chic.

The conversation was moving about as fast as a brush fire on a windless day, so I went over to the bar to get us four drinks. The barman pulled a Carlton, then looked at me under about ten pine plantations of eyebrow.

'So you two blokes finally landed yourselves some sheilas,' he said, emptying one of the schooners of excess froth.

I didn't know what he was on about. I must've signalled incomprehension mighty well, 'cause he nodded his hangover head to our grotto. All I could see was Joe, flanked either side by a floozy. Then it hit me the way a car V-necks a pole. This was the pub where Joe and I would drink a few beers after practice and before he paired up with Kelly all those months back. Funny to think the barman remembered. We'd nicknamed him 'Muzzle Tops' for some reason.

'Oh, right,' I said, picking up the four pots in a cross-formation, feeling their bar-fridge coolness.

'You four looking to make a night of it?' My ears fairly yelped. The barman's voice needed sanding down something shocking. It was all done over in a nicotine patina.

One of the beers I was holding slipped, plunketing the carpeted bartop. It didn't tip but out jumped a good mouthful or two. The barman steadied it with blunt fingers.

'Here, I'll bring two of 'em over for you,' he said. 'You'll be wanting to take the other two to the sheilas.' He shook his head to the side. I followed the flecks of white over to where Kelly and Lydia were standing over by the jukebox, picking tunes. They'd left Joe to his grotto. It struck me how silent it was. But then 'Oh what a Night' flared up, rash and red.

Muzzle Tops nodded to the two remaining beers in my hand.

'Go on, lad,' he said, winking.

I wondered if I should set him straight.

'Don't be shy, son.'

He was still smiling from me to the girls. For a brief second, I wanted to thump the fuck but then I saw I couldn't. Imagine it. It would be so surreal somehow. He wouldn't even have known why – and perhaps I wouldn't have known either. Play back the videotape from the camcorder in the left-hand corner of the room, frame by frame, rewind, then run it back again, and I could see the cops still puzzling over it.

'Why did he hit him?'

I gave up the notion. Sad to say, I bowed to the pressure of lack of supposed motive, left Muzzle Tops' face intact and walked over all manly to the girls. Besides, I'd put aggression behind me, hadn't I? Why was I angry anyway? I guess it was about regretting catching up with Joe again. He was a wrong step I'd taken in a number of bad moves and I didn't want to be repeating mistakes.

Lydia and Kelly were getting on surprisingly well, showing each other little dance steps. At last, they'd found something to prevent them arguing: conversation-free activity. I gave them their beer each then departed but not

217

before saying what an attractive couple they made. I reckon their eyebrows hit the roof.

When I got back to the grotto, there was Joe squared up with Muzzle Tops. I couldn't escape the man! What was it with publicans? Muzzle Tops was an exact facsimile of Wally. But at least Wally didn't assume anything about anyone. I slid under the pine plank, and right up next to Joe. I caught the tail end of what Muzzle Tops was saying. He considered himself a bit of a ladies' man and was liberally giving Joe advice on the girls. Specifically, 'them two sheilas by the jukebox'.

I had a scowl on my face that I reckon would have been scarier than the IQ for the mean intelligence. I reckon Joe, and even Muzzle Tops, detected it quick smart.

'Well, whaddya know, hey?' Muzzle Tops asked me just as if we hadn't spoken a minute before.

I didn't answer straightaway. I don't know much but to list what I do know would still take the best part of a day. What kind of question is that anyway? Whaddya know? A pretty fucking good one according to Muzzle Tops, 'cause he asked it again.

'Know?' answered Joe for me. 'Not much, I guess.'

Muzzle Tops tapped some squared-off fingers on my placemat of table.

'Well, what about your friend then?' he asked Joe, still trying to get me in the conversation. 'Your friend here with the bit of shrapnel in his ear?'

Joe's hand flew to my ear.

'What's wrong?' he asked.

'He means the bolt in my ear,' I said, and his hand fell away. But … but it *was* nice the way it had gotten out of the cage before he'd caught it again.

Muzzle Tops leaned towards me.

'I hope you've got it in the right ear,' he laughed.

'No, the left one,' I said. 'If it's in the right one, you're a fag.'

Joe looked at me, amazed.

'Jeezus, is that right, is it? Right ear and you're a poofta, Barbara. Hear that?'

Barbara was breezing past, picking up clean ashtrays to clean them further.

'Not so loud, Larry. They'll think you're uncouth. That must be what they're thinking about you. Isn't that right, boys?'

I didn't contradict her, but Joe stepped in, six and a half feet tall.

'No, no, not at all.'

I was silent. Don't let me hate. Joe nudged me. I don't want to hate. Barbara squeezed in next to Larry, gripping his hand, but he kept going.

'Christ, so what else means you're a poofta?' he asked. 'The tendons cut in the wrist, eh?'

Larry laughed that yellow-finger laugh.

'So it flops about like this? Get it? Tendons cut?'

Joe laughed too. I couldn't believe it. I had to ball my fists under the table. Don't hate, Sam.

Muzzle Tops turned to me. 'Get this, do you? The bloody tendons cut in the wrist. The hand just flops there like steak.' To Joe, tapping the side of his weaponhead: 'Your friend here's a bit slow.'

I wasn't slow; I was just stone to his wanking hand. Harder than stone. Joe was nudging me, probably jarring his shoulder for his efforts. Muzzle Tops grew louder.

'C'mon, that's right. That's a poofta. What else is? C'mon, there's more of 'em your age.'

Everyone waited. I could see Barbara was doing her share of nudging the other side of the table. At last I let my mouth smile.

219

'A preference for mineral water.'

Joe breathed out. Muzzle Tops slapped the table. He laughed the day's menu.

'Yeah? That's a poofta, is it!' he said, thumping the table. 'Really! That's a poofta, Barbara.'

'Larry,' hissed Barbara.

'So that's a poofta, boss?' said Muzzle Tops to me.

I looked up, dramatic as could be. Like I'd heard him across a valley, for the first time.

'What, mineral water?' I asked, innocent as all heaven, and then the killer, face clenched once more: 'No, boss, a poofta's someone who likes other men.'

'Sam, you shouldn't have done that,' whispered Joe about three minutes later. Muzzle Tops and Barbara had excused themselves back to work. But I didn't care, not a hootenanny. Joe was lucky he still looked so good dressed the way he was. Christ, the man had about as much style as the Pope. Any face, when you look at it long enough, turns ugly.

Muzzle Tops was wiping the beer glasses back at the bar, looking at me and Joe then over to Kelly and Lydia limping at the jukebox. I reckon his mind was working overtime. Good old Babs was replacing the tanks.

Joe sipped his beer. That was the last straw.

'It's not fucking tea,' I said.

'Sam …?'

I got up before I hit him. He could play at straight all he liked, but I didn't have to watch. Kelly and Lydia weren't by the jukebox. Their empty beers were sitting on a windowsill. Maybe they were in the toilet or out the back in the beer garden. But I didn't want to join them either. I walked past the pool table to the pinball machine and computer games. There was this game I liked to play. One of those old ones with a flat glass top. You sit one side, someone else the other. Primitive as hell nowadays, with these 3D games and all, but fun just the same. Moon Buggy. Hell, I remembered when it was hip, the newest, the most revolutionary thing in our small town. The fish and chip shop had it, and I'd always go with mum to get the fish and chips in town 'cause then I could use the twenty cents I'd saved to play the game. Damn near clocked it in the end. 'Cept it broke or something.

Anyway, I got going and was doing pretty well for such a hiatus, but there were voices behind me getting in my ear. It was like someone was turning up the volume, louder and louder, but real slow, slow as a cop. At first I could ignore it, but then there it was, in bloody surround sound.

'What you wanna do,

what you wanna do is,

what you want, mate,

you wanna take that cunt and set fire to his fluffer.'

I looked about. The guy talking (his mates referred to him as Mario) had spiked-up black hair. Next to him a broody, wide feller. And next to him, another, with a mo, a bit shorter. And, behind the three, a fourth guy, who I couldn't get a proper look at. They looked a piece, apart from differing dimensions: spiked up, over-gelled black hair, that would've taken longer to style than a model's; colourful, shiny garments, with zippers in abundance; and enough collective jewellery to open a pawn shop. And silver, lots of silver.

Geez, I was getting pretty sarky. Why?

I hadn't even heard them come in, I was so engrossed in the game. I decided they were loud and annoying. But the feller at the back was quite cute (finally got a good look at him), with his hair over his face. His mobile rang and he had it to his lips two nanoseconds flat.

Mario's antenna-ear swivelled a degree as he paused his pool-stick pre-jab on the green.

The cutie killed his call.

'I gotta go,' he said.

Mario smacked the ball. It grasshoppered to the floor.

'What's fuckin' wrong with you, mate?' yelled Mario. 'You forget your friends? Your mama rings and you're off chasin' pussy? What happens to your mates?'

Something from the cutie. Not that guys stay that cute when they've got girlfriends. Mario went off at the response, whatever it was.

'Yeah, like at that party,' he yelled. 'I mean, you coulda given us a go, mate. I'm talking five minutes, mate. Five minutes tops. Five minutes flat, mate. Yeah, your mama layin' flat, sick mate, sick. I'll hold her for you, brother, I'll spread her for you. I'll guide that cock in, mate. No worries. Just let us watch.'

The cutie said something but I couldn't quite hear. Mario slapped him on the shoulder.

'Nah, forget it, mate. I'm just joking with you, brother. You think I'd fuckin' touch her after you'd been inside her? Getting all the slops? No fuckin' way.'

Mario beefed up against the boy, grabbing him by the shoulder. I thought Mario was going to biff him one. I reckon the cutie did too, 'cause his head went back, but then Mario pulled his punch, bringing an arm round the kid's neck instead. A footy hug, fist still clenched.

'I thought we was friends, mate. Hey, Alexi?'

There, his name.

'You put spadge over me, do ya, mate?'

Spadge?

'Are we playing pool here or what, fellers?' asked Mario, and the others said yes, all pretty much at once. Except for the tall, wide one; he was resolute.

Mario reached for Alexi's fold-out mobile.

'Here, let me take that for you, mate, so you can concentrate on the game. I'll hold it for you, brother.'

Alexi gave it up.

'No worries, mate,' said Mario. 'You'll get it back, bro'. That's guaranteed. Guar-an-teed.'

Alexi sat down. Mario turned back to his two mates still going at it with the blue chalk cube.

'What's stopping you cunts?' he asked.

The guy with the mo' replied, flipping Mario the cue.

'It's your go.'

Mario took the stick and stabbed some balls. Alexi stayed sitting at the table.

'In like Flynn, mate. Alexi, sit over here, mate. You a bit shy? Hey, Alexi, come sit here, mate, next to your buddy.'

Alexi swished in his seat. A real struggle. The broad guy potted three balls in a row. Mario had a word with him.

'Hey, Trepper, you still fucking your mum?'

Trepper was a big guy. He looked up slowly from his next shot.

'I wouldn't tell you if I was, mate,' he said, and proceeded to pot his fourth ball in a row.

Mario turned back to Alexi.

'No manners, brother. Still get abused every day, man?'

Alexi whispered back some response.

'Who by?' shouted Mario. 'Who fucking by? By your fuckin' a-mama, mate. By your mum, every day, mate. Tell your bitch, back off. See this bottle, I'll break it and fuckin' stab you.'

Mario whacked his empty beer bottle on the cushion of the pool table but it failed to break.

'Sick! See that, Trepper, I scared half the fuckers here, man.'

Trepper shook his head slightly. Our eyes connected. Geez, with Mario this was *real* aggro. I didn't ever want to get angry again. It was ugly.

Lydia and Kelly walked in. The guys shushed. Lydia looked at the computer game I was playing and said something about me still being a kid. Kelly waved at Joe. The two girls then noticed the pool players staring at them.

'Well, hel-lo, brother, what have we here?' crooned Mario. 'Would you two lovely ladies like to play?'

No, no, no, Kelly, Lydia, I thought, please God no.

'We'd love to,' said Kelly, and she and Lydia were handed a pool cue each.

I felt pretty sick at that but it seemed to go all right. The guys lifted their game. Mario was a real gentleman and all, even shouting across to me and Joe not to worry, just a friendly game. Our girls were safe. There, that fucked-up assumption again. But I was glad of it this time. Now and then Mario would call over to Alexi but Alexi was sitting at a table way back, hunched forward, feet arched up on a chair. Sulking something heavy. So I was feeling a bit relieved. But then the gay jokes kicked in. They generally do.

My echidna got busy, burrowing way back to my spine. I was worried I had 'gay' written all over. I felt the bolt in my ear. But looking over at those guys, I saw they had more jewellery than me. Appearances don't mean much. I let go of my ear.

The gay jokes were reminding me of that night at Dirk's. This time, I stopped myself from storming off. But Lydia! Every time they threw a gay joke, she'd look over at me. Kelly didn't seem to connect the two. So at least that gave Lydia *some* cred. I must've looked white 'cause she smiled. Lydia smiling at me. Christ, I wanted to scream, don't look over at me every time they make a gay joke. One of these woollies might just join the dots.

So I got stuck into Moon Buggy, or pretended to, like it was the best game on earth, just so Lydia wouldn't look my way.

But Kelly was getting into it, loving the attention.

Things turned green. One beer too many.

Alexi had been roped back into the game. He leant over to play a shot. Mario penguinned up behind him, his arms flapping at his sides for the visual benefit of his mates and the girls, and started thrusting a cushion of air at Alexi's arse. Kelly and the guys laughed. Alexi swivelled round. For the first time that night, I heard what he said.

'Poof.'

Mario roared.

'What?'

I saw Barbara, hunched and watchful, reach under the counter. Obviously with a finger on the 'Trouble' button.

'Ya brushed up against me,' said Alexi, softer now, but still a half-tone up from before.

'Want this pool cue up ya arse, mate?' yelled Mario, his lips practically touching Alexi's.

Alexi didn't budge. Then out came this voice.

'See. You *are* a faggot.'

I think we all expected an explosion. The second hand had counted down the last tock. But nothing forgot itself and fell to pieces. Everything and everyone was still intact. There was just the silence. And, at any moment maybe, the punch. But before it could come, a mobile rang. It rang with one of those stupid, ditzy rings. Neither Mario nor Alexi seemed to know whose it was. Mario grabbed his but it wasn't ringing. But still the jingle – on him! Finally, he remembered. Reaching into his other pocket, which was jiggling like it was home to a mouse, he whipped out Alexi's mobile, which he'd confiscated before, and pressed the answer button. Alexi reached for it but Mario played keepings-off for a bit before jumping on the pool table and saying hello into the mouthpiece. There was a long pause then, finally, a big smile.

'Hey, Alexi, mate, you'd never guess who's on the line?'

The others stood silent. Alexi stopped reaching for his mobile.

'Who?' he asked.

'Ya Mum!'

Laughter. Muzzle Tops put down the phone. Barbara's hand came from under the bar to rest on top of it. Mario tossed Alexi his mobile. Alexi ducked into a corner whispering words of love. Probably his girl on the line.

'You gotta play one more game, girls,' said Mario. 'Leave Alexi over there talking to his sweetheart.'

Then Mario started working his magic on winning the game, *and* the girls. Telling Kelly and Lydia about his car, his cool. Trepper piped in.

'Man, you're not real. You *are* your ethnicity.'

Mario looked at his mate. 'Ethnicity? That's a big word for you, brother.'

Trepper stood up tall. Mario went back to sweet-talking Kelly.

'Lydia, what am I going to do?' bubbled Kelly. 'This is the third time this week some guy's tried to pick me up.'

Don't, I thought, don't. I was thinking so hard I felt Kelly just had to've heard. Don't. Then one of the men sweet-talked her more.

'What can I do?' said Kelly. 'I just seem to attract men. Hey, must just be me.'

Kelly leant over the table, trying to reach for the white ball, halfway out on the green. Mario came behind her, throwing one claw on the small of her back.

'Yeah, stay there, baby.'

Kelly rolled round. Her belt twisted out of Mario's hands.

'Way to go, Mario.'

'Are you going to behave? You're scaring me,' Kelly pleaded.

'Leave her alone,' yelled Lydia.

'Bitch!' screamed Mario. 'Bitches don't fuckin' talk to me like that.'

I got up. Joe came over as well. It was us four against those four. I hadn't heard much from the other two all night but they looked ready for a fight. Trepper alone was a four-man team. We backed our way out. I heard Mario yell after a pause.

'Fuck this,' and this time he managed to smash the bottle.

'Run,' I yelled.

We got in the car, Joe's car: 4-cylinder, brakes rusty, suspension fucked, me driving. They ran out and got in their car: V8, twin-cam, Commodore with mag wheels and a chain steering wheel.

You get the picture. We were fucked.

The chase began.

One of the guys started flashing his dick at us through the passenger-side window. Lydia mimed looking through a magnifying glass. Mario was flashing his arse. Next thing I know, Kelly was flashing her tits in response, and then Lydia. What were they doing, egging them on? But they pulled themselves back into the car when the return gestures became too obscene and the shouts full of violence.

The chase spanned several suburbs. Now, for those few times you speed five *k* over the limit, or speed up through the orange light, there's always a cop car with a speed gun, or an intersection with a red-light camera. But cross two suburbs, with every element of reckless driving, dangerous conduct, high speeds, you name it – and you think there's one cop around?

To cut it short, I outmanoeuvred as much as I could (there was no hope of outgunning them) until I was forced to stop at the intersection of Johnston and Hoddle for a bloody red light.

The hoons surrounded the car: Mario at the front, Trepper at my window, Alexi behind and the fourth guy at the passenger rear door. Trepper had a clublock. The first swing smashed the window; the second, me. Seemed the lights weren't changing any time soon. I ducked the third swing, flooring the car in the process. Mario was thrown up – or half jumped – onto the bonnet. It was car-gauntlet through the crossing.

I tore down a few side streets on the other side, Mario the whole time hanging on to the windscreen wipers. The others were nowhere behind us. By the time they recovered, got back in their car and took off, we were gone.

I braked at the foot of some cyclone fencing rigged up round a demolition site. Mario flew into the wire, like a ball into the net. Let.

We got out of the car.

That whack with the club lock had snapped me out in more ways than one. Mario had got up and was hobbling away. I had his jacket in my hand. Houdini-style, he was out of it, but still fettered at the ankles in pain.

A brick was conveniently near. I picked it up, polo style, hardly breaking my canter. I was over Mario, above him, the brick high in the air. His eyes stared past their lids.

And I dropped it.

Mario didn't wait for reasons. He was up and limping, heading back towards the street. Joe, Lydia and Kelly flanked me either side. Joe had somehow found an iron stake. Lydia threw up a hand.

'Don't you want to smash that fuckhead, Sam! Don't you want to fucking kill him! He's getting away!'

Joe was dribbling.

For the first time, I noticed the other torrent: the blood spilling out of my head.

Kelly was bawling, 'I'm so sorry, Sam. I'm so sorry.'

'What are you sorry for, Kelly?' yelled Lydia. 'Those misogynistic fucks. You should be able to be as sexy as you like. Those cocks shouldn't touch you.'

'Lydia … Lydia … what if we were … what if …' stumbled Kelly.

'If we'd been on an isolated country highway,' said Joe, stepping out in front.

Kelly bawled thanks. 'And if they'd caught us there … we would've been …'

No one needed to finish the sentence.

Lydia stopped pacing. She pursed her lips ten times. She wanted to say more but couldn't get the words out. About ready to explode, she suddenly saw the jacket and grabbed it – the red windcheater of Mario's – with a quick, angry flourish, and pulled from its pocket his mobile and wallet.

'Aha! We've got that guy's address. His filthy friends' numbers, too. I say we go over there and cane the bastard. Smash him up. Well, Sam? All that gay talk. You know, since Joe told us you were, well, you know … I hear it

everywhere now. I mean, jokes about, well, your type …'
She was getting bogged down.

'And they hit you, for Chrissakes,' she went on. 'You should want to fuck them up more than any of us.'

Lydia held up the wallet. That wallet with Mario's address.

Kelly bawled louder. Joe half raised his iron stake.

'Well,' screamed Lydia, 'let's fucking smash that bastard.'

I thought about my smart-missile day. Those cricket balls I'd smashed into the opposing team, hitting silly mid-on in the groin, the wicketkeeper in the chest and finally Charles Acton-Heath in the head.

'I don't want to hate,' I said.

There was silence. Kelly stopped crying. Joe dropped the stake.

'What?' she asked.

'Please, Lydia,' I said, 'I don't want to hate. Don't make me hate.'

And with that, I took the mobile from Lydia's reluctant fingers and sent a blanket text message to every phone number Mario had listed.

Sorry, everyone
4 being such a
fuckhead. I'm
scared and
lonely. Please
don't abandon
me & help me
get thru this time
2 become a
better person.

Lydia wanted to ring a double-o double-five number on Mario's mobile but I put it and the wallet into an old tin and set fire to them. That would cost him enough.

Chapter Eight

Great Expectations by Charles Dickens is another of my favourite books. All through it, the main character, Pip, expects great things for himself. Things he has no right to expect. But he goes on believing they'll come his way anyway. Like this girl, Estella. She's a real beauty, but also an ice queen. Yet Pip goes on liking her, even though she would be no good for him.

Eventually Pip comes to realise that he'll be happy not expecting great things but enjoying the ordinary. And that's a neat and satisfying way to end the book only, unfortunately, it doesn't end there. Pip actually *does* get the girl! He marries Estella! Doesn't that muffle the moral message? Don't expect anything but you still might get what you want anyway?

In the edition Joe owned, there's another ending in the appendices. Pip simply sees Estella riding past in a carriage, knowing he won't have her but having some peace anyway. I like that ending better. I think Dickens got it right there. It's not so nice an ending, maybe, but truer. And you hate to think a book's lied to you.

For the next two weeks after the incident with the hoons, I hung out with Tubby and the others from the cricketing club. As well as making a second attempt at socialising with them, I was also trying to find form. Joe didn't return.

Itching for another 'outing', I tried getting onto Filter but the call kept going straight to Message Bank. Rang Zane a few times but he was too busy to trip because he'd just started some 'night class' and, besides, Filter was apparently his only source of pills anyway. Yeah, right.

As for Tubby and the others as a possible source of illicit substances, they hadn't progressed beyond beer.

One morning I woke up to find that Joe had rung my mobile at three in the morning. I must've slept right through it. He hadn't left a message but hung up. Joe sure as hell wouldn't prove to be a supplier but I knew I should see what his aborted call was about.

I dropped by his house. When no one answered, I pushed my way through the torn flyscreen and walked into his room. Joe looked up from where he was lying on his bed.

'Where have you been?' he asked, and started crying.

God he cried. The whole waterworks. Kept saying the same two things. How he couldn't make anything work. And how he really thought it would this time. I kept asking, what couldn't he make work, although I had a good idea. It was pretty awkward me just standing there, trying to find a spot to sit amidst the mess, him sitting on the bed. What did he really think would work this time? Then he told me: he and Kelly.

Kelly had left.

I didn't feel the least bit cocky. No I-told-you-so's and all that. All I did was ... well, I tried to hug him but he moved so far to the edge of the bed, it made it funny so I gave up.

I knocked over some stuff, trying to sit on the floor. A towel breezed off a brightly-coloured box. Joe almost did himself an injury grabbing for it. And it was this, I reckon, more than any intentional meanness, which made me lunge for the box myself.

' "Staying on the Straight Path",' I read off the lid. ' "Retail Price only $199.95" – Joe, you can't afford that!'

'It was reduced.'

I didn't know what to say. So I said the thing I'd armed myself with as a weapon for jolting Joe out of his rut.

'Me, Jen and Tash are hitting the town tonight. Do you wanna come?'

Joe peeped from behind his fringe of yellow hair.

'Where?'

It was a bar, expensive, with lots of port red on the walls, stainless steel in the fittings, and the tiniest bit of gold-embossing on the trims. Classy, I suppose. Cool? I couldn't say.

There was a tiny detail I'd omitted about the evening. It was actually the cricket crowd, with Jen and Tash thrown in. I'd worried about mixing friendship groups before (once I'd made friendship groups I could worry about mixing!) and here was the test. Surprising that Tash had come, considering her hatred of 'breeders', but perhaps this would be the test of hers and Jen's relationship. Secretly, I hoped so. I didn't think Tash was good for Jen. They still seemed to not talk to each other as often as they talked.

Tubby and Beth were celebrating.

They had reason to.

'Man, these days you don't ask your future father-in-law if you can marry his daughter,' shouted Tubby, 'you ask your mates!'

Laughter all round. The consensus among the guys was that Beth was 'a bit of all right', which meant hot.

'For a woman,' I retorted.

'Man, you're wrong!' shouted Tubby.

Silence followed. Tubby could handle jokes at his own expense, just not about his girlfriend. Not that Beth seemed the least bit offended.

Jen got the scene off pause.

'Now, Sam, you'd have to admit Tubby's pretty hot too.' Long pause. 'For a man!'

That got everyone laughing. Guys, girls, Tubby, everyone. Finally, I'd turned up to his and Beth's fire with my own kindling: friends I'd made myself and was proud of. The night eased in. Only problem was the fawn-coloured leather boxes we had to sit on – trendy I suppose – but no backrest. Jen was still managing to sit up straight; she was enjoying herself. Tash not so much. But she *was* holding up her end, unfortunately.

Joe seemed okay. A few of the blokes were encouraging him to come back to the club. Especially Dizzy, who reckoned Tubby, as an opener, wasn't much chop.

At one point I saw Joe lean over to Jen, whispering: 'You're not worried about what these guys think?'

Jen answered Joe at normal volume.

'Joe, when you tell people you're gay, suddenly *they're* the ones watching what *they* say.'

Joe sat back and pondered that one. So did I. I felt mean about not asking Tubby and Beth to that party Jen and I had all those months back. Worried if they were the right sort of people, if they'd fit in. People can take care of themselves.

The night wasn't as exciting as those trips with Zane and Filter, but cosier somehow. Perhaps my life could still read like a book – without the drugs.

'Joe, I hear you're a Christian,' said Tash.

I half got up, worried Tash was going to have a go at Joe. What Tash said next I never expected.

'I'm a Christian myself.'

Joe looked a bit stunned and Jen turned immediately from the scrum of guys she'd been talking to about 'tips for their ladies'.

'Tash, my dearest, I hate to break it to you, but the only person you worship is yourself.'

'That's exactly right, dear,' answered Tash before turning to Joe again. 'Because God's about love, my friend. And the hardest person to love is yourself. So start there.'

I'd underestimated Tash. There and then, I promised myself never to try to break up her and Jen ever again. They were suited to each other. Besides, maybe there wasn't such a thing as the perfect couple. Just people who could make it work.

Tubby summed up the evening.

'It's that feeling, man. You know that pissy feeling, like everyone's close and all. People aren't so bad.'

So now it was with Joe that I had a couple of weeks hanging out. Sometimes, we'd meet at the train station, leaning against the fence and feeling the wire making soccer ball patterns on our backs. On the train, I'd tell him my stories and he'd tell me his, which weren't his, but from the Bible. I asked about the parables once. What the use of them was. Why they didn't just say their morals up front.

'If you put your message in a story, Sam, people will remember it better.' And we stared out the window at all the houses and factories with their backs to us.

We bowled to each other in the nets, examining our bats afterwards to see how many times they'd been kissed by the ball with lips of seam.

Then we'd rest in the park, him one bench, me the other. I fidgeted but Joe lay still as a pond, picked out in stars.

After one such outing with Joe, I went home to find an envelope under my door. It was from Jen and Tash. They were nowhere in the house. I opened up the envelope, smiled, then closed it again.

Joe and I were standing on the edge of a swimming pool, our bare feet slip-glazed by the hot tiles, psyching ourselves up to dive in. Lydia was floating in the middle on her bright yellow lilo. It was her parent's place, and they were away.

'Oh, Joe, nearly forgot,' I said and retrieved the envelope from my bag. Lydia looked up from her book.

Joe finished reading the envelope's contents, an invite from Jen and Tash for their New Year's Eve party, 2000.

'*I'm* invited?'

'Yes,' I assured him. He looked at the invite again.

'It's got a theme, this party?'

'Yeah, spiritual.'

'Spiritual?'

'Yeah, easy for you,' I joked, 'but not for me. I told Jen that. She's asking a lot.'

'I don't think I've got anything spiritual,' said Joe, alloying a foot blue.

'Rubbish!' I laughed, 'don't you have that cross round your neck? I bet you have. What's that chain there?'

I flicked a chain of silver that hugged his neck. Joe stepped back a space, and lifted the chain from beneath his white T-shirt. There was no cross on it. Nothing.

'Oh no,' said Joe, grabbing at the empty chain, 'I'm naked.'

I fairly howled at that. Rolled round on the ground and everything. I couldn't help it. When I got up and wiped the tears from my eyes, I saw Joe had a grin.

'You meant that?' I asked, prodding him.

Joe nodded.

'Geez, Joe, you made a joke!'

I could've hugged him. A joke, and about religion too. He was easing up. Joe would be okay.

Lydia looked up from her floating bed.

'What's this party?' she asked under her raised sunglasses.

'It's not for a while,' I said, but I could see that didn't satisfy her. Joe nudged me.

'Oh yeah, Lydia,' I added, 'I forgot to tell you, you're invited.'

Lydia lowered her sunglasses and went back to her book. She probably wouldn't even come. But this way, she'd not be coming to a party she *was* invited to. To Lydia, that made all the difference.

New Year's Eve 2000 ... Made me think back to last New Year's Eve with Arny and the cricketers. A whole world gone by. I didn't think I'd remember that New Year's at the time but I did. Something told me I was going to equally remember this one.

Joe had his shirt off and was taking forever to get into the water by way of the shallow end.

I took a faster approach.

'Don't you know it's unsafe to dive-bomb a pool?' yelled Lydia after I'd come up for air. The foam must've made a pretty little ruff round my neck.

'Dive-bomb?' I complained, still gasping with the shock of the cold. '*That*, Lydia, was a dive.'

Lydia made a show of flicking the water-pellets off the cover of her book.

'We obviously have vastly different definitions for words,' she huffed.

I pedalled the water to my right so I could look past her. Joe was at the other end, still trying to get his balls under. It wasn't *that* cold. I had to amuse myself while I waited. One thing I like to do is hold my breath. I've nearly made it to the three-minute mark a few times. So I tried the underside of the water again. Once you were in, the pool was actually pretty warm. Not surprising, really: it was a thirty-degree day.

There I was, in the lotus position, sinking further down with each word bubble I uttered. Lines snaked along the bottom, curving upwards at the walls. The ceiling was a foil of crispy light, except for that one big yellow rectangle, Lydia's lilo.

I thought of Lydia Hamilton floating on her bed of air, floating in a pool of water with the ice taken off but still nicely chilled. Altogether a not so taffeta-and-tied-up-with-a-bow affair as all that, but with the sun in the sky above, pouting its crimson collagen lips, what was ol' Lydia doing?

Reading Proust!

And not just Proust either, but the annotated version.

An idea came to me. On resurfacing, I slapped over to Lydia's floating bed and asked, 'Hey, Lydia, why don't *you* do a dive-bomb?'

Lydia shook the Proust as if the two were incompatible.

Plish-plash. Joe had finally gotten himself in, but was keeping his hair dry. We paddled round a bit but then Lydia asked when I was going to give Joe his present. Joe looked at me. It was his birthday today, and I *had* got him a present but I'd planned to give it to him when the two of us were alone. Seeing that was now pointless, I splashed to the side, grabbed my bag and pulled out his gift.

'You haven't even wrapped it,' sneered Lydia, pulling herself hand over hand up the side of the pool to be next to Joe and me. She'd finally closed Proust on her bookmark – a fifty-dollar note!

Joe took his gift from my hands.

'Thanks, Sam,' he said, pulling out all the different bits on the pocketknife: screwdriver, saw, magnifying glass, tweezers.

'See, Joe, adventurers like us need an all-purpose knife, especially if we're to Huck Finn up the Murray sometime. You know how we were planning?'

'Geez, thanks, Sam.'

Lydia was leaning on Joe's shoulders, looking at the knife.

'Huckleberry Finn?' she snorted. 'You like these Boys' Own Adventure books, don't you, Sam?'

I didn't know what to say. Lydia couldn't stop herself.

'*To Kill a Mockingbird, Wuthering Heights, Great Expectations* – *w*here did you get these favourite books of yours? Off a Year Twelve English syllabus?'

Maybe the pocketknife wasn't such a good present. Probably pretty juvenile. Maybe if we were still kids. Guess I *was* caught up in those books I liked. Was Joe happy with the knife? I kept looking at that thick volume in Lydia's hands.

'Well, Lydia, what did *you* get Joe?' I asked.

Lydia held up the Proust.

'He ... er ... said I could read it first,' she explained.

Joe smiled at me before getting out of the pool, gently drying the knife, and putting it in his jeans pocket where it wouldn't get wet. Then he grabbed a ball before hopping back into the blue.

We started throwing the ball the length of the pool, me at the deep end, he in the shallows, but when it hit Lydia, she ordered us to get out. We didn't just get out of the pool, but off that property altogether, and headed to Joe's place. Sauntering down the road, Joe stopped at a concrete fence cast to look like wood palings and painted green.

'That other night, Sam, with Tubby, Beth, your flatmate Jen, her girlfriend, Tash ... well, you've got great friends,' said Joe. 'I'll never have friends like that.'

'Sure you will, Joe. They're your friends too, now,' I replied and started us walking again.

But were they? My parents unsuccessfully pushing me into my brothers' friendship groups made me think friends were non-transferable. But maybe that wasn't always true. I met Zane through Jen, and Filter through Zane.

Joe's mobile beeped. It was an SMS from Kelly. She was at the pool with Lydia and the two were wondering where the 'heck' we were.

'*They* are my friends,' said Joe, showing me the text message.

I tried to get moving but Joe wouldn't have it. His legs had taken root.

'Hey, they're not so bad, Joe. Give 'em time.'

'You've made it, Sam. I won't make it like you.'

I didn't know what to say. Any of us can make it, whatever that means.

'Joe …' I faltered, 'you say I've got great friends …'

Joe finally looked up.

`Well, you're one of them.'

We arrived at the open flyscreen to Joe's house. But we weren't headed inside. Standing in the driveway, we both looked pointedly at his car.

'Should we go back?' asked Joe.

The next day we took a longer drive. Not back to Lydia's parents' pool but to Joe's parents' house in the country. Joe drove like I wank: at about a million miles an hour. He'd picked this day to come out to his parents.

The Melbourne buildings became blocks of blue in the distance. Moth wing city – there was a face in it – danger!

Were we just another drive-by indifference? There I was, the passenger, looking round for yesterday's smile.

'Slow down, Joe,' I yelled. The car was arguing with each turn, Joe was throwing it around so much. We'd done the Sydney Road stretch and were now on the Hume Highway proper. Joe was determined to get to his folks' before nightfall – but truth was, we'd left it late.

I was getting pretty scared. Joe had his teeth set. Lockjaw pose – not quite holding the line on some of the bends.

He nearly lost it in the gravel on one of them and I grabbed the door handle with my fingers, somehow tasting its metal in my mouth. When Joe took another bend and I felt the car fishtail, I gripped harder. Joe just managed to get the wheels straight. On a downhill stretch, we overtook yet another truck. I didn't know what to do. I thought maybe a joke would work.

'Okay, Joe,' I said, 'you've got heaven to go to. This life is it for me. I'm mortal.'

Luckily Joe laughed.

Then slowed down.

And went at speed.

'Hey, Joe' I said to him, 'we don't have to do this now. There's no hurry.'

Joe stared ahead, squinting into the sun. I tried another tack: *Huck Finn*. We'd both read it so he'd be up to speed.

'It can't be like Huck Finn,' I told him.

'What?'

Joe glanced across at me.

I'd been thinking about how Huck did the right thing and all. By not turning Jim in. Jim, the slave who's done a runner, and hooked thumbs with Mr Finn on the Mississippi. Huck's thinking over the whole thing, ruminating pretty hard. He thinks not dobbing in a runaway slave is pretty bad but he resists all the same. He says 'All right, then, I'll go to hell … It was awful thoughts and awful words, but they was said.' I'd been thinking about this a lot. And this is what I came up with. Huck does the right thing, yeah, but he does the right thing thinking he's doing the wrong thing. So, in a way, he doesn't change. I mean, he never actually believes that what he does is right. He just accepts his lack of racism as a bad habit he won't grow out of because he was brought up for sin anyway. I reckon it's pretty hard to unlearn something. It's pretty damn hard to change, I mean *really* change yourself.

I don't ever want to do the right thing thinking it's the wrong thing. Or the opposite: doing the wrong thing thinking it's right. But it's hard, I know it. Sometimes you just don't know what to do, and unless you want to be a spectator all your life, you've got to do *some*thing, even if it *is* back-handed and across court.

'Tell 'em when you're ready, Joe. I don't reckon you've quite told yourself yet.'

Joe turned his eyes back to the road, which was pretty wise considering we were approaching a bend, and pressed the accelerator that bit harder.

I knew to shut up.

His parents' house was brick-venereal, that gingerbread brown, veranda all round, a few trees dotted about, the land one big flat plain of grass and grass munchers – sheep (I *could* go on). The smell was grassy. We popped our boots off on the veranda. Inside, the smell was talcum. The carpet you could wear round your shoulders, it went that deep.

His parents' car wasn't in the garage. Yet more delay.

There was a note on the fridge: 'Joe, we're at Nanna's.'

It wasn't signed. Joe said his nanna's meant half an hour more's drive. We jumped back in the car. We arrived in twenty minutes with Joe's driving, walked up the steps and knocked. It was about six-thirty. No answer but the door was open. I was halfway in when this voice says, 'Give us a scratch!'

'What?'

I looked about.

'Give us a scratch.'

Well, I'll be blowed; it was a cocky, sitting in its cage. It did this little clown thing, side to side, before jumping onto the grille and using its beak as a third hand. I was a bit scared of it at first, I'll have to say. I don't know, birds can be a bit strange, but Joe popped it out of its cage. He said you had to let it come to you. It sidestepped along Joe's arm and onto mine. I felt all ticklish and nervous.

'Pat it,' said Joe, and I did. It didn't feel quite how I thought it would. I found a magpie when I was a kid, which was as soft as powder, but then it hadn't been long in the world. This bird, the cockatoo, was definitely mature, maybe as old as Joe or I. It was soft, yeah, but there were the feather stalks – or whatever you call them – underneath. Just the texture of the thing told you you had to be ever so gentle.

'Give us a scratch.'

Every time I stopped patting it, it would grab one of my fingers with its claw and put it back under its wing. When you took your fingers away, they were covered in this fine, white, greasy powder. It kept turning its head horse-sideways to look at me with its oyster eye. Joe told me its name was Long John Silver. So-o-o, I wasn't the only one weaned on Boys' Own Adventures!

I looked about the place. There was a thermometer on the wall, in Fahrenheit. A revolving iron chair with a twelve-inch TV backrest by the phone. A number 4 shag carpet you could scrunch your toes in. Paintings of woolsheds. And an aerial photo of Joe's farm, looking like a huge dug-up lawn. The whole place smelled of yellow soap and beeswax.

Then the folks called out. They were in the tiny back courtyard. Joe didn't even introduce me to his parents. He was such a dag. All he said was, 'This is my mum and dad.'

I was going to say hello Mum, hello Dad, but thankfully I didn't.

'So what are your names?' I asked instead.

'What?' asked Joe's father. He was pretty gruff in the way he said it. It quite unnerved me.

'Well, um,' I tried again, 'so I've got something to call you by. Fred, Bill, Jennifer –'

'Sam!' Joe was prodding me.

'What, Joe?'

Long John flurried to my other shoulder, his head mohawked yellow. Joe's parents were staring, mouths slightly open.

'You know my surname,' whispered Joe.

Of course I knew Joe's surname. It was Wilson. Joe Wilson.

Aaaah. Stupid me.

'Mr and Mrs Wilson,' I said, and shook their hands. Mr Wilson's grip was a case of force incommensurate to the need. Mrs Wilson just looked at my hand for a bit then lightly held it. The four of us stood there, stupidly. Over the back fence, I could see the shaded willow flats edging onto the Murray. It was nearly dark. Finally, Mrs Wilson said we should all go into the lounge.

Joe's nanna was already there. She smelt like a long-lived pine tree growing near a beach. I wasn't introduced to her properly either. So I figured she was another Mrs Wilson.

'Hello,' she answered to my hello, lifting a hand for a shake.

I hadn't even bothered to offer my hand this time. When I did, the cocky leapt off my shoulder to perch on my fingers.

'Joe, get that cocky off,' said Mr Wilson.

'No, Mr Wilson, he's okay.'

'Well, if he starts annoying you ...'

'Sure.'

Joe's nanna shook the bird's wing instead. She was wearing pink tracky-dacks with an unmatching aqua top. Her hair was a fancy mess of curls like some people go to the trouble of putting on presents. Colour: blue.

Joe's birthday rites were observed next. He showed his parents the knife I'd given him. They looked at it queerly, Mr Wilson muttering something about how it was time Joe grew up. Geez, it really wasn't a wise gift. Joe then got a present from his parents. It was a book on creationism.

Mr Wilson took a seat, the only high-backed one in the room. The rest of us were consigned to the low-slung woolly couches. Joe's dad was a pretty handsome bloke, I had to admit, but he'd dried out a fair bit in the sun. His arms and neck were an iron red. His hair was all tangled, maybe from wearing a hat most of the time.

'You doing anything with that science degree, Joe?'

'Joe's a great batsman,' I said. 'Just needs to get better at playing the shorter ball.'

Mr Wilson looked at me.

'Turn on the TV,' he said to Joe. 'The news should just be starting.'

And once the TV was on, it didn't go off the whole time I was there. The volume was up pretty loud and no one turned it down. There were a few videos on top of the TV: a couple of biblical tales; several *National Geographic* nature documentaries; and one or two soft-serve classics that wouldn't offend even the pope.

'Hey, Mum,' said Mr Wilson.

'Yes,' said Joe's nanna.

'On TV.'

'Yes.'

'That singer you like.'

'Who?'

'Used to be married to what's-his-name.'

'Oh yes, yes, they say he wasn't nice to her. What's her name?'

Long pause.

'Madonna,' said Joe.

An even longer pause.

'What was her husband's name?' asked Mr Wilson.

No one knew the answer to that one, so there was another bout of silence. Mr Wilson didn't even look away from the TV for his next statement.

'Joe,' he said, 'that book I've given you. Goes into just how wrong evolutionists are. You should give it to Sam after.'

I nearly jumped. Mr Wilson turned to me.

'In it, you read about these people saying Earth's six billion years old. What rot!'

Oh no! Mr Wilson must've thought I was a Christian too. I guess it was an obvious assumption. I didn't know what to say. All I could do was nod stupidly. He went on.

'They say fossils take millions of years to grow! I can make coal like that. Just burn a log.'

'Um, Dad ...' interrupted Joe.

'What, son?'

'Um, Sam's not – '

Mr Wilson turned his head on hearing some clanging in the kitchen.

'Joe, help your mother with the serving up.'

'Oh, *I* can,' I nearly shouted, jumping from my seat.

'Sit down,' commanded Mr Wilson, 'you're the guest.'

'No, that's fine, Mr Wilson. You two must want to catch up.' And I was out of there.

I walked into the kitchen. Mrs Wilson didn't say anything but kept on cooking. So I took the time to have a better look at her. She was pretty attractive, too. Had to be, to pop out a kid like Joe. But she was so done over country-style it was hard to tell. Almost had a she-mullet.

'Want some help?' I asked, and she got me to help her carry the food out to the table. Long John played with the hair about my ears.

Mr Wilson sat at the head of the table, then peeled the tablecloth back to check out the grain.

'Look at that table, Mary,' he said to his wife, 'isn't she a beauty!'

'Yes, Frank, it's lovely,' said Mary.

So those were their names: Frank and Mary. I put down the mutton casserole, then sat down myself.

'Get that bird off your friend,' said Frank.

I said I would myself and took it to its cage. Joe came after me to help. It was like trying to get a blackberry vine off your clothes.

'Good cocky, good cocky, good cocky,' the bird kept screeching.

Between us, Joe and I managed to get it back in the cage. Immediately, it jumped onto the bars.

'Good cocky?' it actually seemed to ask, not just parrot, wondering at its change in fortunes.

'Can it fly?' I asked.

'Dad regularly clips its wings.'

Joe and I moseyed down to the living room.

'We should get a table like that for *our* living room,' Frank was saying. 'Where'd you get this from, Mum?' and Frank ran his tree-root hands along the table's similarly grained surface.

Mary was helping Nanna into her seat. Once settled, Nanna turned to Frank.

'My brother Wal made that,' she said.

'Knew it!' shouted Frank, giving the table's polished top a knock, as if to prove it were wood. 'Handcrafted. Hear that, Mary? We'd never find anything like that, would we? Not a hope. It's all machine-made these days.'

'Pieces of eight,' squawked the cocky from the other room.

'Shut up, bird!' yelled Frank.

249

Long John muttered a dirty streak under his breath. At least I reckon it was all swear words. It was a low-volume wireless sound, half-tuned between stations. Hiss crrks shlllrks.

'Where does that bird learn to swear?' asked Frank.

Joe's nanna very slowly and deliberately tucked her napkin into her top. Maybe *she* was the spark in the family!

'You don't use this table much, do you, Mum?' asked Frank.

Mary brought in the last item of food, sliced white bread, and sat down. With the cook seated, the condiments sprinkled or poured, I grabbed my fork and nearly had a bit of mutton in my mouth when Joe gave me a kick that made me wish I had shin-guards on.

'Joe!' I screamed.

'Shhh!'

And Frank bowed his head after giving me one long, dirty look.

'For what we are about to receive,' he bellowed, 'may the Lord God make us truly thankful. Amen.'

'Amen.'

Christ! 'Amen.' I'd never said grace before in my life! It didn't make sense. I'd seen Mary making the meal myself. If it had been pheasant off the range, maybe …

Frank shot me another look once he'd opened his eyes again. It wasn't a good look. Worse than the first. It was like I'd betrayed him, pretended to be on his side about all that creation stuff then showed my true heathen colours. It was a very dark look. The one he shot Joe wasn't much better. Letting his father step in it!

I waited till he'd buttered his boiled mash before I buttered mine. Mary had scraped the butter into little scalloped twirls.

'So you didn't meet Joe through church?' asked Frank, fixing his X-ray eyes on his mutton, laser-beaming it into tenderness. But the question could only have been directed at me.

'No, um, through cricket.'

'Land ahoy, land ahoy.'

'Shut up, bird!' yelled Frank.

The cocky swore another blue streak. At least, that was my fancy. Frank and Mary blinked at Joe's nanna. She just kept rearranging her plate. I could see Joe holding his giggles under water. Frank observed it, too.

'You got a girlfriend, Sam?' he asked me, after turning his eyes away from his son.

'Well, no, you see, I'm – '

Joe jumped in. 'No, he doesn't.'

The rest of the meal was pretty much eaten in silence. I noticed Joe's nanna didn't eat at all. She just kept pushing her food around. The potato was made to herd the beans. Joe hardly ate either. Perhaps a third of his meal. I couldn't imagine what would happen if he came out to his parents now, between main course and sweets. This place and Joe coming out – the two seemed about as disparate as a greasy carburettor placed on a red leather settee. Frank watched Joe playing with his meal.

'You going to finish that?' he asked.

'Yes,' said Joe.

'It's getting cold.'

'I'll finish it.'

'Don't get cheeky with me, son.'

Joe dutifully shovelled in the rest of his tucker. Afterwards (what felt like a week later), Joe and I volunteered to help wash up. I'd never been so keen to do a chore. Mary washed, we dried. Frank and Nanna stayed

251

in the lounge where Nanna retired to her couch and Frank to his high-backed chair.

Mary's pink-gloved hands churned the bore-water-filled sink like a butter press. She addressed Joe's reflection in the window in front of her.

'Joseph,' she began. (Joseph! Of course, a Biblical name. It never clicked before.) 'Mrs. Drew's daughter's comin' up Tuesday.'

'Mum.'

'You couldn't stay till then?'

'Mum.'

'You and Jess got on well at Sunday school, remember. She's in the Christian choir now.'

'Mum.'

'How's that Bible studies class of Shane's? Must be lots of nice girls you can talk to. No use just looking good.'

Joe said nothing. I continued to dry the plates. Joe was putting them away now. Mary pulled out the plug. The water spiralled in on itself like a snail's shell, leaving a trail of soapsuds. Once Mary shook her hands of foam, she turned round to Joe.

'Joseph, weren't there *any* girls you liked at Sunday class?'

Joe hung the last pot on its hook.

'Lyn Chan was nice.'

'Her!' cried Mrs Wilson. 'Ye-es, nice of course … but you'd think she'd do something about those eyes.'

'Mum!'

'So she can see better.'

'Mum!'

We walked back into the lounge. Frank was ear-bashing Nanna.

'Mum,' he was saying to her, 'it's gonna cost me a fair penny to take that table off your hands. Hobson's gonna want at least a slab to display that table in his antiques shop. You don't think you could see your way to footing the bill, do you? I'll pay the petrol.'

'My brother Wal made that table before he died,' said Nanna.

Frank turned to Joe when he realised we were back in the room. 'Hey, leg it on home, would you, son, and grab the trailer. Bring a few ropes. Clear out some space for Nanna, would you.'

Joe and I about-turned. Mary asked if we could wait. She and Frank would be going to bed soon and, besides, it wasn't every day she had her son home. Frank looked at his wife before nodding at us. We sat down again. *Home Improvement* was playing on TV. Mary disappeared into the kitchen to heat the jug.

'Sean Penn!' screamed Frank.

I nearly jumped for fright.

'What?' asked Joe.

'That was her husband's name,' said Frank. 'Madonna's.'

'Oh, yes, yes,' said Joe's nanna.

'Joe, been selected for the state side yet?' asked Frank. 'All that money you have to spend before you *make* money.'

Mary called from the kitchen to ask what people wanted. We gave our orders.

'Do you want a cup of tea, Mum?' asked Frank. When Joe's nanna didn't answer – she was sitting nearest the TV and, even then, was still cupping an ear – Frank turned to Joe.

'Ask your Nanna if she wants a cup of tea.'

'I will,' I said, and jumped up. Anything to keep busy.

'Would you like a cup of tea, Mrs Wilson?' I asked.

'You'll have to speak up,' said Frank.

'Would you like a cup of tea, Mrs Wilson?'

'She's deaf.'

'Mrs Wilson, would you – '

'Louder!'

'WOULD YOU LIKE A CUP OF TEA?'

Deadly, horrible silence. Mary had even run in from the kitchen. Joe was hiding his face in shock. Frank stared at me the way a farmer would a blowfly infestation. 'That's not very nice,' he said slowly, 'to yell at an old lady.'

'I'm sorry … I just …'

'You've got to get in front of her. So she can read your lips as well. Right round, right round. That's it.'

'Give us a kiss,' screamed the cocky.

Frank's face spasmed into a smile.

'Yes, please,' said Joe's nanna to me, 'that would be lovely.'

Five minutes later and Joe's nanna got her tea. The rest of us were served coffee. Instant. I don't know why Mary insisted we stay the extra half-hour 'cause all we did was watch TV. After a bit, Frank got Joe to help him carry the table outside to the shed so Joe and I wouldn't wake up the house when we came back for it with the trailer. I offered to help, but Frank told me to sit down, saying I was the guest.

When they were gone, I jumped up for a leak. Mary pointed the way. The dunny was outside. I couldn't piss straight away, I was so tensed up. I forced myself to relax, breathe in, all that. Finally! But then halfway through I had to stop. There was a noise, right outside the toilet window. It was Joe and Frank.

'Now son, who's this Sam? Dresses like a bit of a poonce.'

'Dad.'

Silence. I realised I was holding my breath. Come on, come on, speak! I needed to let out the air. Think of yourself under water, Sam, in the pool. You can make that three-minute mark.

'Carson said he'd get you an apprenticeship at Tarrant Estate anytime,' said Frank.

'Dad.'

I breathed out under Frank's following words.

'Put that degree to use. Wine-making is a science. It's all about chemical reactions.'

'Dad.'

I breathed in again.

'Here's his number. Give him a call.'

'Dad.'

'I'm not dictating your life, Joseph. You've got to stand on your own two feet.'

Another pause. I held my breath again.

'Hey, did you get that money I sent you?' asked Frank.

Joe's head must've wilted at the neck.

'Ye-es.'

'Your mother and I will need looking after.'

The conversation must've been finished with a look because next thing I heard was Joe walking back inside. It was definitely his walk, haphazard, unsure. I wanted to flush the toilet but I wasn't sure where Frank was. Maybe he was still standing at the window. Then the worst possible thing happened. Joe started calling me from the house. Then his Mum yelled that I was in the toilet. My position given away! Joe would be out in a second. There was nothing for it. 'Coming!' I yelled, and flushed the toilet. When I stepped out, there was Frank, standing directly in front of the dunny door, staring at me. I stared back a second before rushing inside. I wanted to get in before Joe waltzed out.

Frank now had another reason to hate me, for being an eavesdropper. This was squaring up to be one of the worst social occasions of my life, and I'd chalked up quite a few of those. I ran back into the lounge and sat on the two-seater next to Joe. Nanna was in her own chair, next to mine. Frank and Mary were absent. That made my stomach swill a bit: they were probably discussing me. Quite out of the blue, Nanna started speaking.

'They're pulling out all the old trees now. By the Murray. Oh well. All those nice willows. The young people want to put new ones in; Australian. Oh well, got to move with the times.'

I liked Joe's nanna. I really did.

'Can't complain,' she went on. 'Ye-es, it was a hard life. But a good life. We didn't have all the mod cons you kids have. But we had a good time.' To Joe: 'Your father was always running about, fixing things. The lawns were always mowed. A good kid, really. No, all told, it was a good life.

'Yes, I suppose we had fun,' she added. Joe smiled at me. I wanted to take his hand. Nanna crackled on.

'You didn't really get a say in those days. I worked at Mrs Carew's dressmaking shop. Oh, but I didn't mind. We didn't have the choices you kids have. Oh, I suppose it was easier in a way. If you and Joe want to play cricket then …'

Nanna let her words trail off; Frank and Mary had walked in. I quickly changed the topic of Nanna's monologue.

'What was the thing *you* really liked to do, Mrs Wilson?'

Nanna gave me a look like she had never been asked that question before in her life. I put it to her again.

'What was the thing you liked above everything else? That if you could've earnt a living off it, that's what you would've done and only done?'

I could see Frank and Mary glancing away from the TV. Joe was leaning closer to me to hear Nanna over the ads. She was silent a long time, the whole duration of the ads, which, as we know, is a lifetime.

'Sewing, I guess. Craft things. Used to make the boys all their clothes. Jumpers, sweaters, even their school uniform.'

'They were never quite right,' cut in Frank. 'The shorts with those purple trims. I got a hard time.'

'So they were different, Mrs Wilson?' I nearly yelled, excited by the thought of that look. 'Did you want to go into fashion?'

'You'll have to speak up.'

I nearly told Frank where to go, but stopped myself with nary a centimetre to the precipice.

'Mrs Wilson, did you want to design clothes?' I asked.

'Me …?' suddenly Nanna exploded laughing, but then she put her hand up to her mouth straight away. The idea was a fuse. She turned to look at Joe quite impulsively.

'You're not changing that shirt, Joe, are you? Wouldn't want to throw that out. Could take a few more holes yet!'

Joe examined his dressed-down dagginess then had a squiz at my upmarket chic. I was glad I hadn't 'gone undercover for the occasion'. That, after the Jussy interlude, I'd accepted the clothes Jen helped me choose.

'Why don't you two go out, have fun,' said Nanna. 'Here you go,' and she tried to palm me off twenty bucks from a purse in her lap. I kept saying no but she just let the note fall to the floor. I felt pretty bad taking it but I did in the end. Frank slightly shook his head at that.

'Show my grandson a good time,' said Nanna.

Joe and I got up, with Joe saying it was time to get the trailer.

'Well, it was a hard life, but a good life,' said Nanna as we helped her up. She was retiring to bed. 'Good thing I'll be in the ground, soon.'

Mary's head nearly came off.

'Don't you mean in heaven, Mum?' she asked.

Nanna wiped the sides of her mouth with her silk handkerchief. 'Heaven …? Oh, that.'

They freeze-dried. Joe, Frank and Mary. Nanna shook my hand, then went over to Joe and kissed him good night. She walked through the space that the table, only half an hour before, had occupied. When she'd half-vanished through the door, Frank called out.

'See, Mum,' he said, 'you don't go hitting your leg on that table any more.'

Nanna regarded her son a second before slowly turning away and pulling the door shut behind her.

Frank and Mary went to bed straight after. Joe and I got ready to go, but as we passed Long John in his cage, he jumped forward.

'Weigh anchor?' he squawked.

I asked Joe if we could take him on our mission. We did. We got the trailer. It was half an hour there, half an hour back.

Long-John sat on the dash the whole time, head forward, clipped wings outstretched like he was flying.

When we got back, I had to put him in his cage. 'That's the longest he's been out,' said Joe.

When I took him to the cage he ran right up my arm and behind my neck. Joe had to un-thorn his toes at the back of my shirt. He screeched when we put him inside. I mean, really screeched. Piercing stuff, like your eardrums were going a whole drum solo.

It was an awful, awful sound.

The next morning Joe went to wake up his nanna; she was sleeping in very late. A quarter of an hour later he walked out of her room, red-eyed, and told us she was dead. I remembered the night before how she'd just shifted her meal around on her plate. Nobody said anything straight away. It was the sort of quiet where the background noise gets its short-lived moment front of screen, and you remember fridges hum, and clocks tick. Mary rang the GP. Frank went to the shed to 'check' the knots we tied on the ropes holding the table. When he came back, his lip was trembling.

'I don't believe it,' he said.

'Don't believe what?' said Mary, a little spooked with a corpse in the house.

'Mum … she's … she's made a great big bloody scratch right down the centre of that table!'

Mary rushed to the shed to see. Frank followed.

Joe and I were left alone. He smiled.

I knew then that the pocketknife I'd given Joe was a good present.

Joe and I started out on the road to Melbourne, the land opening up under the disappearing mist like a cold lasagne stripped of its cling-wrap covering. He pulled up at his local train station.

'What are you doing?' I asked.

'I wasn't visiting, Sam,' said Joe. 'I'm staying.'

'You can't go back,' I told him.

As Filter would say, once you wake up to this world, there's no going back to sleep. Joe got out of the car and went round to the boot to get my bag. There was nothing I could do but also get out.

He insisted on carrying my bag till we got inside the station. He then checked out the time of the next train and looked at his watch.

'I thought it ran later,' he said, looking disappointed.

I don't know why he was disappointed. If I was going to be packed on the train, I didn't want to wait for it. Joe handed me my bag. I leant it against my legs – it wasn't worth sitting down. Joe shuffled about on his toes, obviously with something further on his mind. Eventually he got it out.

'Arny will be back soon,' he said.

It came from nowhere and it was the first time Joe had mentioned Arny since inviting me to that ice-skating rink. The next thing he said was even more out of the blue.

'He's "the one", isn't he, Sam?'

It was my turn to shuffle. I didn't know that I believed in 'the one'. My bag fell over and I picked it up. 'The one' would be nice, sure, if it was real. But was it? Even though I'd put Arny out of my head, I guess I still secretly hoped.

'Yes,' I eventually said. 'He's "the one".'

'For you?' asked Joe. The answer was so obviously yes that I didn't bother responding. Joe said a few more strange things, things I didn't really hear at the time, or know how to take in. An announcement was made over the PA: the train was arriving. Joe stopped and looked up the track. There it was.

It wasn't what I wanted to ask – it was probably the least important question – but I asked it anyway.

'What about the cricket?'

'You're the natural, Sam.'

Joe could see my mind working overtime to state my case more cogently. The train pulled up with a hiss and a screech. The other people waiting got on board.

'Just till my parents get over the shock of losing Nanna,' he justified himself.

I also embarked.

'Say hello to Long John for me,' I said. 'Let him out of his cage now and then.'

The doors closed. Joe stood watching for as long as I could see him. Maybe even longer.

Back in Melbourne, I tried ringing Filter. No answer. Same with Zane. I couldn't even intercept Filter at the video store when he was leaving the morning shift and I was arriving for the afternoon shift; the boss was there instead. He told me that Filter had unexpectedly quit.

'Strangely,' he added, 'when I deleted his details on the computer this morning, I realised he quit exactly five years to the day when he started with me.'

That night, I holed up in my room. I was feeling edgy – I couldn't say why. I was angry with Joe, I guess. He was giving up, staying in a place where he couldn't be himself. And that conversation at the train station – was he saying goodbye?

I got out for a golden duck in cricket. My form slump looked like it had set in. Tubby asked me about Joe when he was driving me home. For some reason, an Adam's apple formed in my throat, and water pricked my eyes. I turned sharply to the window on my side, and wound it down so the wind would dry my face. Tubby didn't pursue the subject.

A fortnight passed, time where nothing went right: my game, my friendships. Dizzy cornered me in the nets at training and told me he'd decided he liked me because I wasn't camp.

I told Tubby that when he drove me home.

'Man, maybe the real reason he now likes you is because of your form slump.'

I wondered why I ever wanted to be accepted by the likes of Dizzy.

'Sorry, Sam, but you know what I'm like: "Tubby, telling it like it is".'

'I wouldn't want you any other way, Tubs,' I choked.

Walking to my room, Jen intercepted me in the corridor.

'Sam, a girl's been ringing you.'

'A girl?'

'Her name's Lydia.'

Jen passed me a piece of paper with a number on it.

'Thanks, I know the number,' I said.

Lydia insisted we go out for dinner. We met at this little Thai place. It was very nice. Authentic. An Authentic Thai waitress ran over.

'You friend of Mr Filter, yes?'

My chopsticks missed my mouth, daubing my chin. Filter. This is where he'd taken me one time. *That* time. On the whole beginning, the waking up, the …

'You his friend, yes?'

Lydia was looking at me.

'You tell Mr Filter shame, he not been here a long time.'

I nodded. It *was* a shame. The waitress left.

'Joe's dead,' said Lydia.

'What …? What …?'

'He's dead.'

'Dead? How?'

'He was driving to work, the vineyard – you know how fast he drives – and …' Lydia put a handkerchief to her eyes. 'This food really is spicy.'

I saw her words as crystals. They'd grown halfway across the table. I couldn't speak my side of the bridge.

I called over the waitress.

'Um, please, where's your toilet?' I asked and, because she looked tornadoes at that, I had to add, 'Sorry, I've forgotten.'

'I knew you Mr Filter's friend! Up the hall.'

Even though I was alone in the bathroom, I still had bashful bladder. Did I need a slash? Or a minute alone? What had Lydia said?

Joe – driving to work – the winery – crashed? Yes, that's what she'd said. He was dead. Why did he do it? Driving fast all the time – what was the point in that? The idiot! Things were going well for him. Until he went back to the folks, that is.

I hadn't needed a slash after all, just time to take this in. I tried to leave the bathroom. Dishwashing detergents, scrubs, a mop – must've opened the cupboard door. Turning round, I couldn't see another. That was the only door in the room! That echidna bunched up. Calm down, Sam, calm down. I circled the room. Okay, not another door. I looked at the window. Not even a cat could crawl through it. Right, open the door again: cupboard. Maybe it has a fallback. I went to move a few items but my fully extended arms were still gripping air! How was that possible? Then I realised: the cupboard was set a metre and a half back from the door. The corridor to the toilet doglegged. I hadn't noticed the cupboard to my left coming in. What was wrong with me?

I rejoined Lydia.

'When's the funeral?' I asked.

'Last week – '

'Last week?' I yelled. 'Why wasn't I – ?'

'Sam!' shouted Lydia. 'I only just found out what happened to him myself.'

Lydia explained.

'Yesterday I rang Joe's parents wanting to get onto Joe about his bond for the house. I'm going back to my parents myself, you see, and … and well naturally I wanted Joe to have his money back. He'd told me he didn't want it till I got another flatmate, but … but I couldn't find one.'

Poor Lydia. She and Joe had been a good unit. They could put up with each other.

'You know,' said Lydia, 'when I passed his room this morning, I imagined I could hear him reading *To Kill a Mockingbird* to you. I'm … I'm sorry I made fun of your tastes in books.'

'That's okay, Lydia,' I said, 'I'm sorry, too.'

She reached across for my hand.

I let her take it.

But the truth was, I didn't believe her. Joe dead? I knew what I needed, and it wasn't Thai. It would fill this sudden, yawning chasm that had opened inside me. It would make me feel good.

I rang Zane at work. He seemed surprised. 'Sammy, never at work.'

'All right, but I can't get onto you at home,' I said and was about to hang up.

'Wait,' he whispered. 'Let's go out tonight. Pit. Ten-thirty, *me casa*[1].'

Me casa? The few brief times he'd caught up with me lately, he sure was peppering his talk with foreign words. Now I know this shows my ignorance, but I can't speak any language apart from my own. If I'm reading and the author drops in a sentence in French or a quote in Latin, it's like this real intimate conversation I've been having with them is interrupted when they turn to whisper to a friend behind a hand. Guess that shows my insecurity and I should bloody well just look up the meanings.

Filter was there, spread out in Zane's airport lounge. Zane was on the hash, sucking it through his metal pipe. Filter was chopping up the bar with his pocketknife, one hand bandaged, oddly. Nice-looking pocketknife, though: useful appliances. I'd never really taken note of his pocketknife before. Or had I? Where had I got the idea to give one to Joe?

Joe dead?

When I squeezed between Zane and Filter on the couch, they told me they'd run out of hash.

I picked up the pipe. There was a little dotch. I flicked out the burnt bits with a matchstick. On the carpet I saw a few filings of hash, but I couldn't pick them up with my fingers. Then I saw something to the purpose: the tweezers in Filter's pocketknife.

I got down on the carpet, my eye a microscope, and saved every filigree of hash I could. When I rose up over the coffee table, Zane and Filter were staring at me.

'What?' I asked.

---

[1] Spanish, my house.

A few more shavings of hash in the wood grain – the plastic toothpick from the pocketknife saw to the digging out of those. I'd get a good draw at least.

Zane got up and put on some Stereolab. This was more like it. Beautiful.

I lit the few curls of brown and sucked till my cheeks caved in. Zane and Filter were staring at me. I wheezed out. Not a scent of smoke. I'd swallowed the whole bellows full. The room shifted several degrees to the right. For the first time since the end of the Luke episode, the rush wasn't pleasant, but dislocating. Zane grabbed my unsteady hand. Filter pulled me back onto the couch.

Maybe a hallucinogen wasn't the answer. I needed a euphoric plug. I asked Filter to flip us an E. An E would supercharge the night, like old times.

'I'll square you up later,' I assured him.

Filter didn't answer straight off.

'It's a fookin' journey, these drugs, Sam,' he said at last. 'It's not a journey everyone can take. You're looking at the world, so many ways, most people don't wanna know about.'

'Just an E, Filter?' I said. 'I'm ready for that high again.'

Zane looked at Filter. Filter looked down at his large hands then at me.

'Mate, the other day me and 4play were pill-popping.'

4play was Filter's supplier.

'Without me?'

'You were at cricket, mate. You stick to that. We're the clock-radio controlled automatons, wired up weekdays to turn into weekend warriors. Not you. Now, what happens, right, the first one doesn't kick in. So, what we do? 4play's a supplier, so he's got two more. Well, *he* gets his kicks up, but *I'm* still being cock-teased by the soft-cock. So,

266

what I do? Spend my last bucks on a third. Mates rates and all, but that 4play's still filching me. Anyways, 4play's spastic dancing and I'm in a turmoil, getting the vibration but no buzz. I've gotta have anything – Valium, Temazepam – to knock me out, but 4play doesn't have any concussion grenades, only high explosives. So where'd that leave me on the battlefield? In a pay phone, calling every number on my mobile (no credit left) for a housewife drug.'

'Did you score?'

'For fook's sake, Sam! Me fookin' mother digits are in me mobile. I was so fookin' wired, I still don't know if I called her.'

Filter raised a bandaged hand.

'But I do know this, mate: I wasn't asking down the line; I was fookin' screaming.'

I asked about the hand. He'd cut it smashing the glass. Filter sure had a dark side. Witness the Greenpeace guy whose teeth he wanted to smash.

Zane told me Filter might lose movement in his hand.

'Being a musician, it's vital that Filter – '

But Filter cut Zane off, telling him to hush. There was a dark look between those two, now. Great, wherever I went, I was trouble.

It's so hard to get on top of your game, and I'm not just talking cricket. I mean life. You work out how you're gonna play it, you take the crease, the first few overs are easy, but then the opposition goes and changes tactics! Walking home with Zane from The Pit that night, that night when we'd resolved to enjoy ourselves, and actually did – well, that felt like the start, the start of a mature Sam, a Sam who was finally getting good at life. And here I was, not even a couple of months later, being kept back a year for failing to make the mark.

We wrapped up the night; it wasn't going anywhere.

A whole week passed before Zane, Filter and I reunited, this time at Filter's apartment. In the meantime, I'm embarrassed to say, I got in the habit of getting drunk with Dizzy and some of the other cricketers I didn't like so much. Well, what choice had I? Zane and Filter were becoming real stay-at-homes. The TV would be on next. After a lot of whinging on my part, Filter weeded out some weed for me, which I stuffed into the end of a crumpled cigarette

Someone buzzed the downstairs door. Turned out to be 4play. When he got up to the room, he and Filter did some complicated handshake. Started off like a shake but you slid your hand back, gripped then punched. He gave me a nod. Filter introduced him to me, then to Zane. So those two hadn't met before? Their nod was brief.

4play looked round for a seat but there wasn't one. Zane and I always had to clear away Filter's junk to get a seat. So 4play stood, his clothes making swishing noises. He was wearing a yellow parka and looked like a lilo. He had a chain round his neck and rings prominent as knuckle dusters on his fingers. Filter inquired after a piece 4play had resurrected that day (don't think that's the right lingo, but anyway).

'They've got some mad loops happening, man. That stuff is the shit. Amuck, Aura and Assist were doin' all this freestylin' and stuff, man. It was so cool. Man, you should've seen their groupies. They had joyform tits.'

Zane shook his head.

Filter asked 4play if he'd scored.

'Nah, man, these bitches were skanky as. You needed three condoms on apiece just to fuck the bitches.'

'Pencil dick,' uttered Zane from the corner.

4play swivelled his baseball cap veranda-backwards, scoping Zane in the half-light. Zane hadn't liked Jussy pretty much on sight either. Maybe I should take note this time.

'Yeah, those mother-fucking bitches want 4play bad, man. So what's up with my nigger-bitch, Filter? When you coming Westside again? I gotta come Eastside to dope you up. No money?' asked 4play when Filter remained unmoved. 'What about some bling bling? Nice watch.'

Filter exploded.

'You want me watch, wigga? My fookin' mother gave me that watch!' he shouted, waving his bandaged hand.

4play backed off. Filter proceeded to explain that he wasn't in the 'buying and selling' business anymore. That raised eyebrows from everyone and a few voiced objections from myself. I saw 4play took good notice of those.

'Yeah, well, mah homes, gotta get back to my bitches. They want 4play bad.'

'Yeah, but I bet they wish you'd get down to the fookin'!'

And with that, 4play left.

Zane asked Filter to elaborate. Seemed Filter was venturing into telemarketing. A five-days-a-week, nine-to-five occupation. A former career of selling drugs was the perfect résumé.

I couldn't understand Filter. He was the one who told me that once you wake up to the world, there's no going back to sleep. Yet, here he was, in comatosia. He'd done what he'd dissed all his same-age friends for doing: trading the homey spine for the corporate carapace.

Filter stood up and took off his jacket.

'You don't get it, do you, Sammy? Reason we had a fookin' good time, mate, was 'cause it's rare. Do that every day, mate, I seen it, it's not pretty. It's not fun then. You've got to do it, then let it go.'

'You're the one telling me to stay interested,' I yelled, 'Well, how the fuck do I stay interested now?'

'How do you stay interested, Sam? How da fuck would I know? *I'm* bored.'

'Sam,' interjected Zane. 'Rules to stop yourself from becoming a pedestrian: soon as you get into a routine, change it.'

'Keep interested, mate,' added Filter tersely. 'But other ways.'

He softened almost immediately, like Brie in the microwave, and leaned over, grabbing my elbow.

'We've been living a week in a moment, Sam. We've got to cut back to a day a day.'

A day a day? The very thought made me feel kind of stuck, the way I'd feel at tram-stops, waiting for the next one to come but knowing where it would be going anyway. But what about those moments? Everything momentous, packed with meaning.

'Sammy, darling, there is a flipside to drugs,' put in Zane.

'Yeah, like fucking what?'

Filter and Zane were silent. Eventually Zane answered me.

'Uncontrollable mood swings.'

Uncontrollable …? My hands waved for my attention. The bone had worn through white at the knuckles. So I *was* agitated. Why? I was angry. Very angry. And I knew why.

Joe.

The anger coloured every other emotion. I stubbed out my impromptu joint in a beer bottle top. It was only tobacco left anyway.

Walking home alone, I thought back to that parting at the train station. He'd asked about Arny – whether he was 'the one'.

He'd also said something I couldn't process at the time.

'If I'd found "the one" in Melbourne, Sam, I could go back. That would give me the courage. Arny's lucky. I haven't found *my* Sam.'

I stopped, two houses from my front door, a sword falling through my centre. No, it wasn't fair to put to me what I didn't realise at the time was an ultimatum. I wasn't going to be anyone's reason for living … or not. It wasn't fair – I didn't believe in 'the one' – and I hated him.

I rang Filter, leaving a message on his mobile about that months-old promise to accompany him to the gym. It was about the tenth message I'd left without reply. So much for *that* resolution. I buzzed Zane next, at work. I could hear the rustle of his hand cupping the mouthpiece.

'Sammy, I only gave you this number for emergencies.'

'What's the story with corporate Filter?' I asked.

'I guess he wants a steady job.'

Zane sounded so different when he was at work. Neutral tone.

'What about his music?' I asked.

'He's made his decision.'

Zane obviously didn't want this to be a long conversation.

'Dinner?' I said, hopeful. I needed to get out of the house.

'No.'

'No?'

The real Zane came back.

'Sammy, darling, it's Spanish class tonight.'

Silence.

'Tell you what, I'll meet you at The Pit afterwards. *Hablo a menudo de Vd.*[2]

Whatever. I hung up.

On the way, I ran into 4play, still dressed as a human lifeboat.

'What's the story with Filter?' he asked. 'I called his digits. "Hi, you've rung Timothy Bain at LectraVision." Timothy Bain!'

I'd heard the same message myself when trying to get onto so-called 'Filter'. The truth is always plainer.

'You chasin'?' asked 4play.

I told him drugs had stopped having the desired effect on me.

'Maybe you need to up the dosage,' said 4Play.

Matter, though generally distributed throughout the cosmos …

Objects fighting for space.

Can you hear me? LIFT OFF. Counting down now. Your decision?

You decide. Your decision? You decide. Counting down now.

FIVE, FOUR, THREE – counting down – ONE, IGNITION –

Blast!

It wasn't kicking in.

Zane eyed me carefully.

We were at the The Pit, Pulse Night For Men, standing at the railing, looking down at the rice cooker. There was this one, long, slim piece of picturesque youth bopping about with a girl.

---

[2] Spanish: I often speak of you.

272

'You like that one, Sammy?' asked Zane.

'Him!' I laughed. 'Oh God no. He's just come out and that girl he's dancing with – *she's* his supportive sister. He's all in the flush of excitement – he thinks he's over the one and only hurdle in his life – coming out. Give him a while. He'll be bitter and twisted. He still thinks being gay is exciting.'

Zane laughed. 'I *am* your father.'

We both played up to that. I can do a pretty good Darth Vader voice, and what with Zane breathing heavily, it kept us going for a few secs, but then it kind of wheezed away. We just watched the lights and dancing. I popped my second pill. Zane frowned. Then spoke.

'The gay world isn't holding much for me any more, Sammy. Oh, when I was young and gorgeous. But now I'm a fat bitch. And taking boys home – who can be bothered? It just means messy sheets and no sleep. What will I do when I'm too old for the clubs?'

I suddenly got frightened. I remembered that time we'd made an effort, and how everyone had been attracted to us.

'We're not slipping backwards, are we, Zane?'

Zane pushed himself away from the railing into a standing position.

'Sammy, we're like a dog that's been de-sexed. It still tries to rut the bitch called Life, but it just isn't getting the same pleasure out of it. Taking drugs in the park, those nights here at The Pit, when we worked to make it work … well, time to find the newer something to do, Sammy.'

No, not yet. I wasn't ready to say goodbye. What was taking so long with that first pill? The forty-five minutes were well and truly up.

'Life isn't very literary,' I whinged.

'You shouldn't read so much, Sammy. *Pocos libros hay que le sean útiles*[3].

'What's with all the French?' I asked him.

'Spanish.'

'Well, Spanish then. Are you planning on …?'

Zane's guilty smile was answer enough.

That's why he was doing the Spanish classes.

Started hanging out with 4play after that. Had to, with Zane and Filter turning adult overnight. Smoked dope, popped pills, got up to mischief. Broke into the *Nylex* tower. When I say 'broke in', I mean we climbed a fence and hurdled through a window, nothing smashed or jimmied. I got to the very top, looking out over the neon sign. Kind of poetic; or would've been if it wasn't for 4play and his wiggas below, talking their 'gangsta rap'. Could've kept going back, except Happy – one of 4play's space-monkeys, that's what he called his 'crew' – smashed some of the brewery piping on the way down. Next night, the spaces in the steps you swung under were already welded over.

It was adrenalin-etched so far as its illegality, but not profound. All action, no subtext. The life of books? A grunge novel, maybe.

Next night, we hooked up at Richmond Station. The 7 o'clock Flinders Street hauled in, a spitfire spray down the tracks: the result of 4play's starter-caps taped to the rails (4play had bummed the starter-caps off Filter – he no longer needed them, apparently). The bangs washed the commuters the other side of the platform. With the cops and MetGestapo on-scene and occupied, our gang caught the train going the opposite direction, to Prahran. Never seen a more efficient demolition squad, like a nest of

---

[3] Spanish: There are few books which are of use to you.

termites in a block of wood. First, two of them prized the doors open; another ripped the top off a Coke can and shoved it under one of the doors, preventing them from closing. Next, a blade withdrawn and the rubber cut out of a window. The glass sucked in, a plastic bag over a face. Then the glass swallowed whole, leaving the mouth of night gasping. 4play ordered me, his mate Happy and another space-monkey to take a corner each of a seat. We rocked it till it broke, and started carrying it. Then I saw where to.

'Hey, wait …'

Too late, it was out the window.

That night, 4play offered me a new drug. At least it was new to me. But I'd seen the face of someone who well and truly knew it: Kev, Cinder's boyfriend, all those months back.

'Wanna try some horse, Sam?'

Back at the oval in the morning, we played another match. A duck. My fourth in a row. I was setting records, just all the wrong ones. Tubby left me at my locker. I glanced round at a poster that caught my attention. It was moving! Calming down, I saw it wasn't a poster; it was the window, and the coach was motioning me to come outside.

He took me to the stands, the ones where the wooden planks on the seat are each painted a different colour. Scrolling colour bars on a dodgy set.

'Not getting enough sleep there, Big Feller?' asked the coach, his sausage dog limbs tiny at the joints.

I cocked my head.

'You've got more rings under your eyes than I have in my bathtub.'

I'd say he only noticed my eyes 'cause I'd drawn attention to them myself. There was a strand of hair I kept pulling at.

The coach leaned forward.

'I'm going to have to let you go, Sam.'

Go? I leant back an equal distance to that which he'd leant in. Going would probably mean having to go back home. I didn't have the job at the library any more and my boss at the video store was hinting at doing my shifts to cut back on wages. Going home would mean starting again. All over. Finding another escape route.

'One more chance?' I asked, still pulling at that strand of damn hair.

The coach stood up, scoped me a second longer, and walked away.

The hair over my eye wasn't a hair at all but the shadow of a power cord looping from the speaker in the stand to a pole ten metres away. Hallucinations when *not* on drugs?

At home, Tash and Jen confronted me about some money that had gone missing. Tash had put it on the table as her contribution for the water bill. I shrugged and went into my room.

Sitting on my mattress, I looked at the lone needle mark on my arm. I'd watched 4play cut open the plastic that contained the syringe, so I was safe there.

And I remembered back to when I'd asked Filter about heroin. It wasn't long after that night we'd seen the drag queen. And it wasn't long after I'd asked about heroin, that he and Zane started dissociating themselves from me. Maybe that was why.

It was at Filter's, the three of us smoking hash.

'Filter, if E gives you such a high, what must horse be like?'

Filter sat up on his bed.

'Horse?' he laughed. 'Ha, he's even got the lingo?' he said to Zane. He then turned back to me again. 'Mate, wot you talking about horse for? You don't wanna know the ho' slow.

'Have *you* known slow?'

He started to rap to the theme, hitting his drums.

'Have I known the ho' slow? In my veins like water in drains, collecting, pooling, suspecting? The needle tip, the love of it? Oh god yes, the ultimate slut to get you in the rut. As soon as she's yours, you're *her* whore. That very street corner you've bought her on, you'll meet, you're gone. Nothing else matters. Nothing at all. And you'll lie because she's the only truth. O God, I wanted her. I wanted her, to be with her – *her*, I wanted. To be us, us two, together, forever, then dead together. Dead. I wanted to be fed then fled. I wanted to be *her*, and *her* me, but each of us surprising, a mystery. I wanted her to know me at my best and the rest? – the rest, shed. I wanted, wanted, more than I wanted, to want, to wonder, to know the ho' slow.'

He stopped beating his drums.

'Thank god for soft-serve drugs to part-fill the hole. If I had to be completely clean, I'd go mad with this scene.'

And he toked his metal pipe. Zane was staring at me worriedly from his dark corner.

'Sammy, darling, I wish I'd never introduced you to drugs.'

Filter exhaled, his face turning serious and angry. He turned from Zane to me, worry also on his face.

'Mate, what you talking about the ho' slow for? Humans – we're not meant to feel that good. Ever.'

Chapter Nine

4play opened the bag of magic mushrooms. He and Happy examined them, trying to suss out if they'd picked the genuine articles. There were all these checks: right colour, right cap, right shape. Their stalks were meant to go blue-vein or something when picked. If you got it wrong and picked a deadly toadstool, you could die. Filter had refused to pick the mushrooms with 4play, apparently, to show him what to look for. He didn't want the 'responsibility'.

'Yeah, no, they're right,' said Happy.

It was night and we were in that park with the kiddies' fort – a touch 4play had stolen from Filter.

We chewed down the mushrooms, and started walking. Walking would pump the blood through our systems and bring on the trip faster, according to 4play. Filter had always warned about forcing the feeling.

'Sammy D,' smiled 4play, 'Mr L L Filtrated water, Monsieur H_2O to go, on the rocks with his cock's sock unmatched, says your sideways snatch can bust some mad rhymes?'

Mad rhymes? What was he talking about? Where were we going?

My world was unhinging, 4play's impinging. We trod the bitumen path, green grass leaning over the edges like the front rows of a mosh pit onto a stage. Maybe this was a bad idea.

'So watcha gonna teach us?' shouted 4play. 'Can you reach us? Tell us about your crumbed sausage sex on the beaches, the beats, the heat, the snap, the thaw. Come on, yo! I can smell that liverwurst breath, 'cause you been suckin' on the dick of death!'

'Large it up, dawg,' laughed Happy.

They were talking about me, weren't they?

And the pace, the race? Why were we walking so fast, our fleet-footed hooves flinting fire? A thousand coconut castanets. Or was it the cicadas, disguised as leaves in the trees beside us?

'Man, Filter said you had some mad rhymes, but you're mad wak. Happy, give him a few more toadstools.'

'No, I …'

'And another, yo.'

I stuffed them down.

'Happy, start your beatbox.'

The trees were at my knees, the path river-wide. Hurtling, hurrying forward. Whoosh-whoosh, the wind.

'Don't you know it!' said 4play. 'He's all hush. You gotta own it, Sam!'

Needed to get home. Tried to break my steam-engine legs, the endless rotations. A lilo hand grabbed me, coupling me in front.

'Hello, ah no, don't you go. Come back to the community where you got immunity. Let's hear your rub-a-dub-dub, back scrubber.'

Back scrubber?

'Filter reckons you can rhyme more lyrical than the spiritual Mr Me. But I don't see it, no.'

Feet spinning. Locked between the two.

'My chin tastes funny,' laughed Happy, licking his chin.

Carried up the bank, getting to an intersection, stopped at the crossing.

Had that car been waiting too long at the lights? It had, hadn't it? Oh God, maybe they were onto us. Don't panic, Sam, don't. They don't. 4play and Happy seem snappy. Don't let on. Don't. A panic of you (in you) could beset a panic of them and you – don't.

Surely the lights had changed ten times already, and still the car waiting? It was onto us, they were onto us. How many? I counted ten faces too many, all looking out that car's windows.

Did Joe go too fast or did he mean to crash? Put away your stash.

I scream, they scream, we all scream for – I scream!

'Yo, honky! Wazzup?' asked 4play, the human road hazard sign in his fluoro yellow. His yellow peril. Reaching out with lollypop hand, dragging me across the zebra steam-rolled flat, Happy flat-chat behind us, the city lights flashed red-green, red-green. Only a quarter of the way across the road, the green-man intersection to go.

It must be green, that light, by now, and still the car waiting? They were onto us. No, wait! Moving, gaining speed, disappearing, gone.

'Come on, niggas, let's cross.'

But now, what's this?

Watch those fence palings, each a sentry box. And now that boom gate, a Checkpoint Charlie. See that man with the machine gun, rat-a-tat-tat? 4play jamming a twenty-cent coin in the boom arm. Ring ring ring, slow train, colour of dust for fingerprints. Not mine, oh not mine. Don't let that rail blow.

'You'll kill them!'

Why'd we drop that chair out the train window?
Where'd it fall?

'Where what?' asked Happy. Where had his eyebrows
flown?

Wiping the boom arm of my prints. Boom arm? Wait,
this no high-wall, barbwire, border crossing. No, that,
Sam, that's the railway crossing. And that? That is the
wind's hissing, between and off afar. It's okay, okay? Man
with the machine gun is just a signal box with a circle
head.

Must be dead.

'Quick,' yelled 4play.

Ducking down an alley, 'The pigs!' squealed Happy.

The pigs, oink, oink? Sirens sidling past streets like
parents past doors, looking in to wish you asleep. Me,
4play, Happy crouched down and overshadowed in the
eaves. The factory walls in permanent high-falls.

'Wow the constabulary with your vocabulary, Sammy
D,' said 4play.

'Pardon?'

'I said, even Jesus got a hard-on.'

'Pardon?'

'Yeah, seeing what your ma done!'

4play and Happy standing up now, the sirens faded. Me
still foetus-scared, balled up on pavement.

This wasn't that high-tide poetry of the first time, with
Zane and Filter, feeling the moment momentous, packed
with meaning, but that last time with them, pulling hand
guns on lovers innocent, indiscriminate bullying. Where
had the poetry gone, gone to?

They were laughing about me, weren't they? Tried to
wipe my face. Where's my hand? I moved my hand, I'm
sure, but it hasn't moved …? Paralysed! Oh my God. No,

there it goes. Time delay? The whole world stopped? Or just me, falling behind in the past? *Can* see 4play, Happy, steps ahead, but put on pause, shimmering.

And someone else? The third who walks beside them. Get up, Sam. Follow. Who's that someone else?

Me …?

Seeing … me, externally!

Richmond Industrial area, that's where we are. Smell the hops. 'Carlton United' ushers the way. Okay, so I know where I am, but where am I? Still outside myself. Pizza tossing views, 4play, Happy, back, side, profile, front. All at once. Too much, too much! Multiple flipping realities. Somewhere, something eats. Possum in the garbage. Sound so loud, can't hear the others. Possum so far away but sound so loud.

Get back to your body, Sam. Don't fall behind.

My eyes about my ankles, my ankles at my waist.

Can't feel my body, can't feel, keep that boy walking, pull that puppet string persona. Looking down a black tunnel of myself, seeing Happy a little circle at the end.

'You there?' he asks.

'Keep … keep … keep talking. Say normal … say.'

And he talks, but it's as mad as me.

So afraid. Get through that tunnel. Almost at my nose, a pink/black line – like when you go cross-eyed. Nearly there. It's okay, okay? Keep looking at 4play, looking at the tree, Happy at the ready.

Where are we now? A park. A park where?

Forgetting, forgetting, oh God, already. Where am I? Where? There am I, there. Two steps behind myself, out of body. You can make it back to yourself, Sam.

How does the foggy universe of atoms …

How does …

Become the tangible world of things and people?

Lost in light. Dissipating.

Get through it, Sam, get through this, don't miss ...

Miss what? Just keep walking.

Don't lose 4play and Happy, don't. Out of the park, in the city. Pedestrians are there, their streams forward and back. Can see where they've been and are, and were. Did Joe swerve? Miss, Sam, miss them. Stay in the present.

Keep walking behind 4play, Happy. Keep them in sight.

Back in alleys, the dark, not much easier.

'Can we sit, please, sit?'

'My head feels funny,' said Happy. 'Oh look, your ears are falling off. Lulla-lulla-la.'

It's not funny. This ain't funny, this.

Get that seat to solidify before sitting on it, Sam. Everything peeling away. Doily shadows on walls, the plaster, bricks, the whole world transparent. Seeing to the horizon in every direction, seeing through people, houses, trees!

Choking visually.

Help, help, help!

'Man, everything's dripping,' said 4play. We were all going mad, were we? We were. Grabbing Happy.

'We're in trouble?'

'Trouble double! No man, this is cool!'

Cool? Coolly dooly. They were okay.

'This is mad clean,' said 4play.

They were okay, just me, then, me. My nose in focus then ... then ...

Back inside myself! There I am – no, here I am – with ... With who?

Couch-dancing on the seat, 4play and Happy dancing, before me, I must ask: 'Um, excuse me, but ... but how do I know you?'

'You shitting me?' cried 4play.

'How do I know you two?'

'Uh oh,' smiled Happy, 'don't do this to me. You're spinning me out.'

'No, please, how do I know you?'

'This must be that mad shit Filter said you hang on people,' said 4play.

'Filter? How do I … know *him* …? Who knows who of you two?'

'Who knows who? We know you!' they laughed, Acca Dacca-style.

But still the questions. How do I know you two? Who do I know you through? What do I know that's true? What do I know?

Who am I?

Who *am* I!

I don't even know that. No, this isn't happening. Think it through. Who am I? Begins with … No, no, no, sounds like … like … tram. Can I remember? I was born, that much … And one time – four, I think it was – discarding my floaties, I jumped in a pool, sinking all the way to the bottom and as the water filled my lungs, I felt myself forgetting before I had much to remember. How peaceful it was. I can't believe how peaceful it was. But this time, peddling the water, cycling the waves, chopped up with surf, not wanting to drown eternally, I was yanked up, Dirk my brother, a first slap of baby breath bringing me to the norm. 'Hey, hey, can you hear me …?'

Yes, can you hear me (prompting him) …?

'Sam!'

Oh, thank God.

My name is Sam. Sam the man on hand at hand, the man is Sam.

Going down an escalator, metal monsters screaming past. We're in the underground now, Sam. Hang in there. Happy scabbing money for chips. Reaching in pockets. Shaking the machine. Packet of Doritos.

Happy and I munching them down. For some reason, 4play not eating. He and Happy sharing looks, with 4play shaking his head. After, hearing him ask Happy, 'You can get Hep B from sharing saliva with them, can't you?' That meant me, didn't it? Did it? Hid it – had I hid it? That I *knew* knew. That I knew that they knew that I knew what they did? Had I kept it hid?

Getting on the train, swaying in at a million pounds.

This is the world.

What world?

This is the world that God built. Who built? He built. And these are the men who cry in the night

– Because they are lorn

Who cry in the night

– From dark to dawn

Who love and hate

– With equal scorn

Yes these are the men that,

armed to the hilt,

destroy the world

that God built.

What built? *He* built. Who? Was He listening, listening to my thoughts? Get out of my head! Telling the girl on the train, it wasn't fair, didn't she know it was rude to listen in to other people's thoughts? Her getting up and moving away. 4play, Happy laughing. When will this stop? Her huddling by the doors. When will I think straight again? When?

Then …? 4play, Happy, dragging me off the train.

'Filter reckons you got mad rhyming style,' said 4play. 'But you're just fronting like you're all that. But me? My style's like butta. It's so good I gotta spread it round. You ain't jack shit.'

'You dissing him?' said Happy.

'Shak his world,' said 4play to Happy. 'Boo-yakka,' he yelled at me. 'Give the cunt chop chop, yuk yuk. That guy's a lick. Oi, flosser? You think you're so dope, but you're a no-hope, fuckin' joke!'

I recoiled.

'Ha! Sook.'

'4play, man!' said Happy, putting a hand on his mate's lilo. 4play shook it off.

'Happy, there's a difference between a surf*er* and a surf*ie*.'

Up the ramp, outside again, feet so sore. No longer night. Cold porridge clouds. The day in segments. Morning. The sun was comeuppance.

'You okay, man?' asked Happy, reaching to light a cigarette, 4play reaching to bum one off him.

'I was … it was hard,' I tried to say.

'You seemed fine.'

'It was … I'm okay.'

And I tried to walk away. Happy nudged 4play.

'Yo!' shouted 4play. 'Big ups to my man, Sammy D. That guy gets nuff rezpect. He's fresh. Got mad style. Dope. Made.'

He gripped my hand. I untangled it.

'Increase the peace,' called Happy behind me.

Got away. Hadn't let on. Finding a supermarket. In the supermarket. What for? What am I doing? Here for … Heretofore I'd been here to … Which aisle? Noodles, sauces, pickles. Shopping to shop. What is that music? Why does it sing so softly, Softly, Baby Powder, Fabulon?

Can't take that can. Can't take the second last can-can, tinned-soup, spaghetti. Who's the one left gonna dance with? How's he gonna cope? Can't take the last, man. Can't, shan't, won't, varmint.

Doggone it, darn it. Which aisle? So many. Getting escorted out, don't shout.

'Should we call the cops?' a big man's saying, Brilliantine swells piled mile high on that impossible head.

Am I dead?

'I'm okay – okay.'

Them sparring, me hooking back the light. Them against the sun, two broad boats, sailing on.

Sitting on the concrete, something real. Feel it, Sam, it's real. Baked so hot, so hard, it must be real. It must be, mustn't it?

And I knew the black-backed reality of the thing.

And I knew its sound and I knew its ring.

That it was real and that I was alive.

That if time was infinite then none could be dead longer than another.

That the great-great grandson would be dead as long as his great-great-grandmother.

That is, if time were infinite.

Getting up, hitting a bin. Clink.

'Twenty cents for your empty bottles.'

That is, if there were an infinite number of bottles – and there were – if there were an infinite number of bottles hanging on the wall, an infinite number of bottles hanging on the wall, and one such bottle should accidentally fall, then there'd be an infinite number of bottles still hanging on the wall.

Getting back to the flat. Bottles of this. Cellared memory number ten. A good year, that, that year Dad pulled him from under the house, the feral kitten, black and brown like a wooden cupboard with half the paint stripped back. The mother shot dead. The other kittens drowned in a bucket, him too if I hadn't cried out.

'Your brothers aren't blubbin',' he said.

'Give it to him, Neil.'

Dad looked at Mum, Mum at Dad. Dad kneeled down, kitten held by the scruff of the neck. Me taking it in my arms. Dad standing. Kitten clawing my arms and biting me. Blood starting out on my hand. A yelp, from me. Dad turning round, stepping forward, frowning, picking up the bucket. Me stepping back, him reaching for the kitten, it biting harder. My hand hurting, having to let the hurt out, but this time with a yap like I was happy.

'It's not a pup,' said Dad, and he put the bucket back down. I breathed out. My palm was wet. Little streams of red welled up between my fingers. I pressed them close together to stop the flow, worried Dad could see but he turned round and emptied the bucket out over by the dam. My brothers went off after him, picking up sticks for something to poke with. I put my hand over the kitten's eyes at that. Mum saw and smiled. When I took my hand away, the kitten had a little red mask. That got me laughing, for real that time.

A little red mask?

A little red bath? A little pink?

I got the blade out of my razor.

Zorro was a great kitten and a better cat. That's the way I'd wanted it with me. All right now, but nicer later. Somehow it had all gone awry. Why?

Yet …?

Yet Zorro was the best you could get.

Used to be a real terror, but. Hardly ever purred. You had to pat and pat and pat him before there was even a chance of getting a sound out of 'im. And then it would come, usually by scratching under his chin: that bit where the jaw meets in a triangle, right up – oh well, you know. You'd pat and pat and pat and then this little growl. So soft, it was. Like trying to hear your own heart beating. But it was there. You'd win and you'd feel so happy.

And then guess what he would do? This Zorro? He'd have had enough so he'd just scratch you. Or bite. That was it. That was his way of telling you, 'Thanks again, Sam, but don't push it.'

Later, Dad would see all the red dots and dashes on my arm and tell me to give the cat a good belting next time it happened. I know my brothers did, but it didn't go back to them much after that. Anyhow, I didn't reckon I wanted to follow after them. Being youngest, you've got to set out on your own. No, I had a better way. I'd take Zorro up to the cubby house and talk it out with him. How it wasn't so nice. How we could be the best of friends, Zorro and me, Defenders of Justice. Anyways, I thought of those dots and dashes on my arm as Zorro's way of communicatin' something. Morse code for cats, if you like. So I'd read away – for hours. It said all this stuff about what he'd get up to – mostly at night, it was. Used to just sleep in the day. But boy, what nights he'd have! Going down by the creek, exploring in the caves, climbing the trees and scratching at the sliver of moon like it was the lighted rim of a manhole onto the sky.

Zorro.

Geez, I loved that cat. He did his own thing. Never needed anyone.

Or so I thought. 'Cause Zorro was a different kitten a year later. Well, he was a cat now. It didn't happen all at

289

once but so slow it was hard to notice; but he changed. He used to sit up with me on the couch, when I was watching the telly or something. He'd sit on the armchair, a yellow thing if I recollect right, and with him being mostly black and all, he looked like one of those Egyptian cats. Bast, I think. Some sort of god, anyway, but regal as all hell. There he'd sit – didn't matter how uncomfortable (he could be bridging two armchairs with a Grand Canyon gap between them), and still he'd look like you couldn't ruffle him in a million years. He was the king, cool as could be.

Even Mum and Dad took a liking to him in the end. They used to call out, 'Zorro, Zorro, here pussy.'

Here pussy? That wasn't how you talked to Zorro! You couldn't expect anything out of him if you spoke like that. What you had to do was, was totally ignore the terror. Not even look his way. Never say a word. And then, you'd be getting into the TV, there he was – on your lap!

And that's how he'd changed. He no longer bit or scratched when you patted him. Gone was the Morse code for cats.

But then, just when things seemed done, they undid.

Because there were lumps in Zorro's stomach.

'Yes,' said Mum, 'I'm afraid so. This is probably the beginning of the end, Sam. It's hard coming into this world and it's hard going out of it.'

Mum made an appointment for the vet's at five, the last one for the day. It was ten at the time. That gave me seven hours minus travel to spend with Zorro.

I gave Zorro all his drugs at once. It pepped him up no end. He was on a high.

It was 10:30 am. Had obviously been a long night for Jen and Tash, who still weren't in. An even longer night for me. I headed out of the house and looked for the swankest eatery I could find on Lygon Street.

Knew I'd get a hiding – stealing those chicken wings from the fridge for Zorro. But it was worth it, worth it for Zorro. He had his appetite back for the first time. Only ate half of what he used to, but he damn near purred doing it.

12 midday. Tiramisu. Love that dessert. Figured I'd splash out on a meal. Couldn't afford it but what would it matter? I worked out my ideal order and pretty much got most of it. It was early for lunch but I could stretch it.

I took Zorro to his favourite spot. He was a funny cat 'cause he would go for walks with you, but at a distance. I tried to put him on the lead one time but he clawed into the ground and I gave up. If he wanted to walk behind, that was okay. You'd stop for him to catch up, but he'd just stop as well, those ten or more metres back. The whole boogieman in the park thing.

2:30. Not much time. I paid my bill, over-tipping. I tried to think what would be *my* favourite place. I reckoned it would be the same spot as Zorro's but since I was about a million miles from where I grew up it'd have to be in the city somewhere. Finally I opted for the top of the Manchester Unity building. Love that place. The bit I like best isn't the view so much as the air-conditioner thing. Unit, I guess. It's this round can-like thing with another round-can-like thing on top, separated by stilts. It's wonderfully green and the whole bottom of the second can drips all over and down into the coffee-filter-type thing on the bottom one. Pretty futuristic. A legionnaires hell, probably, but a bit special.

Zorro's favourite place was this gum with just two branches shaped like the legs of an athlete doing a cartwheel. You could see all the red/brown scratches in the blue/white bark. I helped him up and he pricked it more than ripped.

3pm. I looked over the side of the building but it fell away onto the street. And already it was pretty busy with the pre-5-o'clock crowd, the school kids buying milkshakes at Maccas, and the suits getting in some beers before home-time TV.

4pm. Sitting in the living room as Mum laid out a rug in the back of the car, Zorro in my lap. The drugs wearing off. I gave him that pat he liked. Up under the chin, but ever so gentle.

4:10pm. Home again. Jen and Tash still out. Good. No one knew I was there.

4:15pm. Carrying Zorro out to the car wrapped in his favourite blanket. The car taking off. Mum avoiding every pothole, going slow over each bump. I wanted to read to Zorro but I didn't have a book.

4:40pm. Sun almost dead. Turned on just the lamps in my room and looked about for my favourite book, *To Kill a Mockingbird*. Couldn't read all of it. There wasn't time.

So I just looked at the cover. I love the cover: orange, with a kid's picture of a bird and black titles. Joe and me liked those best. Books without pictures on the front, I mean, unless they're picture books of course and that's different. Don't ask me why. Just 'cause. Anyhow, this had a good cover. Bare, you see. Some aren't, and that's bad. The ones with 'artists' impressions' – we don't like those. I had a copy of *Bridge to Terabithia* with the cover ripped off 'cause it was all wrong. Gave me the irrits. The forest, Jess, Leslie – it wasn't them. Somehow, if you draw one of these people in books, they're less alive, not more so. Can't say why, exactly. I guess … Well, once something's made flesh it's mortal. Christ, I'm glad I never slung that crap at Joe. He'd think he had a chance with me. Now take Joe, while we're onto him. If ever they publish this malarkey, I'm gonna tell them not to put any pictures on the cover. Not even Joe. Might sell the damn thing but no, forget it. You've probably got your own idea of how we shape up and that's enough. That's better. Well, for me anyhow.

4:45. Coming into the town. Getting to the vet's.

4:50. Putting down *To Kill a Mockingbird*. Not much time.

4:55. The vet letting out a lady with her lame dog. The vet saying to me, 'We can just take him for you.'
I held Zorro closer. 'Mum, I want to be there.' Mum nodding. Us both going in.

4:56. Lifting the blade off the bathroom sink.

4:57. Lifting Zorro onto the bench, still in his rug. The vet shaving his leg, putting in the cannulas.

4:58. The bath almost full.

4:59. The vet flicking the needle. Mum asking if I wanted to leave. 'No, I have to be there, right to the end.'
'Okay, Sam.'

293

5:00. The needle going in. Zorro sagging into my arms. I wanted so much for me to be the last thing he saw, but his head twisted up to the ceiling and white.

5:00. One slash and pain. Searing red pain.
All pain.
Dead.

For a long time there was just blackness.

Then a voice, mum's voice, reading *To Kill a Mockingbird*.

When she finished the last page, I asked her what happened next.

'What do you mean?' she asked back.

'Mum, what happens to Scout an' Jem an' Boo an' all the rest of 'em? I reckon Scout just had to've become a lawyer. Well, did she?'

Mum put down the book and got up.

'It's just a story. Nothing happened afterwards.'

And it was like she'd killed them.

Was I still asleep? Above I heard a herd of horses.

And all those castanets going clickety-clop. I wanted to shoo the horses off the roof, but Dad said it wouldn't be right. All that red-righteous clay, clinkering to pieces, mum wouldn't be happy. Better clear your head, Sam, said Dad. I can do something about it then. If they're the facts … Fact is … What?

'Hello, hello?'

Someone slapping my arm.

'Hello, hello. Can you hear us? Tell us your name.'

Someone slapping my face.

'Your name?'

'Zorro.'

294

Dead grass like straws. I was walking in the grass back on the farm, but an adult now. Jen walked up to me, counter-clockwise to the current. Here was someone from my present drop-parachuted to a pozzie in my past.

'Sam,' she said, '95% of how people see you, is how you see yourself. So it's in your hands. How do you see you?'

I've been a ... (but my lips weren't moving).

'Who do you see?'

I've been a baggage handful. (But I couldn't mouth a word.)

Jen smiled sweetly and laughed, but gently, stepped over to third-slip position and was gone.

Zane on the scene now. Zane! Couldn't imagine *him* being sporty but he even had the gloves on – wicketkeeping. 'Sammy, darling, I hate to break it to you like this, but living *is* fighting. At the end of the day, there's no choice but to cope.'

'I've been a ...'

'Yes, Sammy?'

'I've been a baggage handful.'

Suddenly he too was gone. The oval was earth-wide, the pitch pitched passed grief. Arny at the other end now! I asked him what was happening. It was getting too scary.

'You stepped back on your stumps, Sam. It *is* still Sam's Sam ...?'

'Arny,' I tried to tell him, 'if I had known what you had known ...' but fumbled straightaway. I tried again. 'Arny, if you had been ... I mean, if we had seen ...'

'Sam's Sam,' laughed Arny, tut-tutting.

I tried for the last time. 'Arny, if *I* had known what *you* had known, there and then ...'

'Where and when, Sam?' laughed Arny. 'Every day's today.'

295

And he was away, gone too far down the pitch to see. I was at his end and Filter at mine, bat in hand.

'What you doing, Samster? Stepping back on your own stumps, mate. You had to go through this, Sam. Someone can say to you, some oldie can say to you, don't expect too much, mate. Now you know the sense of it, you can see what he means, but it's all brain, right? You've got to expect a hell of a lot of things first, thinking things are your right, just 'cause you're you and all, and get a million disappointments in the process. And *then* you think back to that oldie, and what he said, and for the first time it's real to you, 'cause you've lived through it, and you think why couldn't you bloody well have shown me that then and there and saved me a lot of bovver? But of course he couldn't. He knew that himself, but he was trying, mate.'

The whole Pip and Estella thing.

Where was Joe in this line-up? I wanted to see him, for him to answer a few questions. Was he down by the boundary line? Off the field for a moment?

Another noise, someone behind me. Tubby bringing out drinks. 'Man, this shit ain't right. They've called the third umpire.'

Tubby had a hand to his neck, as if caressing a gunshot wound; he was nervous.

The third umpire? So was I.

'Man, this is fucked up. They're replaying it every way. Back and forth. Fast forward, rewind, slow-motion. When are they going to make a bloody decision?'

'What's happened?' I asked Tubby, but my voice was so shaky it came out a slur.

'Man, they're saying you stepped back on your own stumps.'

My stomach heaved upwards through a tube.

Tubby was looking at the replay. Again and again. A sound was building in my ears, loud, unbearable.

I heard a siren, then I saw a green light.

They'd reached their verdict.

Not out.

Somewhere down near the botanicals, there was a siren. An ambulance siren. Like a noise sticking out in the night. A siren with me in it.

As I lay in the stretcher, the ambo sitting next to me kept looking out the back window, but he knew I was coming to, pretty groggily. I kept trying to hook his eye but he kept turning away. I wanted to say something and all. I knew I'd put a lot of people out. I'd wanted to not put people out anymore. And here I was, twice the nuisance I used to be. So I was pretty grateful and all, if not for the actual rescue, then at least for the thought.

'Can't even get this right,' I said, opting for humour.

The ambo finally looked at me then quickly to the two guys in front. They were busy with the road. The ambo leaned over me and whispered.

'You're too bloody right about that, mate,' he said. 'You know where I should be right now?'

I couldn't say anything. He went on.

'Saving the life of someone *actually* in need.'

And I kind of wanted to die, for the second time that night.

'Man, I'm so guilty over you. What you go and do that for?' asked Filter when he and Zane visited the hospital.

'No more pills for you, Sammy,' said Zane, slapping down the other side of the bed.

'Too right,' added Filter, slapping my thigh for good measure. 'You, my son, you've got talent, with a capital T. Gold capped at that. Now, you know what I'm up to when I say, Filter here is having a bat, but you, my boy, you're doing the real thing, whipping the willow.'

Zane smiled at me, but I had to take Filter up on his claim. I hadn't told him about my form slump. I'd only told him about my previous batting prowess. The good, never the bad.

'You've never even seen me play,' I countered.

'Hey, bitch, I don't need to.' And Filter got up to walk to the window.

'Sammy, darling,' said Zane, 'I know I give boys the impression I can live without them, but it's just a front. I've taken up niceness. Hang in there, sista, 'cause you're one of the tough ones!'

Zane got up and puffed my pillows for me. Filter was staring out the window.

'We heard about your friend Joe,' said Filter. 'Was it that or the drugs that made you … made you go over the edge, Sam?'

I'd been avoiding thinking about Joe ever since I heard of his death. Actually, even earlier, when we parted for the last time. I didn't know the answer but I could see Filter and Zane needed to. They had their own issues of conscience. If my behaviour was due to the latter reason, drugs, how much were *they* responsible?

'I don't know,' I answered as truthfully as I could. 'Both, neither.'

This seemed to ease Filter's mind. Zane's, too, from the way he breathed out long and hard.

'Hey, saw a top piece of graff, Sam,' laughed Filter. 'Know what it said? "Don't take drugs … eventually." Ha!'

When his belly stopped wobbling, I asked Filter why he'd dissociated himself from me and Zane. It was pretty hard the way he'd turned his back on me.

'Getting off drugs isn't just about not taking them, Sam. It's getting away from the atmosphere. And you were just too much fun to trip with.'

Was that a good enough excuse? I looked down at the white bed sheet and thought about the company *I'd* been keeping lately. After me, 4play, Happy & Co. threw that seat out of the moving train into the Yarra below, I spent the next few days at Jen's library trawling through every newspaper article I could, just to make sure it hadn't hit anyone. The private school kids row along that river.

There were no reported injuries.

I was worried 'cause I remembered a story from a few years before about a couple of kids, not even teenagers, dropping stones off a highway overpass. One stone smashed a small hole through a car windscreen, hitting the male driver in the chest and stopping his heart.

We do a lot of stupid things when we're young. Most of us get away with them.

'Sam?'

I looked up from the white bed sheet. Zane and Filter were staring at me. When I explained I was thinking about those kids on the highway overpass, Filter left the ward for a moment, saying he was getting a drink. Zane got up. I joined him by the window, feeling the stitches pull on my wrists when I rested my hands on the sill. It was like I was wearing a long-sleeved shirt when I wasn't. Filter ambled back in.

'Mate, that was a fookin' wakeup call.'

He threw his rusted screwdriver in the bin.

Filter had been dealing for a long time. He'd once had to resuscitate a customer he'd sold heroin to. Perhaps there were a few smashed windscreens in his life.

Several days later, I was discharged from hospital. Jen and Tash made me as welcome as possible, cooking and washing clothes for me till I was doing it for myself. But, despite it all, there was still the thought of Joe. I couldn't very well go up country and drop in on his grave – I didn't even know for sure that he was buried, although that was more likely than cremation – so one time I visited a spot we used to hang out: the park. The play equipment was sooty with night, but I could see easily enough that Joe wasn't on top of the slide. With nowhere I could put a face to the force, I looked up at the starless sky and attached a stamp. Maybe the postcard would return to sender, but it was sent nonetheless. It read: I hope it was an accident, Joe. But either way, if there's someplace you go when you go, I hope you're at peace.

The scars on my wrists meant I was forced to get even more trendy: Jen and Tash bought me bracelets and things – 'till you don't need them at all, Sam.' With the stitches out, the skin still pulled a bit, and I was told it would till it stretched enough to stop stretching.

I went to the bank and withdrew just about my last reserves of cash. I left the money on the coffee table in the lounge room, saying I'd found it – it must've been Tash's that went missing. Jen and Tash didn't quiz me over it, but just took it.

That afternoon, I went to The Union, which is a pub. With Zane leaving, I'd have to get used to going to gay venues on my own. At least till I found a new buddy. Tell you what, if you can pull it off and not look too self-conscious, in some ways it's better. Guess Zane and I did look like a long-term couple out to find some three-way action. This way, I was advertising my availability with less confusion. It was an older set. No dancing, just guys sitting at high tables on their high stools. I ordered a beer at the bar. While it was being poured, this guy with ears like butterflies batting for a raise, and eyes a baffled-blue, watched me, smiling. He was sitting chatting with a woman who looked like she'd just come from work, hubcap shoulders.

As I went past their table, beer in hand, the woman spoke to me.

'Hello handsome,' she laughed, then turned to her friend. 'Time I went. Hey, you don't want to come, do you?' she asked, turning her attention back to me. 'I won't tell anyone you're gay in the morning.'

I think I blushed.

She gave the man a kiss and hug, telling him to drop by next time he was in Melbourne, and was gone.

The man introduced himself.

'Maddy – short for Madison. Don't ask.'

We shook hands.

'All right,' he explained, 'I was born in New York – 39th Street. Not even near Madison Square Gardens.'

'Sam,' I said.

He told me I looked like a Sam. He said he'd never looked like a Madison.

'You look like a Maddy, though.'

We chatted a bit more. Turned out he was living in the Top End. He was down in Melbourne for a bit of business. I told him I wouldn't mind travelling north myself one day – maybe beginning with Sydney.

'I should give you the name of a few good places in Sydney I go when I'm feeling naughty. I went to one spot and there were all these guys with their shirts off. I thought, hello, this is the place for me.'

That seemed strange, talking about scoring other guys when I thought, hey, aren't you trying to score me?

'I've been trying to get in some Me time down here. Oh, I'd just like some sun so much. To lie on the beach naked all day.'

Melbourne was hardly the place.

He asked if I wanted to come back to his hotel room.

'I … I don't do this … much,' I said. 'I mean, it seems a bit sordid.'

He chuckled.

'One night stands can be good. If you both know it's one night. It can be just this giving moment between strangers and then they're gone. I've only had one night where I didn't feel comfortable.'

Poking me in the ribs: 'So where do *you* go when you get horny? I can't imagine you at a beat. You'd be so cute hiding in the bushes! Last time in Melbourne I met this guy I had this very raunchy time with at Wet & Slippery. We get together sometimes when I'm down but it's getting a bit safe. His idea of sex is slapping his dick against my chest.'

'Oh, that's not my idea,' I said boldly, and was surprised by it. I was feeling powerfully attracted to him.

'What I wonder is, where do hetties' – (I raised an eyebrow) – 'heterosexual males go to get their kicks? They don't have their clubs like us. Prostitutes, I suppose.'

Was the whole monogamy thing just a straight convention? Did it have to be that way? How many guys had open relationships like Jussy and Dorian? Or 'parallel-processed' like Zane? It was hard to know what to think.

302

'Have you ever thought about going to a prostitute?' Maddy added. 'You don't really need to as a gay male.'

We went to his hotel room and kissed. I was feeling that echidna in my stomach again, but this time it was readjusting for warmth, not bristling its back. It was rubbing its tummy inside of mine.

'Is it all right if we don't do anything?' I asked.

'Sure,' he said. And because he said sure, I wanted to do everything. Holding each other afterwards, feeling where we'd been, I thought how our bodies had simply fitted together.

'Cuddleslut,' he said, as I moved closer into his chest, then started nibbling.

'Uh oh, not *again*!'

I looked up into his eyes.

'Oh, look at that look of yours! So mischievous. Such cute little eyes. You and your rushed sex, how about more in the morning?'

And he held me tighter to him.

'It's so nice holding you,' he crooned. 'Your arms wrap nicely round me. Someone the same height, not have to stoop to kiss or arch your neck!'

We took a little duck bath. In the morning he made me a drink with his portable juicer and bread with plenty of jam. He got my number then asked if I wanted to hang out with him late in the day when he'd finished his business.

'Where are you going for your date?' asked Jen.

'We're going swimming.' A bit of a pause. 'That's okay, isn't it?'

'Sammy, darling,' said Zane, 'that's what you call an action date. Plenty of time to go to the pictures later. When you've nothing left to talk about.'

303

Always the cynic. I could see Jen thought so too. Zane was over at the house, and he and Jen were writing letters together. *I* was the interruption. Seemed pretty weird that they should be writing letters together but then I recognised the symbol on the letterheads.

'Amnesty International.'

'Sammy darling,' sighed Zane, 'I flatter myself that I have beautiful handwriting.'

Beautiful handwriting! That Zane was a mystery. Maybe he was onto the key to personal happiness. Thinking outside yourself. Guess that's a pretty selfish way of looking at it, really.

Ha, I make myself laugh.

You know what book I take after most? Or books I should say? Anything by Tolstoy. He's always got characters in them talking about the answer to life, and mostly that answer's to work. To 'busy oneself'.

But then what if your work's boring?

The video job was boring. At least to me. I'd started my shifts again. Even though Filter had his new job, he'd somehow managed to cover for me while I was in hospital so I'd have a job to return to.

Dad rang the store.

'Just wanted to wish you good luck for the last two weeks of the year.'

It took me a minute to work out what he was referring to. Cricket! I didn't have the heart to tell him I'd been kicked off the team. The last update I gave him was that I wasn't getting out for ducks anymore, but I wasn't making many runs either, which was itself a lie. This time round, I spun the same spiel.

'A bit of a Yallop,' he said. 'You've probably progressed further than you think, Sam. You and I, we're similar. Lots of little victories. Late starters. But we win big in the end.'

I wondered if there wasn't something Dad was getting at that I was missing. I remembered being at the top of the hill with Arny, and wanting to get the moment desperately, understand its significance at the time, but I didn't till too late. When I was actually playing cricket, the last thing I wanted to do was talk about it.

'I'll try my best, Dad,' I said, and that made it worse.

I rang Maddy from the hotel reception.

'Oh, it's so lovely to hear your voice. Which one are you again? The hairy midget? No, wrong match.'

Maddy and I found that we were both pretty good at holding our breaths. We timed ourselves in the hotel pool.

'I nearly panicked today,' said Maddy after I'd come up for breath. 'This is the second day I've seen you in a row! What does it mean? I like the term special friends. Is that okay with you?'

I nodded, the water still dripping off my eyelids.

We showered, got changed, went to dinner and up to his room.

'These young people who like to wear their jeans round their arses so you can see their y-fronts,' he said, putting his hands down my trousers, 'I don't know.'

In the morning, Maddy rolled over and mussed my hair.

'Hey, you look so cute when you smile. I don't know what's going on in your head. How are those two lesbians of yours?'

Jen and Tash were about the only people from my life I'd mentioned to Maddy. They seemed to need the least explanation. Besides, it was good not having a history.

'They're very up and down,' I said, snuggling into him.

'Fighting is good. It can be painful at the time but it can sort a lot out. You'll find out when you've got a boyfriend.'

I sat up.

'When I've got…?'

I got out of bed, searching for my clothes. Maddy sat up slowly.

'Sam, I'm going back to Darwin tomorrow.'

'Life just doesn't live up to dream, does it?' I blurted, trying unsuccessfully to get even one sock on. 'It's pointless! There aren't angels and unicorns. There aren't even vampires and devils,' I added, thinking of Joe's conception of a hell of fire and fiends.

Maddy was looking sideways at these last few comments. I condensed my thoughts to my original point: 'Life's meaningless!'

Maddy chuckled, unfurling his legs from rumpled sheets.

'Life is meaningless!' he roared. 'What about that brilliant headjob you gave me this morning? You didn't have to do that.'

'Yeah, the memory still chokes me up.'

Maddy got out of bed, walked over and pinched my cheek.

'Sam, I bet you're the sort of person who kicks a one-night stand out of bed the moment you come?'

I thought back to that guy I'd taken home after my failure with Jussy. Yes, I had tossed him out straightaway. Compared to me, Maddy was a consummate romantic.

'So, are you going to throw me out?' I asked.

Maddy smiled.

'I haven't come yet.'

Things seemed to be getting better, I was getting closer.

'That's assuming there is any place to *get to*, Sammy darling.'

No, that was Zane talking. I was. Getting closer, I mean.

So.

Arny. The right book but read too early.

Luke. The wrong book I wanted desperately to be the right one. (Like misinterpreting *The Prince* as a Buddhist text.)

Jussy. The wrong book, time, everything.

Maddy. The wrong book but the right time.

And Joe?

Poor Joe was dead.

Chapter Ten

Days go but this one came and I remembered it. I found a bird, injured, so took it under my wing. Nurse and saviour to three birds previously, I felt up to the challenge. Dad said to keep it in a cage till its wounds healed. It was a criminally small cage, the only one we had. The bird squawked and flapped about so much, I shifted it to the shade house. I reckoned it would be nice and cool there, and could stretch and yawn. I've always hated cramped spaces myself.

The next day I found it gone. I searched for days and Dad told me how stupid I was.

Since then, I see birds' bodies splashed on roads all the time. It amazes me, this, 'cause all the years I've driven I've never hit one. Or any animal, for that matter. I've always slowed, beeped and swerved. I reckon some people run the birds down on purpose.

One day Dad showed me the bird. It was unmistakably the same one, with frayed feather and twisted claw. Its eyes were missing and ants filled their place.

'See what you've done? You never listen to me.'

Dad needn't have said that. I went back to my room and tried to cry.

It was Saturday and the second last match of the year. Probably already under way. It was a home game, on the other side of town. Public transport on a Sunday …? I rang Maddy and asked for a favour.

Maddy drove me to the match in his hire-car. His next destination was the airport and Darwin. Balwyn was in the complete opposite direction but he was cool about it. The drive was all too short. Most of our conversation involved me giving directions and then giving further directions on how to get to the airport after I'd been unloaded.

I kept looking at him out of the corner of my eye, thinking, wondering, is skin on skin as close as you can get to someone, no closer? There's the getting to know someone, then there's the getting to know over time. I'd had the former, but I would never have the latter with Maddy. You can keep dividing the present down to the smallest moment, but even that moment will have smaller moments still.

A kind of song ran through my head.

What do I know about you? Who do I know you through? What do I know that's true?

How do I live while I'm alive? Where do I go when I die? The future won't last forever. Today is all we have.

It got me upset but then I thought, no, I'd had a good time with Maddy. With him, there'd been no pain.

Maddy pulled up slowly at the oval but there's only so slow a speed you can go before stalling. He gave me a big kiss. I could see a few cricketers and their folks staring at us but I didn't care.

I opened the door, just about to leave, but had one more thing to say.

'Thanks, Maddy. Being with you has shown me I can have a fun time with a stranger.'

Maddy laughed, boomingly.

'Right, get out of here before I *do* fall in love with you.'

I had to watch his car all the way down the road. You know that way you get it into your head that you've got to watch a boat to the horizon? Or when you wake up in the middle of the night and the clock radio says 1:59 and you've just got to wait that extra minute 'cause those two noughts look so perfect together? Well, I watched Maddy's car till it got so I thought I was watching a different car altogether, then none at all but a big blur. I wiped my eyes and made my way to the lockers.

Tears make you lighter.

Passing the assorted spectators, I tried to think about my batting approach – that is, if I was to ever get another chance. But how could I feel free to make a big score, smash the ball, when I was worried I might hit one of my opponents again?

The lockers smelt clean for once. The guys had washed their whites, even ironed them (or got their mums or partners to). Tubby was reading something as he stood at his locker, with the locker door held open like the dust jacket to a hard cover. When he saw me coming, he quickly threw whatever it was inside, shut the door and met me halfway across the floor.

'Sam, the coach sees you here, he'll cane you,' said Tubby.

'I'm finally ready to play my game,' I told him.

Tubby snorted before walking over to the drink fountain.

Dizzy opened his own locker two doors down. He looked a few times my way, itching to say something. Finally, he got it out.

'We don't need you any more, Sam. Roger's got your position for now. And when Arny comes back, which will be next week, he'll take over.'

Arny? My body eloped for an instant. I turned round to face Tubby, who was quaffing his paper cup of ice-cold water. Maybe I *would* have the fairytale ending. Don't want it, Sam, don't hope.

'Hey, Tubby,' I said. Quietly. 'Why didn't you tell me Arny had given you a date for his return?'

It sounded pathetic even to me.

'Shit, Sam, you hardly return my calls.'

He was right. I'd been treating Tubby the way Filter had treated me. Snubbed. The coach walked in, his hotdog face over-stuffed with extras.

'Get out.'

It was pretty unequivocal. I made to move.

'Wait,' said Tubby quietly, but with force.

The coach turned on him sharply. Tubby went to his locker, removed the 'literature' he'd been reading – a postcard – and handed it to the coach.

'We're gonna need Sam after all,' said Tubby.

The coach read the postcard carefully then, after a long pause, handed it to me.

'You may be right,' he said.

On the front of the postcard was a beautiful picture of No. 10 Downing Street in the fog. I turned it over to read the back.

Hey, Tubby, good and bad news, I'm afraid. The good news is that I've got a place in County cricket in England! The bad news is that it means I won't be coming back! Come and visit some time. You'll love the pints, and you'd be able to meet my man, Trevor!

Hope Sam's all right. One day I might be playing against him – against both of you.

Funny how things work out.

Arny.

Somewhere, slow, a creek.
Don't cry, Sam, don't cry.
A creek, and water running.
Don't cry, Sam.
And a magpie.
Don't cry.
With ants for eyes.
Don't.
Streaming black tears.
Its eyes missing and ants in their place.

The coach told Tubby and Dizzy to leave and not let anyone back into the clubhouse. He took the postcard from me and pinned it to the 'fun board'. He sat down on the bench and gestured to me to sit opposite.

'You've got a lot of talent, Sam. You could be brilliant.'

I was still wiping my eyes. 'But it doesn't – it doesn't make me happy,' I said.

'Okay, that's a point, but I'd love to have your ability. Every player on this team would love to have your ability. Take Dizzy. A case in point.'

For the first time, it amazed me how clued in the coach was, not just to our strengths on-field, but off.

'Maybe he's happier than me,' I lobbed.

The coach slapped his thigh.

'You've got a fucking gift, Sam. The rest of us are just fucking about. Maybe Tubby, a bit, but you!'

'It doesn't make me happy, though,' I countered, this time almost yelling. The coach breathed in, serving his next sentence many decibels below mine, which was quite a feat because his voice wasn't open-cut but shaft-deep.

'It's *not* going to make you happy, Sam. 'Cause you want to be the best at it. But what else are you going to do?'

I started to mention the nine-to-five, but he saw it coming and cut me off.

'You couldn't live that life, Sam. You wouldn't be happy with that.'

His sausage-dog limbs sizzled on the bench before flipping into action.

'Sam, you've got an opportunity most never get. How many people do you reckon want to play cricket for their state? And maybe one day for their country? 'Cause that's where you're headed, Big Feller.'

Where *you're* headed?

'Does that mean I'm to be given one last chance?'

The coached eyed me carefully.

'I don't ask that you enjoy the game, Sam; I expect that you love it.'

I thought about Filter and his music. How many people get to do what they really love?

'I *do* love it,' I told the coach.

'Well, you can't play today, obviously. But you know next week's the last match of the year, and it's absolutely *your* last chance to knuckle down and prove yourself.'

I nodded. 'Thanks.'

'Don't thank me yet.'

The day of the match. A lot of families had come to watch. The stands were filled, the lawns covered. The other team had made an almost unbeatable three-hundred plus score before finally being bowled out in the last over before lunch. The coach gave me another rousing one-on-one pep talk. I told him I was confident I could do okay, but 'okay' wouldn't prove anything, he said, and I knew he was right. I thought how I'd underestimated the coach – hadn't even figured him – as counting. Everyone can surprise you.

What had I told that shrink in the hospital? How I wanted to compose perfect strings of moments, how I wanted to be the best at life, to live the life of books, every moment momentous, packed with meaning. But I couldn't. In the end, I'd have to settle for something less than that life, and maybe that could be cricket. If I could get anything perfect, perhaps it would be my game.

Lunch ended. It was our side's turn to bat. Everyone was low, Tubby the lowest. His bowlers had let him down, especially his strike-bowler and vice-captain, Dizzy. It was almost never heard of, the follow-up side chasing down over three-hundred runs.

Tubby and I made our way out of the clubhouse and down the stairs. He shuffled up beside me. Always the gossip, he wanted to know what the coach had said. We passed through the gate. The green oval opened up beneath us.

'Why do all these people have such faith in me, Tubby? I haven't really done anything to warrant it.'

'What is this shit? Sure you have, Sam. Anyway, it's not what you've done so much, but how you've done it, and what that says about what you *will* do.'

We were almost at the pitch. I was still getting used to the weight of the pads again, the feel of the bat through gloves. The other side already had their players spread out across the green.

Three hundred runs? Impossible. But I'd do my best. If I ever wanted to ditch that part-time video store job, I'd have to lift my game, if for no other reason than to prove to myself that I could. For once, I'd actually remembered to put some talc in my gloves so they wouldn't slip. It was a small thing, but it made me feel strong just knowing I'd thought to do it.

'Want me to open?' asked Tubby, looking at my fidgeting.

I shook my head, taking my place at the crease, marking my spot. Finally, I lowered my bat.

The leggy gaited in. It was unusual to open with a spinner but the pitch was pretty scuffed up. The ball spun back. It hit me on the pad. There was a murmur of 'Ooh' among the fielders. Dangerous not to offer a shot.

I tried to watch the next one from the bowler's fingers. He unexpectedly sped it up. The wrong 'un. It beat the inside edge of my bat, narrowly passing over middle stump. Tubby was practically de-clawing his talons at the other end. The next ball I met with a sweep shot. Luckily I hadn't got much bat on it, because they had a man placed forty-five degrees on the angle for just that shot. The ball fell a few yards in front of him.

Concentrate, Sam. Come on, concentrate! I had to play my natural game, be aggressive, but controlled aggression. By playing defensively, I was sure to get out.

The leggy dropped another in short. Somehow I swept it square of the wicket for one. I was glad to get off strike, and while Tubby faced the next few shots, I tried to get the field placements in my head.

A maiden over. A swapping of ends. Me facing again.

To win, we'd need better than six an over.

The second bowler was Charles Acton-Heath, the guy I'd smashed in the head with a beautiful cover-drive and team captain. The quickie some were saying was clocking speeds of up to one-forty. Not bad for District Cricket.

The first was a very nasty bouncer I only just ducked under.

'Ooh, nice one, Charlie,' crooned the keeper through dank teeth.

315

Charles grinned nastily at me before turning to find the beginning of his run-up, his battleship hairdo tipped with breakers at the bow.

Right, I was going to take the challenge to the ball – not *him*, the ball. The ball is the enemy, Sam. But Charles saw me coming, bowled it quicker, and kept it short. I almost got it too high on the bat. I took my right hand off fast as I could to kill it, but the ball popped up the other end of the pitch. Tubby stepped sideways, Charles's caught-and-bowl hopes ending in a two-man sprawl. Hisses and spitting from his team. A bit of chesting between Charles and Tubby, like they were pigeons – just one arm lifted and it would degenerate into an all-out punch-up.

I couldn't have Tubby cheating for me. Come on, Sam, concentrate.

The next ball I hooked but it wasn't really there for the hook. More out of a fieldsman fumbling, than any real skill, we got two runs.

Three balls to go in the over. My shoulder was hurting. I'd gone against the ball instead of with it – tried to force the moment.

Come on, Sam, come on. Concentrate.

Tubby found a need to tie up his shoelaces in the path of the bowler. Charles killed his run short. Time. Tubby was giving me time.

I thought back to the previous night, with Maddy, how we'd wrestled each other onto the bed, upsetting the ever-so-perfect folds of hotel linen. He was pinning my arms to the side, sitting astride me, but I was resisting, deliciously.

Maddy chuckled.

'I'll have to show you this move in Aikido, Sam,' he said, sliding off the bed and pulling me to my feet. 'It's where you use your opponent's force against them. You can just lift up your arm and let them smash into it or you can step aside slightly and direct them on.'

He showed me how to do it.

'So you can block like this or go with the blow?' I asked.

'That's it,' he boomed, and I used the force of his punch to flip him onto the bed.

'What's that?' Maddy asked, when he saw he'd pulled one of my bracelets free.

'Morse code for cats.'

'Sam!'

Tubby was shouting at me. I lowered my bat. The crowd was a planter of particoloured coral, the air an ocean of vents and currents. The field spread out. Charles ran in. He mustered all the speed he had. The ball was loosed. I thought to smash it but that would be force against force. I simply deflected it into the pitch. It gave a dry dock whistle and asphyxiated at my feet. There was a pause before Tubby yelled 'run'. We ran and we'd made the distance before the closest fielder managed to run in. Tubby scored a single next ball. Then Charles bowled a high one, tempting me in to the pull shot, but I merely stepped back and gave it a top edge over the wicketkeeper for four. All that one hundred and forty kilometres an hour of effort from Charles, I'd turned to my advantage.

Tubby and I were working ourselves into the game.

I was seeing the oval from above. Seeing every point, every fielder in space and time. Guiding the ball through the easiest path, the least pain, getting it to the fence every time. Seeing the ball off *their* pitch, out of *their* hands, and into *mine*. Working through every permutation. Re-routing bad connections. Feeling muscles I'd never felt before. Involuntary becoming voluntary and vice versa. A million choices, all real till decided.

Another ball. Another. Another. Knowing the ones worth going for; letting the others through. A Jussy – leaving, letting it go. A coy ball, like Luke, spinning wide of the bat – knowing it wasn't for me; leaving, letting it go. A Joe, opposite spin; gently slapping it on its path for three. A full-toss – Maddy – giving it my all; a sweet cover-drive over the bowler for six.

Maybe I finally was good at life.

The field reset. Bowlers came and went. There was nothing they could do.

I was vaguely aware of Tubby making jokes to the crowd. Should he just leave his bat at the crease? He wasn't getting much of a hit, anyway.

I stayed in the whole innings, making over eighty per cent of the runs. Tubby stayed in with me. We wandered back to the stands, Tubby with the stumps under his arms. The applause signalled amazement.

Walking back out for the end-of-game ceremonies, I saw two people bumbling through the crowd.

'Mum, Dad!'

They shook hands with me. Pretty strange shaking hands with your parents. Dad's suit was shiny with age, Mum's dress yet to catch up with her weight. But they'd put in an effort, Sunday-best.

'Sam, um, your mum and I, well … look, I'm just saying … we should've been more supportive – about your cricket, I mean. You're obviously talented. We should've been more supportive, that's all.'

Dad drove me to sport every Saturday …

'I mean … it's your gift. Your mother and I … we could've helped out more.'

… and picked me up after practice Wednesday nights …

'I mean, recognised your … er … talent.'

… every Christmas, a new bat, one size up.

I shook hands with him again to shut him up. Mum looped an arm under my elbow. In the gravity of the moment, we were a three-pronged spiral galaxy. The crowd knew to make its path elliptical to ours. But then the stars flew out of orbit once more and found their own trajectories.

Hadn't I seen a similar image on one of my trips? Me, Zane and Filter passing as comets through our own and other people's wakes, sometimes connecting at the head, sometimes only at the very tail.

Tubby yelled at me to get moving. They were announcing Man of the Match.

'The house where you're living's very nice,' said Mum.

That dingy place.

'Hey, Mum, I'd better go.' I could see the team gathering on the green.

'You're flatmate's very nice – Jen,' said Mum, still holding my elbow.

'She is.'

'And her friend. She's nice too.'

Her friend? Ah – Tash.

'Oh, you mean her *girl*friend?'

'We're trying, Sam.'

Man of the Match was announced. I had to collect my trophy.

'Thanks for coming, Mum, Dad,' I said, turning, but then turned back again. 'Thank you.'

Mum let go of my arm.

There was a fair bit of revelry in the clubhouse afterwards. The beer was at full tide. Finally, someone thought to ask: 'Did anyone get a relly to videotape the game?'

No one had. There was this long silence. All the faces took an hour to turn to me. But I was smiling. Just then, I knew I loved cricket. Not only because I'd got my form back – that would come and go – but because I was home, where I wanted to be. Happiness is knowing it at the time.

'Cricket's in-the-moment stuff,' I said, 'best enjoyed at the time.'

The coach looked in.

'Hey, Big Feller, guess who I spoke to in the stands?'

'Who?'

'The selectors for the Victorian Bushrangers.'

There was a hush over all my teammates.

'So, I guess we better call this your farewell drinks.'

Every one of those players clinked stubbies with me. Even Dizzy. Poor old Tubby had a tear in his eye, not that he'd admit to it.

The next day, I went over to Zane's. Knowing I was on a health kick, he poured me Evian water. Never mind that H_2O ran from the taps. He had a new look, too: socks with their tops bitten off so you could barely see them above the cushion of his sneakers.

'Neat?' he asked. He was standing on a stool, pulling down his posters. I was on the couch, looking up at him. I was about to ask what he was doing when he let slip that he'd been to the game. I asked why he didn't come to the clubhouse afterwards and he just gave me a look.

'Fair enough,' I said, and then, without meaning to, added, 'Hey, I wish Joe had been there.'

Zane stopped tearing at a poster, and turned to me.

'The thing is, Sammy, these freaks can't stand themselves. So why should *we* stand *them*?'

I stood up from the couch, joining him at the whitening wall.

'Zane,' I said very seriously, 'there was a time when *we* couldn't stand ourselves. When I met you, you'd talk about yourself in third person as "the bitch".'

'That's because I *am* a tubby queen, Sammy darling.'

Another thick, crackling poster took its magic carpet ride to the floor. Zane noted my gaze. 'Very messy,' he agreed and, 'not at all like *moi*.' He asked me to fetch his rubber bands – a tiny wooden box of them next to his computer.

I handed it to him. Maddy had left, I said, but I was okay with it. Maddy had it sorted. Whoever came along – beats, saunas …

'Another slut in a rut,' mused Zane.

That shut me up.

Zane chuckled as he noosed a wound-up poster with a rubber band.

'That's what I like about you, Sammy Sausage: you keep thinking you've found the answer.'

I bowed my head. He knighted me with the poster.

'Sir Stupid.'

'I'm trying too hard still, aren't I?' I asked.

Zane smiled. '*Tres vous*[4].'

The bell rang. It was Tash, pageboy hairdo for once instead of vertical with gel. Button-nose normally in the air – also dropped. Was everyone changing? She stood looking at the empty white walls, then down at the posters of semi-naked men. The only poster left was one I'd given Zane of a cricketer in a very un-gentlemanly pose. Joe and I had found it on one of our forays. Zane got back on his stool and started tearing it down.

'Zane's going undercover,' Tash said to me.

I looked a question mark at this.

---

[4] French: very you.

321

Tash squealed. 'Hasn't he told you? His parents are visiting!'

Zane? His parents? Zane who said, 'I have no parents'? Finally it made sense. He wasn't out to them.

'They don't know you're gay?' I asked.

Zane looked away, for the first time uncomfortable.

'My parents know nothing about me, Sam, nothing. They don't know a thing about my life.'

Did Joe's parents know a thing about *his* life? Had he ever given them the chance to reject him? Did my parents know mine?

'Well, of course they don't know a thing about you,' I said bitterly to Zane. 'How could they?'

'Telling them won't make any difference, Sammy,' he said, quickly gathering up the posters of muscly men. 'They don't know the *real* me.'

'Exactly.'

'I warn you, we're going to fall out over this.'

'Then I'll just say one thing more. Maybe we shouldn't decide things for others. It's prejudging them.'

We said nothing more on the topic but I noticed Zane didn't take down his last poster. And for the first time, Tash was almost cordial with me.

Zane and I went to The Pit that night, greeting the door staff on the way in.

'*Yea, Yorgos, nos easai?*[5]' said Zane. One of the guys was apparently of Greek descent.

'Yeah, thanks, I'm good, mate,' the guy replied.

The two laughed.

Half a night later and Zane wanted to keep dancing. Before, at The Pit, I had rarely wanted to leave his side. Now I was happy to wander on my own.

---

[5] Greek: Hi, George, how are you?

That's probably why I met Oscar.

'Koori? Nah, I'm Murri – Murri mob, up north.'

I asked Oscar if he was on his own. It was a new policy I was trying.

'Some Tassie just asked if I was on my own. Felt like saying, you're not really alone if you've got a brain. Nah, only gammin'.'

Gammin'?

'He wanted to know if I was visiting Melbourne. 'Cause, yeah, all real Aborigines live in the bush, fuckyas. Aw, don't, poor thing. He was just trying to be friendly.'

'I've got off to a bad start already, haven't I?' I asked.

'Nah, you're all right. So what's your game?'

I told him I played for the State Cricket Team.

'Aw, true?'

I couldn't quite nod: yes. It wasn't strictly true, not yet. I told him it was looking hopeful that I'd be selected. He laughed, half of it to the ceiling, as he bent his head back.

'You been gammin' you play for State Team and that? Gammin' confident, that's what you bin' doin'. That's okay, mate. Big-noting. We know all about that.'

He was right. There I was, skiting already! People don't really change.

'Nah, I believe ya,' laughed Oscar. 'You're deadly, know that?'

He smiled. His hair was longer than most gay guys wore theirs: dark curls to the collar. His shirt was patchwork black and tan, tight across the chest. Somehow we got onto oldies. There were a few veteran attendees in the place and that made me think of Filter making fun of the frizzled and friendless.

'You white fellers can't wait to get rid of your elders. We blackfellers listen to our mob. Our ancestors' voices.

Walking about like you own the place. Some places you shouldn't walk in.'

'How do you know where not to?' I asked.

'You'll know.'

I told him a story about the farm. An anthropologist visited once and showed us some Aboriginal paintings in a cave we'd never looked in before. We never looked in that cave again.

'See, weren't meant to. Listen to your ancestors.'

'Yeah, but look at what *my* ancestors did: crash your party.'

'But nah, Sam, there still be some good mob among them. You don't listen to spirit ways and that? Songlines?'

I shook my head.

'Some day I tell you 'bout them, maybe, when you ready to listen, not before.'

This was hopeful. Talking like a minute's acquaintance was a prolonged friendship. If he was a cricket delivery, what type would he be? Something told me a yorker, going straight for my feet. His next bowl confirmed it.

'You're a big spunk, know that?'

'Um … thanks.' I went red, which got another good laugh from Oscar. What with him and Maddy, seemed I was meeting happier people lately. That was a good sign.

'Tell us 'bout your hobbies. Cricket's okay,' he said, 'for a colonial sport.'

Hadn't thought of it that way before. There's a million angles on everything, but you can't look at them all at once. I'd had that on mushrooms and it nearly sent me mad. So I told Oscar about my love affair – okay, obsession – with books, and how I'd tried to write my life as one.

'You write spirit things down, they don't change so easy after that.'

I thought of Joe's literal bible.

'They don't live no more. We got the dreaming. You dream, too, brother, I see that. You spiritual person, you're just gammin' like you're not and that.'

I had to get to the bottom of this word.

'Gammin'?' I asked.

'Fakin'.'

Zane's skin-tight aqua top announced itself through the mostly dark colours of the punters. He was holding up the queue to the bar by chatting up the bar staff. He really was taking this friendliness resolution to its extreme! Seeing the guy he was, I couldn't help but compare him to the one I'd imagined. All that time back (not even a year – ten months), walking to my first date with Zane, my very first meeting with him, I was thinking over the night before it had actually happened. But of course the script wasn't going to turn out how I'd written it. And that's the best thing about actual people anyway; you could never invent a character more complex than a person in real life.

I turned and looked full eyes at the reality before me.

Oscar and I swapped numbers. He left. Zane walked over, handing me a beer. He had a Stollie in his.

'*Guten Rutsch*[6], you old queen! You've found a replacement buddy for poor old Zane already.'

'No one could replace you, Zane. You're unique.'

He clinked my glass in agreement.

'Do you know, Sammy, that gentleman has given you the eye when you've come in here before?'

I thought back. He had. Round the time of Luke. Guess I wasn't ready then to smile back.

A week later, Oscar and I had seen each other every day and night except for Christmas Eve and Christmas

---

[6] German: Good year.

325

Day. Being such a dyed-in-the-wool atheist, I found it a bit hard to come at some of what he said.

'People telling me rocks and things, they inanimate, they don't know. Everything's got life, even pollies. That's what I am, Sam: local member for the Greens.'

'What do you think about the present incumbents?' I asked, sitting up straight in bed. We were at his place, the light burning through the Venetian blinds like toaster bands on a slice of bread.

'In Canberra, you mean?' he asked. 'That's blowfly country.'

'Why do you say that?'

'They're the only bit of Australia that lives off the rest of us, aren't they? Nah, but serious. If you don't allow you might be wrong, you're never gonna be right, fuckyas.'

I pulled the pillow from behind my back and mock-hit him before lying down again. It wasn't quite time to get up. Oscar emerged over my shoulder like the sun. I stared up into his glare.

We went shopping later – not for clothes, but food. Ho-hum domestic. We found a trolley, but it needed a one-dollar coin to free it from the rest of the chain gang. Oscar searched his pockets for coins. I quickly reached in mine. Oscar withdrew empty hands.

'Oi, can I have a few bob?' he asked.

I filtered my empty pockets.

'Aw, don't, I so shame. We only going out one week; already I'm hitting you for cash. You better watch that, bub, that's blackfeller ways. What's yours is mine. Nah, only gammin'; I got the shrapnel on me.'

And he dug from his bag the bond for the itinerant trolley. His mobile rang the generic dial tone as he slotted the gold in place.

'What am I doin'? he said into his phone. 'I'm here with Mullaga.'

'What's Mullaga?' I asked when he'd rung off.

'Boyfriend.'

The roots were showing in Jen's hair; she was a blonde. I'd never known that. She was growing out the black and, with it, the Goth. Gone, also, were the spider web glasses; back were the sensible specs. Her ears had lost some rings but not their tally of holes. Her lips were their real red. She was beautiful.

Growing up or growing old? Funny that this new look reminded me of Jen as I saw her first, at the ice-skating rink.

Tash had moved in with Jen and me 'officially', and that meant a lot of her furniture as well. Already, practically every wall of our rental was covered with a cupboard, dresser or bookcase of Jen's. Since I owned nothing in the house apart from what was in my room, I really was in the position of 'boarder'. I'd have to move out soon; leave Jen and Tash to themselves.

Wanting a rest from all the shifting of Tash's stuff, we somehow managed to find room in the kitchen, sitting at the fifties laminate table, warm coffee mugs imparting their warmth to our hands, the smell of things cooking adding spice to our conversation.

Suddenly Jen laughed.

'Remember the scared little things we used to be, Sam, going to our first gay clubs, sitting in the corner, looking like the hetero-couple that had walked into the wrong bar?'

I laughed because I remembered.

'Did you think we could ever be so strong?'

I was spending a lot of time at Oscar's and gradually getting used to his way of sleeping. He didn't like the top sheet tucked in round his legs. Kept the blinds open so the morning sun could let itself in in the morning. Guess I'd over-romanticised the idea of a relationship. Much of it was mere forbearance. He was perfectly quiet in his sleep. I hadn't been the night before. I'd dreamt a dingo had walked past the open blinds and stared in.

When the dingo was satisfied, it moved on because, for the first time, everything was fine just as it was. No red-pen markings, no rewrites, just first-draft wonders, stream-of-consciousness. Oscar and I were stepping through every shape and circumstance we could bring, let loose in loveliness.

On waking, I put the dingo down to nothing more than the influence of some of the photos and pictures on Oscar's bedroom wall. Oscar saw more in it. But what the heck? I hadn't had a dream in a long time. Was Oscar my dream?

'No you haven't given up your dreams, Sammy,' said Zane that afternoon. I'd gone over to his place for 'mid-morning post-breakfast pre-lunch'. Filter, Jen and Tash were there also, retiring on those monstrous black leather couches.

'Your standards have actually risen since you met me,' continued Zane. 'You won't take shit from anyone any more. You want someone as good as you finally. I'm … I'm glad I met you! Ugh, ugh, no hugging. You know how I hate man-sweat.'

I hugged him all the same.

'I've only just got it together, Zane,' I said. 'Some people out there, well, they've had a girlfriend since they were eighteen, they've got jobs now, careers … I'm hopeless. It's taken me so – '

Tash cut me off by whispering loudly in Jen's ear.

'Don't you hate it when people come out of their shells?'

Zane and Filter laughed.

'You lot!' sighed Jen.

'Sam has corrupted Zane,' said Tash.

'No,' said Jen, pushing Tash back in her place. 'Sam's softened Zane. You've softened, too, since you met me.'

The fact that Tash couldn't answer showed she knew it. Jen turned to me.

'Well, off you go, Sam,' she said. 'Your date's waiting.'

'I don't know,' I faltered. 'It's all been so painless with Oscar.'

'Well, what you want, mate?' chipped in Filter, hoola-hooping his belly with mirth. 'Another Jussy? Fuck that. This new guy's a champ. And he's paying you the highest compliment those other tosspots never did. He's taking a chance on you, Sammy. Not a half-arsed pisstake but a real one hundred per cent bet. That's a show of confidence. You've got a shit load more to offer than you did, Sammy mate. 'Cause you can take care of yourself, now. Hell, I'd have you if I batted for your team.'

'Yeah, I'd fuck you,' said Jen.

'Yeah, all right, I'd fuck you,' said Tash, once Jen nudged her.

'Hear, hear,' said Zane, a little red. 'Again!'

'See, we all wanna fuck you, Sam. You've come a long way, mate.'

'I have, haven't I?'

'Now don't go fucking milking it.' And Filter gave me a clip on the ear.

New Year's Eve. This was it, the millennium party 2000. All year I'd been gunning for the biggest party ever, and now that night was here. Jen and Tash were trying to get me to come to their party. The lads – Zane and Filter – were spending New Year's on the beach. But, true to form, not the popular one: down by Williamstown.

Oscar and I each wanted the other to come to his New Year's Eve get-together. But no one likes spending New Year's Eve with a whole bunch of people they don't know. Here was my first real taste of having to take someone else into account when making decisions. Guess this was where compromise came into it. Luckily, Oscar was as forthright as me. We'd go separate ways.

'That doesn't seem like compromise, does it? More like disagreement,' I said.

Oscar worked out a solution. Share a countdown ahead of time, then separate for the actual countdown.

Seemed a good relationship.

'5 – 4 – 3 – 2 – 1. Happy New Year!'

Oscar and I were sitting in a restaurant in Williamstown and the rest of the clientele thought we were daft – it was only six o' clock. The waiters cleared our table the second we were finished, hoping to sell our seats to the queuing punters outside. I wondered what they were getting paid to work on this night. Finishing up, Oscar and I walked outside, pausing on the pavement. Oscar gave the concept of the shared New Year's Eve one more try. He had a party with his mob and I was welcome. But did I want to go? Zane would be overseas soon, Filter interstate (his success in telemarketing had got him a promotion). Little time with both. I turned to Oscar.

'Mind if I spend the night with them?'

'Cheers, that's how you feel!'

I nearly backed down but he jumped in.

'Nah, only gammin'. You do what you have to, bub. You dreamed about a dingo. That's the luckiest thing you can dream about. That dingo's taking you home, bub. You follow him. You're deadly, know that?'

'You're deadly too.'

Zane was in his tight Mooks top, Filter in his 'fat people clothing', a tent-like Adidas sweater. Filter had brought his guitar, which was unexpected. He and Zane were sitting either side of a park bench, their respective six-packs between them, already out of their plastic placentas and the bottles empty.

Our posse was soon to be disbanded. The road forked ahead where I'd come to see it as undivided. Soon, Zane and Filter would be hanging out with different people in different places. In his own way, Filter already was with his telemarketing.

'State Cricket will mean more travel,' I said out loud, 'at least interstate. And with First Class Cricket, I'll see the world.'

'Keep your dreams to yourself,' hissed Filter.

Zane and I looked at each other. Perhaps you shouldn't broadcast your happiness. But then should you hide it? Filter doused the awkwardness with a splash of guitar. It was the happiest combo you ever ate with your ears. I thought maybe a gentle dig might ease the tension between us, since Filter wouldn't appreciate a soppy angle.

'Thought all your music was multi-layered electronica?' I asked.

Filter smiled at his guitar.

'Sam, some of the best songs are written with three chords.'

He was a genius all right, living with obscurity every day of his life. I told him so, and I reckon he was glad to hear it coming from someone other than himself.

'What kind of a world is it,' crooned Filter, 'where greatness can actually hold you back?'

When Filter wound down his song, I asked Zane how it had gone with his olds. Zane waved me away. Not so well then.

'At least they now know,' he said. 'If they were honest with themselves, they would accept they always knew. I was a glamour queen at three!'

Zane then asked about Oscar. I told him how well it was going.

'Does this now mean the two of you have stopped parallel-processing?'

Filter lifted his head from his guitar and stared at Zane.

'What does that mean?' he asked Zane.

'Seeing other people. I know you, Sammy; you want monogamy. Have you raised that question?'

'He … he believes in *emotional* monogamy,' I faltered.

'I see.'

I looked at the bench beneath my hands. Something settled on me, a bird, caged, heavy. What if there *was* such a thing as 'the one' and it had never been Arny? What if, all that time, 'the one' was Joe? Had I ever really grabbed life, or totally missed it instead? When had I felt best, really embraced the moment? I remembered the times me, Zane and Filter took magic mushrooms together, and how fun that was. And the highest I'd ever felt, that one hit of heroin. I brought this up with Filter.

'Maybe we could pop an E each for old time's sake? An E is a fraction of the high you feel on heroin but …'

Filter stopped strumming.

'Drugs don't change your reality, Sam; just your perception of it. You've still got to go back to the real thing, mate.'

'I'll never feel as high again,' I said.

'No, mate,' agreed Filter. 'You've landed. Make sure you keep those wings regularly clipped.'

I shook myself to get some sense into me. I was onto a good thing with Oscar.

'Sammy,' said Zane, 'I hate to deflower your rosy view of life, but those times – we were just three bums in a park. There is no satisfying conclusion to life unless you call death a great ending. Life is just a series of readjustments to disappointment.'

That irritated me. I arced up.

'Zane,' I said, about to repeat words he'd used on me once before, 'you should never assume someone feels as you do. I'm optimistic about Oscar, but it isn't blind optimism. I'll see where things go.'

Zane looked like he was deciding between being offended or amused.

'Sammy, darling, you are not alone in your loneliness,' he said at last, with a smile.

Zane and Filter got themselves some fish and chips – from the cheapest joint they could find. Filter was still a miser, even though he was going into a higher wage bracket. I saw what that meant: with more responsibility comes more hours. I put a question to him.

'Won't this promotion take you further from your dream?'

'What's that, Samster? Drugs I've quit. But guess what? Now I'm addicted to the number one pedestrian drug,' and he shouted his next slogan to the background city: 'Oi, society, ask yourself this: Capitalism – can you afford it?'

'*Toujours*[7],' laughed Zane. 'In mourning for the lives we can't have; being led by the ones we lead. I will write to my buddies. Filter responding is doubtful,' he said, looking over his bottle at Filter; Filter looked up from his guitar, 'though he'll try; Sammy more likely, because he'll want to join me some time. Here, Sammy darling, throw the last of these chips to the rats of the sea.'

The seagulls were already gathered for the foreign food source. Adaptation.

I stood on the jetty. The sun washed her hair in the sea. A strand of it completed my bridge to the horizon. As the sun subsided beneath the waves altogether, I wanted then to become the many sucking noises the crabs made, or the slaps the waters gave themselves. The sun gave of itself in its reflection on the waves, serrated waves which peeled it like an orange.

Filter called, stubbie in hand, and I joined him and Zane on the ocean's edge. They'd sourced some hard rubbish from the beachfront verge. Two beds and a cupboard were our bonfire.

I fell in the sand between them. Zane tapped his Stollie against Filter's Coopers. I clinked my VB against each.

We talked till midnight and beyond. Filter tapped his watch five minutes past the hour. We were already into the next century. No street lamps fizzled out, or planes fell out of the sky. Perhaps Y2K wasn't such a worry after all, like most things.

'This is what it's fookin' all about,' said Filter, half sloshed and launching a beer into the air. 'Nights like this, sitting round, good food, good company.'

---

[7] French: always.

We turned to the fire. As it grew, its warmth drew us in. I felt sorry for those people who were missing out on pleasures like this. People sitting at home, night after night, and even on this night, watching their videos. The people Filter and I would talk about, who'd get their weekly videos week in, week out, hoping for warmth. The customers who spent so long in the video store we should've been charging them for rent.

'That's profound, Filter,' I said. 'Times like this …' and I repeated his words. "This is what it's fookin' about … sitting round, good food, good company".'

'Uh oh,' sighed Zane, 'dope revelations and we're not even doped up.'

'You know, Sam, Zane,' said Filter, raising his beer again, 'I'm not where I thought I'd fookin' be – no fame, no assets, no girl – but, funny thing to say, I'm happy where I've gotten to. It's been a fookin' journey!'

There was another round of toasting. The beer helped to sift the lump in my throat. I saw I'd fallen in with a good crowd, good people. I was so glad I'd taken that key, let myself out of my prison and gone this far. I wondered where I'd be if I'd stayed with Arny at the top of that hill. I wouldn't be who I was now. I'd still be that same old Sam who didn't understand things but was lucky enough to make the right choice by chance. You've got to do the right thing thinking it's right.

And further up the sand I saw Joe lying on a park bench. He lay still as a pond, picked out in stars.

'If you put your message in a story, Sam,' said Joe, 'people will remember it better.'

And you know, I reckon that's about right.